Nora Roberts is the *N...* more than 190 novels. U... is author of the *New Yo...* pense series, which featu... Roarke. There are more than 300 million copies of her books in print, and she has had more than 150 *New York Tim...* ...tsellers.

Visit... ...r website at www.nora-roberts.co.uk

By Nora Roberts

Homeport
The Reef
River's End
Carolina Moon
The Villa
Midnight Bayou
Three Fates
Birthright
Northern Lights
Blue Smoke
Montana Sky
Angels Fall
High Noon
Divine Evil
Tribute
Sanctuary

Three Sisters Island Trilogy:
Dance Upon the Air
Heaven and Earth
Face the Fire

Chesapeake Bay Quartet:
Sea Swept
Rising Tides
Inner Harbour
Chesapeake Blue

The Key Trilogy:
Key of Light
Key of Knowledge
Key of Valour

In the Garden Trilogy:
Blue Dahlia
Black Rose
Red Lily

The Irish Trilogy:
Jewels of the Sun
Tears of the Moon
Heart of the Sea

The Circle Trilogy:
Morrigan's Cross
Dance of the Gods
Valley of Silence

The Dream Trilogy:
Daring to Dream
Holding the Dream
Finding the Dream

The Sign of Seven Trilogy:
Blood Brothers
The Hollow
The Pagan Stone

The Born In Trilogy:
Born in Fire
Born in Ice
Born in Shame

As J. D. Robb:

Naked in Death
Glory in Death
Immortal in Death
Rapture in Death
Ceremony in Death
Vengeance in Death
Holiday in Death
Conspiracy in Death
Loyalty in Death
Witness in Death
Judgement in Death
Betrayal in Death
Seduction in Death
Reunion in Death
Purity in Death
Portrait in Death
Imitation in Death
Divided in Death
Visions in Death
Survivor in Death
Origin in Death
Memory in Death
Born in Death
Innocent in Death
Creation in Death
Strangers in Death

By Nora Roberts and J. D. Robb:

Remember When

BORN IN ICE

Nora Roberts

PIATKUS

PIATKUS

First published in the US in 1995 by Jove Books, an imprint of
the Berkeley Publishing Group
First published in Great Britain in 2009 by Piatkus
This paperback edition published in 2009 by Piatkus
Reprinted 2009

A CIP catalogue record for this book
is available from the British Library

ISBN 978-0-7499-2890-2

Typeset by Phoenix Photosetting, Chatham, Kent
www.phoenixphotosetting.co.uk
Printed and bound in Great Britain by CPI Mackays, Chatham, ME5 8TD

Papers used by Piatkus are natural, renewable and recyclable
products sourced from well-managed forests and certified
in accordance with the rules of the Forest Stewardship Council.

Mixed Sources
Product group from well-managed
forests and other controlled sources
www.fsc.org   Cert no. SGS-COC-004081
© 1996 Forest Stewardship Council

Piatkus
An imprint of
Little, Brown Book Group
100 Victoria Embankment
London EC4Y 0DY

An Hachette UK Company
www.hachette.co.uk

www.piatkus.co.uk

To all my ancestors who traveled across the foam

Dear Reader,

Ireland holds a special place in my heart. The rolling green fields under heavy skies, the criss-crossing gray of stone fences, the majestic tumble of a ruined castle, most likely sacked by those damned Cromwellians. I love the way the sun can shine gold through the rain, and the flowers bloom wildly in gardens and fields. It's a land of violent cliffs and dim, smoky pubs. Of magic and legend and heartbreak. There is a beauty even in the air.

And the west of Ireland is the most stunning landscape of a stunning country.

There, the traffic jams are often the cows being led to field by the farmer. There, a winding country road, closed in tight with hedgerows of wild fuchsia, can lead you any-where. There, the River Shannon gleams like silver and the sea crashes like thunder.

But beyond the countryside, the most magnificent thing in Ireland are the Irish. True, it's a land of poets and war-riors and dreamers, but it is also a land that opens its arms to strangers. Irish hospitality is simple and kind. That is, or should be, the definition of the word welcome.

In writing *Born in Ice*, Brianna Concannon's story, I hoped to reflect that incomparable generosity of spirit, the simplicity of an open door, and the strength of love. So come and sit for a while in front of the fire, take a drop of whiskey in your tea. Put your feet up and let your worries rest. I'd like to tell you a story.

Nora Roberts

Look for the other books in the trilogy . . .

BORN IN FIRE
BORN IN SHAME

I've been a wild rover for many the year

THE WILD ROVER

Prologue

The wild wind raced cursing across the Atlantic and pounded its fists over the fields of the west counties. Hard, needle-point bullets of rain beat on the ground and sliced through a man's flesh to batter his bones. Flowers that had bloomed brilliantly from spring through autumn blackened under the killing frost.

In cottages and pubs, people gathered around fires and talked of their farms and their roofs, the loved ones who had emigrated to Germany or the States. It hardly mattered whether they had left the day before, or a generation. Ireland was losing its people, as it had all but lost its language.

There was occasional talk about The Troubles, that endless war in the north. But Belfast was far from the village of Kilmilhil, in miles, and in emotion. People worried more about their crops, their animals, and the weddings and wakes that would come with winter.

A few miles out of the village, in a kitchen warmed with the heat and scents of baking, Brianna Concannon looked out of the window as the ice-edged rain attacked her garden.

'I'll lose the columbine, I'm thinking. And the foxglove.' It broke her heart to think of it, but she'd dug up what she could and stored the plants in the crowded little cabin out back. The gale had come so quickly.

'You'll plant more in spring.' Maggie studied her sister's profile. Brie worried about her flowers like a mother over her babes. With a sigh, Maggie rubbed her own bulging belly. It still astonished her that it was she who was married and carrying a child, and not her home-loving sister. 'You'll love every minute of it.'

'I suppose. What I need is a greenhouse. I've been looking at pictures. I think it could be done.' And she could probably afford it by spring, if she was careful. Daydreaming a little about the plants that would flourish in their new glass enclosure, she slipped a fresh batch of cranberry muffins from the oven. Maggie had brought her the berries all the way from a Dublin market. 'You'll take this home with you.'

'I will, yes.' Maggie grinned and snatched one from the basket, tossing it from hand to hand to cool it enough before she bit in. 'After I've eaten my fill. I swear to you, Rogan all but weighs every morsel I put in my mouth.'

'He wants you and the baby healthy.'

'Oh, he does. And I think he's worrying about how much of me is baby and how much is fat.'

Brianna eyed her sister. Maggie had grown round and soft, and there was a rosy contentment about her as she approached the last trimester of her pregnancy that was a sharp contrast to the bundle of energy and nerve Brianna was accustomed to.

She's happy, Brianna thought, in love. And knows her love is well returned. 'You have put on more than a few, Margaret Mary,' Brianna said and watched wicked humor rather than temper light Maggie's eyes.

'I'm having a contest with one of Murphy's cows, and I'm winning.' She finished off the muffin, reached shamelessly for another. 'In a few weeks I'll not be able to see past my belly to the end of my pipe to blow glass. I'll have to switch to lamp work.'

'You could take a vacation from your glass,' Brianna pointed out. 'I know Rogan's told you you've enough done already for all of his galleries.'

'And what would I do, besides die of boredom? I've got an idea for a special piece for the new gallery here in Clare.'

'Which won't open until spring.'

'By then Rogan will have made good on his threat to tie me to the bed if I make a move toward my shop.' She sighed, but Brie suspected Maggie didn't mind the threat so much. Didn't mind Rogan's subtle domineering ways. She was afraid she was mellowing. 'I want to work while I can,' Maggie added. 'And it's good to be home, even in such weather. I suppose you've got no guests coming.'

'As it happens, I do. A Yank, next week.' Brianna freshened Maggie's cup of tea, then her own, before sitting down. The dog, who had been waiting patiently beside her chair, laid his big head in her lap.

'A Yank? Just one? A man?'

'Mmmm.' Brianna stroked Concobar's head. 'It's a writer. He's booked a room, wants board as well, for an indefinite period. He's paid a month in advance.'

'A month! At this time of year?' Amused, Maggie looked out as the wind shook the kitchen windows. Welcoming weather it wasn't. 'And they say artists are eccentric. What sort of writer is he, then?'

'A mystery type. I've read a few, and he's good. He's won awards and had films made from them.'

'A successful writer, a Yank, spending the dead of winter at a B and B in Clare County. Well, they'll have plenty to say about that at the pub.'

Maggie licked crumbs from her fingers and studied her sister with an artist's eye. Brianna was a lovely woman, all rose and gold with creamy skin and a fine, trim figure. A classic oval face, a mouth that was soft, unpainted, and often too serious. Pale green eyes that tended to dream, long, fluid limbs, hair that held quiet fire – thick, slippery hair that often escaped its pins.

And she was soft-hearted, Maggie thought. Entirely too naive, despite her contact with strangers as the owner of a

3

B and B, about what went on out in the world beyond her own garden gate.

'I don't know as I like it, Brie, you alone in the house with a man for weeks at a time.'

'I'm often alone with guests, Maggie. That's how I make my living.'

'You rarely have only one, and in the middle of winter. I don't know when we might have to go back to Dublin, and –'

'Not be here to look after me?' Brianna smiled, more amused than offended. 'Maggie, I'm a grown woman. A grown businesswoman who can look after herself.'

'You're always too busy looking after everyone else.'

'Don't start on about Mother.' Brianna's lips tightened. 'I do very little now that she's settled with Lottie in the cottage.'

'I know exactly what you do,' Maggie tossed back. 'Running every time she wags her finger, listening to her complaints, dragging her off to the doctor's every time she imagines herself with a new fatal disease.' Maggie held up a hand, furious at herself for being sucked, yet again, into the anger and the guilt. 'That's not my concern just now. This man –'

'Grayson Thane,' Brianna supplied, more than grateful the topic had turned away from their mother. 'A respected American author who has designs on a quiet room in a well-run establishment in the west of Ireland. He doesn't have designs on his landlady.' She picked up her tea, sipped. 'And he's going to pay for my greenhouse.'

Chapter One

It wasn't unusual for Brianna to have a guest or two at Blackthorn Cottage during the worst of winter's storms. But January was slow, and more often than not her home was empty. She didn't mind the solitude, or the hell-hound howl of the wind, or even the leaden sky that spewed rain and ice day after bitter day. It gave her time to plan.

She enjoyed travelers, expected or not. From a business standpoint the pounds and pence counted. But beyond that, Brianna liked company, and the opportunity to serve and make a temporary home for those who passed her way.

She had, in the years since her father died and her mother moved out, turned the house into the home she had longed for as a child, with turf fires and lace curtains and the scents of baking coming from the kitchen. Still, it had been Maggie, and Maggie's art, that had made it possible for Brianna to expand, bit by bit. It wasn't something Brianna forgot.

But the house was hers. Their father had understood her love and her need for it. She tended her legacy as she would a child.

Perhaps it was the weather that made her think of her father. He had died on a day very much like this. Now and again, at odd moments when she found herself alone, she discovered she still carried little pockets of grief, with memories, good and bad, tucked into them.

Work was what she needed, she told herself, turning away from the window before she could brood for long.

With the rain pelting down, she decided to postpone a trip into the village and instead tackle a task she had put off for too long. No one was expected that day, and her single reservation wasn't due until the end of the week. With her dog trooping behind her, Brianna carted broom, bucket, rags, and an empty carton up to the attic.

She cleaned up here with regularity. No dust was allowed in Brianna's house for long. But there were boxes and trunks she had ignored in her day-to-day routine. No more, she told herself and propped open the attic door. This time she would make a clean sweep. And she would not allow sentiment to prevent her from dealing with left-over memories.

If the room was cleaned out properly once and for all, she thought, she might be able to afford the materials and labor necessary to remodel it. A cozy loft room it could be, she mused, leaning on her broom. With one of those ceiling windows, and perhaps a dormer. Soft yellow paint to bring the sun inside. Polish and one of her hooked rugs on the floor.

She could already see it, the pretty bed covered by a colorful quilt, a sugan chair, a little writing table. And if she had . . .

Brianna shook her head and laughed at herself. She was getting ahead of herself.

'Always dreaming, Con,' she murmured, rubbing the dog's head. 'And what's needed here is elbow grease and ruthlessness.'

Boxes first, she decided. It was time to clean out old papers, old clothes.

Thirty minutes later she had neat piles. One she would take to the church for the poor; another would be rags. The last she would keep.

'Ah, look at this, Con.' Reverently she took out a small white christening gown, gently shaking out the folds. Faint wisps of lavender haunted the air. Tiny buttons and narrow edges of lace decorated the linen. Her grandmother's handiwork, Brianna knew, and smiled. 'He saved it,' she

murmured. Her mother would never had given such sentimental thought to future generations. 'Maggie and I would
have worn this, you see. And Da packed it away for our
children.'

There was a pang, so familiar she barely felt it. There
was no babe sleeping in a cradle for her, no soft bundle
waiting to be held and nursed and loved. But Maggie, she
thought, would want this. Taking care, she folded the
gown again.

The next box was filled with papers that made her sigh.
She would have to read them, scan them at least. Her father
had saved every scrap of correspondence. There would be
newspaper clippings as well. His ideas, he would have said,
for new ventures.

Always a new venture. She set aside various articles he'd
clipped out, on inventions, foresting, carpentry, shopkeep-
ing. None on farming, she noticed with a smile. A farmer
he'd never been. She found letters from relatives, from
companies he'd written to in America, in Australia, in
Canada. And here the proof of purchase for the old truck
they'd had when she'd been a child. One document
stopped her, made her frown in puzzlement. It looked like
some sort of stock certificate. Triquarter Mining, in Wales.
From the date it seemed he'd purchased it only a few weeks
before he died.

Triquarter Mining? Another venture, Da, she mused,
spending money we barely had. Well, she would have to
write to this Triquarter company and see what was to be
done. It was unlikely the stock was worth more than the
paper it was printed on. Such had always been Tom Concannon's luck with business deals.

That bright brass ring he'd forever reached for had never
fit the palm of his hand.

She dug further into the box, amused herself with letters

from cousins and uncles and aunts. They had loved him. Everyone had loved him. Almost, she corrected, thinking of her mother.

Pushing that thought aside, she took out a trio of letters tied with a faded red ribbon. The return address was New York, but that was no surprise. The Concannons had a number of friends and relations in the States. The name, however, was a mystery to her. Amanda Dougherty.

Brianna unfolded the letter, scanned the neat, convent-school writing. As her breath caught in her throat, she read again, carefully, word for word.

> *My darling Tommy,*
>
> *I told you I wouldn't write. Perhaps I won't send this letter, but I need to pretend, at least, that I can talk to you. I've been back in New York for only a day. Already you seem so far away, and the time we had together all the more precious. I have been to confession and received my penance. Yet in my heart, nothing that passed between us is a sin. Love cannot be a sin. And I will always love you. One day, if God is kind, we will find a way to be together. But if that never happens, I want you to know that I'll treasure every moment we were given. I know it's my duty to tell you to honor the sacrament of your marriage, to devote yourself to the two babies you love so much. And I do. But, however selfish it is, I also ask that sometime, when spring comes to Clare, and the Shannon is bright with sunlight, you think of me. And how for those few short weeks, you loved me. And I love you . . .*
>
> *Always,*
> *Amanda*

Love letters, she thought dully. To her father. Written, she saw, staring at the date, when she was an infant.

Her hands chilled. How was a woman, a grown woman of twenty-eight years, supposed to react when she learned her father had loved a woman other than his wife? Her father, with his quick laugh, his useless schemes. These were words written for no one's eyes but his. And yet, how could she not read them?

With her heart pounding thickly in her chest, Brianna unfolded the next.

> *My darling Tommy,*
> *I have read and read your letter until I can see every word in my head. My heart breaks to think of you so unhappy. I, too, often look out to sea and picture you gazing across the water toward me. There is so much I wish to tell you, but I'm afraid it will only add to your heartache. If there is no love with your wife, there must be duty. There is no need for me to tell you that your children are your first concern. I know, have known all along, that they are first in your heart, and in your thoughts. God bless you, Tommy, for thinking also of me. And for the gift you gave me. I thought my life would be empty, now it will never be anything but full and rich. I love you now even more than I did when we parted. Don't grieve when you think of me. But think of me.*
>
> *Always,*
> *Amanda*

Love, Brianna thought as her eyes welled with tears. There was such love here, though so little had been said. Who had she been, this Amanda? How had they met? And how often had her father thought of this woman? How often had he wished for her?

Dashing a tear away, Brianna opened the last letter.

My darling,

I have prayed and prayed before writing this. I've asked the Holy Mother to help me know what is right. What is fair to you, I can't be sure. I can only hope that what I tell you will give you joy, not grief.

I remember the hours we spent together in my little room at the inn overlooking the Shannon. How sweet and gentle you were, how blinded we both were by the love that swept through us. I have never known, nor will I know again, that deep, abiding love. So am I grateful that though we can never be together, I will have something precious to remind me that I was loved. I'm carrying your child, Tommy. Please be happy for me. I'm not alone, and I'm not afraid. Perhaps I should be ashamed. Unmarried, pregnant by another woman's husband. Perhaps the shame will come, but for now, I am only full of joy.

I have known for weeks, but could not find the courage to tell you. I find it now, feeling the first quickening of the life we made inside me. Do I have to tell you how much this child will be loved? I have already imagined holding our baby in my arms. Please, my darling, for the sake of our child, let there be no grief or guilt in your heart. And, for the sake of our child, I am going away. Though I will think of you every day, every night, I will not write again. I will love you all of my life, and whenever I look at the life we created in those magic hours near the Shannon, I will love you more.

Give whatever you feel for me to your children. And be happy.

Always,
Amanda

A child. As her eyes swam with tears, Brianna covered her mouth with her hand. A sister. A brother. Dear God. Somewhere, there was a man or woman bound to her by blood. They would be close in age. Perhaps share the same coloring, the same features.

What could she do? What could her father have done, all those years ago? Had he searched for the woman and his baby? Had he tried to forget?

No. Gently Brianna smoothed the letters. He hadn't tried to forget. He'd kept her letters always. She closed her eyes, sitting in the dimly lit attic. And, she thought, he had loved his Amanda. Always.

She needed to think before she told Maggie what she'd found. Brianna thought best when she was busy. She could no longer face the attic, but there were other things that could be done. She scrubbed and polished and baked. The simple hominess of chores, the pleasure of the scents they created, lightened her spirits. She added turf to the fires, brewed tea, and settled down to sketch out ideas for her greenhouse.

The solution would come, in time, she told herself. After more than twenty-five years, a few days of thought would hurt no one. If a part of the delay was cowardice, a weak need to avoid the whip of her sister's emotions, she recognized it.

Brianna never claimed to be a brave woman.

In her practical way, she composed a polite, businesslike letter to Triquarter Mining in Wales and set it aside to be posted the next day.

She had a list of chores for the morning, rain or shine. By the time she'd banked the fires for the night, she was grateful Maggie had been too busy to drop by. Another day, perhaps two, Brianna told herself, and she would show her sister the letters.

But tonight she would relax, let her mind empty. An indulgence was what she needed, Brianna decided. In truth her back was aching just a bit from overdoing her scrubbing. A long bath with some of the bubbles Maggie had brought her from Paris, a cup of tea, a book. She would use the big tub upstairs and treat herself like a guest. Rather than her narrow bed in the room off the kitchen, she would sleep in splendor in what she thought of as the bridal suite.

'We're kings tonight, Con,' she told the dog as she poured bubbles lavishly under the stream of water. 'A supper tray in bed, a book written by our soon-to-be guest. A very important Yank, remember,' she added as Con thumped his tail on the floor.

She slipped out of her clothes and into the hot, fragrant water. The sigh rose up from her toes. A love story might be more appropriate to the moment, she thought, than a thriller with the title of *The Bloodstone Legacy*. But Brianna settled back in the tub and eased into the story of a woman haunted by her past and threatened by her present.

It caught her. So much so that when her water had chilled, she held the book in one hand, reading, as she dried off with the other. Shivering, she tugged on a long flannel nightgown, unpinned her hair. Only ingrained habit had her setting the book aside long enough to tidy the bath. But she didn't bother with the supper tray. Instead, she snuggled into bed, pulling the quilt up close.

She barely heard the wind kick at the windows, the rain slash at them. Courtesy of Grayson Thane's book, Brianna was in the sultry summer of the southern United States, hunted by a murderer.

It was past midnight when fatigue defeated her. She fell asleep with the book still in her hands, the dog snoring at the foot of the bed and the wind howling like a frightened woman.

She dreamed, of course, of terror.

Grayson Thane was a man of impulses. Because he recognized it, he generally took the disasters that grew from them as philosophically as the triumphs. At the moment he was forced to admit that the impulse to drive from Dublin to Clare, in the dead of winter, in the face of one of the most bad-tempered storms he'd ever experienced, had probably been a mistake.

But it was still an adventure. And he lived his life by them.

He'd had a flat outside of Limmerick. A puncture, Gray corrected. When in Rome, speak the lingo. By the time he'd changed the tire, he'd looked and felt like a drowned rat, despite the macintosh he'd picked up in London the week before.

He'd gotten lost twice, finding himself creeping down narrow, winding roads that were hardly more than ditches. His research had told him that getting lost in Ireland was part of its charm.

He was trying hard to remember that.

He was hungry, soaked to the skin, and afraid he would run out of gas — petrol — before he found anything remotely like an inn or village.

In his mind he went over the map. Visualizing was a talent he'd been born with, and he could, with little effort, reproduce every line of the careful map his hostess had sent him.

The trouble was, it was pitch dark, the rain washed over his windshield like a roaring river, and the wind was buffeting his car on this godforsaken excuse for a road as if the Mercedes was a Tinkertoy.

He wished violently for coffee.

When the road forked, Gray took his chances and guided the car to the left. If he didn't find the inn or something like in it another ten miles, he'd sleep in the damn car and try again in the morning.

It was a pity he couldn't see any of the countryside. He had a feeling in the dark desolation of the storm it would be exactly what he was looking for. He wanted his book here, among the cliffs and fields of western Ireland, with the fierce Atlantic threatening, and the quiet villages huddled against it. And he might just have his tired, world-weary hero arriving in the teeth of a gale.

He squinted into the gloom. A light? He hoped to Christ it was. He caught a glimpse of a sign, swinging hard in the wind. Gray reversed, aimed the headlights, and grinned.

The sign read Blackthorn Cottage. His sense of direction hadn't failed him after all. He hoped his hostess proved out the legend of Irish hospitality – he was two days early after all. And it was two in the morning.

Gray looked for a driveway, saw nothing but soaked hedges. With a shrug, he stopped the car in the road, pocketed the keys. He had all he'd need for the night in a knapsack on the seat beside him. Swinging it with him, he left the car where it was and stepped into the storm.

It slapped him like an angry woman, all teeth and nails. He staggered, almost plowed through the drenched hedges of fuchsia, and through more luck than design all but ran into the garden gate. Gray opened it, then fought it closed again. He wished he could see the house more clearly. There was only an impression of shape and size through the dark, with that single light shining in the window upstairs.

He used it like a beacon and began to dream of coffee.

No one answered his knock. With the wind screaming, he doubted anyone would hear a battering ram. It took him less than ten seconds to decide to open the door himself.

Again, there were only impressions. The storm at his back, the warmth within. There were scents – lemon, polish, lavender, and rosemary. He wondered if the old Irishwoman who ran the inn made her own potpourri. He wondered if she'd wake up and fix him a hot meal.

Then he heard the growl – deep, feral – and tensed. His head whipped up, his eyes narrowed. Then his mind, for one stunning moment, blanked.

Later, he would think it was a scene from a book. One of his own perhaps. The beautiful woman, the long white gown billowing, her hair spilling like fired gold down her shoulders. Her face was pale in the swaying light of the candle she held in one hand. Her other hand was clutched at the collar of a dog that looked and snarled like a wolf. A dog whose shoulders reached her waist.

She stared down at him from the top of the steps, like a vision he had conjured. She might have been carved from marble, or ice. She was so still, so utterly perfect.

Then the dog strained forward. With a movement that rippled her gown, she checked him.

'You're letting the rain in,' she said in a voice that only added to the fantasy. Soft, musical, lilting of the Ireland he'd come to discover.

'Sorry.' He fumbled behind him for the door, shutting it so that the storm became only a backdrop.

Her heart was still thudding. The noise and Con's response had wakened her from a dream of pursuit and terror. Now, Brianna stared down at a man in black, shapeless but for his face, which was shadowed. When he stepped closer, she kept her trembling hand tight on Con's collar.

A long, narrow face, she saw now. A poet's face with its dark, curious eyes and solemn mouth. A pirate's face, hardened by those prominent bones and the long sun-streaked hair that curled damp around it.

Silly to be afraid, she scolded herself. He was just a man, after all.

'Are you lost, then?' she asked him.

'No.' He smiled, slow, easy. 'I'm found. This is Blackthorn Cottage?'

'It is, yes.'

'I'm Grayson Thane. I'm a couple days early, but Miss Concannon's expecting me.'

'Oh.' Brianna murmured something to the dog Gray didn't catch, but it had the effect of relaxing those bunched canine muscles. 'I was looking for you on Friday, Mr. Thane. But you're welcome.' She started down the steps, the dog at her side, the candlelight wavering. 'I'm Brianna Concannon.' She offered a hand.

He stared at it a moment. He'd been expecting a nice, homey woman with graying hair tucked back in a bun. 'I woke you,' he said foolishly.

'We usually sleep here in the middle of the night. Come in by the fire.' She walked to the parlor, switching on the lights. After setting the candle aside, blowing it out, she turned to take his wet coat. 'It's a terrible night for traveling.'

'So I discovered.'

He wasn't shapeless under the mac. Though he wasn't as tall as Brianna's uneasy imagination had made him, he was lean and wiry. Like a boxer, she thought, then smiled at herself. Poet, pirate, boxer. The man was a writer, and a guest. 'Warm yourself, Mr. Thane. I'll make you some tea, shall I? Or would you rather I . . .' She'd started to offer to show him to his room, and remembered that she was sleeping in it.

'I've been dreaming of coffee for the last hour. If it isn't too much trouble.'

'It's not a problem. No problem at all. Make yourself comfortable.'

It was too pretty a scene to spend alone, he decided. 'I'll just come in the kitchen with you. I feel bad enough about dragging you out of bed at this hour.' He held out a hand for Con to sniff. 'This is some dog. For a minute I took him for a wolf.'

'A wolfhound, he is.' Her mind was busy figuring details. 'You're welcome to sit in the kitchen. Are you hungry, then?'

He rubbed Con's head and grinned down at her. 'Miss Concannon, I think I love you.'

She flushed at his compliment. 'Well, you give your heart easily then, if for no more than a bowl of soup.'

'Not from what I've heard of your cooking.'

'Oh?' She led the way into the kitchen and hung his dripping coat on a hook by the rear door.

'A friend of a cousin of my editor stayed here a year or so ago. The word was that the hostess of the Blackthorn cooked like an angel.' He hadn't heard she looked like one as well.

'That's a fine compliment.' Brianna put on the kettle, then ladeled soup into a pot for heating. 'I'm afraid I can only offer you plain fare tonight, Mr. Thane, but you'll not go to your bed hungry.' She took soda bread from a bin and sliced it generously. 'Have you traveled long today?'

'I started out late from Dublin. I'd planned to stay another day, but I had the itch.' He smiled, taking the bread she set on the table and biting into the first piece before she could offer him butter. 'It was time to get on the road. Do you run this place alone?'

'I do. I'm afraid you'll have a lack of company this time of year.'

'I didn't come for company,' he said, watching as she measured out coffee. The kitchen was beginning to smell like heaven.

'For work, you said. I think it must be wonderful to be able to tell stories.'

'It has its moments.'

'I like yours.' It was simply said as she reached into a cupboard for a stoneware bowl glazed in deep blue.

He raised a brow. People usually began to ask dozens of questions at this point. How do you write, where do you get your ideas – the most hated of questions – how do you get published? And questions were usually followed up by the deathless information that the inquirer had a story to tell.

But that was all she said. Gray found himself smiling again. 'Thanks. Sometimes I do, too.' He leaned forward, sniffed deeply when she set the bowl of soup in front of him. 'It doesn't smell like plain fare to me.'

'It's vegetable, with a bit of beef. I can make you a sandwich if you like.'

'No, this is great.' He sampled, sighed. 'Really great.' He studied her again. Did her skin always look so soft and flushed? he wondered. Or was it sleepiness? 'I'm trying to be sorry I woke you,' he said and continued to eat. 'This is making it tough.'

'A good inn's always open to a traveler, Mr. Thane.' She set his coffee beside him, signaled the dog who immediately stood from his perch beside the kitchen table. 'Help yourself to another bowl if you like. I'll tend to your room.'

She hurried out, quickening her steps as she came to the stairs. She'd have to change the sheets on the bed, the towels in the bath. It didn't occur to her to offer him one of the other rooms. As her only guest, he was entitled to the best she had.

18

She worked quickly and was just plumping the pillows in their lace-edged cases when she heard the sound at the door.

Her first reaction was distress to see him standing in the doorway. Her next was resignation. It was her home, after all. She had a right to use any part of it.

'I was giving myself a bit of a holiday,' she began and tugged at the quilt.

Odd, he thought, that a woman performing the simple task of tucking in sheets should look so outrageously sexy. He must be more tired than he'd thought.

'I seemed to have dragged you from your bed in more ways than one. It wasn't necessary for you to move out.'

'This is the room you're paying for. It's warm. I've built the fire up, and you've your own bath. If you –'

She broke off because he'd come up behind her. The prickling down her spine had her stiffening, but he only reached for the book on the night table.

Brianna cleared her throat and stepped back. 'I fell asleep reading it,' she began, then went wide-eyed in distress. 'I don't mean to say it put me to sleep. I just –' He was smiling, she noted. No, he was grinning at her. The corners of her mouth tugged in response. 'It gave me nightmares.'

'Thank you.'

She relaxed again, automatically turning sheets and quilt down in welcome. 'And you coming in from the storm had me imagining the worst. I was sure the killer had popped right out of the book, bloody knife in hand.'

'And who is he?'

She cocked a brow. 'I can't say, but I've my suspicions. You've a clever way of twisting the emotions, Mr. Thane.'

'Gray,' he said, handing her the book. 'After all, in a convoluted sort of way, we're sharing a bed.' He took her hand before she could think of how to respond, then left her unsettled by raising it to his lips. 'Thanks for the soup.'

'You're welcome. Sleep well.'

He didn't doubt he would. Brianna had hardly gone out and closed his door when he stripped off his clothes and tumbled naked into the bed. There was a faint scent of lilacs in the air, lilacs and some summer meadow scent he recognized as Brianna's hair.

He fell asleep with a smile on his face.

Chapter Two

It was still raining. The first thing Gray noticed when he pried his eyes open in the morning was the gloom. It could have been any time from dawn to dusk. The old clock on the stone mantel said nine-fifteen. He was optimistic enough to bet it was A.M.

He hadn't studied the room the night before. Travel fatigue, and the pretty sight of Brianna Concannon making his bed, had fuzzed his brain. He did so now, warm under the pooling quilt. The walls were papered so that tiny sprigs of violets and rosebuds climbed from floor to ceiling. The fire, gone cold now, had been set in a stone hearth, and bricks of turf were set in a painted box beside it.

There was a desk that looked old and sturdy. Its surface was polished to a high gloss. A brass lamp, an old inkwell, and a glass bowl of potpourri stood on it. A vase of dried flowers was centered on a mirrored dresser. Two chairs, covered in a soft rose, flanked a small occasional table. There was a braided rug on the floor that picked up the muted tones of the room and prints of wildflowers on the wall.

Gray leaned against the headboard, yawned. He didn't need ambience when he worked, but he appreciated it. All in all, he thought he'd chosen well.

He considered rolling over, going back to sleep. He hadn't yet closed the cage door behind him – an analogy he often used for writing. Chilly, rainy mornings anywhere in the world were meant to be spent in bed. But he thought of his landlady, pretty, rosy-cheeked Brianna. Curiosity about her had him gingerly setting his feet on the chilly floor.

At least the water ran hot, he thought as he stood groggily under the shower. And the soap smelled lightly, and practically, of a pine forest. Traveling as he did, he'd faced a great many icy showers. The simple hominess of the bath, the white towels with their charming touch of embroidery suited his mood perfectly. Then again, his surroundings usually suited him, from a tent in the Arizona desert to plush hotels on the Riviera. Gray liked to think he twisted his setting to fit his needs – until, of course, his needs changed.

For the next few months he figured the cozy inn in Ireland would do just fine. Particularly with the added benefit of his lovely landlady. Beauty was always a plus.

He saw no reason to shave, and pulled on jeans and a tattered sweatshirt. Since the wind had died considerably, he might take a tramp over the fields after breakfast. Soak up a little atmosphere.

But it was breakfast that sent him downstairs.

He wasn't surprised to find her in the kitchen. The room seemed to have been designed for her – the smoky hearth, the bright walls, the neat-as-a-pin counters.

She'd scooped her hair up this morning, he noted. He imagined she thought the knot on top of her head was practical. And perhaps it was, he mused, but the fact that strands escaped to flutter and curl around her neck and cheeks made the practical the alluring.

It probably was a bad idea all around to be allured by his landlady.

She was baking something, and the scent of it made his mouth water. Surely it was the scent of food and not the sight of her in her trim white apron that had his juices running.

She turned then, her arms full of a huge bowl, the contents of which she continued to beat with a wooden spoon. She blinked once in surprise, then smiled in cautious welcome. 'Good morning. You'll want your breakfast.'

'I'll have whatever I'm smelling.'

'No, you won't.' In a competent manner he had to admire, she poured the contents of a bowl into a pan. 'It's not done yet, and what it is is a cake for tea.'

'Apple,' he said, sniffing the air. 'Cinnamon.'

'Your nose is right. Can you handle an Irish breakfast, or will you be wanting something lighter?'

'Light isn't what I had in mind.'

'Fine, then, the dining room's through the door there. I'll bring you in some coffee and buns to hold you.'

'Can I eat in here?' He gave her his most charming smile and leaned against the doorjamb, 'Or does it bother you to have people watch you cook?' Or just watch her, he thought, do anything at all.

'Not at all.' Some of her guests preferred it, though most liked to be served. She poured him coffee she already had heating. 'You take it black?'

'That's right.' He sipped it standing, watching her. 'Did you grow up in this house?'

'I did.' She slid fat sausages in a pan.

'I thought it seemed more of a home than an inn.'

'It's meant to. We had a farm, you see, but sold off most of the land. We kept the house, and the little cottage down the way where my sister and her husband live from time to time.'

'From time to time?'

'He has a home in Dublin as well. He owns galleries. She's an artist.'

'Oh, what kind?'

She smiled a little as she went about the cooking. Most people assumed artist meant painter, a fact which irritated Maggie always. 'A glass artist. She blows glass.' Brianna gestured to the bowl in the center of the kitchen table. It bled with melting pastels, its rim fluid, like rain-washed petals. 'That's her work.'

'Impressive.' Curious, he moved closer, ran a finger tip around the wavy rim. 'Concannon,' he murmured, then chuckled to himself. 'Damn me, M. M. Concannon, the Irish sensation.'

Brianna's eyes danced with pleasure. 'Do they call her that, really? Oh, she'll love it.' Pride flashed in. 'And you recognized her work.'

'I ought to, I just bought a – I don't know what the hell it is. A sculpture. Worldwide Galleries, London, two weeks ago.'

'Rogan's gallery. Her husband.'

'Handy.' He went to the stove to top off his cup himself. The frying sausages smelled almost as good as his hostess. 'It's an amazing piece. Icy white glass with this pulse of fire inside. I thought it looked like the Fortress of Solitude.' At her blank look, he laughed. 'You're not up on your American comic books, I take it. Superman's private sanctum, in the Artic, I think.'

'She'll like that, she will. Maggie's big on private sanctums.' In an unconscious habit she tucked loose hair back into pins. Her nerves were humming a little. She supposed it was due to the way he stared at her, that frank and unapologetic appraisal that was uncomfortably intimate. It was the writer in him, she told herself and dropped potatoes into the spitting grease.

'They're building a gallery here in Clare,' she continued. 'It'll be open in the spring. Here's porridge to start you off while the rest is cooking.'

Porridge. It was perfect. A rainy morning in an Irish cottage and porridge in a thick brown bowl. Grinning, he sat down and began to eat.

'Are you setting a book here, in Ireland?' She glanced over her shoulder. 'Is it all right to ask?'

'Sure. That's the plan. Lonely countryside, rainy fields,

24

towering cliffs.' He shrugged. 'Tidy little villages. Postcards. But what passions and ambitions lie beneath.'

Now she laughed, turning bacon. 'I don't know if you'll find our village passions and ambitions up to your scope, Mr. Thane.'

'Gray.'

'Yes, Gray.' She took an egg, broke it one-handed into the sizzling skillet. 'Now, mine ran pretty high when one of Murphy's cows broke through the fence and trampled my roses last summer. And as I recall, Tommy Duggin and Joe Ryan had a bloody fistfight outside O'Malley's pub not long back.'

'Over a woman?'

'No, over a soccer game on the television. But then, there were a wee bit drunk at the time, I'm told, and made it up well enough once their heads stopped ringing.'

'Well, fiction's nothing but a lie anyway.'

'But it's not.' Her eyes, softly green and serious, met his as she set a plate in front of him. 'It's a different kind of truth. It would be your truth at the time of the writing, wouldn't it?'

Her perception surprised and almost embarrassed him. 'Yes. Yes, it would.'

Satisfied, she turned back to the stove to heap sausage, a rasher of bacon, eggs, potato pancakes onto a platter. 'You'll be a sensation in the village. We Irish are wild for writers, you know.'

'I'm no Yeats.'

She smiled, pleased when he transferred healthy portions of food onto his plate. 'But you don't want to be, do you?'

He looked up, crunching into his first slice of bacon. Had she pegged him so accurately so quickly? he wondered. He, who prided himself on his own aura of mystery – no past, no future.

Before he could think of a response, the kitchen door crashed open and a whirlwind of rain and woman came in. 'Some knothead left his car smack in the middle of the road outside the house, Brie.' Maggie stopped, dragged off a dripping cap, and eyed Gray.

'Guilty,' he said, lifting a hand. 'I forgot. I'll move it.'

'No rush now.' She waved him back into his seat and dragged off her coat. 'Finish your breakfast, I've time. You'd be the Yank writer, would you?'

'Twice guilty. And you'd be M. M. Concannon.'

'I would.'

'My sister, Maggie,' Brianna said as she poured tea. 'Grayson Thane.'

Maggie sat with a little sigh of relief. The baby was kicking up a storm of its own. 'A bit early, are you?'

'Change of plans.' She was a sharper version of Brianna, Gray thought. Redder hair, greener eyes – edgier eyes. 'Your sister was kind enough not to make me sleep in the yard.'

'Oh, she's a kind one, Brie is.' Maggie helped herself to a piece of the bacon on the platter. 'Apple cake?' Maggie asked, sniffing the air.

'For tea.' Brianna took one pan out of the oven, slipped another in. 'You and Rogan are welcome to some.'

'Maybe we'll come by.' She took a bun from the basket on the table and began to nibble. 'Plan to stay awhile, do you?'

'Maggie, don't harass my guest. I've some extra buns if you want to take some home.'

'I'm not leaving yet. Rogan's on the phone, will be as far as I can tell until doomsday's come and gone. I was heading to the village for some bread.'

'I've plenty to spare.'

Maggie smiled, bit into the bun again. 'I thought you

might.' She turned those sharp green eyes on Gray. 'She bakes enough for the whole village.'

'Artistic talent runs in the family,' Gray said easily. After heaping strawberry jam on a piece of bread, he passed the jar companionably to Maggie. 'You with glass, Brianna with cooking.' Without shame, he eyed the cake cooling on top of the stove. 'How long until tea?'

Maggie grinned at him. 'I may like you.'

'I may like you back.' He rose. 'I'll move the car.'

'If you'd just pull it into the street.'

He gave Brianna a blank look. 'What street?'

'Beside the house – the driveway you'd call it. Will you need help with your luggage?'

'No, I can handle it. Nice to have met you, Maggie.'

'And you.' Maggie licked her fingers, waited until she heard the door shut. 'Better to look at than his picture in back of his books.'

'He is.'

'You wouldn't think a writer would have a build like that – all tough and muscled.'

Well aware Maggie was looking for a reaction, Brianna kept her back turned. 'I suppose he's nicely put together. I wouldn't think a married woman going into her sixth month of pregnancy would pay his build much mind.'

Maggie snorted. 'I've a notion every woman would pay him mind. And if you haven't, we'd best be having more than your eyes checked.'

'My eyes are fine, thank you. And aren't you the one who was worried about me being alone with him?'

'That was before I decided to like him.'

With a little sigh Brianna glanced toward the kitchen doorway. She doubted she had much time. Brianna moistened her lips, kept her hands busy with tidying the breakfast dishes. 'Maggie, I'd be glad if you could find time to come by later. I need to talk to you about something.'

'Talk now.'

'No, I can't.' She glanced at the kitchen doorway. 'We need to be private. It's important.'

'You're upset.'

'I don't know if I'm upset or not.'

'Did he do something? The Yank?' Despite her bulk, Maggie was out of her chair and ready to fight.

'No, no. It's nothing to do with him.' Exasperated, Brianna set her hands on her hips. 'You just said you liked him.'

'Not if he's upsetting you.'

'Well, he's not. Don't press me about it now. Will you come by later, once I'm sure he's settled?'

'Of course I will.' Concerned, Maggie brushed a hand over Brianna's shoulder. 'Do you want Rogan to come?'

'If he can. Yes,' Brianna decided, thinking of Maggie's condition. 'Yes, please ask him to come with you.'

'Before tea, then — two, three o'clock?'

'That would be good. Take the buns, Maggie, and the bread. I want to help Mr. Thane settle in.'

There was nothing Brianna dreaded more than confrontations, angry words, bitter emotions. She had grown up in a house where the air had always simmered with them. Resentments boiling into blowups. Disappointments flashing into shouts. In defense she had always tried to keep her own feelings controlled, steering as far to the opposite pole as possible from the storms and rages that had served as her sister's shield to their parents' misery.

She could admit, to herself, that she had often wished to wake one morning and discover her parents had decided to ignore church and tradition and go their separate ways. But more often, too often, she had prayed for a miracle. The miracle of having her parents discover each other again, and reigniting the spark that had drawn them together so many years before.

Now, she understood, at least in part, why that miracle could never have happened. Amanda. The woman's name had been Amanda.

Had her mother known? Brianna wondered. Had she known that the husband she'd come to detest had loved another? Did she know there was a child, grown now, who was a result of that reckless, forbidden love?

She could never ask. Would never ask, Brianna promised herself. The horrible scene it would cause would be more than she could bear.

Already she had spent most of the day dreading sharing what she'd discovered with her sister. Knowing, for she knew Maggie well, that there would be hurt and anger and soul-deep disillusionment.

She'd put it off for hours. The coward's way, she knew, and it shamed her. But she told herself she needed time to settle her own heart before she could take on the burden of Maggie's.

Gray was the perfect distraction. Helping him settle into his room, answering his questions about the nearby villages and the countryside. And questions he had, by the dozen. By the time she pointed him off toward Ennis, she was exhausted. His mental energy was amazing, reminding her of a contortionist she'd once seen at a fair, twisting and turning himself into outrageous shapes, then popping out only to twist and turn again.

To relax, she got down on hands and knees and scrubbed the kitchen floor.

It was barely two when she heard Con's welcoming barks. The tea was steeping, her cakes frosted, and the little sandwiches she'd made cut into neat triangles. Brianna wrung her hands once, then opened the kitchen door to her sister and brother-in-law.

'Did you walk over, then?'

'Sweeney claims I need exercise.' Maggie's face was rosy, her eyes dancing. She took one long, deep sniff of the air. 'And I will, after tea.'

'She's greedy these days.' Rogan hung his coat and Maggie's on hooks by the door. He might have worn old trousers and sturdy walking shoes, but nothing could disguise what his wife would have termed the Dublin in him. Tall, dark, elegant, he would be in black tie or rags. 'It's lucky you asked us for tea, Brianna. She's cleaned out our pantry.'

'Well, we've plenty here. Go sit by the fire and I'll bring it out.'

'We're not guests,' Maggie objected. 'The kitchen'll do for us.'

'I've been in it all day.' It was a lame excuse. There was no more appealing room in the house for her. But she wanted, needed, the formality of the parlor for what needed to be done. 'And there's a nice fire laid.'

'I'll take the tray,' Rogan offered.

The minute they were settled in the parlor, Maggie reached for a cake.

'Take a sandwich,' Rogan told her.

'He treats me more like a child than a woman who's carrying one.' But she took the sandwich first. 'I've been telling Rogan about your very attractive Yank. Long gold-tipped hair, sturdy muscles, and big brown eyes. Isn't he joining us for tea?'

'We're early for tea,' Rogan pointed out. 'I've read his books,' he said to Brianna. 'He has a clever way of plunging the reader into the turmoil.'

'I know.' She smiled a little. 'I fell asleep last night with the light on. He's gone out for a drive, to Ennis and about. He was kind enough to post a letter for me.' The easiest way, Brianna thought, was often through the back door. 'I found some papers when I was up in the attic yesterday.'

'Haven't we been through that business before?' Maggie asked.

'We left a lot of Da's boxes untouched. When Mother was here, it seemed best not to bring it up.'

'She'd have done nothing but rant and rave.' Maggie scowled into her tea. 'You shouldn't have to go through his papers on your own, Brie.'

'I don't mind. I've been thinking I might turn the attic into a loft room, for guests.'

'More guests.' Maggie rolled her eyes. 'You're overrun with them now, spring and summer.'

'I like having people in the house.' It was an old argument, one they would never see through the same eyes. 'At any rate, it was past time to go through things. There were some clothes as well, some no more than rags now. But I found this.' She rose and went to a small box. She took out the lacy white gown. 'It's Granny's work, I'm sure. Da would have saved it for his grandchildren.'

'Oh.' Everything about Maggie softened. Her eyes, her mouth, her voice. She held out her hands, took the gown into them. 'So tiny,' she murmured. Even as she stroked the linen, the baby inside her stirred.

'I thought your family might have one put aside as well, Rogan, but –'

'We'll use this. Thank you, Brie.' One look at his wife's face had decided him. 'Here, Margaret Mary.'

Maggie took the handkerchief he offered and wiped her eyes. 'The books say it's hormones. I always seem to be spilling over.'

'I'll put it back for you.' After replacing the gown, Brianna took the next step and offered the stock certificate. 'I found this as well. Da must have bought it, or invested, whatever it is, shortly before he died.'

A glance at the paper had Maggie sighing. 'Another of his moneymaking schemes.' She was nearly as sentimental over the stock certificate as she'd been over the baby gown. 'How like him. So he thought he'd go into mining, did he?'

'Well, he'd tried everything else.'

Rogan frowned over the certificate. 'Would you like me to look into this company, see what's what?'

'I've written to them. Mr. Thane's posting the letter for me. It'll come to nothing, I imagine.' None of Tom Concannon's schemes ever had. 'But you might keep the paper for me until I hear back.'

'It's ten thousand shares,' Rogan pointed out.

Maggie and Brianna smiled at each other. 'And if it's worth more than the paper it's printed on, he'll have broken his record.' Maggie shrugged and treated herself to a cake. 'He was always after investing in something, or starting a new business. It was his dreams that were big, Rogan, and his heart.'

Brianna's smile dimmed. 'I found something else. Something I need to show you. Letters.'

'He was famous for writing them.'

'No,' Brianna interrupted before Maggie could launch into one of her stories. Do it now, she ordered herself when her heart shied back. Do it quickly. 'These were written to him. There are three of them, and I think it's best if you read them for yourself.'

Maggie could see Brianna's eyes had gone cool and remote. A defense, she knew, against anything from temper to heartache. 'All right, Brie.'

Saying nothing, Brianna picked up the letters, put them in Maggie's hand.

Maggie had only to look at the return address on the first envelope for her heartbeat to thicken. She opened the letter.

Brianna heard the quick sound of distress. The fingers she'd locked together twisted. She saw Maggie reach out, grip Rogan's hand. A change, Brianna thought with a little sigh. Even a year before Maggie would have slapped any comforting hand aside.

'Amanda.' There were tears in Maggie's voice. 'It was Amanda he said before he died. Standing there at the cliffs at Loop Head, at that spot he loved so much. We would go there and he would joke about how we'd hop in a boat and our next stop would be a pub in New York.' Now the tears spilled over. 'In New York. Amanda was in New York.'

'He said her name.' Brianna's fingers went to her mouth. She stopped herself, barely, before she gave into her child-hood habit of gnawing her nails. 'I remember now that you said something about that at his wake. Did he say anything more, tell you anything about her?'

'He said nothing but her name.' Maggie dashed at tears with a furious hand. 'He said nothing then, nothing ever. He loved her, but he did nothing about it.'

'What could he do?' Brianna asked. 'Maggie —'

'Something.' There were more tears and more fury when Maggie lifted her head. 'Anything. Sweet Jesus, he spent his life in hell. Why? Because the Church says it's a sin to do otherwise. Well, he'd sinned already, hadn't he? He'd committed adultery. Do I blame him for that? I don't know that I can, remembering what he faced in this house. But by God, couldn't he have followed through on it? Couldn't he have finally followed through?'

'He stayed for us.' Brianna's voice was tight and cold. 'You know he stayed for us.'

'Is that supposed to make me grateful?'

'Will you blame him for loving you?' Rogan asked quietly. 'Or condemn him for loving someone else?'

Her eyes flashed. But the bitterness that rose up in her throat died into grief. 'No, I'll do neither. But he should have had more than memories.'

'Read the others, Maggie.'

'I will. You were barely born when these were written,' she said as she opened the second letter.

'I know,' Brianna said dully.

'I think she loved him very much. There's a kindness here. It isn't so much to ask, love, kindness.' Maggie looked at Brianna then, for some sign. She saw nothing but that same cool detachment. With a sigh, she opened the final letter while Brianna sat stiff and cold. 'I only wish he . . .' Her words faltered. 'Oh, my God. A baby.' Instinctively her hand went to cover her own. 'She was pregnant.'

'We have a brother or sister somewhere. I don't know what to do.'

Shock and fury had Maggie lurching to her feet. Teacups rattled as she pushed back to stalk around the room. 'What to do? It's been done, hasn't it? Twenty-eight years ago to be exact.'

Distressed, Brianna started to rise, but Rogan covered her hand. 'Let her go,' he murmured. 'She'll be better for it after.'

'What right did she have to tell him this and then go away?' Maggie demanded. 'What right did he have to let her? And now, are you thinking it falls to us? To us to follow it through? This isn't some abandoned fatherless child we're speaking of now, Brianna, but a person grown. What have they to do with us?'

'Our father, Maggie. Our family.'

'Oh, aye, the Concannon family. God help us.' Overwhelmed, she leaned against the mantel, staring blindly into the fire. 'Was he so weak, then?'

'We don't know what he did, or could have done. We may never know.' Brianna took a careful breath. 'If Mother had known —'

Maggie interrupted with a short, bitter laugh. 'She didn't. Do you think she wouldn't have used a weapon like this to beat him into the ground? God knows she used everything else.'

'Then there's no point in telling her now, is there?'

Slowly Maggie turned. 'You want to say nothing?'

'To her. What purpose would it serve to hurt her?'

Maggie's mouth thinned. 'You think it would?'

'Are you so sure it wouldn't?'

The fire went out in Maggie as quickly as it had flared. 'I don't know. How can I know? I feel as if they're both strangers now.'

'He loved you, Maggie.' Rogan rose now to go to her. 'You know that.'

'I know that.' She let herself lean. 'But I don't know what I feel.'

'I think we should try to find Amanda Dougherty,' Brianna began, 'and —'

'I can't think.' Maggie closed her eyes. There were too many emotions battering inside her to allow her to see, as she wanted, the right direction to take. 'I need to think about this, Brie. It's rested this long. It can rest awhile longer.'

'I'm sorry, Maggie.'

'Don't take this on your shoulders as well.' A bit of the bite and briskness came back into Maggie's voice. 'They're burdened enough. Give me a few days, Brie, then we'll decide together what's to be done.'

'All right.'

'I'd like to keep the letters, for now.'

'Of course.'

Maggie crossed over, laid a hand on Brianna's pale cheek. 'He loved you, too, Brie.'

'In his way.'

'In every way. You were his angel, his cool rose. Don't worry. We'll find a way to do what's best.'

Gray didn't mind when the leaden sky began to spit rain again. He stood on a parapet of a ruined castle looking out on a sluggish river. Wind whistled and moaned through chinks in the stone. He might have been alone, not simply in this spot, but in this country, in the world.

It was, he decided, the perfect place for murder.

The victim could be lured here, could be pursued up ancient winding stone steps, could flee helplessly up, until any crumb of hope would dissolve. There would be no escape.

Here, where old blood had been spilled, where it seeped into stone and earth so deep, yet not so deep, fresh murder would be done. Not for God, not for country. But for pleasure.

Gray already knew his villain, could picture him there, slicing down so that the edge of his knife glinted silver in the dull light. He knew his victim, the terror and the pain. The hero, and the woman he would love, were as clear to Gray as the slow run of the river below.

And he knew he would have to begin soon to create them with words. There was nothing he enjoyed in writing more than making his people breathe, giving them flesh and blood. Discovering their backgrounds, their hidden fears, every twist and turn of their pasts.

It was, perhaps, because he had no past of his own. He had made himself, layer by layer, as skillfully and as meticulously as he crafted his characters. Grayson Thane was who he had decided to be, and his skill in storytelling had provided a means to become who and what he wanted, in some style.

He would never consider himself a modest man, but considered himself no more than a competent writer, a spinner of tales. He wrote to entertain himself first, and acknowledged his luck in hitting some chord in the public.

Brianna had been right. He had no desire to be a Yeats. Being a good writer meant he could make a living and do as he chose. Being a great one would bring responsibilities and expectations he had no desire to face. What Gray didn't choose to face, he simply turned his back on.

But there were times, such as this, when he wondered what it might be like to have roots, ancestry, a full-blooded devotion to family or country. The people who had built this castle that still stood, those who had fought there, died there. What had they felt? What had they wished for? And how could battles fought so long ago still ring, as clear as the fatal music of sword against sword, in the air?

He'd chosen Ireland for this, for the history, for the people whose memories were long and roots were deep. For people, he admitted, like Brianna Concannon.

It was an odd and interesting bonus that she should be so much what he was looking for in his heroine.

Physically she was perfect. That soft, luminous beauty, the simple grace and quiet manner. But beneath the shell, in contrast to that open-handed hospitality, was a remoteness, and a sadness. Complexities, he thought, letting the rain slap his cheeks. He enjoyed nothing better than contrasts and complexities – puzzles to be solved. What had put that haunted look in her eyes, that defensive coolness in her manner?

It would be interesting to find out.

Chapter Three

He thought she was out when he came back. As focused as a hound on a scent, Gray headed to the kitchen. It was her voice that stopped him – soft, quiet, and icy. Without giving a thought to the ethics of eavesdropping, he shifted and moved to the doorway of the parlor.

He could see her on the phone. Her hand twisted in the cord, a gesture of anger or nerves. He couldn't see her face, but the stiff set of her back and shoulders was indication enough of her mood.

'I've just come in, Mother. I had to pick up a few things in the village. I've a guest.'

There was a pause, Gray watched as Brianna lifted a hand, rubbed it hard at her temple.

'Yes, I know. I'm sorry it upsets you. I'll come around tomorrow. I can –'

She broke off, obviously interrupted by some sharp comment on the other end of the phone. Gray pushed back an urge to move into the room and soothe those tensed shoulders.

'I'll take you wherever you want to go tomorrow. I never said I was too busy, and I'm sorry you're not feeling well. I'll do the marketing, yes, it's no problem. Before noon, I promise. I have to go now. I have cakes in the oven. I'll bring you some, shall I? Tomorrow, Mother, I promise.' She muttered a goodbye and turned. The weary distress on her face turned to shock when she saw Gray, then a flush crept into her cheeks. 'You move quiet,' she said with the faintest trace of annoyance in the tone. 'I didn't hear you come in.'

'I didn't want to interrupt.' He had no shame about listening to her conversation, nor about watching her varying reactions flicker over her face. 'Your mother lives nearby?'

'Not far.' Her voice was clipped now, edged with the anger that stirred inside her. He'd listened to her personal misery and didn't think it important enough to apologize for. 'I'll get your tea now.'

'No hurry. You've got cakes in the oven.'

She leveled her eyes at his. 'I lied. I should tell you that I open my home to you, but not my private life.'

He acknowledged this with a nod. 'I should tell you, I always pry. You're upset, Brianna. Maybe you should have some tea.'

'I've had mine, thank you.' Her shoulders remained stiff as she crossed the room and started to move past him. He stopped her with the faintest of brushes of his hand on her arm. There was curiosity in his eyes – and she resented it. There was sympathy – she didn't want it.

'Most writers have as open an ear as a good bartender.'

She shifted. It was only the slightest movement, but it put distance between them, and made her point. 'I've always wondered about people who find it necessary to tell their personal problems to the man who serves them ale. I'll bring your tea into the parlor. I've too much to do in the kitchen for company.'

Gray ran his tongue around his teeth as she walked away. He had, he knew, been put ever so completely in his place.

Brianna couldn't fault the American for curiosity. She had plenty of her own. She enjoyed finding out about the people who passed through her home, hearing them talk about their lives and their families. It might have been unfair, but she preferred not to discuss hers. Much more comfortable was the role of onlooker. It was safer that way.

But she wasn't angry with him. Experience had taught her that temper solved nothing. Patience, manners, and a quiet tone were more effective shields, and weapons against most confrontations. They had served her well through the evening meal, and by the end of it, it seemed to her that she and Gray had resumed their proper positions of landlady and guest. His casual invitation to join him at the village pub had been just as casually refused. Brianna had spent a pleasant hour finishing his book.

Now, with breakfast served and the dishes done, she prepared to drive to her mother's and devote the rest of the morning to Maeve. Maggie would be annoyed to hear it, Brianna thought. But her sister didn't understand that it was easier, certainly less stressful to simply meet their mother's need for time and attention. Inconvenience aside, it was only a few hours out of her life.

Hardly a year earlier, before Maggie's success had made it possible to set Maeve up with a companion in her own home, Brianna had been at her beck and call twenty-four hours a day, tending to imaginary illnesses, listening to complaints on her own shortcomings.

And being reminded, time after time, that Maeve had done her duty by giving Brianna life.

What Maggie couldn't understand, and what Brianna continued to be guilty about, was that she was willing to pay any price for the serenity of being the sole mistress of Blackthorn Cottage.

And today the sun was shining. There was a teasing hint of far-off spring in the mild breeze. It wouldn't last, Brianna knew. That made the luminous light and soft air all the more precious. To enjoy it more fully, she rolled down the windows of her ancient Fiat. She would have to roll them up again and turn on the sluggish heater when her mother joined her.

She glanced over at the pretty little Mercedes Gray had leased – not in envy. Or perhaps with just the slightest twinge of envy. It was so efficiently flashy and sleek. And suited its driver, she mused, perfectly. She wondered what it would be like to sit behind the wheel, just for a moment or two.

Almost in apology she patted the steering wheel of her Fiat before turning the key. The engine strained, grumbled, and coughed.

'Ah, now, I didn't mean it,' she murmured and tried the key again. 'Come on, sweetheart, catch hold, will you? She hates it when I'm late.'

But the engine merely stuttered, then died off with a moan. Resigned, Brianna got out and lifted the hood. She knew the Fiat often displayed the temperament of a cranky old woman. Most usually she could coax it along with a few strokes or taps with the tools she carried in the trunk.

She was hauling out a dented toolbox when Gray strolled out the front door.

'Car trouble?' he called.

'She's temperamental.' Brianna tossed back her hair and pushed up the sleeves of her sweater. 'Just needs a bit of attention.'

Thumbs tucked in the front pocket of his jeans, he crossed over, glanced under the hood. It wasn't a swagger – but it was close. 'Want me to take a look?'

She eyed him. He still hadn't shaved. The stubble should have made him look unkempt and sloppy. Instead, the combination of it and the gold-tipped hair pulled back in a stubby ponytail fit Brianna's image of an American rock star. The idea made her smile.

'Do you know about cars then, or are you offering because you think you should – being male, that is.'

His brow shot up, and his lips quirked as he took the toolbox from her. He had to admit he was relieved she wasn't angry with him any longer.

'Step back, little lady,' he drawled in a voice thick with

the rural South. 'And don't worry that pretty head of yours. Let a man handle this.'

Impressed, she tilted her head. 'You sounded just as I imagined Buck sounded in your book.'

'You've a good ear.' He flashed her a grin before he ducked under the hood. 'He was a pompous red-necked ass, wasn't he?'

'Mmm.' She wasn't sure, even though they were discussing a fictional character, if it was polite to agree. 'Usually it's the carburetor,' she began. 'Murphy promised to rebuild it when he has a few hours to spare.'

Already head and shoulders under the hood, Gray simply turned his head and gave her a dry look. 'Well, Murphy's not here, is he?'

She had to admit he was not. Brianna bit her lip as she watched Gray work. She appreciated the offer, truly she did. But the man was a writer, not a mechanic. She couldn't afford to have him, with all good intentions, damage something.

'Usually if I just prop open that hinge thing there with a stick' – to show him, she leaned in alongside Gray and pointed – 'then I get in and start it.'

He turned his head again, was eye to eye and mouth to mouth with her. She smelled glorious, as fresh and clean as the morning. As he stared, color flushed into her cheeks, her eyes widened fractionally. Her quick and obviously unplanned reaction to him might have made him smile, if his system hadn't been so busy going haywire.

'It's not the carburetor this time,' he said and wondered what she would do if he pressed his lips just where the pulse in her throat was jumping.

'No?' She couldn't have moved if her life had been threatened. His eyes had gold in them, she thought foolishly, gold streaks along the brown, just as he had in his hair. She fought to get a breath in and out. 'Usually it is.'

He shifted, a test for both of them, until their shoulders brushed. Those lovely eyes of hers clouded with confusion, like a sea under uncertain skies. 'This time it's the battery cables. They're corroded.'

'It's . . . been a damp winter.'

If he leaned just the slightest bit toward her now, his mouth would be on hers. The thought of it shot straight to her stomach, flipped over. It would be rough – he would be rough, she was certain. Would he kiss like the hero in the book she had finished the night before? With teeth nipping, tongue thrusting? All fierce demand and wild urgency while his hands . . .

Oh, God. She'd been wrong, Brianna discovered, she could move if her life was threatened. It felt as if it had been, though he hadn't moved, hadn't so much as blinked. Giddy from her own imagination, she jerked back, only to make a small, distressed sound in her throat when he moved with her.

They stood, almost embracing, in the sunlight.

What would he do? she wondered. What would *she* do?

He wasn't sure why he resisted. Perhaps it was the subtle waves of fear vibrating from her. It might have been the shock of discovering he had his own fear, compressed in a small tight ball in the pit of his stomach.

It was he who took a step back, a very vital step back.

'I'll clean them off for you,' he said. 'And we'll try her again.'

Her hands reached for each other until her fingers were linked. 'Thank you. I should go in and call my mother, let her know I'll be a little late.'

'Brianna.' He waited until she stopped retreating, until her eyes lifted to his again. 'You have an incredibly appealing face.'

As compliments went, she wasn't sure how this one fit. She nodded. 'Thank you. I like yours.'

He cocked his head. 'Just how careful do you want to be about this?'

It took her a moment to understand, and another to find her voice. 'Very,' she managed. 'I think very.'

Gray watched her disappear into the house before he turned back to the job at hand. 'I was afraid of that,' he muttered.

Once she was on her way – the Fiat's engine definitely needed an overhaul – Gray took a long walk over the fields. He told himself he was absorbing atmosphere, researching, priming himself to work. It was a pity he knew himself well enough to understand he was working off his response to Brianna.

A normal response, he assured himself. She was, after all, a beautiful woman. And he hadn't been with a woman at all for some time. If his libido was revving, it was only to be expected.

There had been a woman, an associate with his publishing house in England, whom he might have tumbled for. Briefly. But he'd suspected that she'd been much more interested in how their relationship might have advanced her career than in enjoying the moment. It had been distressingly easy for him to keep their relationship from becoming intimate.

He was becoming jaded, he supposed. Success could do that to you. Whatever pleasure and pride it brought carried a price. A growing lack of trust, a more jaundiced eye. It rarely bothered him. How could it when trust had never been his strong point in any case? Better, he thought, to see things as they were rather than as you wanted them to be. Save the *I wants* for fiction.

He could turn his reaction to Brianna around just that way. She would be his prototype for his heroine. The lovely, serene, and composed woman, with secrets in her eyes and ice floes, banked fires, and conflicts stirring beneath the shell.

What made her tick? What did she dream of, what did she fear? Those were questions he would answer as he built a woman out of words and imagination.

Was she jealous of her stunningly successful sister? Did she resent her demanding mother? Was there a man she wanted and who wanted her?

Those were questions he needed to answer as he discovered Brianna Concannon.

Gray began to think he would need to combine them all before he could tell his tale.

He smiled to himself as he walked. He would tell himself that, he thought, because he wanted to know. And he had no qualms whatsoever about prying into someone's private thoughts and experiences. And no guilt about hording his own.

He stopped, turned a slow circle as he looked around him. Now this, he decided, was a place a person could lose himself in. Roll after roll of glistening green fields bisected with gray stone walls, dotted with fat cows. The morning was so clear, so shining, that he could see the glint of window glass in cottages in the distance, the flap of clothes hung out on lines to dry in the breeze.

Overhead the sky was a bowl of swimming blue – postcard perfect. Yet already, at the west rim of that bowl, clouds were swarming together, their purple-edged tips threatened storm.

Here, in what seemed to be the center of a crystalized world, he could smell grass and cow, hints of the sea carried on the air, and the faint, faint scent of smoke from a cottage chimney. There was the sound of wind in the grass, the swish of cows' tails, and the steady trumpet of a bird who celebrated the day.

He almost felt guilty about bringing even fictional murder and mayhem to such a place. Almost.

He had six months, Gray thought. Six months before his next book hit the stands and he flung himself, as cheerfully as possible, into the fun house ride of book tours and press. Six months to create the story that was already growing inside his head. Six months to enjoy this little spot in the world, and the people in it.

Then he would leave it, as he had left dozens of other spots, hundreds of other people, and go on to the next. Going on was something he excelled at.

Gray swung over a wall and crossed the next field.

The circle of stones caught his eye and his imagination immediately. He had seen greater monuments, had stood in the shadow of Stonehenge and felt the power. This dance was hardly more than eight feet, the king stone no taller than a man. But finding it here, standing silent among grazing, disinterested cows, seemed wonderful to him.

Who had built it, and why? Fascinated, Gray rounded the outside circumference first. Only two of the lintels remained in place, the others having fallen off in some long-ago night. At least he hoped it had been at night, during a storm, and the sound of them crashing to earth would have vibrated like a roar of a god.

He laid a hand on the king stone. It was warm from the sun, but carried an underlying iciness that thrilled. Could he use this, he wondered? Somehow weave this place and the echoes of ancient magic into his book?

Would there be murder done here? He stepped into the circle, into the center. A sacrifice of sorts, he mused. A self-serving ritual where blood would splash the thriving green grass, stain the base of the stones.

Or perhaps it would be love done here. A desperate and greedy tangle of limbs — the grass cool and damp beneath, the full white moon swimming overhead. The stones standing guard as the man and woman lost themselves in need.

He could imagine both with equal clarity. But the second appealed more, so much more, he could all but see Brianna lying on the grass, her hair fanned out, her arms lifted up. Her skin would be pale as milk, soft as water.

Her slim hips would arch, her slender back bow. And when he drove himself into her, she would cry out. Those neat, rounded nails would score his back. Her body would plunge like a mustang under his, faster, deeper, stronger, until . . .

'Good morning to you.'

'Jesus.' Gray jolted back. His breathing was unsteady, his mouth dust dry. Later, he promised himself, later it would be amusing, but for now he fought to rip himself out of erotic fantasy and focus on the man approaching the circle of stones.

He was dark, strikingly handsome, dressed in the rough, sturdy clothes of a farmer. Perhaps thirty, Gray judged, one of the stunning Black Irish who claimed jet hair and cobalt eyes. The eyes seemed friendly enough, a little amused.

Brianna's dog was prancing happily at his heels. Recognizing Gray, Con galloped into the circle to greet him.

'An interesting spot,' the man said in a musical west county brogue.

'I didn't expect to find it here.' Rubbing Con's head, Gray came through a space between stones. 'It isn't listed on any of the tourist maps I have.'

'It isn't, no. It's our dance, you see, but we don't mind sharing it occasionally. You'd be Brie's Yank.' He offered a big, work-roughened hand. 'I'm Murphy Muldoon.'

'Of the rose-trampling cows.'

Murphy winced. 'Christ, she'll never forget it. And didn't I replace every last bush? You'd think the cows had stepped on her firstborn.' He looked down at Con for support. The dog sat, tilted his head, and kept his own counsel. 'You've settled into Blackthorn, then?'

'Yes. I'm trying to get a feel for the area.' Gray glanced around again. 'I guess I crossed over onto your land.'

'We don't shoot trespassers often these days,' Murphy said easily.

'Glad to hear it.' Gray studied his companion again. There was something solid here, he thought, and easily approachable. 'I was in the village pub last night, O'Malley's, had a beer with a man named Rooney.'

'You mean you bought him a pint.' Murphy grinned.

'Two.' Gray grinned back. 'He earned them, with the payment of village gossip.'

'Some of which was probably truth.' Murphy took out a cigarette, offered one.

After shaking his head, Gray tucked his hands in his pockets. He only smoked when he was writing. 'I believe your name was mentioned.'

'I won't doubt you.'

'What young Murphy is missing,' Gray began in such a deadly mimic of Rooney that Murphy snorted with laughter, 'is a good wife and strong sons to be working the land with him. He's after perfection, is Murphy, so he's spending his nights alone in a cold bed.'

'This from Rooney who spends most of his nights in the pub complaining that his wife drives him to drink.'

'He did mention that.' Gray eased into the question he was most interested in. 'And that since the jackeen had snapped Maggie out from under your nose, you'd be courting her younger sister before long.'

'Brie?' Murphy shook his head as he expelled smoke.

48

'It'd be like cuddling my baby sister.' He smiled still, but his eyes were sharp on Gray's. 'Is that what you wanted to know, Mr. Thane?'

'Gray. Yes, that's what I wanted to know.'

'Then I'll tell you the way's clear there. But mind your step. I'm protective of my sisters.' Satisfied his point was made, Murphy took another comfortable drag. 'You're welcome to come back to the house for a cup of tea.'

'I appreciate the offer, but I'll take a raincheck. There are things I need to get done today.'

'Well, then, I'll let you get to them. I enjoy your books,' he said in such an offhand way that Gray was doubly complimented. 'There's a bookstore in Galway you may like to visit if you travel that way.'

'I intend to.'

'You'll find it then. Give my best to Brianna, will you? And you might mention that I've not a scone left in my pantry.' His grin flashed. ' 'Twill make her feel sorry for me.'

After whistling for the dog who fell into place beside him, he walked away with the easy grace of a man crossing his own land.

It was midafternoon when Brianna returned home, frazzled, drained, and tense. She was grateful to find no trace of Gray but for a note hastily scrawled and left on her kitchen table.

Maggie called. Murphy's out of scones.

An odd message, she thought. Why would Maggie call to tell her Murphy wanted scones? With a sigh Brianna set the note aside. Automatically she put on the kettle for tea before setting out the ingredients she needed to go with the free-range chicken she'd found – like a prize – at the market.

Then she sighed, gave in. Sitting down again, she folded her arms on the table, laid her head on them. She didn't weep. Tears wouldn't help, wouldn't change anything. It had been one of Maeve's bad days, full of snipes and complaints and accusations. Maybe the bad days were harder now, because over the last year or so there had been nearly as many good ones.

Maeve loved her little house, whether or not she ever admitted to it. She was fond of Lottie Sullivan, the retired nurse Brianna and Maggie had hired as her companion. Though the devil would never be able to drag that simple truth from Maeve's lips. She had found as much contentment as Brianna imagined she was capable of.

But Maeve never forgot, never, that Maggie was responsible for nearly every bite of bread their mother enjoyed. And Maeve could never seem to stop resenting that.

This had been one of the days when Maeve had paid her younger daughter back by finding fault with everything. With the added strain of the letters Brianna had found, she was simply exhausted.

She closed her eyes and indulged herself for a moment by wishing. She wished her mother could be happy. She wished Maeve could recapture whatever joy and pleasure she'd had in her youth. She wished, oh, she wished most of all that she could love her mother with an open and generous heart instead of with cold duty and dragging dispair.

And she wished for family, for her home to be filled with love and voices and laughter. Not simply for the transient guests who came and went, but for permanence.

And, Brianna thought, if wishes were pennies, we'd all be as rich as Midas. She pushed back from the table, knowing the fatigue and depression would fade once she began to work.

Gray would have a fine roast chicken for dinner, stuffed with herbed bread and ladeled with rich gravy.

And Murphy, bless him, would have his scones.

Chapter Four

In a matter of days Brianna had grown accustomed to Gray's routine and adjusted her schedule accordingly. He liked to eat, rarely missing a meal – though she soon discovered he had little respect for timetables. She understood he was hungry when he began to haunt her kitchen. Whatever the time, she fixed him a plate. And had to admit she appreciated watching him enjoy her cooking.

Most days he went out on what she thought of as his rambles. If he asked, she gave him directions, or made suggestions on some sight he might like to see. But usually he set out with a map, a notebook, and a camera.

She saw to his rooms when he was out. Anyone who tidies up after another begins to learn things. Brianna discovered Grayson Thane was neat enough when it came to what belonged to her. Her good guest towels were never tossed on the floor in a damp heap; there were never any wet rings on her furniture from a forgotten glass or cup. But he had a careless disregard for what he owned. He might scrape off his boots before he came in out of the mud and onto her floors. Yet he never cleaned the expensive leather or bothered to polish them.

So she did it herself.

His clothes carried labels from fine shops around the world. But they were never pressed and were often tossed negligently over a chair or hung crookedly in the wardrobe.

She began to add his laundry to her own, and had to admit it was pleasant to hang his shirts on the line when the day was sunny.

He kept no mementos of friends or family, made no attempt to personalize the room he now lived in. There were books, boxes of them – mysteries, horror novels, spy thrillers, romances, classics, nonfiction books on police procedures, weapons and murder, psychology, mythology, witchcraft, auto mechanics – that made her smile – and subjects as varied as architecture and zoology.

There seemed to be nothing that didn't interest him.

She knew he preferred coffee but would drink tea in a pinch if it was strong enough. He had the sweet tooth of a ten-year-old boy – and the energy of one.

He was nosy – there was to be no question he wouldn't ask. But there was an innate kindness in him that made him hard to rebuff. He never failed to offer to do some chore or errand for her – and she'd seen him sneaking tidbits of food to Con when he thought she wasn't looking.

All in all, it was an excellent arrangement – he provided her company, income, and the work she loved. She gave him a smoothly running base. Yet she could never quite relax around him. He had never referred to that one moment of mind-numbing attraction between them. But it was there – in the way her pulse jumped if she walked into a room and found him there unexpectedly. In the way her body heated when he turned those gilded eyes in her direction and simply looked at her.

Brianna blamed herself for it. It had been a long, long time since she had been deeply attracted to a man. Not since Rory McAvery had left her with a scar on her heart and a hole in her life had she felt such a wicked stirring for any man.

Since she was feeling it for a guest, Brianna had decided it was her responsibility to still it.

But as she smoothed the quilt on his bed, fluffed his pillows, she wondered where his ramblings were taking him today.

He hadn't gone far. Gray had decided to travel on foot that morning and wandered down the narrow road under gloomy, threatening skies. He passed a couple of outbuildings, saw a tractor shelter, hay bales stacked out of the weather. Murphy's, he imagined and began to wonder what it would be like to be a farmer.

Owning land, he mused, being responsible for it. Plowing, planting, tending, watching things grow. Keeping an eye on the sky, sniffing the air for a turn in the weather.

Not a life for Grayson Thane, he thought, but imagined some would find it rewarding. There'd been that simple pride of ownership in Murphy Muldoon's walk — a man who knew his feet were planted on his own.

But owning land — or anything — meant being tied to it. He'd have to ask Murphy how he felt about that.

Gray could see the valley from this spot, and the rise of hills. From the distance came the quick, happy bark of a dog. Con, perhaps, out looking for adventure before heading home to lay his head in Brianna's lap.

Gray had to envy the dog the privilege.

Grimacing, Gray tucked his hands in his pockets. He'd been working hard to keep those hands off his subtly sexy landlady.

He told himself she didn't wear those prim aprons or pin her hair up in those fall-away knots to charm him. But it worked. It was unlikely she fussed around the house smelling of wildflowers and cloves to drive him crazy. But he was suffering.

Beyond the physical — which was difficult enough — there was that air of secrets and sadness. He'd yet to slip through that thin wall of reserve and discover what was troubling her. Whatever it was haunted her eyes.

Not that he intended to get involved, Gray assured himself. He was just curious. Making friends was something he did easily by way of sincere interest and a sympathetic nature. But close friends, the kind a man kept in touch with through the years, worried over, missed when he was away, weren't in the master plan.

Grayson Thane traveled light, and he traveled frequently.

The little cottage with the boldly painted front door had Gray pausing. An addition had been framed in on the south side that was as big as the original house. The earth that had been displaced was now a hill of mud that would have delighted any five-year-old.

The little place down the road? he wondered. Where Brianna's sister and brother-in-law lived from time to time? He decided the magenta door was Maggie's doing and went through the gate for a closer look.

For the next few minutes he pleased himself poking through the new construction. Someone knew what they were doing here, he thought. The frame was sturdy, the materials top of the line. Adding on for the baby, he assumed, working his way to the rear. It was then he spotted the building out in the back.

Her glass shop. Pleased with his new discovery, he stepped off the planking and crossed the dew-dampened lawn. Once he reached it, Gray cupped his hands against the window and peered in. He could see furnaces, benches, tools that whet his curiosity and imagination. Shelves were loaded with works in progress. Without a qualm he stepped back and reached for the door.

'Are you wanting your fingers broken?'

He turned. Maggie stood in the rear doorway of the cottage, a steaming cup in one hand. She wore a bagging sweater, worn cords, and a scowl. Gray grinned at her.

'Not especially. Is this where you work?'

'It is. How do you treat people who pop uninvited into your studio?'

'I haven't got a studio. How about a tour?'

She didn't bother to muffle the oath, or the sigh. 'You're

a bold one, aren't you? All right, then, since I don't seem to be doing anything else. The man goes off,' she complained as she crossed the grass. 'Doesn't even wake me. Leaves me a note is all he does, telling me to eat a decent breakfast and keep my feet up.'

'And did you?'

'I might have if I hadn't heard somebody tramping around my property.'

'Sorry.' But still he grinned at her. 'When's the baby due?'

'In the spring.' Despite herself she softened. It took only the mention of the baby. 'I've weeks yet, and if the man keeps trying to pamper me, I'll have to murder him. Well, come in, then, since you're here.'

'I see that gracious hospitality runs in the family.'

'It doesn't.' Now a smile tugged at her lips. 'Brianna got all the niceness. Look,' she said as she opened the door. 'Don't touch, or I will break those fingers.'

'Yes, ma'am. This is great.' He started to explore the minute he stepped in, moving to the benches, bending down to check out the furnace. 'You studied in Venice, did-n't you?'

'I did, yes.'

'What started you off? God, I hate when people ask me that. Never mind.' He laughed at himself and strolled toward her pipes. His fingers itched to touch. Cautious, he looked back at her, measured. 'I'm bigger than you.'

She nodded. 'I'm meaner.' But she relented enough to take up a pontil herself and hand it to him.

He hefted it, twirled it. 'Great murder weapon.'

'I'll keep that in mind the next time someone interrupts my work.'

'So what's the process?' He glanced toward drawings spread out on a bench. 'You sketch out ideas?'

'Often.' She sipped at her tea, eyeing him. In truth, there was something about the way he moved, light and fluid without any fuss, that made her yearn for her sketchpad. 'After a quick lesson?'

'Always. It must get pretty hot in here when the furnaces are fired. You melt the stuff in there, and then what?'

'I make a gather,' she began. For the next thirty minutes she took him step by step through the process of hand-blowing a vessel.

The man was full of questions, she thought. Intriguing questions, she admitted, the kind that made you go beyond the technical processes and into the creative purpose behind them. She might have been able to resist that, but his enthusiasm was more difficult. Instead of hurrying him along, she found herself answering those questions, demonstrating, and laughing with him.

'Keep this up and I'll draft you as pontil boy.' Amused, she rubbed a hand over her belly. 'Well, come in and have some tea.'

'You wouldn't have any of Brianna's cookies – biscuits.' Maggie's brow arched. 'I do.'

A few moments later Gray was settled at Maggie's kitchen table with a plate of gingersnaps. 'I swear she could market these,' he said with his mouth full. 'Make a fortune.'

'She'd rather give them to the village children.'

'I'm surprised she doesn't have a brood of her own.' He waited a beat. 'I haven't noticed any man coming around.'

'And you're the noticing sort, aren't you, Grayson Thane?'

'Goes with the territory. She's a beautiful woman.'

'I won't disagree.' Maggie poured boiling water into a warmed teapot.

'You're going to make me yank it out,' he muttered. 'Is there someone or not?'

'You could ask her yourself.' Miffed, Maggie set the pot on the table, frowned at him. Oh, he had a talent, she thought, for making you want to tell him what he wanted to know. 'No,' she snapped out and slapped a mug on the table in front of him. 'There's no one. She brushes them off, freezes them out. She'd rather spend all her time tending to her guests or running out to Ennis every time our mother sniffles. Self-sacrificing is what our Saint Brianna does best.'

'You're worried about her,' Gray murmured. 'What's troubling her, Maggie?'

' 'Tis family business. Let it alone.' Belatedly she poured his cup, then her own. She sighed then, and sat. 'How do you know she's troubled?'

'It shows. In her eyes. Just like it's showing in yours now.'

'It'll be settled soon enough.' Maggie made a determined effort to push it aside. 'Do you always dig into people?'

'Sure.' He tried the tea. It was strong enough to stand up and dance. Perfect. 'Being a writer's a great cover for just being nosy.' Then his eyes changed, sobered. 'I like her. It's impossible not to. It bothers me to see her sad.'

'She can use a friend. You've a talent for getting people to talk. Use it on her. But mind,' she added before Gray could speak, 'she's soft feelings underneath. Bruise them, and I'll bruise you.'

'Point taken.' And time, he thought, to change the subject. He kicked back, propping a booted foot on his knee. 'So, what's the story with our pal Murphy? Did the guy from Dublin really steal you out from under his nose?'

It was fortunate that she'd swallowed her tea or she might have choked. Her laugh started deep and grew into guffaws that had her eyes watering.

'I missed a joke,' Rogan said from the doorway. 'Take a breath, Maggie, you're turning red.'

'Sweeney.' She sucked in a giggling breath and reached

for his hand. 'This is Grayson Thane. He was wondering if you stepped over Murphy's back to woo me.'

'Not Murphy's,' he said pleasantly, 'but I had to step all over Maggie's – ending with her head, which needed some sense knocked into it. It's nice meeting you,' he added, offering Gray his free hand. 'I've spent many entertaining hours in your stories.'

'Thanks.'

'Gray's been keeping me company,' Maggie told him. 'And now I'm in too fine a mood to yell at you for not waking me this morning.'

'You needed sleep.' He poured tea, winced after the first sip. 'Christ, Maggie, must you always brew it to death?'

'Yes.' She leaned forward, propped her chin on her hand. 'What part of America are you from, Gray?'

'No part in particular. I move around.'

'But your home?'

'I don't have one.' He bit into another cookie. 'I don't need one with the way I travel.'

The idea was fascinating. Maggie tilted her head and studied him. 'You just go from place to place, with what – the clothes on your back?'

'A little more than that, but basically. Sometimes I end up picking up something I can't resist – like that sculpture of yours in Dublin. I rent a place in New York, kind of a catchall for stuff. That's where my publisher and agent are based, so I go back about once, maybe twice a year. I can write anywhere,' he said with a shrug. 'So I do.'

'And your family?'

'You're prying, Margaret Mary.'

'He did it first,' she shot back to Rogan.

'I don't have any family. Do you have names picked out for the baby?' Gray asked, neatly turning the subject.

Recognizing the tactic, Maggie frowned at him. Rogan

gave her knee a squeeze under the table before she could speak. 'None that we can agree on. We hope to settle on one before the child's ready to go to university.'

Smoothly Rogan steered the conversation into polite, impersonal topics until Gray rose to leave. Once she was alone with her husband, Maggie drummed her fingers on the table.

'I'd have found out more about him if you hadn't interfered.'

'It's none of your business.' He leaned over and kissed her mouth.

'Maybe it is. I like him well enough. But he gets a look in his eyes when he speaks of Brianna. I'm not sure I like *that*.'

'That's none of your business, either.'

'She's my sister.'

'And well able to take care of herself.'

'A lot you'd know about it,' Maggie grumbled. 'Men always think they know women, when what they know is a pitiful nothing.'

'I know you, Margaret Mary.' In a neat move he scooped her out of the chair and into his arms.

'What are you about?'

'I'm about to take you to bed, strip you naked, and make incredibly thorough love with you.'

'Oh, are you?' She tossed back her hair. 'You're just trying to distract me from the subject at hand.'

'Let's see how well I can do.'

She smiled, wound her arms around his neck. 'I suppose I should at least give you the chance.'

When Gray strolled back into Blackthorn Cottage, he found Brianna on her hands and knees rubbing paste wax into the parlor floor in slow, almost loving circles. The little gold cross she sometimes wore swung like a pendulum from its thin chain and caught quick glints of light. She had music on, some lilting tune she was singing along with in Irish. Charmed, he crossed over and squatted down beside her.

'What do the words mean?'

She jolted first. He had a way of moving that no more than stirred the air. She blew loose hair out of her eyes and continued to polish. 'It's about going off to war.'

'It sounds too happy to be about war.'

'Oh, we're happy enough to fight. You're back earlier than usual. Are you wanting tea?'

'No, thanks. I just had some at Maggie's.'

She looked up then. 'You were visiting Maggie?'

'I thought I'd take a walk and ended up at her place. She gave me a tour of her glass house.'

Brianna laughed, then seeing he was serious, sat back on her haunches. 'And how in sweet heaven did you manage such a feat as that?'

'I asked.' And grinned. 'She was a little cranky about it at first, but she fell in.' He leaned toward Brianna, sniffed. 'You smell of lemon and beeswax.'

'That's not surprising.' She had to clear her throat. 'It's what I'm polishing the floor with.' She made a small, strangled sound when he took her hand.

'You ought to wear gloves when you do heavy work.'

'They get in my way.' She shook her hand, but he held on. Though she tried to look firm, she only managed to look distressed. 'You're in my way.'

'I'll get out of it in a minute.' She looked so damned pretty, he thought, kneeling on the floor with her polishing rag and her flushed cheeks. 'Come out with me tonight, Brie. Let me take you to dinner.'

'I've a – I've mutton,' she said, fumbling, 'for making Dingle Pies.'

'It'll keep, won't it?'

'It will, yes, but . . . If you're tired of my cooking –'

'Brianna.' His voice was soft, persuasive. 'I want to take you out.'

'Why?'

'Because you've got a pretty face.' He skimmed his lips over her knuckles and made her heart stick in her throat. 'Because I think it might be nice for you to have someone else do the cooking and the washing up for one night.'

'I like to cook.'

'I like to write, but it's always a kick to read something someone else has sweated over.'

'It's not the same.'

'Sure it is.' Head tilted, he aimed that sudden razor-sharp gaze at her. 'You're not afraid to be alone with me in a public restaurant, are you?'

'What a foolish thing to say.' What a foolish thing, she realized, for her to feel.

'Fine then, it's a date. Seven o'clock.' Wise enough to know when to retreat, Gray straightened and strolled out.

She told herself not to worry over her dress, then fretted about it just the same. In the end she chose the simple hunter green wool that Maggie had brought her back from Milan. With its long sleeves and high neck, it looked plain, even serviceable, until it was on. Cannily cut, the thin, soft wool had a way of draping over curves and revealing every bit as much as it concealed.

Still, Brianna told herself, it suited a dinner out, and that it was a sin she'd yet to wear it when Maggie had gone to the trouble and expense. And it felt so lovely against her skin.

Annoyed at the continued flutter of nerves, she picked up her coat, a plain black with a mended lining, and draped it over her arm. It was simply the offer of a meal, she reminded herself. A nice gesture from a man she'd been feeding for more than a week.

Taking one last steadying breath, she stepped out of her room into the kitchen, then started down the hall. He'd just come down the stairs. Self-conscious, she paused.

He stopped where he was, one foot still on the bottom step, his hand on the newel post. For a moment they only stared at each other in one of those odd, sliding instants of awareness. Then he stepped forward and the sensation rippled away.

'Well, well.' His lips curved into a slow, satisfied smile. 'You make a picture, Brianna.'

'You're wearing a suit.' And looked gorgeous in it.

'I drag one on now and again.' He took her coat, slipped it over her shoulders.

'You never said where we were going.'

'To eat.' He put an arm around her waist and swept her out of the house.

The interior of the car made her sigh. It smelled of leather, and the leather was soft as butter. She skimmed her fingers over the seat as he drove.

'It was kind of you to do this, Gray.'

'Kindness had nothing to do with it. I had an urge to go out, and I wanted you with me. You never come into the pub at night.'

She relaxed a little. So that's where they were going. 'I haven't lately. I do like stopping in now and then, seeing everyone. The O'Malleys had another grandchild this week.'

'I know. I was treated to a pint to celebrate.'

'I just finished a bunting for the baby. I should have brought it with me.'

'We're not going to the pub. What's a bunting?'

'It's a kind of saque; you button the baby into it.' As they passed through the village she smiled. 'Look, there's Mr. and Mrs. Conroy. More than fifty years married, and they still hold hands. You should see them dance.'

'That's what I was told about you.' He glanced at her. 'You won contests.'

'When I was a girl.' She shrugged it off. Regrets were a foolish indulgence. 'I was never serious about it. It was just for fun.'

'What do you do for fun now?'

'Oh, this and that. You drive well for a Yank.' At his bland look, she chuckled. 'What I mean is that a lot of your people have some trouble adjusting to our roads and driving on the proper side.'

'We won't debate which is the proper side, but I've spent a lot of time in Europe.'

'You don't have an accent I can place – I mean other than American. I've made kind of a game out of it, you see, from guessing with my guests.'

'It might be because I'm not from anywhere.'

'Everyone's from somewhere.'

'No, they're not. There are more nomads in the world than you might think.'

'So, you're claiming to be a gypsy.' She pushed her hair back and studied his profile. 'Well, that's one I didn't think of.'

'Meaning?'

'The night you came. I thought you looked a bit like a pirate – then a poet, even a boxer, but not a gypsy. But that suits, too.'

'And you looked like a vision – billowing white gown, tumbled hair, courage and fear warring in your eyes.'

'I wasn't afraid.' She glimpsed the sign just before he turned off the road. 'Here? Drumoland Castle? But we can't.'

'Why not? I'm told the cuisine's exquisite.'

'Sure and it is, and very dear.'

He laughed, slowing to enjoy the view of the castle, gray and glorious on the slope of the hill, glinting under lights. 'Brianna, I'm a very well paid gypsy. Stunning, isn't it?'

'Yes. And the gardens . . . you can't see them well now, and the winter's been so harsh, but they've the most beautiful gardens.' She looked over the slope of lawn to a bed of dormant rosebushes. 'In the back is a walled garden. It's so lovely it doesn't seem real. Why didn't you stay at a place like this?'

He parked the car, shut it off. 'I nearly did, then I heard about your inn. Call it impulse.' He flashed a grin at her. 'I like impulses.'

He climbed out of the car, took her hand to lead her up the stone steps into the great hall.

It was spacious and lush, as castles should be, with dark wood and deep red carpets. There was the smell of woodsmoke from the fire, the glint of crystal, the lonely sound of harp music.

'I stayed in a castle in Scotland,' he began, moving toward the dining room with his fingers twined with hers. 'And one in Cornwall. Fascinating places, full of shades and shadows.'

'You believe in ghosts?'

'Of course.' His eyes met hers as he reached out to take her coat. 'Don't you?'

'I do, yes. We have some, you know, at home.'

'The stone circle.'

Even as she felt surprise, she realized she shouldn't. He would have been there, and he would have felt it. 'There, yes, and other places.'

Gray turned to the maître d'. 'Thane,' he said simply.

They were welcomed, shown to their table. As Gray

accepted the wine list, he glanced at Brianna. 'Would you like wine?'

'That would be nice.'

He took a brief glance, smiled up at the sommelier. 'The Chassagne-Montrachet.'

'Yes, sir.'

'Hungry?' he asked Brianna, who was all but devouring the menu.

'I'm trying to memorize it,' she murmured. 'I dined here once with Maggie and Rogan, and I've come close to duplicating this chicken in honey and wine.'

'Read it for pleasure,' he suggested. 'We'll get a copy of the menu for you.'

She eyed him over the top. 'They won't give one to you.'

'Sure they will.'

She gave a short laugh and chose her meal at random. Once they'd placed their orders and sampled the wine, Gray leaned forward. 'Now, tell me.'

She blinked. 'Tell you what?'

'About the ghosts.'

'Oh.' She smiled a little, running a finger down her wineglass. 'Well, years ago, as it happened, there were lovers. She was betrothed to another, so they met in secret. He was a poor man, a simple farmer so they say, and she the daughter of the English landlord. But they loved, and made desperate plans to run off and be together. This night, they met at the stone circle. There, they thought, at that holy place, that magic place, they would ask the gods to bless them. She carried his child now, you see, and they had no time to lose. They knelt there, at the center, and she told him she was with child. It's said they wept together, with joy and with fear as the wind whispered cold and the old stones sheltered them. And there they loved each other a last time. He would go, he told her, and take his horse from his plow, gather whatever he could, and come back for her. They would leave that very night.'

Brianna sighed a little, her eyes dreamy. 'So he left her there, in the center of the circle of stones. But when he reached his farm, they were waiting for him. The men of the English landlord. They cut him down so that his blood stained the land, and they burned his house, his crops. His only thought as he lay dying was of his love.'

She paused, with the innate timing of one who knows and spins tales. The harpist in the far corner plucked softly at a ballad of ill-fated love. 'And she waited there, in the center of the circle of stones. While she waited, she grew cold, so cold she began to tremble. Her lover's voice came across the fields to her, like tears in the air. She knew he was dead. And knowing, she laid down, closed her eyes, and sent herself to him. When they found her the next morning, she was smiling. But she was cold, very cold, and her heart was not beating. There are nights, if you stand in the center of the circle of stones, you can hear them whisper their promises to each other and the grass grows damp with their tears.'

Letting out a long breath, Gray sat back and sipped at his wine. 'You have talent, Brianna, for storytelling.'

'I tell you only as it was told to me. Love survives, you see. Through fear, through heartache, even through death.'

'Have you heard them whispering?'

'I have. And I've wept for them. And I've envied them.' She sat back, shook off the mood. 'And what ghosts do you know?'

'Well, I'll tell you a story. In the hills not far from the field of Culladon a one-armed Highlander roams.'

Her lips curved. 'Is this truth, Grayson, or made up?'

He took her hand, kissed it. 'You tell me.'

Chapter Five

She'd never had an evening quite like it. All the elements added up to one wonderful memory – the gorgeous man who seemed fascinated by her every word, the romantic trappings of a castle, without the medieval inconveniences, glorious French food, delicate wine.

She wasn't sure how she would ever pay him back for it – particularly for the menu Gray had charmed out of the maître d'.

She began the only way she knew, by planning a special breakfast.

When Maggie came in, the kitchen was filled with sizzling scents, and Brianna was singing.

'Well, you're having a fine morning, I see.'

'I am, yes.' Brianna flipped over a thick slab of spiced toast. 'Will you have some breakfast, Maggie? There's more than enough.'

'I've eaten already.' It was said with some regret. 'Is Gray about?'

'He isn't down yet. Usually he's sniffing at the skillets by this time of day.'

'Then we're alone for the moment.'

'Yes.' Her light mood plummeted. Carefully Brianna set the last piece of bread on the platter and put the meal into the oven to keep warm. 'You've come to talk about the letters.'

'I've kept you worrying over it long enough, haven't I? I'm sorry for that.'

'We both needed to think.' Brianna folded her hands over her apron, faced her sister. 'What do you want to do, Maggie?'

'What I want to do is nothing, to pretend I've never read them, that they don't exist.'

'Maggie –'

'Let me finish,' she snapped out and began to roam the kitchen like an ill-tempered cat. 'I want to go on as we are, and to keep my memories of Da my own. I don't want to wonder or worry about a woman he knew and bedded a lifetime ago. I don't want to think about a grown brother or sister somewhere. You're my sister,' she said passionately. 'You're my family. I tell myself this Amanda made a life for herself and her child somewhere, somehow, and they wouldn't thank us for poking into it now. I want to forget it, I want it to go away. That's what I want, Brianna.'

She stopped, leaning back on the counter and sighing. 'That's what I want,' she repeated, 'but it's not what must be done. He said her name – almost the last thing he said in life was her name. She has the right to know that. I have the right to curse her for it.'

'Sit down, Maggie. It can't be good for you to be so upset.'

'Of course I'm upset. We're both upset. We have different ways of dealing with it.' With a shake of her head she waved Brianna off. 'I don't need to sit. If the baby isn't used to my temper by now, he'll have to learn.' Still she made an effort, taking a couple of calming breaths. 'We'll need to hire an investigator, a detective, in New York. That's what you want, isn't it?'

'I think it's what we have to do,' Brianna said carefully. 'For ourselves. For Da. How will we go about it?'

'Rogan knows people. He'll make calls. He's wonderful at making calls.' Because she could see Brianna needed it, she managed a smile. 'That'll be the easy part. As to finding them, I don't know how long that might take. And God only knows what we'll do if and when we're faced with them. She might have married, this Amanda, and have a dozen children and a happy life.'

'I've thought of that. But we have to find out, don't we?'

'We do.' Stepping forward, Maggie laid her hands gently on Brianna's cheeks. 'Don't worry so, Brie.'

'I won't if you won't.'

'It's a pact.' Maggie kissed her lightly to seal it. 'Now go feed your lazy Yank. I've fired my furnace and have work to do.'

'Nothing heavy.'

Maggie tossed back a grin as she turned for the door. 'I know my limits.'

'No, you don't, Margaret Mary,' Brianna called out as the door slammed shut. She stood for a moment, lost in thought until Con's steady tail thumping roused her. 'Want out, do you? Fine, then. Go see what Murphy's up to.'

The minute she opened the door, Con streaked out. After one satisfied bark, he was loping toward the fields. She closed the door on the damp air and debated. It was after ten, and she had chores. If Gray wasn't coming down to breakfast, she'd take it up to him.

A glance at the menu on the table had her smiling again. She was humming as she arranged the breakfast tray. Hefting it, she carried it upstairs. His door was closed and made her hesitate. She knocked softly, got no response, and began to gnaw her lip. Perhaps he was ill. Concerned, she knocked again, more loudly, and called his name.

She thought she heard a grunt, and shifting the tray, eased the door open.

The bed looked as though it had been the scene of a small war. The sheets and blankets were tangled into knots, the quilt trailing over the footboard onto the floor. And the room was stone cold.

Stepping over the threshold, she saw him, and stared.

He was at the desk, his hair wild, his feet bare. There was a heap of books piled beside him as his fingers raced over the keys of a small computer. At his elbow was an ashtray overflowing with cigarette butts. The air reeked of them.

'Excuse me.' No response. The muscles in her arms were beginning to ache from the weight of the tray. 'Grayson.'

'What?' The word shot out like a bullet, taking her back a step. His head whipped up.

It was the pirate again, she thought. He looked dangerous and inclined to violence. As his eyes focused on her, without any sign of recognition, she wondered if he might have gone mad during the night.

'Wait,' he ordered and attacked the keyboard again. Brianna waited, baffled, for nearly five full minutes. He leaned back then, rubbed his hands hard over his face like a man just waking from a dream. Or, she thought, a nightmare. Then he turned to her again, with that quick, familiar smile. 'Is that breakfast?'

'Yes, I . . . It's half past ten, and when you didn't come down . . .'

'Sorry.' He rose, took the tray from her, and set it on the bed. He picked up a piece of English bacon with his fingers. 'I got it in the middle of the night. It was the ghost story that clicked it, I think. Christ, it's cold in here.'

'Well, 'tis no wonder. You're after catching your death with nothing on your feet and the fire out.'

He only smiled as she knelt at the hearth and began to arrange new turf. She'd sounded like a mother scolding a foolish child. 'I got caught up.'

'That's all fine and good, but it's not healthy for you to be sitting here in the cold, smoking cigarettes instead of eating a decent meal.'

'Smells better than decent.' Patient, he crouched down beside her, ran a carelessly friendly hand down her back. 'Brianna, will you do me a favor?'

'If I can, yes.'

'Go away.'

Stunned, she turned her head. Even as she gaped at him, he was laughing and taking her hands in his.

'No offense, honey. It's just that I tend to bite if my work's interrupted, and it's cooking for me right now.'

'I certainly don't mean to be in your way.'

He winced, bit back on annoyance. He was trying to be diplomatic, wasn't he? 'I need to hang with it while it's moving, okay? So just forget I'm up here.'

'But your room. You need the linens changed, and the bath —'

'Don't worry about it.' The fire was glowing now, and so was the impatience inside him. He raised her to her feet. 'You can shovel it out when I hit a dry spell. I'd appreciate it if you'd drop some food off outside the door now and again, but that's all I'll need.'

'All right, but —' He was already guiding her to the door. She huffed. 'You don't have to be booting me out, I'm going.'

'Thanks for breakfast.'

'You're —' He shut the door in her face. 'Welcome,' she said between her teeth.

For the rest of that day and two more she didn't hear a peep out of him. She tried not to think of the state of the room, if he'd remembered to keep the fire going or if he bothered to sleep. She knew he was eating. Each time she brought up a fresh tray, the old one was outside the door. He rarely left so much as a crumb on a plate.

She might have been alone in the house — if she hadn't been so aware of him. She doubted very much that he gave her a moment's thought.

She'd have been right. He did sleep now and again, cat-naps that were ripe with dreams and visions. He ate, fueling his body as the story fueled his mind. It was storming through him. In three days he had more than a hundred pages. They were rough, sometimes static, but he had the core of it.

He had murder, gleeful and sly. He had hopelessness and pain, desperation and lies.

He was in heaven.

When it finally ground to a halt, he crawled into bed, pulled the covers over his head, and slept like the dead.

When he woke, he took a long look at the room and decided a woman as strong as Brianna was unlikely to faint at the sight of it. The sight of him, however, as he studied himself in the bathroom mirror, was another matter. He rubbed a hand over the stubble on his chin. He looked, he decided, like something that had crawled out of a bog.

He peeled off his shirt, winced at the smell of it, and himself, and stepped into the shower. Thirty minutes later he was pulling on fresh clothes. He felt a little light-headed, more than a little stiff from lack of exercise. But the excitement was still on him. He pushed open the bedroom window and took a deep gulp of the rainy morning.

A perfect day, he thought. In the perfect place.

His breakfast tray was outside the door, the food gone cold. He'd slept through that, he realized, and lifting it, hoped he could charm Brianna into heating it up for him again.

And maybe she'd go for a walk with him. He could use some company. Maybe he could talk her into driving into Galway, spending the day with him in crowds. They could always –

He stopped in the kitchen doorway, and his grin spread from ear to ear. There she was, up to her wrists in bread dough, her hair scooped up, her nose dusted with flour.

It was such a wonderful picture, and his mood was high. He set the tray down with a rattle that had her jolting and looking up. She had just begun to smile when he strode to her, framed her face firmly in his hands, and kissed her hard on the mouth.

Her hands fisted in the dough. Her head spun. Before she could react, he'd pulled away. 'Hi. Great day, isn't it? I feel incredible. You can't count on it coming like that, you know. And when it does, it's like this train highballing right through your head. You can't stop it.' He picked up a piece of cold toast from his tray, started to bite in. It was halfway to his mouth before it hit him. His eyes locked on hers again. He let the toast fall back to the plate.

The kiss had merely been a reflection of his mood, light, exuberant. Now, some sort of delayed reaction was setting in, tightening his muscles, skimming up his spine.

She simply stood there, staring at him, her lips still parted in shock, her eyes huge with it.

'Wait a minute,' he murmured and moved to her again. 'Wait just a minute.'

She couldn't have moved if the roof had caved in. She could barely breathe as his hands framed her face again, gently this time, like a man experimenting with texture. His eyes stayed open, the expression in them not entirely pleased as he leaned toward her this time.

She felt his lips brush hers, soft, lovely. The kind of touch that shouldn't have kindled a fire in the blood. Yet her blood heated. He turned her, just enough so that their bodies met, tipped her head back just enough so that the kiss would deepen.

Some sound, distress or pleasure, hummed in her throat before her fisted hands went limp.

Hers was a mouth to savor, he realized. Full, generous, yielding. A man shouldn't hurry a mouth such as this. He scraped his teeth lightly over her bottom lip and thrilled to the low, helpless purr that answered him. Slowly, watching her eyes glaze and close, he traced her lips with his tongue, dipped inside.

So many subtle flavors.

It was wonderful, the way he could feel her skin warm, her bones soften, her heart pound. Or maybe it was his heart. Something was roaring in his head, throbbing in his blood. It wasn't until greed began to grow, with the crafty violence that mated with it, that he drew back.

She was trembling, and instinct warned him that if he let himself go, he'd hurt them both. 'That was better than I imagined it would be,' he managed. 'And I've got a hell of an imagination.'

Staggered, she braced a hand on the counter. Her knees were shaking. Only fear of mortification kept her voice from shaking as well. 'Is this how you always behave when you come out of your cave?'

'I'm not always lucky enough to have a beautiful woman handy.' He tilted his head, studying her. The pulse in her throat was still jumping, and her skin was still flushed. But, unless he was off the mark, she was already rebuilding that thin, defensive wall. 'That wasn't ordinary. There isn't any point in pretending it was.'

'I'm not ordinarily kissed by a guest while I'm making bread. I wouldn't know what's ordinary for you, would I?' His eyes changed, darkening with a hint of temper. When he stepped forward, she stepped back. 'Please, don't.'

Now those dark eyes narrowed. 'Be more specific.'

'I have to finish this. The dough needs to rise again.'

'You're evading, Brianna.'

'All right, don't kiss me like that again.' She let out a choppy breath, drew another in. 'I don't have the right defenses.'

'It doesn't have to be a battle. I'd like to take you to bed, Brianna.'

To occupy her nervous hands, she snatched up a towel and rubbed at the dough clinging to her fingers. 'Well, that's blunt.'

'It's honest. If you're not interested, just say so.'

'I don't take things as casually as you, with a yes or a no, and no harm done.' Fighting for calm, she folded the towel neatly, set it aside. 'And I've no experience in such matters.'

Damn her for being cool when his blood was raging. 'What matters?'

'The one you're speaking of. Now move aside, so I can get back to my bread.'

He simply took her arm and stared into her eyes. A virgin? he wondered, letting the idea circle around and take root. A woman who looked like this, who responded like this?

'Is something wrong with the men around here?' He said it lightly, hoping to cut some of the tension. But the result was a flash of pain in her eyes that made him feel like a slug.

'It's my business, isn't it, how I live my life?' Her voice had chilled. 'Now, I've respected your wishes and your work these past days. Would you do me the same and let me get on with mine?'

'All right.' He let her go, stepped back. 'I'm going out for a while. Do you want me to pick up anything for you?'

'No, thank you.' She plunged her hands into the dough again and began to knead. 'It's raining a bit,' she said evenly. 'You might want a jacket.'

He walked to the doorway, turned back. 'Brianna.' He waited until she'd lifted her head. 'You never said whether or not you were interested. I'll have to assume you're thinking about it.'

He strode out. She didn't let out her next breath until she heard the door close behind him.

★

Gray worked off excess energy with a long drive and a visit to the Cliffs of Mohr. To give them both time to settle, he stopped in for lunch at a pub in Ennis. He walked off a heavy dose of fish and chips by wandering along the narrow streets. Something in a shop window caught his eyes, and following impulse he stepped inside and had it boxed.

By the time he returned to Blackthorn, he'd nearly convinced himself that what he'd experienced in the kitchen with Brianna was more a result of his joy over his work than chemistry.

Still, when he stepped into his room and found her kneeling on the edge of his bathroom floor, a bucket beside her and a rag in her hand, the scales tipped the other way. If a man wasn't dazzled with sex, why else would such a picture make his blood pump?

'Do you have any idea how often I come across you in that position?'

She looked over her shoulder. 'It's an honest living.' She blew her hair back. 'I'll tell you this, Grayson Thane, you live like a pig when you're working.'

He cocked a brow. 'Is that the way you talk to all your guests?'

He had her there. She flushed a little and slapped her rag back on the floor. 'I'll be done here soon if you've a mind to get back to it. I've another guest coming in this evening.'

'Tonight?' He scowled at the back of her head. He liked having the place to himself. Having her to himself. 'Who?'

'A British gentleman. He called shortly after you left this morning.'

'Well, who is he? How long's he staying?' And what the hell did he want?

'A night or two,' she said easily. 'I don't interrogate my guests, as you should know.'

'It just seems to me that you should ask questions. You can't just let strangers waltz into your home.'

Amused, she sat back and shook her head at him. A combination of the scruffy and elegant, she thought, with his gold-tipped hair pulled back piratelike, those lovely eyes of his sulky, the pricey boots, worn jeans, and crisp shirt. 'That's exactly what I do. I believe you waltzed in yourself, in the dead of night, not so long ago.'

'That's different.' At her bland look, he shrugged. 'It just is. Look, would you get up and stop that? You could eat off the damn floor.'

'Obviously today's rambling didn't put a smile on your face.'

'I was fine.' He prowled the room, then snarled. 'You've been messing with my desk.'

'I cleaned off an inch of dust and cigarette ash, if that's what you're meaning. I didn't touch your little machine there except to lift it up and set it down again.' Though she'd been tempted, sorely, to open the lid and take a peek at the works.

'You don't have to clean up after me all the time.' He hissed out a breath, stuffed his hands in his pockets when she simply stood, bucket in hand, and looked at him. 'Goddamn it, I thought I'd figured this out. It's not doing my ego any good to know you're not even trying to tie me up in knots.' He closed his eyes, let out a breath. 'Okay, let's try this again. I brought you a present.'

'Did you? Why?'

'Why the hell not?' He snatched the bag he'd put on the bed and handed it to her. 'I saw it. I thought you'd like it.'

'That was kind of you.' She slipped the box from the bag and began to work at the tape that held it closed.

She smelled of soap and flowers and disinfectant. Gray set his teeth. 'Unless you want me to toss you on the bed you've just tidied up, you'd be wise to step back.'

She looked up, startled, her hands freezing on the box. 'I'm serious.'

Cautious, she moistened her lips. 'All right.' She took a step back, then another. 'Is this better?'

The absurdity of it finally struck. Helpless to do otherwise, he grinned at her. 'Why do you fascinate me, Brianna?'

'I have no idea. None at all.'

'That might be why,' he murmured. 'Open your present.'

'I'm trying.' She loosened the tape, turned back the lid, and dug into the tissue paper. 'Oh, it's lovely.' Pleasure lit her face as she turned the porcelain cottage in her hands. It was delicately made, the front door open in welcome, a tidy garden with each tiny petal perfect. 'It looks as though you could move right in.'

'It made me think of you.'

'Thank you.' Her smile was easier now. 'Did you buy it to soften me up?'

'Tell me if it worked first.'

Now she laughed. 'No, I won't. You have advantage enough as it is.'

'Do I?'

Warned by the purr in his tone, she concentrated on replacing the cottage in the bed of tissue. 'I have dinner to tend to. Will you be wanting a tray?'

'Not tonight. The first wave's past.'

'The new guest is expected by five, so you'll have company with your meal.'

'Terrific.'

Gray had been prepared to dislike the British gentleman on sight, rather like a stud dog, he realized, exercising territorial rights. But it was difficult to feel threatened or irritated with the tidy little man with the shiny bald pate and the snooty public school accent.

His name was Herbert Smythe-White, of London, a retired widower who was in the first stages of a six-month tour of Ireland and Scotland.

'Pure indulgence,' he told Gray over dinner. 'Nancy and I weren't blessed with children, you see. She's been gone nearly two years now, and I find myself brooding about the house. We'd planned to make a trip like this, but work always kept me too busy.' His smile was laced with regret. 'I decided to make it myself as a sort of tribute to her. I think she would have liked that.'

'Is this your first stop?'

'It is. I flew into Shannon, leased a car.' He chuckled, taking off his wire-rimmed glasses and polishing the lenses on a handkerchief. 'I'm armed with the tourist's weapons of maps and guidebooks. I'll take a day or two here before heading north.' He set his glasses back on his prominent nose. 'I'm very much afraid I'm taking the best first, however. Miss Concannon sets an excellent table.'

'You won't get an argument from me.' They were sharing the dining room and a succulent salmon. 'What work were you in?'

'Banking. I'm afraid I spent too much of my life worried about figures.' He helped himself to another spoonful of potatoes in mustard sauce. 'And you, Mr. Thane. Miss Concannon tells me you're a writer. We practical sorts always envy the creative ones. I've never taken enough time to read for pleasure, but will certainly pick up one of your books now that we've met. Are you traveling, also?'

'Not at the moment. I'm based here for now.'

'Here, at the inn?'

'That's right.' He glanced up as Brianna came in.

'I hope you've room for dessert.' She set a large bowl of trifle on the table.

'Oh, my dear.' Behind his polished lenses, Smythe-

White's eyes danced with pleasure, and perhaps a little greed. 'I'll be a stone heavier before I leave the room.'

'I put magic in it, so the calories don't count.' She dished generous portions into bowls. 'I hope your room's comfortable, sir. If there's anything you need, you've only to ask.'

'It's exactly what I want,' he assured her. 'I must come back when your garden's in bloom.'

'I hope you will.' She left them a coffeepot and a decanter of brandy.

'A lovely woman,' Smythe-White commented.

'Yes, she is.'

'And so young to be running an establishment alone. One would think she'd have a husband, a family.'

'She's nothing if not efficient.' The first spoonful of trifle melted on Gray's tongue. *Efficient* wasn't the word, he realized. The woman was a culinary witch. 'She has a sister and brother-in-law just down the road. And it's a close community. Someone's always knocking on the kitchen door.'

'That's fortunate. I imagine it could be a lonely place otherwise. Still, I noticed as I was driving in that neighbors are few and far between.' He smiled again. 'I'm afraid I'm spoiled by the city, and not at all ashamed that I enjoy the crowds and the pace. It may take me awhile to grow accustomed to the night quiet.'

'You'll have plenty of it.' Gray poured brandy into a snifter, then, at his companion's nod, into a second. 'I was in London not long ago. What part are you from?'

'I have a little flat near Green Park. Didn't have the heart to keep the house after Nancy went.' He sighed, swirled brandy. 'Let me offer some unsolicited advice, Mr. Thane. Make your days count. Don't invest all your efforts in the future. You miss too much of the now.'

'That's advice I live on.'

★

Hours later it was thoughts of leftover trifle that pulled Gray away from his warm bed and a good book. The house moaned a bit around him as he dug up a pair of sweats, pulled them on. He padded downstairs in his bare feet with greedy dreams of gorging.

It certainly wasn't his first middle-of-the-night trip to the kitchen since he'd settled into Blackthorn. None of the shadows or creaking boards disturbed him as he slipped down the hall and into the dark kitchen. He turned on the stove light, not wanting to awaken Brianna.

Then he wished he hadn't thought of her, or of the fact that she was sleeping just a wall beyond. In that long, flannel nightgown, he imagined, with the little buttons at the collar. So prim it made her look exotic – certainly it made a man, a red-blooded one, wonder about the body all that material concealed.

And if he kept thinking along those lines, all the trifle in the country wouldn't sate his appetite.

One vice at a time, pal, he told himself. And got out a bowl. A sound from the outside made him pause, listen. Just as he was about to dismiss it as old house groans, he heard the scratching.

With the bowl in one hand, he went to the kitchen door, looked out, and saw nothing but night. Suddenly the glass was filled with fur and fangs. Gray managed to stifle a yelp and keep himself from overbalancing onto his butt. On something between a curse and a laugh, he opened the door for Con.

'Ten years off my life, thanks very much.' He scratched the dog's ears, and since Brianna wasn't around to see, decided to share the trifle with his canine companion.

'What do you think you're up to?'

Gray straightened, rapped his head against the cupboard

door he'd failed to close. A spoonful of trifle plopped into the dog's bowl and was gobbled up.

'Nothing.' Gray rubbed his throbbing head. 'Jesus Christ, between you and your wolf I'll be lucky if I live to see my next birthday.'

'He's not to be eating that.' Brianna snatched the bowl away from Gray. 'It isn't good for him.'

'*I* was going to eat it. Now I'll settle for a bottle of aspirin.'

'Sit down and I'll have a look at the knot on your head, or the hole in it, whatever the case may be.'

'Very cute. Why don't you just go back to bed and –'

He never finished the thought. From his stance between them, Con abruptly tensed, snarled, and with a growl bursting from his throat leaped toward the hallway door. It was Gray's bad luck that he happened to be in the way.

The force of a hundred and seventy pounds of muscle had him reeling back and smashing into the counter. He saw stars as his elbow cracked against the wood, and dimly heard Brianna's sharp command.

'Are you hurt?' Her tone was all soothing maternal concern now. 'Here now, Grayson, you've gone pale. Sit down. Con, heel!'

Ears ringing, stars circling in front of his eyes, the best Gray could do was slide into the chair Brianna held out for him. 'All this for a fucking bowl of cream.'

'There now, you just need to get your breath back. Let me see your arm.'

'Shit!' Gray's eyes popped wide as she flexed his elbow and pain radiated out. 'Are you trying to kill me just because I want to get you naked?'

'Stop that.' The rebuke was mild as she tut-tutted over the bruise. 'I've got some witch hazel.'

'I'd rather have morphine.' He blew out a breath and

stared narrow-eyed at the dog. Con continued to stand, quivering and ready at the doorway. 'What the hell is with him?'

'I don't know. Con, stop being a bloody fool and sit.' She dampened a cloth with witch hazel. 'It's probably Mr. Smythe-White. Con was out roaming when he got in. They haven't been introduced. It's likely he caught a scent.'

'It's lucky the old man didn't get a yen for trifle then.'

She only smiled and straightened up to look at the top of Gray's head. He had lovely hair, she thought, all gilded and silky. 'Oh, Con wouldn't hurt him. He'd just corner him. There, you'll have a fine bump, you will.'

'You don't have to sound so pleased about it.'

'It'll teach you not to give the dog sweets. I'll just make you an ice pack and —' She squealed as Gray yanked her into his lap. The dog's ears pricked up, but he merely wandered over and sniffed at Gray's hands.

'He likes me.'

'He's easily charmed. Let me up or I'll tell him to bite you.'

'He wouldn't. I just gave him trifle. Let's just sit here a minute, Brie. I'm too weak to bother you.'

'I don't believe that for a minute,' she said under her breath, but relented.

Gray cradled her head on his shoulder and smiled when Con rested his on her lap. 'This is nice.'

'It is.'

She felt a little crack around her heart as he held her quietly in the dim light from the stove while the house settled in sleep around them.

Chapter Six

Brianna needed a taste of spring. It was chancy, she knew, to begin to early, but the mood wouldn't pass. She gathered the seeds she'd been hording and her small portable radio and carted them out to the little shed she'd rigged as a temporary greenhouse.

It wasn't much, and she'd have been the first to admit it. No more than eight feet square with a floor of hard-packed dirt, the shed was better used for storage than planting. But she'd imposed on Murphy to put in glass and a heater. The benches she'd built herself with little skill and a great deal of pride.

There wasn't room, nor was there equipment for the kind of experimentation she dreamed of. Still, she could give her seeds an early start in the peat pots she'd ordered from a gardening supply catalog.

The afternoon was hers, after all, she told herself. Gray was closeted with his work, and Mr. Smythe-White was taking a motor tour of the Ring of Kerry. All the baking and mending were done for the day, so it was time for pleasure.

There was little that made her happier than having her hands in soil. Grunting a bit, she hefted a bag of potting mix onto the bench.

Next year, she promised herself, she'd have a professional greenhouse. Not a large one, but a fine one nonetheless. She'd take cuttings and root them, force bulbs so that she could have spring any time of year she liked. Perhaps she'd even attempt some grafting. But for the moment she was content to baby her seeds.

In days, she mused, humming along with the radio, the first tender sprigs would push through the soil. True it was a horrid expense, the luxury of fuel to warm them. It would have been wiser to use the money to have her car overhauled.

But it wouldn't be nearly so much fun.

She sowed, gently patting dirt, and let her mind drift.

How sweet Gray had been the night before, she remembered. Cuddling with her in the kitchen. It hadn't been so frightening, nor, she admitted, so exciting, as when he'd kissed her. This had been soft and soothing, and so natural it had seemed, just for a moment, that they'd belonged there together.

Once, long ago, she'd dreamed of sharing small, sweet moments like that with someone. With Rory, she thought with an old, dull pang. Then she'd believed she'd be married, have children to love, a home to tend to. What plans she'd made, she thought now, all rosy and warm with happy ever after at the end of them.

But then, she'd only been a girl, and in love. A girl in love believed anything. Believed everything. She wasn't a girl now.

She'd stopped believing when Rory had broken her heart, snapped it into two aching halves. She knew he was living near Boston now, with a wife and a family of his own. And, she was sure, with no thought whatever of the young sweet springtime when he'd courted her, and promised her. And pledged to her.

That was long ago, she reminded herself. Now she knew that love didn't always endure, and promises weren't always kept. If she still carried a seed of hope inside that longed to bloom, it hurt no one but herself.

'Here you are!' Eyes dancing, Maggie burst into the shed. 'I heard the music. What in the world are you up to in here?'

'I'm planting flowers.' Distracted, Brianna swiped the

back of her hand over her cheek and smeared it with soil. 'Close the door, Maggie, you're letting the heat out. What is it? You look about to burst.'

'You'll never guess, not in a thousand years.' With a laugh, Maggie swung around the small shed, grabbing Brianna's arms to twirl her. 'Go ahead. Try.'

'You're having triplets.'

'No! Praise God.'

Maggie's mood was infectious enough to have Brianna chuckle and fall into the rhythm of the impromptu jig. 'You've sold a piece of your glass for a million pounds, to the president of the United States.'

'Oh, what a thought. Maybe we should send him a brochure. No, you're miles off, you are, miles. I'll give you a bit of a hint then. Rogan's grandmother called.'

Brianna blew her tumbling hair out of her eyes. 'That's a hint?'

'It would be if you'd put your mind to it. Brie, she's getting married. She's marrying Uncle Niall, next week, in Dublin.'

'What?' Brianna's mouth fell open on the word. 'Uncle Niall, Mrs. Sweeney, married?'

'Isn't it grand? Isn't it just grand? You know she had a crush on him when she was a girl in Galway. Then after more than fifty years they meet again because of Rogan and me. Now, by all the saints in heaven, they're going to take vows.' Tossing back her head, she cackled. 'Now as well as being husband and wife, Rogan and I will be cousins.'

'Uncle Niall.' It seemed to be all Brianna could manage.

'You should have seen Rogan's face when he took the call. He looked like a fish. His mouth opening and closing and not a word coming out.' Snorting with laughter, she leaned against Brianna's workbench. 'He's never gotten accustomed to the idea that they were courting. More than courting, if it comes to that – but I suppose it's a difficult thing for a man to imagine his white-haired granny snuggled up in sin.'

'Maggie!' Overcome, Brianna covered her mouth with her hand. Giggles turned into hoots of laughter.

'Well, they're making it legal now, with an archbishop no less officiating.' She took a deep breath, looked around. 'Have you anything to eat out here?'

'No. When is it to be? Where?'

'Saturday next, in her Dublin house. A small ceremony, she tells me, with just family and close friends. Uncle Niall's eighty if he's a day, Brie. Imagine it.'

'I think I can. Oh, and I do think it's grand. I'll call them after I've finished here and cleaned up.'

'Rogan and I are leaving for Dublin today. He's on the phone right now, God bless him, making arrangements.' She smiled a little. 'He's trying to be a man about it.'

'He'll be happy for them, once he gets used to it.' Brianna's voice was vague as she began to wonder what sort of gift she should buy the bride and groom.

'It's to be an afternoon ceremony, but you may want to come out the night before so you'll have some time.'

'Come out?' Brianna focused on her sister again. 'But I can't go, Maggie. I can't leave. I have a guest.'

'Of course you'll go.' Maggie straightened from the bench, set her jaw. 'It's Uncle Niall. He'll expect you there. It's one bloody day, Brianna.'

'Maggie, I have obligations here, and no way to get to Dublin and back.'

'Rogan will have the plane take you.'

'But –'

'Oh, hang Grayson Thane. He can cook his own meals for a day. You're not a servant.'

Brianna's shoulders stiffened. Her eyes turned cool. 'No,

I'm not. I'm a businesswoman who's given her word. I can't dance off for a weekend in Dublin and tell the man to fend for himself.'

'Then bring him along. If you're worried the man will fall over dead without you to tend him, bring him with you.'

'Bring him where?' Gray pushed open the door, eyed both women cautiously. He'd seen Maggie go dashing into the shed from his bedroom window. Curiosity had eventually brought him out, and the shouting had done the rest.

'Shut the door,' Brianna said automatically. She fought back embarrassment that he should have walked in on a family argument. She sighed once. The tiny shed was now crowded with people. 'Was there something you needed, Grayson?'

'No.' He lifted a hand, brushing his thumb over the dirt on her cheek — a gesture that had Maggie's eyes narrowing. 'You have dirt on your face, Brie. What are you up to?'

'I'm trying to put in some seeds — but there's hardly room for them now.'

'Mind your hands, boy-o,' Maggie muttered.

He only grinned and stuck them in his pockets. 'I heard my name mentioned. Is there a problem?'

'There wouldn't be if she wasn't so stubborn.' Maggie tossed up her chin and decided to dump the blame at Gray's feet. 'She needs to go to Dublin next weekend, but she won't leave you.'

Gray's grin turned into a satisfied smile as his gaze shifted from Maggie to Brianna. 'Won't she?'

'You've paid for room and board,' Brianna began.

'Why do you need to go to Dublin?' he interrupted.

'Our uncle's getting married,' Maggie told him. 'He'll want her there, and that's as it should be. I say if she won't leave you behind, she should take you along.'

'Maggie, Gray doesn't want to be going off to a wedding, with people he doesn't know. He's working, and he can't just –'

'Sure he does,' Gray cut her off. 'When do we leave?'

'Good. You'll stay at our house there. That's settled.' Maggie brushed her hands together. 'Now, who's going to tell Mother?'

'I –'

'No, let me,' Maggie decided before Brianna could answer. She smiled. 'She'll really hate it. We'll have the plane take her out Saturday morning so you won't be badgered by her the whole trip. Have you a suit, Gray?'

'One or two,' he murmured.

'Then you're set, aren't you?' She leaned forward, kissed Brianna firmly on both cheeks. 'Plan to leave Friday,' she ordered. 'I'll call you from Dublin.'

Gray ran his tongue around his teeth as Maggie slammed out. 'Bossy, isn't she?'

'Aye.' Brianna blinked, shook her head. 'She doesn't mean it. It's just that she's always sure she's right. And she has a deep fondness for Uncle Niall and for Rogan's grandmother.'

'Rogan's grandmother.'

'That's who he's marrying.' She turned back to her potting, hoping to clear her mind with work.

'That sounds like a story.'

'Oh, it is. Gray, it's kind of you to be so obliging, but it's not necessary. They won't miss me, really, and it's a lot of trouble for you.'

'A weekend in Dublin's no trouble for me. And you want to go, don't you?'

'That's not the point. Maggie put you in a difficult position.'

He put a hand under her chin, lifted it. 'Why do you

have such a hard time answering questions? You want to go, don't you? Yes or no.'

'Yes.'

'Okay, we go.'

Her lips started to curve, until he leaned toward them. 'Don't kiss me,' she said, weakening.

'Now, that's a lot of trouble for me.' But he reined himself in, leaned back. 'Who hurt you, Brianna?'

Her lashes fluttered down, shielding her eyes. 'It may be I don't answer questions because you ask too many of them.'

'Did you love him?'

She turned her head, concentrated on her pots. 'Yes, very much.'

It was an answer, but he found it didn't please him. 'Are you still in love with him?'

'That would be foolish.'

'That's not an answer.'

'Yes, it is. Do I breathe down your neck when you're working?'

'No.' But he didn't step back. 'But you have such an appealing neck.' To prove it, he bent down to brush his lips over the nape. It didn't hurt his ego to feel her tremble. 'I dreamed of you last night, Brianna. And wrote of it today.'

Most of her seeds scattered on the workbench instead of in the soil. She busied herself rescuing them. 'Wrote of it?'

'I made some changes. In the book you're a young widow who's struggling to build on a broken past.'

Despite herself, she was drawn and turned to look at him. 'You're putting me in your book?'

'Pieces of you. Your eyes, those wonderful, sad eyes. Your hair.' He lifted a hand to it. 'Thick, slippery hair, the color of the coolest sunset. Your voice, that soft lilt. Your body, slim, willowy, with a dancer's unconscious grace. Your skin, your hands. I see you when I write, so I write of you. And beyond the physical, there's your integrity, your loyalty.' He smiled a little. 'Your tea cakes. The hero's just as fascinated with her as I am with you.'

Gray set his hands on the bench on either side of her, caging her in. 'And he keeps running into that same shield you both have. I wonder how long it'll take him to break it down.'

No one had ever said such words about her before, such words to her. A part of her yearned to wallow in them, as if they were silk. Another part stood cautiously back.

'You're trying to seduce me.'

He lifted a brow. 'How'm I doing?'

'I can't breathe.'

'That's a good start.' He leaned closer until his mouth was a whisper from hers. 'Let me kiss you, Brianna.'

He already was in that slow, sinking way he had that turned all her muscles to mush. Mouth to mouth. It was such a simple thing, but it tilted every thing in her world. Further and further until she was afraid she would never right it again.

He had skill, and with skill a patience. Beneath both was the shimmer of repressed violence she once sensed in him. The combination seeped into her like a drug, weakening, dizzying.

She wanted, as a woman wanted. She feared, as innocence feared.

Gently he took the fingers she gripped on the edge of the bench, soothed them open. With his mouth skimming over hers, he lifted her arms.

'Hold me, Brianna.' God he needed her to. 'Kiss me back.'

Like a crack of a whip, his quiet words spurred her. Suddenly she was clinging to him, her mouth wild and willing. Staggered, he rocked back, gripping her. Her lips were hot, hungry, her body vibrating like a plucked harp string. The eruption of her passion was like lava spewing through ice, frenzied, unexpected, and dangerous.

There was the elemental smell of earth, the wail of Irish pipes from the radio, the succulent flavor of woman in his mouth, and the quivering temptation of her in his arms.

Then he was blind and deaf to all but her. Her hands were fisted in his hair, her panting breaths filling his mouth. More, only wanting more, he slammed her back against the shed wall. He heard her cry out – in shock, pain, excitement – before he muffled the sound, devouring it, devouring her.

His hands streaked over her, hotly possessive, invasive. And her pants turned to moans: Please . . . She wanted to beg him for something. Oh, please. Such an ache, a deep, grinding, glorious ache. But she didn't know the beginning of it, or how it would end. And the fear was snapping like a wolf behind it – fear of him, of herself, of what she'd yet to know.

He wanted her skin – the feel and taste of her flesh. He wanted to pound himself inside of her until they were both empty. The breath was tearing through his lungs as he gripped her shirt, his hands poised to rip and rend.

And his eyes met hers.

Her lips were bruised and trembling, her cheeks pale as ice. Her eyes were wide with terror and need warring in them. He looked down, saw his knuckles were white from strain. And the marks his greedy fingers had put on her lovely skin.

He jerked back as if she'd slapped him, then held up his hands. He wasn't sure what or who he was warding off.

'I'm sorry,' he managed while she stood pressed back into the wall, gulping air. 'I'm sorry. Did I hurt you?'

'I don't know.' How could she know where there was nothing but this horrible pulsing ache. She hadn't dreamed she could feel like this. Hadn't known it was possible to feel so much. Dazed, she brushed at the dampness on her cheeks.

'Don't cry.' He dragged an unsteady hand through his hair. 'I feel filthy enough about this.'

'No, it's not –' She swallowed the tears. She had no idea why she should shed them. 'I don't know what happened to me.'

Of course she didn't, he thought bitterly. Hadn't she told him she was innocent? And he'd gone at her like an animal. In another minute he would have dragged her down on the dirt and finished the job.

'I pushed you, and there's no excuse for it. I can only tell you I lost my head and apologize for it.' He wanted to go back to her, brush the tangled hair from her face. But didn't dare. 'I was rough, and frightened you. It won't happen again.'

'I knew you would be.' She was steadier now, perhaps because he seemed so shaken. 'All along I knew. It wasn't that, Grayson. I'm not the fragile sort.'

He found he could smile after all. 'Oh, but you are, Brianna. And I've never been quite so clumsy. This may seem like an awkward time to tell you, but you don't have to be afraid of me. I won't hurt you.'

'I know. You –'

'And I'm going to try my damnedest not to rush you,' he interrupted. 'But I want you.'

She discovered she had to concentrate to breath evenly again. 'We can't always have what we want.'

'I've never believed that. I don't know who he was, Brie, but he's gone. I'm here.'

She nodded. 'For now.'

'There's only now.' He shook his head before she could argue. 'This is as odd a place for philosophy as it is for sex. We're both a little wired up, right?'

'I suppose you could say that.'

'Let's go inside. This time I'll make *you* some tea.'

Her lips curved. 'Do you know how?'

'I've been watching you. Come on.' He held out a hand. She looked at it, hesitated. After another cautious glance at his face – it was calm now, without that odd feral light that was so frightening and exciting – she slipped her hand into his.

'Maybe it's a good thing we've got a chaperone tonight.'

'Oh?' She turned her head as they stepped outside.

'Otherwise you might sneak up to my room tonight and take advantage of me.'

She let out a short laugh. 'You're too clever for anyone to take advantage of you.'

'Well, you could try.' Relieved neither of them were trembling now, he slung a companionable arm around her shoulders. 'Why don't we have a bit of cake with the tea?'

She slid her eyes toward him as they reached the kitchen door. 'Mine, or the one the woman makes in your book?'

'Hers is only in my imagination, darling. Now, yours –' He froze when he pushed the door open. Instinctively he shoved Brianna behind him. 'Stay here. Right here.'

'What? Are you – oh, sweet Jesus.' Over his shoulder she could see the chaos of her kitchen. Tins had been turned over, cupboards emptied. Flour and sugar, spices and tea were swept onto the floor.

'I said stay here,' he repeated as she tried to shove by him.

'I'll not. Look at this mess.'

He blocked her with an arm across the doorway. 'Do you keep money in your tins? Jewelry?'

'Don't be daft. Of course I don't.' She blinked up at him.

'You think someone was after stealing something? I've nothing to steal and no one would.'

'Well, someone did, and they could still be in the house. Where's that damn dog?' he muttered.

'He'd be off with Murphy,' she said dully. 'He goes off to visit most afternoons.'

'Run over to Murphy's then, or to your sister's. I'll take a look around.'

She drew herself up. 'This is my home, I'll remind you. I'll look myself.'

'Stay behind me,' was all he said.

He checked her rooms first, ignoring her expected shriek of outrage when she saw the pulled-out drawers and tumbled clothes.

'My things.'

'We'll see if there's anything missing later. Better check the rest.'

'What sort of mischief is this?' she demanded, her temper heating as she trailed behind Gray. 'Oh, damn them,' she swore when she saw the parlor.

It had been a quick, hurried, and frantic search, Gray mused. Anything but professional and foolishly risky. He was thinking it through when another idea slammed into him.

'Shit.' He took the stairs two at a time, burst into the mess of his own room, and bolted straight for his laptop. 'Somebody will die,' he muttered, booting it up.

'Your work.' Brianna stood pale and furious in the doorway. 'Did they harm your work?'

'No.' He skimmed through page after page until he was satisfied. 'No, it's here. It's fine.'

She let out a little sigh of relief before turning away to check Mr. Smythe-White's room. His clothes had been turned out of the drawers and closet, his bed pulled apart. 'Mary, Mother of God, how will I explain this to him?'

'I think it's more to the point to ask what they were looking for. Sit down, Brianna,' Gray ordered. 'Let's think this through.'

'What's to think about?' But she did sit, on the edge of the tilted mattress. 'I've nothing of value here. A few pounds, a few trinkets.' She rubbed her eyes, impatient with herself for the tears she couldn't manage to stem. 'It wouldn't have been anyone from the village or nearby. It had to be a vagrant, a hitchhiker perhaps, hoping to find a bit of cash. Well . . .' She let out a shaky breath. 'He'll have been disappointed in what he found here.' She looked up abruptly, paling again. 'You? Did you have any?'

'Mostly traveler's checks. They're still here.' He shrugged. 'He got a few hundred pounds, that's all.'

'A few — hundred?' She bolted off the bed. 'He took your money?'

'It's not important. Brie —'

'Not important?' she cut in. 'You're living under my roof, a guest in my home, and had your money stolen. How much was it? I'll make it good.'

'You certainly will not. Sit down and stop it.'

'I said I'll make it good.'

Patience snapped, he took her firmly by the shoulders and shoved her down on the bed. 'They paid me five million for my last book, before foreign and movie rights. A few hundred pounds isn't going to break me.' His eyes narrowed when her lips quivered again. 'Take a deep breath. Now. Okay, another.'

'I don't care if you've gold dripping from your fingers.' Her voice broke, humiliating her.

'You want to cry some more?' He sighed lustily, sat down beside her, and braced for it. 'Okay, let it rip.'

'I'm not going to cry.' She sniffled, used the heels of her hands to dry her cheeks. 'I've got too much to do. It'll take hours to put things right here.'

'You'll need to call the police?'

'For what?' She lifted her hands, let them fall. 'If anyone saw a stranger lurking about, my phone would already be ringing. Someone needed money, and they took it.' She scanned the room, wondering how much her other guest might have lost, and how big a hole it would put in her precious savings. 'I want you to say nothing to Maggie about this.'

'Goddamn it, Brie —'

'She's six months along. I won't have her upset. I mean this.' She gave him a steady look through eyes still shimmering with tears. 'Your word, please.'

'Fine, whatever you want. I want yours that you'll tell me exactly what's missing.'

'I will. I'll phone to Murphy and tell him. He'll ask about. If there's something to know, I'll know it by nightfall.' Calm again, she rose. 'I need to start putting things in order. I'll start with your room so you can get to your work.'

'I'll see to my own room.'

'It's for me to —'

'You're pissing me off, Brianna.' He unfolded himself slowly until he stood toe to toe with her. 'Let's get this straight. You're not my maid, my mother, or my wife. I can hang up my own clothes.'

'As you please.'

Swearing, he grabbed her arm before she could walk out on him. She didn't resist, but stood very still, looking just over his shoulder. 'Listen to me. You have a problem here and I want to help you. Can you get that through your head?'

'Want to help, do you?' She inclined her head and spoke with all the warmth of a glacier. 'You might go borrow some tea from Murphy. We seem to be out.'

'I'll call him for you,' Gray said evenly. 'And ask him to bring some over. I'm not leaving you alone here.'

'Whatever suits you. His number's in the book in the kitchen by the . . .' She trailed off as the image of her lovely little room flashed into her head. She closed her eyes. 'Gray, would you leave me alone for a little while? I'll be better for it.'

'Brianna.' He touched her cheek.

'Please.' She'd crumble completely, humiliatingly, if he was kind now. 'I'll be fine again once I'm busy. And I'd like some tea.' Opening her eyes, she managed to smile. 'Truly, I would.'

'All right, I'll be downstairs.'

Grateful, she got to work.

Chapter Seven

Gray sometimes toyed with the idea of buying himself a plane. Something very much along the lines of the sleek little jet Rogan had left at his and Brianna's disposal for the trip to Dublin might be just the ticket. He could have it custom-decorated to suit him, play with the engine himself occasionally. There was nothing to stop him from learning how to fly it.

It would certainly be an interesting toy, he mused as he settled into the comfortable leather seat beside Brianna. And having his own transportation would eliminate the minor headache of arranging for tickets and being at the mercy of the hiccups of the airlines.

But owning something – anything – equaled the responsibility of maintaining that something. That was why he rented or leased, but had never actually owned a car. And though there was something to be said for the privacy and convenience of a neat little Lear, he thought he would miss the crowds and company and all the odd expected glitches of a commercial flight.

But not this time. He slipped his hand over Brianna's as the plane began to taxi.

'Do you like to fly?'

'I haven't done it very often.' The anticipation of spearing up into the sky still gave her stomach an intriguing little flip. 'But yes, I think I do. I like looking down.' She smiled at herself as she watched the ground tilt away below. It fascinated her, always, to picture herself above her own home, the hills, streaking through the clouds to somewhere else. 'I suppose it's second nature to you.'

'It's fun, thinking about where you're going.'

'And where you've been.'

'I don't think about that much. I've just been there.'

As the plane climbed, he put a hand under her chin, turned her face toward his to study it. 'You're still worried.'

'It doesn't feel right, going off like this, and so luxuriously, too.'

'Catholic guilt.' The gilt in his eyes deepened when he grinned. 'I've heard of that particular phenomenon. It's like if you're not doing something constructive, and actually enjoying not doing it, you're going to hell. Right?'

'Nonsense.' She sniffed, irritated that it was even partially true. 'I've responsibilities.'

'And shirking them.' He tsked and fingered the gold cross she wore. 'That's like the near occasion of sin, isn't it? What is the near occasion of sin, exactly?'

'You are,' she said, batting his hand away.

'No kidding?' The idea of that appealed enormously. 'I like it.'

'You would.' She tucked a loose pin into place. 'And this has nothing to do with that. If I'm feeling guilty, it's because I'm not used to just packing up and going on a moment's notice. I like to plan things out.'

'Takes half the fun out of it.'

'It stretches out the fun to my way of thinking.' But she gnawed on her lip. 'I know it's important that I be in Dublin for the wedding, but leaving home just now . . .'

'Murphy's dog sitting,' Gray reminded her. 'And keeping an eye on the place.' A sharp eye, Gray was certain, since he'd talked to Murphy privately. 'Old Smythe-White left days ago, so you don't have any customers to worry about.'

'Guests,' she said automatically, brow creasing. 'I can't imagine he'll be recommending Blackthorn after what happened. Though he was terribly good about it.'

'He didn't lose anything. "Never travel with cash, you

know," ' Gray said in a mimic of Smythe–White's prissy voice. ' "It's an invitation for trouble." '

She smiled a little, as he'd hoped. 'He may not have had anything stolen, but I doubt he spent a peaceful night knowing his room had been broken into, his possessions pawed through.' Which was why she'd refused to charge him for his stay.

'Oh, I don't know. I haven't had any trouble.' He unfastened his seat belt and rose to wander into the galley. 'Your brother-in-law's a classy guy.'

'He is, yes.' Her brow furrowed when Gray came back with a bottle of champagne and two glasses. 'You're not going to open that. 'Tis only a short flight and –'

'Sure I'm going to open it. Don't you like champagne?'

'I like it well enough, but –' Her protest was cut off by the cheerful sound of a popping cork. She sighed, as a mother might seeing her child leap into a mud puddle.

'Now then.' He sat again, poured both glasses. After handing her one, he tapped crystal to crystal and grinned. 'Tell me about the bride and groom. Did you say they were eighty?'

'Uncle Niall, yes.' Since there could be no putting the cork back into the bottle, she sipped. 'Mrs. Sweeney's a few years younger.'

'Imagine that.' It tickled him. 'Entering the matrimonial cage at their age.'

'Cage?'

'It has a lot of restrictions and no easy way out.' Enjoying the wine, he let it linger on his tongue before swallowing. 'So, they were childhood sweethearts?'

'Not exactly,' she murmured, still frowning over his description of marriage. 'They grew up in Galway. Mrs. Sweeney was friends with my grandmother – she was Uncle Niall's sister, you see. And Mrs. Sweeney had a bit of a crush on Uncle Niall. Then my grandmother married and moved to Clare. Mrs. Sweeney married and went to Dublin. They lost track of each other. Then Maggie and Rogan began working together, and Mrs. Sweeney made the connection between the families. I wrote of it to Uncle Niall, and he brought himself down to Dublin.' She smiled over it, hardly noticing when Gray refilled her glass. 'The two of them have been close as bread and jam ever since.'

'The twists and turns of fate.' Gray raised his glass in toast. 'Fascinating, isn't it?'

'They love each other,' she said simply, sighed. 'I only hope –' She cut herself off and stared out the window again.

'What?'

'I want them to have a fine day, a lovely one. I'm worried my mother will make it awkward.' She turned to him again. However it embarrassed her, it was best he knew so that he wouldn't be too shocked if there was a scene. 'She wouldn't go out to Dublin today. Wouldn't sleep in Maggie's Dublin house. She told me she'd come tomorrow, do her duty, then go back immediately.'

He lifted a brow. 'Not happy in cities?' he asked, though he sensed it was something entirely different.

'Mother's not a woman who finds contentment easily anywhere at all. I should tell you she may be difficult. She doesn't approve, you see, of the wedding.'

'What? Does she think those crazy kids are too young to get married?'

Brianna's lips curved, but her eyes didn't reflect it. 'It's money marrying money, as she sees it. And she . . . well, she has strong opinions about the fact that they've been living together in a way outside the sacrament.'

'Living together?' He couldn't stop the grin. 'In a way?'

'Living together,' she said primly. 'And as Mother will tell you, if you give her the chance, age hardly absolves them from the sin of fornication.'

He choked on his wine. He was laughing and whooping for air when he caught the glint of Brianna's narrowed gaze. 'Sorry – I can see that wasn't meant to be a joke.'

'Some people find it easy to laugh at another's beliefs.'

'I don't mean to.' But he couldn't quite get the chuckles under control. 'Christ, Brie, you've just told me the man's eighty and his blushing bride is right behind him. You don't really believe they're going to some firey hell because they . . .' He decided he'd better find a delicate way of putting it. 'They've had a mature, mutually satisfying physical relationship.'

'No.' Some of the ice melted from her eyes. 'No, I don't, of course. But Mother does, or says she does, because it makes it easier to complain. Families are complicated, aren't they?'

'From what I've observed. I don't have one to worry about myself.'

'No family?' The rest of the ice melted into sympathy. 'You lost your parents?'

'In a manner of speaking.' It would have been more apt, he supposed, to say they had lost him.

'I'm sorry. And you've no brothers, no sisters?'

'Nope.' He reached for the bottle again to top off his glass.

'But you've cousins, surely.' Everyone had someone, she thought. 'Grandparents, or aunts, uncles.'

'No.'

She only stared, devastated for him. To have no one. She couldn't conceive of it. Couldn't bear it.

'You're looking at me like I'm some foundling bundled in a basket on your doorstep.' It amused him, and oddly, it touched him. 'Believe me, honey, I like it this way. No ties, no strings, no guilts.' He drank again, as if to seal the words. 'Simplifies my life.'

Empties it, more like, she thought. 'It doesn't bother you, having no one to go home to?'

'It relieves me. Maybe it would if I had a home, but I don't have one of those, either.'

The gypsy, she recalled, but she hadn't taken him literally until now. 'But, Grayson, to have no place of your own –'

'No mortgage, no lawn to mow or neighbor to placate.' He leaned over her to glance out the window. 'Look, there's Dublin.'

But she looked at him, felt for him. 'But when you leave Ireland, where will you go?'

'I haven't decided. That's the beauty of it.'

'You've got a great house.' Less than three hours after landing in Dublin, Gray stretched his legs out toward the fire in Rogan's parlor. 'I appreciate your putting me up.'

'It's our pleasure.' Rogan offered him a snifter of after-dinner brandy. They were alone for the moment, as Brianna and Maggie had driven to his grandmother's to help the bride with last-minute arrangements.

Rogan still had trouble picturing his grandmother as a nervous bride-to-be. And more trouble yet, imagining the man even now haranguing the cook as his future step-grandfather.

'You don't look too happy about it.'

'What?' Rogan glanced back at Gray, made himself smile. 'No, I'm sorry, it's nothing to do with you. I'm a bit uneasy about tomorrow, I suppose.'

'Giving-the-bride-away jitters?'

The best Rogan could come up with was a grunt.

Reading his host well, Gray tucked his tongue in his cheek and stirred the unease. 'Niall's an interesting character.'

'A character,' Rogan muttered. 'Indeed.'

'Your grandmother had stars in her eyes at dinner.'

Now Rogan sighed. She had never looked happier. 'They're besotted with each other.'

'Well . . .' Gray swirled his brandy. 'There are two of us and one of him. We could overpower him, drag him off to the docks, and put him on a ship bound for Australia.'

'Don't think I haven't considered it.' But he smiled now, easier. 'There's no picking family, is there? And I'm forced to admit the man adores her. Maggie and Brie are delighted, so I find myself outgunned and outvoted.'

'I like him,' Gray said in grinning apology. 'How can you not like a man who wears a jacket the shade of a Halloween pumpkin with tasseled alligator shoes?'

'There you are.' Rogan waved an elegant hand. 'In any case, we're pleased to be able to provide you with a wedding during your stay in Ireland. You're comfortable at Blackthorn?'

'Brianna has a knack for providing the comfortable.'

'She does.'

Gray's expression sobered as he frowned into his drink. 'Something happened a few days ago that I think you should know. She didn't want me to mention it, particularly to Maggie. But I'd like your take on it.'

'All right.'

'The cottage was broken into.'

'Blackthorn?' Startled, Rogan set his brandy aside.

'We were outside, in that shed she uses for potting. We might have been in there for half an hour, maybe a little longer. When we went back in, someone had tossed the place.'

'Excuse me?'

'Turned it upside down,' Gray explained. 'A fast, messy search, I'd say.'

'That doesn't make sense.' But he leaned forward, worried. 'Was anything taken?'

'I had some cash in my room.' Gray shrugged it off. 'That seems to be all. Brianna claims none of the neighbors would have come in that way.'

'She'd be right.' Rogan sat back again, picked up his brandy but didn't drink. 'It's a closely knit community, and Brie's well loved there. Did you inform the garda?'

'She didn't want to, didn't see the point. I did speak with Murphy, privately.'

'That would tend to it,' Rogan agreed. 'I'd have to think it was some stranger passing through. But even that seems out of place.' Dissatisfied with any explanation, he tapped his fingers against the side of his glass. 'You've been there some time now. You must have gotten a sense of the people, the atmosphere.'

'Next stop Brigadoon,' Gray murmured. 'Logic points to a one-shot deal, and that's how she's handling it.' Gray moved his shoulders. 'Still, I don't think it would hurt for you to keep an eye out when you come back.'

'I'll do that.' Rogan frowned into his brandy. 'You can be sure of it.'

'You've a fine cook, Rogan me boy.' Niall strolled in carting a tray loaded with china and a huge chocolate torte. He was a large man, sporting his thirty extra pounds like a badge of honor. And did indeed look somewhat like a jolly jack-o'-lantern in his orange sport coat and lime-green tie. 'A prince of a man, he is.' Niall set down the tray and beamed. 'He's sent out this bit of sweet to help calm my nerves.'

'I'm feeling nervous myself.' Grinning, Gray rose to cut into the torte himself.

Niall boomed out with a laugh and slapped Gray heartily on the back. 'There's a lad. Good appetite. Why don't we tuck into this, then have a few games of snooker?' He winked at Rogan. 'After all, it's my last night as a free man. No more carousing with the boy-os for me. Any whiskey to wash this down with?'

'Whiskey.' Rogan looked at the wide, grinning face of his future grandfather. 'I could use a shot myself.'

They had several. And then a few more. By the time the second bottle was opened, Gray had to squint to see the balls on the snooker table, and then they still tended to weave. He ended by closing one eye completely.

He heard the balls clack together, then stood back. 'My point, gentlemen. My point.' He leaned heavily on his cue.

'Yank bastard can't lose tonight.' Niall slapped Gray on the back and nearly sent him nose first onto the table. 'Set 'em up again, Rogan me boy. Let's have another.'

'I can't see them,' Rogan said slowly before lifting a hand in front of his face and peering at it. 'I can't feel my fingers.'

'Another whiskey's what you need.' Like a sailor aboard a pitching deck, Niall made his way to the decanter. 'Not a drop,' he said sadly as he upended the crystal. 'Not a bleeding drop left.'

'There's no whiskey left in Dublin.' Rogan pushed himself away from the wall that was holding him up, then fell weakly back. 'We've drank it all. Drunk it all. Oh, Christ. I can't feel my tongue, either. I've lost it.'

'Let's see.' Willing to help, Gray laid his hands heavily on Rogan's shoulders. 'Stick it out.' Eyes narrowed, he nodded. ' 'S okay, pal. It's there. Fact is, you've got two of 'em. That's the problem.'

'I'm marrying my Chrissy tomorrow.' Niall stood, teetering dangerously left, then right, his eyes glazed, his smile brilliant. 'Beautiful little Chrissy, the belle of Dublin.'

He pitched forward, falling like a redwood. With their arms companionably supporting each other, Rogan and Gray stared down at him.

'What do we do with him?' Gray wondered.

Rogan ran one of his two tongues around his teeth. 'Do you think he's alive?'

'Doesn't look like it.'

'Don't start the wake yet.' Niall lifted his head. 'Just get me on me feet, lads. I'll dance till dawn.' His head hit the floor again with a thud.

'He's not so bad, is he?' Rogan asked. 'When I'm drunk, that is.'

'A prince of a man. Let's haul him up. He can't dance on his face.'

'Right.' They staggered over. By the time they'd hefted Niall to his knees, they were out of breath and laughing like fools. 'Get up, you dolt. It's like trying to shift a beached whale.'

Niall opened his bleary eyes, tossed back his head, and began, in a wavering but surprisingly affecting tenor, to sing.

'And it's all for me grog, me jolly, jolly grog. It's all for me beer and tobacco.' He grunted his way up on one foot, nearly sent Gray flying. 'Well, I spent all me tin on lassies drinking gin. Far across the Western ocean I must wander.'

'You'll be lucky to wander to bed,' Rogan told him.

He simply switched tunes. 'Well, if you've got a wingo, take me up to ringo where the waxies singo all the day.'

Well insulated by whiskey, Rogan joined in as the three of them teetered on their feet. 'If you've had your fill of porter and you can't go any further −'

That struck Gray as wonderfully funny, and he snickered his way into the chorus.

With the harmony and affection of the drunk, they staggered their way down the hall. By the time they reached the base of the stairs, they were well into a whiskey-soaked rendition of 'Dicey Riley.'

'Well, I wouldn't say it was only poor old Dicey Riley who'd taken to the sup, would you, Brie?' Maggie stood halfway down the stairs with her sister, studying the trio below.

'I wouldn't, no.' Folding her hands neatly at her waist, Brianna shook her head. 'From the looks of them, they've dropped in for several little drops.'

'Christ, she's beautiful, isn't she?' Gray mumbled.

'Yes.' Rogan grinned brilliantly at his wife. 'Takes my breath away. Maggie, my love, come give me a kiss.'

'I'll give you the back of my hand.' But she laughed as she started down. 'Look at the lot of you, pitiful drunk. Uncle Niall, you're old enough to know better.'

'Getting married, Maggie Mae. Where's my Chrissy?' He tried to turn a circle in search and had his two supporters tipping like dominoes.

'In her own bed sleeping, as you should be. Come on, Brie, let's get these warriors off the field.'

'We were playing snooker.' Gray beamed at Brianna. 'I won.'

'Yank bastard,' Niall said affectionately, then kissed Gray hard on the mouth.

'Well, that's nice, isn't it?' Maggie managed to get an arm around Rogan. 'Come on now, that's the way. One foot in front of the other.' Somehow they managed to negotiate the steps. They dumped Niall first.

'Get Rogan off to bed, Maggie,' Brianna told her. 'I'll tuck this one in, then come back and pull off Uncle Niall's shoes.'

'Oh, what heads they'll have tomorrow.' The prospect made Maggie smile. 'Here we go, Sweeney, off to bed. Mind your hands.' Since she considered him harmless in his current state, the order came out with a chuckle. 'You haven't a clue what to do with them in your state.'

'I'll wager I do.'

'Oh, but you smell of whiskey and cigars.' Brianna sighed and draped Gray's arm over her shoulders, braced him. 'The man's eighty, you know. You should have stopped him.'

'He's a bad influence, that Niall Feeney. We had to toast Chrissy's eyes, and her lips, and her hair, and her ears. I think we toasted her toes, too, but things get blurry about then.'

'And small wonder. Here's your door. Just a bit farther now.'

'You smell so good, Brianna.' With what he thought was a smooth move, he sniffed doglike at her neck. 'Come to bed with me. I could show you things. All sorts of wonderful things.'

'Mmm-hmm. Down you go. That's the way.' Efficiently, she lifted his legs onto the bed and began to take off his shoes.

'Lie down with me. I can take you places. I want to be inside you.'

Her hands fumbled at that. She looked up sharply, but his eyes were closed, his smile dreamy. 'Hush now,' she murmured. 'Go to sleep.'

She tucked a blanket around him, brushed the hair from his brow, and left him snoring.

Suffering was to be expected. Overindulgence had to be paid for, and Gray was always willing to pay his way. But it seemed a little extreme to have to take a short, vicious trip to hell because of one foolish evening.

His head was cracked in two. It didn't show, a fact that relieved him considerably when he managed to crawl into the bathroom the following morning. He looked haggard, but whole. Obviously the jagged break in his skull was on the inside.

He'd probably be dead by nightfall.

His eyes were small, hard balls of fire. The inside of his mouth had been swabbed with something too foul to imagine. His stomach clutched and seized like a nervous fist.

He began to hope he'd be dead long before nightfall.

Since there was no one around, he indulged himself in a few whimpers as he stepped under the shower. He'd have sworn the smell of whiskey was seeping out of his pores.

Moving with the care of the aged or infirm, he climbed out of the tub, wrapped a towel around his waist. He did what he could to wash the hideous taste out of his mouth.

When he stepped into the bedroom, he yelped, slapped his hands over his eyes in time – he hoped – to keep them from bursting out of his head. Some sadist had come in and opened his drapes to the sunlight.

Brianna's own eyes had gone wide. Her mouth had fallen open. Other than the towel hanging loosely at his hips, he wore nothing but a few lingering drops of water from his shower.

His body was . . . the word *exquisite* flashed into her mind. Lean, muscled, gleaming. She found herself linking her fingers together and swallowing hard.

'I brought you a breakfast tray,' she managed. 'I thought you might be feeling poorly.'

Cautious, Gray spread his fingers just enough to see through. 'Then it wasn't the wrath of God.' His voice was rough, but he feared the act of clearing it might do permanent damage. 'For a minute I thought I was being struck down for my sins.'

'It's only porridge, toast, and some coffee.'

'Coffee.' He said the word like a prayer. 'Could you pour it?'

'I could. I brought you some aspirin.'

'Aspirin.' He could have wept. 'Please.'

'Take them first then.' She brought him the pills with a small glass of water. 'Rogan looks as sad as you,' she said as Gray gobbled down the pills – and she fought to keep her hand from stroking over all that wet, curling dark hair. 'Uncle Niall's fit as a fiddle.'

'Figures.' Gray moved cautiously toward the bed. He eased down, praying his head wouldn't roll off his neck. 'Before we go any further, do I have anything to apologize for?'

'To me?'

'To anyone. Whiskey's not my usual poison, and I'm fuzzy on details after we started on the second bottle.' He squinted up at her and found she was smiling at him. 'Something funny?'

'No – well, yes, but it's not very kind of me to find it funny.' She did give in then, sleeking a hand over his hair as she might over that of a child who had overindulged in cakes. 'I was thinking it was sweet of you to offer to apologize right off that way.' Her smile warmed. 'But no, there's nothing. You were just drunk and silly. There was no harm in it.'

'Easy for you to say.' He supported his head. 'I don't make a habit of drinking like that.' Wincing, he reached for the coffee with his free hand. 'In fact, I don't believe I've ever had that much at one time, or will again.'

'You'll feel better when you've had a bite to eat. You have a couple of hours before you have to drive over for the wedding – if you're up to it.'

'Wouldn't miss it.' Resigned, Gray picked up the porridge. It smelled safe. He took a tentative bite and waited to see if his system would accept it. 'Aren't I going with you?'

'I'm leaving in a few minutes. There's things to be done. You'll come over with Rogan and Uncle Niall – since it's doubtful the three of you can get into any trouble on such a short drive.'

He grunted and scooped up more porridge.

'Do you need anything else before I go?'

'You've hit most of the vital points.' Tilting his head, he studied her. 'Did I try to talk you into going to bed with me last night?'

'You did.'

'I thought I remembered that.' His smile was quick and easy. 'I can't imagine how you resisted me.'

'Oh, I managed. I'll be off, then.'

'Brianna.' He sent her one quick, dangerous look. 'I won't be plastered next time.'

Christine Rogan Sweeney might have been on the verge of becoming a great-grandmother, but she was still a bride. No matter how often she told herself it was foolish to be nervous, to feel so giddy, her stomach still jumped.

She was to be married in only a few minutes more. To pledge herself to a man she loved dearly. And to take his pledge to her. And she would be a wife once again, after so many years a widow.

'You look beautiful.' Maggie stood back as Christine turned in front of the chevel glass. The pale rose suit gleamed with tiny pearls on the lapels. Against Christine's shining white hair sat a jaunty, matching hat with a finger-tip veil.

'I feel beautiful.' She laughed and turned to embrace Maggie, then Brianna. 'I don't care who knows it. I wonder if Niall could be as nervous as I am.'

'He's pacing like a big cat,' Maggie told her. 'And asking Rogan for the time every ten seconds.'

'Good.' Christine drew in a long breath. 'That's good, then. It is nearly time, isn't it?'

'Nearly.' Brianna kissed her on each cheek. 'I'll be going down now to make sure everything's as it should be. I wish you happiness . . . Aunt Christine.'

'Oh, dear.' Christine's eyes filled. 'How sweet you are.'

'Don't do that,' Maggie warned. 'You'll have us all going. I'll signal when we're ready, Brie.'

With a quick nod Brianna hurried out. There were caterers, of course, and a houseful of servants. But a wedding was a family thing, and she wanted it perfect.

The guests were milling in the parlor – swirls of color, snatching of laughter. A harpist was playing in soft, dreamy notes. Garlands of roses had been twined along the banister, and pots of them were artistically decked throughout the house.

She wondered if she should slip into the kitchen, just to be certain all was well, when she spotted her mother and Lottie. Fixing a bright smile on her face, she went forward.

'Mother, you look wonderful.'

'Foolishness. Lottie nagged me into spending good money on a new dress.' But she brushed a hand fussily along the soft linen sleeve.

'It's lovely. And so's yours, Lottie.'

Maeve's companion laughed heartily. 'We splurged sinfully, we did. But it isn't every day you go to such a fancy wedding. The archbishop,' she said with a whisper and a wink. 'Imagine.'

Maeve sniffed. 'A priest's a priest no matter what hat he's wearing. Seems to me he'd think twice before officiating at such a time. When two people have lived in sin –'

'Mother.' Brianna kept her voice low, but icily firm. 'Not today. Please, if you'd only –'

'Brianna.' Gray stepped up, took her hand, kissed it. 'You look fabulous.'

'Thank you.' She struggled not to flush as his fingers

locked possessively around hers. 'Mother, Lottie, this is Grayson Thane. He's a guest at Blackthorn. Gray, Maeve Concannon and Lottie Sullivan.'

'Mrs. Sullivan.' He took Lottie's hand, making her giggle when he kissed it. 'Mrs. Concannon. My congratulations on your lovely and talented daughters.'

Maeve only scowled. His hair was as long as a girl's, she observed. And his smile had more than a bit of the devil in it. 'A Yank, are you?'

'Yes, ma'am. I'm enjoying your country very much. And your daughter's hospitality.'

'Paying tenants don't usually come to family weddings.'

'Mother —'

'No, they don't,' Gray said smoothly. 'That's another thing I find charming about your country. Strangers are treated as friends, and friends never as strangers. May I escort you to your seats?'

Lottie was already hooking her arm through his. 'Come ahead, Maeve. How often are we going to get an offer from a fine-looking young man like this? You're a book writer, are you?'

'I am.' He swept both women off, sending a quick, smug smile to Brianna over his shoulder.

She could have kissed him. Even as she sighed in relief, Maggie signaled from the top of the stairs.

As the harpist switched to the wedding march, Brianna slipped to the back of the room. Her throat tightened as Niall took his place in front of the hearth and looked toward the stairs. Perhaps his hair was thin and his waist thick, but just then he looked young and eager and full of nerves.

The room hummed with anticipation as Christine walked slowly down the stairs, turned, and with her eyes bright behind her veil, went to him. The archbishop blessed them, and the ceremony began.

'Here.' Gray slipped up beside Brianna a few moments later and offered his handkerchief. 'I had a feeling you'd need this.'

'It's beautiful.' She dabbed at her eyes. The words sighed through her. *To love. To honor. To cherish.*

Gray heard *Till death do us part.* A life sentence. He'd always figured there was a reason people cried at weddings. He put an arm around her shoulders and gave her a friendly squeeze. 'Buck up,' he murmured. 'It's nearly over.'

'It's only beginning,' she corrected and indulged herself by resting her head on his shoulder.

Applause erupted when Niall thoroughly, and enthusiastically, kissed the bride.

Chapter Eight

Trips on private planes, champagne, and glossy society weddings were all well and good, Brianna supposed. But she was glad to be home. Though she knew better than to trust the skies or the balmy air, she preferred to think the worst of the winter was over. She dreamed of her fine new greenhouse as she tended her seedlings in the shed. And planned for her converted attic room while she hung the wash.

In the week she'd been back from Dublin, she all but had the house to herself. Gray was closeted in his room working. Now and again he popped off for a drive or strolled into the kitchen sniffing for food.

She wasn't sure whether to be relieved or miffed that he seemed too preoccupied to try to charm more kisses from her.

Still, she was forced to admit that her solitude was more pleasant knowing he was just up the stairs. She could sit by the fire in the evening, reading or knitting or sketching out her plans, knowing he could come wandering down to join her at any time.

But it wasn't Gray who interrupted her knitting one cool evening, but her mother and Lottie.

She heard the car outside without much surprise. Friends and neighbors often stopped in when they saw her light on. She'd set her knitting aside and started for the door when she heard her mother and Lottie arguing outside it.

Brianna only sighed. For reasons that escaped her, the two women seemed to enjoy their bickering.

'Good evening to you.' She greeted them both with a kiss. 'What a fine surprise.'

'I hope we're not disturbing you, Brie.' Lottie rolled her merry eyes. 'Maeve had it in her head we would come, so here we are.'

'I'm always pleased to see you.'

'We were out, weren't we?' Maeve shot back. 'Too lazy to cook, she was, so I have to drag myself out to a restaurant no matter how I'm feeling.'

'Even Brie must tire of her own cooking from time to time,' Lottie said as she hung Maeve's coat on the hall rack. 'As fine as it is. And it's nice to get out now and again and see people.'

'There's no one I need to see.'

'You wanted to see Brianna, didn't you?' It pleased Lottie to score a small point. 'That's why we're here.'

'I want some decent tea is what I want, not that pap they serve in the restaurant.'

'I'll make it.' Lottie patted Brianna's arm. 'You have a nice visit with your ma. I know where everything is.'

'And take that hound to the kitchen with you.' Maeve gave Con a look of impatient dislike. 'I won't have him slobbering all over me.'

'You'll keep me company, won't you, boy-o?' Cheerful, Lottie ruffled Con between the ears. 'Come along with Lottie, now, there's a good lad.'

Agreeable, and ever hopeful for a snack, Con trailed behind her.

'I've a nice fire in the parlor, Mother. Come and sit.'

'Waste of fuel,' Maeve muttered. 'It's warm enough without one.'

Brianna ignored the headache brewing behind her eyes. 'It's comforting with one. Did you have a nice dinner?'

Maeve gave a snort as she sat. She liked the feel and the look of the fire, but was damned if she would admit it.

'Dragged me off to a place in Ennis and orders pizza, she does. Pizza of all things!'

'Oh, I know the place you're speaking of. They have lovely food. Rogan says the pizza tastes just as it does in the States.' Brianna picked up her knitting again. 'Did you know that Murphy's sister Kate is expecting again?'

'The girl breeds like a rabbit. What's this – four of them?'

' 'Twill be her third. She's two boys now and is hoping for a girl.' Smiling, Brianna held up the soft pink yarn. 'So I'm making this blanket for luck.'

'God will give her what He gives her, whatever color you knit.'

Brianna's needles clicked quietly. 'So He will. I had a card from Uncle Niall and Aunt Christine. It has the prettiest picture of the sea and mountains on it. They're having a lovely time on their cruise ship, touring the islands of Greece.'

'Honeymoons at their age.' And in her heart Maeve yearned to see the mountains and foreign seas herself. 'Well, if you've enough money you can go where you choose and do what you choose. Not all of us can fly off to warm places in the winter. If I could, perhaps my chest wouldn't be so tight with cold.'

'Are you feeling poorly?' The question was automatic, like the answers to the multiplication tables she'd learned in school. It shamed her enough to have her look up and try harder. 'I'm sorry, Mother.'

'I'm used to it. Dr. Hogan does no more than cluck his tongue and tell me I'm fit. But I know how I feel, don't I?'

'You do, yes.' Brianna's knitting slowed as she turned over an idea. 'I wonder if you'd feel better if you could go away for some sun.'

'Hah. And where am I to find sun?'

'Maggie and Rogan have that villa in the south of

France. It's beautiful and warm there, they say. Remember, she drew me pictures.'

'Went off with him to that foreign country before they were married.'

'They're married now,' Brianna said mildly. 'Wouldn't you like to go there, Mother, you and Lottie, for a week or two? Such a nice rest in the sunshine you could have, and the sea air's always so healing.'

'And how would I get there?'

'Mother, you know Rogan would have the plane take you.'

Maeve could imagine it. The sun, the servants, the fine big house overlooking the sea. She might have had such a place of her own if . . . If.

'I'll not ask that girl for any favors.'

'You needn't. I'll ask for you.'

'I don't know as I'm fit to travel,' Maeve said, for the simple pleasure of making things difficult. 'The trip to Dublin and back tired me.'

'All the more reason for you to have a nice vacation,' Brianna returned, knowing the game well. 'I'll speak to Maggie tomorrow and arrange it. I'll help you pack, don't worry.'

'Anxious to see me off, are you?'

'Mother.' The headache was growing by leaps and bounds.

'I'll go, all right.' Maeve waved a hand. 'For my health, though the good Lord knows how it'll affect my nerves to be among all those foreigners.' Her eyes narrowed. 'And where is the Yank?'

'Grayson? He's upstairs, working.'

'Working.' She huffed out a breath. 'Since when is spinning a tale working, I'd like to know. Every other person in this county spins tales.'

'Putting them on paper would be different, I'd think. And there are times when he comes down after he's been at it for a while he looks as though he's been digging ditches. He seems that tired.'

'He looked frisky enough in Dublin – when he had his hands all over you.'

'What?' Brianna dropped a stitch and stared.

'Do you think I'm blind as well as ailing?' Spots of pink rode high on Maeve's cheeks. 'Mortified I was to see the way you let him carry on with you, in public, too.'

'We were dancing,' Brianna said between lips that had gone stiff and cold. 'I was teaching him some steps.'

'I saw what I saw.' Maeve set her jaw. 'And I'm asking you right now if you're giving your body to him.'

'If I'm . . .' The pink wool spilled onto the floor. 'How can you ask me such a thing?'

'I'm your mother, and I'll ask what I please of you. No doubt half the village is talking of it, you being here alone night after night with the man.'

'No one is talking of it. I run an inn, and he's my guest.'

'A convenient path to sin – I've said so since you insisted on starting this business.' She nodded as if Grayson's presence there only confirmed her opinion. 'You haven't answered me, Brianna.'

'And I shouldn't, but I'll answer you. I haven't given my body to him, or to anyone.'

Maeve waited a moment, then nodded again. 'Well, a liar you've never been, so I'll believe you.'

'I can't find it in me to care what you believe.' It was temper she knew that had her knees trembling as she rose. 'Do you think I'm proud and happy to have never known a man, to have never found one who would love me? I've no wish to live my life alone, or to forever be making baby things for some other woman's child.'

'Don't raise your voice to me, girl.'

'What good does it do to raise it?' Brianna took a deep breath, fought for calm. 'What good does it do not to? I'll help Lottie with the tea.'

'You'll stay where you are.' Mouth grim, Maeve angled her head. 'You should thank God on your knees for the life you lead, my girl. You've a roof over your head and money in your pocket. It may be I don't like how you earn it, but you've made some small success out of your choice in what many would consider an honest living. Do you think a man and babies can replace that? Well, you're wrong if you do.'

'Maeve, what are you badgering the girl about now?' Wearily Lottie came in and set down the tea tray.

'Stay out of this, Lottie.'

'Please.' Cooly, calmly, Brianna inclined her head. 'Let her finish.'

'Finish I will. I had something once I could call mine. And I lost it.' Maeve's mouth trembled once, but she firmed it, hardened it. 'Lost any chance I had to be what I'd wanted to be. Lust and nothing more, the sin of it. With a baby in my belly what could I be but some man's wife?'

'My father's wife,' Brianna said slowly.

'So I was. I conceived a child in sin and paid for it my whole life.'

'You conceived two children,' Brianna reminded her.

'Aye, I did. The first, your sister, carried that mark with her. Wild she was and will always be. But you were a child of marriage and duty.'

'Duty?'

With her hands planted on either arm of her chair, Maeve leaned forward, and her voice was bitter. 'Do you think I wanted him to touch me again? Do you think I enjoyed being reminded why I would never have my heart's desire? But the Church says marriage should produce children. So I did my duty by the Church and let him plant another child in me.'

'Duty,' Brianna repeated, and the tears she might have shed were frozen in her heart. 'With no love, no pleasure. Is that what I came from?'

'There was no need to share my bed with him when I knew I carried you. I suffered another labor, another birth, and thanked God it would be my last.'

'You never shared a bed with him. All those years.'

'There would be no more children. With you I had done what I could to absolve my sin. You don't have Maggie's wildness. There's a coolness in you, a control. You'll use that to keep yourself pure – unless you let some man tempt you. It was nearly so with Rory.'

'I loved Rory.' She hated knowing she was so near tears. For her father, she thought, and the woman he had loved and let go.

'You were a child.' Maeve dismissed the heartbreak of youth. 'But you're a woman now, and pretty enough to draw a man's eye. I want you to remember what can happen if you let them persuade you to give in. The one upstairs, he'll come and he'll go as he pleases. Forget that, and you could end up alone, with a baby growing under your apron and shame in your heart.'

'So often I wondered why there was no love in this house.' Brianna took in a shuddering breath and struggled to steady her voice. 'I knew you didn't love Da, couldn't somehow. It hurt me to know it. But then when I learned from Maggie about your singing, your career, and how you'd lost that, I thought I understood, and could sympathize for the pain you must have felt.'

'You could never know what it is to lose all you've ever wanted.'

'No, I can't. But neither can I understand a woman, any

woman, having no love in her heart for the children she carried and birthed.' She lifted her hands to her cheeks. But they weren't wet. Dry and cold they were, like marble against her fingers. 'Always you've blamed Maggie for simply being born. Now I see I was nothing more than a duty to you, a sort of penance for an earlier sin.'

'I raised you with care,' Maeve began.

'With care. No, it's true you never raised your hand to me the way you did with Maggie. It's a miracle she didn't grow to hate me for that alone. It was heat with her, and cold discipline with me. And it worked well, made us, I suppose, what we are.'

Very carefully she sat again, picked up her yarn. 'I've wanted to love you. I used to ask myself why it was I could never give you more than loyalty and duty. Now I see it wasn't the lack in me, but in you.'

'Brianna.' Appalled, and deeply shaken, Maeve got to her feet. 'How can you say such things to me? I've only tried to spare you, to protect you.'

'I've no need of protection. I'm alone, aren't I, and a virgin, just as you wish it. I'm knitting a blanket for another woman's child as I've done before, and will do again. I have my business, as you say. Nothing has changed here, Mother, but for an easing of my conscience. I'll give you no less than I've always given you, only I'll stop berating myself for not giving more.'

Dry-eyed again, she looked up. 'Will you pour the tea, Lottie? I want to tell you about the vacation you and Mother will be taking soon. Have you been to France?'

'No.' Lottie swallowed the lump in her throat. Her heart bled for both the women. She sent a look of sorrow toward Maeve, knowing no way to comfort. With a sigh she poured the tea. 'No,' she repeated. 'I've not been there. Are we going, then?'

'Yes, indeed.' Brianna picked up the rhythm of her knitting. 'Very soon if you like. I'll be talking to Maggie about it tomorrow.' She read the sympathy in Lottie's eyes and made herself smile. 'You'll have to go shopping for a bikini.'

Brianna was rewarded with a laugh. After setting the teacup on the table beside Brianna, Lottie touched her cold cheek. 'There's a girl,' she murmured.

A family from Helsinki stayed the weekend at Blackthorn. Brianna was kept busy catering to the couple and their three children. Out of pity, she scooted Con off to Murphy. The towheaded three-year-old couldn't seem to resist pulling ears and tail – an indignity which Concobar suffered silently.

Unexpected guests helped keep her mind off the emotional upheaval her mother had stirred. The family was loud, boisterous, and as hungry as bears just out of hibernation.

Brianna enjoyed every moment of them.

She bid them goodbye with kisses for the children and a dozen tea cakes for their journey south. The moment their car passed out of sight, Gray crept up behind her.

'Are they gone?'

'Oh.' She pressed a hand to her heart. 'You scared the life out of me.' Turning, she pushed at the stray wisps escaping her topknot. 'I thought you'd come down to say goodbye to the Svensons. Little Jon asked about you.'

'I still have little Jon's sticky fingerprints over half my body and most of my papers.' With a wry grin Gray tucked his thumbs in his front pockets. 'Cute kid, but, Jesus, he never stopped.'

'Three-year-olds are usually active.'

'You're telling me. Give one piggyback ride and you're committed for life.'

Now she smiled, remembering. 'You looked very sweet with him. I imagine he'll always remember the Yank who played with him at the Irish inn.' She tilted her head. 'And he was holding the little lorry you bought him yesterday when he left.'

'Lorry – oh, the truck, right.' He shrugged. 'I just happened to see it when I was taking a breather in the village.'

'Just happened to see it,' she repeated with a slow nod. 'As well as the two dolls for the little girls.'

'That's right. Anyway, I usually get a kick out of OPKs.'

'OPKs?'

'Other people's kids. But now' – he slipped his hands neatly around her waist – 'we're alone again.'

In a quick defensive move she pressed a hand to his chest before he could draw her closer. 'I've errands to do.'

He looked down at her hand, lifted a brow. 'Errands.'

'That's right, and I've a mountain of wash to do when I get back.'

'Are you going to hang out the wash? I love to watch you hang it on the line – especially when there's a breeze. It's incredibly sexy.'

'What a foolish thing to say.'

His grin only widened. 'There's something to be said for making you blush, too.'

'I'm not blushing.' She could feel the heat in her cheeks. 'I'm impatient. I need to be off, Grayson.'

'How about this, I'll take you where you need to go.' Before she could speak, he lowered his mouth, brushed it lightly over hers. 'I've missed you, Brianna.'

'You can't have. I've been right here.'

'I've missed you.' He watched her lashes lower. Her shy, uncertain responses to him gave him an odd sense of power. All ego, he thought, amused at himself. 'Where's your list?'

'My list?'

'You've always got one.'

Her gaze shifted up again. Those misty-green eyes were aware, and just a little afraid. Gray felt the surge of heat spear up from the balls of his feet straight to the loins. His fingers tightened convulsively on her waist before he forced himself to step back, let out a breath.

'Taking it slow is killing me,' he muttered.

'I beg your pardon?'

'Never mind. Get your list and whatever. I'll drive you.'

'I don't have a list. I've only to go to my mother's and help her and Lottie pack for their trip. There's no need for you to take me.'

'I could use the drive. How long will you be there?'

'Two hours, perhaps three.'

'I'll drop you off, pick you up. I'm going out anyway,' he continued before she could argue. 'It'll save petrol.'

'All right. If you're sure. I'll just be a minute.'

While he waited, Gray stepped into the path of the front garden. In the month he'd been there, he'd seen gales, rain, and the luminous light of the Irish sun. He'd sat in village pubs and listened to gossip, traditional music. He'd wandered down lanes where farmers herded their cows from field to field, and had walked up the winding steps of ruined castles, hearing the echos of war and death. He'd visited grave sites and had stood on the verge of towering cliffs looking out on the rolling sea.

Of all the places he'd visited, none seemed quite so appealing as the view from Brianna's front garden. But he wasn't altogether certain if it was the spot or the woman he was waiting for. Either way, he decided, his time here would certainly be one of the most satisfying slices of his life.

★

127

After he dropped Brianna off at the tidy house outside Ennis, he went wandering. For more than an hour he clambered over rocks at the Burren, taking pictures in his head. The sheer vastness delighted him, as did the Druid's Altar that drew so many tourists with their clicking cameras.

He drove aimlessly, stopping where he chose – a small beach deserted but for a small boy and a huge dog, a field where goats cropped and the wind whispered through tall grass, a small village where a woman counted out his change for his candy bar purchase with curled, arthritic fingers, then offered him a smile as sweet as sunlight.

A ruined abbey with a round tower caught his eye and had him pulling off the road to take a closer look. The round towers of Ireland fascinated him, but he'd found them primarily on the east coast. To guard, he supposed, from the influx of invasions across the Irish Sea. This one was whole, undamaged, and set at a curious slant. Gray spent some time circling, studying, and wondering how he could use it.

There were graves there as well, some old, some new. He had always been intrigued by the way generations could mingle so comfortably in death when they rarely managed it in life. For himself, he would take the Viking way – a ship out to sea and a torch.

But for a man who dealt in death a great deal, he preferred not to linger his thoughts overmuch on his own mortality.

Nearly all of the graves he passed were decked with flowers. Many of them were covered with plastic boxes, misty with condensation, the blossoms within all no more than a smear of color. He wondered why it didn't amuse him. It should have. Instead he was touched, stirred by the devotion to the dead.

They had belonged once, he thought. Maybe that was the definition of family. Belong once, belong always.

He'd never had that problem. Or that privilege.

He wandered through, wondering when the husbands, the wives, the children came to lay the wreaths and flowers. On the day of death? The day of birth? The feast day of the saint the dead had been named for? Or Easter maybe. That was a big one for Catholics.

He'd ask Brianna, he decided. It was something he could definitely work into his book.

He couldn't have said why he stopped just at that moment, why he looked down at that particular marker. But he did, and he stood, alone, the breeze ruffling his hair, looking down at Thomas Michael Concannon's grave.

Brianna's father? he wondered and felt an odd clutch around his heart. The dates seemed right. O'Malley had told him stories of Tom Concannon when Gray had sipped at a Guinness at the pub. Stories ripe with affection, sentiment, and humor.

Gray knew he had died suddenly, at the cliffs at Loop Head, with only Maggie with him. But the flowers on the grave, Gray was certain, was Brianna's doing.

They'd been planted over him. Though the winter had been hard on them, Gray could see they'd been recently weeded. More than a few brave blades of green were spearing up, searching for the sun.

He'd never stood over a grave of someone he'd known. Though he often paid visits to the dead, there'd been no pilgrimage to the resting place of anyone he'd cared for. But he felt a tug now, one that made him crouch down and brush a hand lightly over the carefully tended mound.

And he wished he'd brought flowers.

'Tom Concannon,' he murmured. 'You're well remembered. They talk of you in the village, and smile when they say your name. I guess that's as fine an epitaph as anyone could ask for.'

Oddly content, he sat beside Tom awhile and watched sunlight and shadows play on the stones the living planted to honor the dead.

He gave Brianna three hours. It was obviously more than enough as she came out of the house almost as soon as he pulled up in front of it. His smile of greeting turned to a look of speculation as he got a closer look.

Her face was pale, as he knew it became when she was upset or moved. Her eyes, though cool, showed traces of strain. He glanced toward the house, saw the curtain move. He caught a glimpse only, but Maeve's face was as pale as her daughter's, and appeared equally unhappy.

'All packed?' he said, keeping his tone mild.

'Yes.' She slipped into the car, her hands tight around her purse — as if it was the only thing that kept her from leaping up. 'Thank you for coming for me.'

'A lot of people find packing a chore.' Gray pulled the car out and for once kept his speed moderate.

'It can be.' Normally, she enjoyed it. The anticipation of going somewhere, and more, the anticipation of returning home. 'It's done now, and they'll be ready to leave in the morning.'

God, she wanted to close her eyes, to escape from the pounding headache and miserable guilt into sleep.

'Do you want to tell me what's upset you?'

'I'm not upset.'

'You're wound up, unhappy, and as pale as ice.'

'It's personal. It's family business.'

The fact that her dismissal stung surprised him. But he only shrugged and lapsed into silence.

'I'm sorry.' Now she did close her eyes. She wanted

peace. Couldn't everyone just give her a moment's peace? 'That was rude of me.'

'Forget it.' He didn't need her problems in any case, he reminded himself. Then he glanced at her and swore under his breath. She looked exhausted. 'I want to make a stop.'

She started to object, then kept her eyes and mouth closed. He'd been good enough to drive her, she reminded herself. She could certainly bear a few minutes longer before she buried all this tension in work.

He didn't speak again. He was driving on instinct, hoping the choice he made would bring the color back to her cheeks and the warmth to her voice.

She didn't open her eyes again until he braked and shut the engine off. Then she merely stared at the castle ruins. 'You needed to stop here?'

'I wanted to stop here,' he corrected. 'I found this my first day here. It's playing a prominent part in my book. I like the feel of it.'

He got out, rounded the hood, and opened her door. 'Come on.' When she didn't move, he leaned down and unfastened her seat belt himself. 'Come on. It's great. Wait till you see the view from the top.'

'I've wash to do,' she complained and heard the sulkiness of her own voice as she stepped out of the car.

'It's not going anywhere.' He had her hand now and was tugging her over the high grass.

She didn't have the heart to point out that the ruins weren't likely to go anywhere, either. 'You're using this place in your book?'

'Big murder scene.' He grinned at her reaction, the uneasiness and superstition in her eyes. 'Not afraid are you? I don't usually act out my scenes.'

'Don't be foolish.' But she shivered once as they stepped between the high stone walls.

There was grass growing wild on the ground, bits of green pushing its way through chinks in the stone. Above her, she could see where the floors had been once, so many years ago. But now time and war left the view to the sky unimpeded.

The clouds floated silently as ghosts.

'What do you suppose they did here, right here?' Gray mused.

'Lived, worked. Fought.'

'That's too general. Use your imagination. Can't you see it, the people walking here? It's winter, and it's bone cold. Ice rings on the water barrels, frost on the ground that snaps like dry twigs underfoot. The air stings with smoke from the fires. A baby's crying, hungry, then stops when his mother bares her breast.'

He drew her along with him, physically, emotionally, until she could almost see it as he did.

'Soldiers are drilling out there, and you can hear the ring of sword to sword. A man hurries by, limping from an old wound, his breath steaming out in cold clouds. Come on, let's go up.'

He pulled her toward narrow, tight winding stairs. Every so often there would be an opening in the stone, a kind of cave. She wondered if people had slept there, or stored goods. Or tried to hide, perhaps, from the enemy who would always find them.

'There'd be an old woman carrying an oil lamp up here, and she has a puckered scar on the back of her hand and fear in her eyes. Another's bringing fresh rushes for the floors, but she's young and thinking of her lover.'

Gray kept her hand in his, stopping when they came to a level midway. 'It must have been the Cromwellians, don't you think, who sacked it. There'd have been screams, the stench of smoke and blood, that nasty thud of metal hack-

ing into bone, and that high-pitched shriek a man makes
when the pain slices him. Spears driving straight through
bellies, pinning a body to the ground where the limbs
would twitch before nerves died. Crows circling overhead,
waiting for the feast.'

He turned, saw her eyes were wide and glazed – and
chuckled. 'Sorry, I get caught up.'

'It's not just a blessing to have an imagination like that.'
She shivered again and fought to swallow. 'I don't think I
want you to make me see it so clear.'

'Death's fascinating, especially the violent type. Men are
always hunting men. And this is a hell of a spot for murder
– of the contemporary sort.'

'Your sort,' she murmured.

'Mmm. He'll toy with the victim first,' Gray began as he
started to climb again. He was caught up in his own mind,
true, but he could see Brianna was no longer worrying
over whatever had happened at her mother's. 'Let the
atmosphere and those smoky ghosts stir into the fear like a
slow poison. He won't hurry – he likes the hunt, craves it.
He can scent the fear, like any wolf, he can scent it. It's the
scent that gets in his blood and make it pump, that arouses
him like sex. And the prey runs, chasing that thin thread of
hope. But she's breathing fast. The sound of it echoes, car-
ries on the wind. She falls – the stairs are treacherous in the
dark, in the rain. Wet and slick, they're weapons themselves.
But she claws her way up them, air sobbing in and out of
her lungs, her eyes wild.'

'Gray –'

'She's nearly as much as an animal as he now. Terror's
stripped off layers of humanity, the same as good sex will,
or true hunger. Most people think they've experienced all
three, but it's rare even to know one sensation fully. But she
knows the first now, knows that terror as if it was solid and

alive, as if it could wrap its hands around her throat. She wants a bolt hole, but there's nowhere to hide. And she can hear him climbing, slowly, tirelessly behind her. Then she reaches the top.'

He drew Brianna out of the shadows onto the wide walled ledge where sunlight streamed.

'And she's trapped.'

She jolted when Gray swung her around, nearly screamed. Roaring with laughter, he lifted her off her feet. 'Christ, what an audience you are.'

' 'Tisn't funny.' She tried to wiggle free.

'It's wonderful. I'm planning on having him mutilate her with an antique dagger, but . . .' He hooked his arm under Brianna's knees and carried her to the wall. 'Maybe he should just dump her over the side.'

'Stop!' Out of self-preservation she threw her arms around him and clung.

'Why didn't I think of this before? Your heart's pounding, you've got your arms around me.'

'Bully.'

'Got your mind off your troubles, didn't it?'

'I'll keep my troubles, thank you, and keep out of that twisted imagination of yours.'

'No, no one does.' He snuggled her a little closer. 'That's what fiction's all about, books, movies, whatever. It gives you a break from reality and lets you worry about someone else's problems.'

'What does it do for you who tells the tale?'

'Same thing. Exactly the same thing.' He set her on her feet and turned her to the view. 'It's like a painting, isn't it?' Gently, he drew her closer until her back was nestled against him. 'As soon as I saw this place, it grabbed me. It was raining the first time I came here, and it almost seemed as if the colors should run.'

She sighed. Here was the peace she'd wanted after all. In his odd roundabout way he'd given it to her. 'It's nearly spring,' she murmured.

'You always smell of spring.' He bent his head to rub his lips over the nape of her neck. 'And taste of it.'

'You're making my legs weak again.'

'Then you'd better hold on to me.' He turned her, cupped a hand at her jaw. 'I haven't kissed you in days.'

'I know.' She built up her courage, kept her eyes level. 'I've wanted you to.'

'That was the idea.' He touched his lips to hers, stirred when her hands slipped up his chest to frame his face.

She opened for him willingly, her little murmur of pleasure as arousing as a caress. With the wind swirling around them, he drew her closer, careful to keep his hands easy, his mouth gentle.

All the strain, the fatigue, the frustration had vanished. She was home, was all that Brianna could think. Home was always where she wanted to be.

On a sigh she rested her head on his shoulder, curved her arms up his back. 'I've never felt like this.'

Nor had he. But that was a dangerous thought, and one he would have to consider. 'It's good with us,' he murmured. 'There's something good about it.'

'There is.' She lifted her cheek to his. 'Be patient with me, Gray.'

'I intend to. I want you, Brianna, and when you're ready . . .' He stepped back, ran his hands down her arms until their fingers linked. 'When you're ready.'

Chapter Nine

Gray wondered if his appetite was enhanced due to the fact that he had another hunger that was far from satisfied. He thought it best to take it philosophically – and help himself to a late-night feast of Brianna's bread-and-butter pudding. Making tea was becoming a habit as well, and he'd already set the kettle on the stove and warmed the pot before he scooped out pudding into a bowl.

He didn't think he'd been so obsessed with sex since his thirteenth year. Then it had been Sally Anne Howe, one of the other residents of the Simon Brent Memorial Home for Children. Good old Sally Anne, Gray thought now, with her well blossomed body and sly eyes. She'd been three years older than he, and more than willing to share her charms with anyone for smuggled cigarettes or candy bars.

At the time he thought she was a goddess, the answer to a randy adolescent's prayers. He could look back now with pity and anger, knowing the cycle of abuse and the flaws in the system that had made a pretty young girl feel her only true worth was nestled between her thighs.

He'd had plenty of sweaty dreams about Sally Anne after lights out. And had been lucky enough to steal an entire pack of Marlboros from one of the counselors. Twenty cigarettes had equaled twenty fucks, he remembered. And he'd been a very fast learner.

Over the years, he'd learned quite a bit more, from girls his own age, and from professionals who plied their trade out of darkened doorways that smelled of stale grease and sour sweat.

He'd been barely sixteen when he'd broken free of the orphanage and hit the road with the clothes on his back and twenty-three dollars worth of loose change and crumpled bills in his pocket.

Freedom was what he'd wanted, freedom from the rules, the regulations, the endless cycle of the system he'd been caught in most of his life. He'd found it, and used it, and paid for it.

He'd lived and worked those streets for a long time before he'd given himself a name, and a purpose. He'd been fortunate enough to have possessed a talent that had kept him from being swallowed up by other hungers.

At twenty he'd had his first lofty, and sadly autobiographical, novel under his belt. The publishing world had not been impressed. By twenty-two, he'd crafted out a neat, clever little whodunit. Publishers did not come clamoring, but a whiff of interest from an assistant editor had kept him holed up in a cheap rooming house battering at a manual typewriter for weeks.

That, he'd sold. For peanuts. Nothing before or since had meant as much to him.

Ten years later, and he could live as he chose, and he felt he'd chosen well.

He poured the water into the pot, shoveled a spoonful of pudding into his mouth. As he glanced over at Brianna's door, spotted the thin slant of light beneath it, he smiled.

He'd chosen her, too.

Covering his bases, he set the pot with two cups on a tray, then knocked at her door.

'Yes, come in.'

She was sitting at her little desk, tidy as a nun in a flannel gown and slippers, her hair in a loose braid over one shoulder. Gray gamely swallowed the saliva that pooled in his mouth.

'Saw your light. Want some tea?'

'That would be nice. I was just finishing up some paperwork.'

The dog uncurled himself from beside her feet and walked over to rub against Gray. 'Me, too.' He set down the tray to ruffle Con's fur. 'Murder makes me hungry.'

'Killed someone today, did you?'

'Brutally.' He said it with such relish, she laughed.

'Perhaps that's what makes you so even tempered all in all,' she mused. 'All those emotional murders purging your system. Do you ever –' She caught herself, moving a shoulder as he handed her a cup.

'Go ahead, ask. You rarely ask anything about my work.'

'Because I imagine everyone does.'

'They do.' He made himself comfortable. 'I don't mind.'

'Well, I was wondering, if you ever make one of the characters someone you know – then kill them off.'

'There was this snotty French waiter in Dijon. I garotted him.'

'Oh.' She rubbed a hand over her throat. 'How did it feel?'

'For him, or me?'

'For you.'

'Satisfying.' He spooned up pudding. 'Want me to kill someone for you, Brie? I aim to please.'

'Not at the moment, no.' She shifted and some of her papers fluttered to the floor.

'You need a typewriter,' he told her as he helped her gather them up. 'Better yet, a word processor. It would save you time writing business letters.'

'Not when I'd have to search for every key.' While he read her correspondence, she cocked a brow, amused. ' 'Tisn't very interesting.'

'Hmm. Oh, sorry, habit. What's Triquarter Mining?'

'Oh, just a company Da must have invested in. I found the stock certificate with his things in the attic. I've written them once already,' she added, mildly annoyed. 'But had no answer. So I'm trying again.'

'Ten thousand shares.' Gray pursed his lips. 'That's not chump change.'

'It is, if I think I know what you're saying. You had to know my father – he was always after a new moneymaking scheme that cost more than it would ever earn. Still, this needs to be done.' She held out a hand. 'That's just a copy. Rogan took the original for safekeeping and made that for me.'

'You should have him check it out.'

'I don't like to bother him with it. His plate's full with the new gallery – and with Maggie.'

He handed her back the copy. 'Even at a dollar a share, it's fairly substantial.'

'I'd be surprised if it was worth more than a pence a share. God knows he couldn't have paid much more. More likely it is that the whole company went out of business.'

'Then your letter would have come back.'

She only smiled. 'You've been here long enough to know the Irish mails. I think –' They both glanced over as the dog began to growl. 'Con?'

Instead of responding, the dog growled again, and the fur on his back lifted. In two strides Gray was at the windows. He saw nothing but mist.

'Fog,' he muttered. 'I'll go look around. No,' he said when she started to rise. 'It's dark, it's cold, it's damp, and you're staying put.'

'There's nothing out there.'

'Con and I will find out. Let's go.' He snapped his fingers, and to Brianna's surprise, Con responded immediately. He pranced out at Gray's heels.

She kept a flashlight in the first kitchen drawer. Gray snagged it before he opened the door. The dog quivered once, then at Gray's murmured, 'go,' leaped into the mist. In seconds the sound of his racing feet was muffled to silence.

The fog distorted the beam from the flash. Gray moved carefully, eyes and ears straining. He heard the dog bark, but from what direction or distance he couldn't say.

He stopped by Brianna's bedroom windows, playing the light on the ground. There, in her neat bed of perennials, was a single footprint.

Small, Gray mused, crouching down. Nearly small enough to be a child's. It could be as simple as that — kids out on a lark. But when he continued to circle the house, he heard the sound of a engine turning over. Cursing, he quickened his pace. Con burst through the mist like a diver spearing through the surface of a lake.

'No luck?' To commiserate, Gray stroked Con's head as they both stared out into the fog. 'Well, I'm afraid I might know what this is about. Let's go back.'

Brianna was gnawing on her nails when they came through the kitchen door. 'You were gone so long.'

'We wanted to circle the whole way around.' He set the flashlight on the counter, combed a hand through his damp hair. 'This could be related to your break-in.'

'I don't see how. You didn't find anyone.'

'Because we weren't quick enough. There's another possible explanation.' He jammed his hands in his pockets. 'Me.'

'You? What do you mean?'

'I've had it happen a few times. An overenthusiastic fan finds out where I'm staying. Sometimes they come calling like they were old pals — sometimes they just trail you like a shadow. Now and again, they break in, look for souvenirs.'

'But that's dreadful.'

'It's annoying, but fairly harmless. One enterprising woman picked the lock on my hotel room at the Paris Ritz, stripped, and crawled into bed with me.' He tried for a grin. 'It was . . . awkward.'

'Awkward,' Brianna repeated after she'd managed to close her mouth. 'What – no, I don't think I want to know what you did.'

'Called security.' His eyes went bright with amusement. 'There are limits to what I'll do for my readers. Anyway, this might have been kids, but if it was one of my adoring fans, you might want me to find other accommodations.'

'I do not.' Her protective instincts snapped into place. 'They've no right to intrude on your privacy that way, and you'll certainly not leave here because of it.' She let out a huff of breath. 'It's not just your stories, you know. Oh, they draw people in – it all seems so real, and there's always something heroic that rises above all the greed and violence and grief. It's your picture, too.'

He was charmed by her description of his work and answered absently. 'What about it?'

'Your face.' She looked at him then. 'It's such a lovely face.'

He didn't know whether to laugh or wince. 'Really?'

'Yes, it's . . .' She cleared her throat. There was a gleam in his eyes she knew better than to trust. 'And the little biography on the back – more the lack of it. It's as if you came from nowhere. The mystery of it's appealing.'

'I did come from nowhere. Why don't we go back to my face?'

She took a step in retreat. 'I think there's been enough excitement for the night.'

He just kept moving forward until his hands were on her shoulders and his mouth lay quietly on hers. 'Will you be able to sleep?'

'Yes.' Her breath caught, expelled lazily. 'Con will be with me.'

'Lucky dog. Go on, get some sleep.' He waited until she

and the dog were settled, then did something Brianna hadn't done in all the years she'd lived in the house.

He locked the doors.

The best place to spread news or to garner it was, logically, the village pub. In the weeks he'd been in Clare County, Gray had developed an almost sentimental affection for O'Malley's. Naturally, during his research, he'd breezed into a number of public houses in the area, but O'Malley's had become, for him, as close to his own neighborhood bar as he'd ever known.

He heard the lilt of music even as he reached for the door. Murphy, he thought. Now, that was lucky. The moment Gray stepped in, he was greeted by name or a cheery wave. O'Malley began to build him a pint of Guinness before he'd planted himself in a seat.

'Well, how's the story telling these days?' O'Malley asked him.

'It's fine. Two dead, no suspects.'

With a shake of his head, O'Malley slipped the pint under Gray's nose. 'Don't know how it is a man can play with murder all the day and still have a smile on his face of an evening.'

'Unnatural, isn't it?' Gray grinned at him.

'I've a story for you.' This came from David Ryan who sat on the end of the bar and lighted one of his American cigarettes.

Gray settled back amid the music and smoke. There was always a story, and he was as good a listener as he was a teller.

'Was a maid who lived in the countryside near Tralee. Beautiful as a sunrise, she was, with hair like new gold and eyes as blue as Kerry.'

Conversation quieted, and Murphy lowered his music so that it was a backdrop for the tale.

'It happened that two men came a-courting her,' David went on. 'One was a bookish fellow, the other a farmer. In her way, the maid loved them both; for she was as fickle of heart as she was lovely of face. So, enjoying the attention, as a maid might, she let them both dangle for her, making promises to each. And there began to grow a blackness in the heart of the young farmer, side by side with his love of the maid.'

He paused, as storytellers often do, and studied the red glow at the end of his cigarette. He took a deep drag, expelled smoke.

'So one night he waited for his rival along the roadside, and when the bookish fellow came a-whistling – for the maid had given him her kisses freely – the farmer leaped out and bore the young lover to the ground. He dragged him, you see, in the moonlight across the fields, and though the poor sod still breathed, he buried him deep. When dawn came, he sowed his crop over him and put an end to the competition.'

David paused again, drew deep on his cigarette, reached for his pint.

'And?' Gray asked, caught up. 'He married the maid.'

'No, indeed he didn't. She ran off with a tinker that very day. But the farmer had the best bloody crop of hay of his life.'

There were roars of laughter as Gray only shook his head. He considered himself a professional liar and a good one. But the competition here was fierce. Amid the chuckles, Gray picked up his glass and went to join Murphy.

'Davey's a tale for every day of the week,' Murphy told him, gently running his hands along the buttons of his squeeze box.

'I imagine my agent would scoop him up in a heartbeat. Heard anything, Murphy?'

'No, nothing helpful. Mrs. Leery thought she might have seen a car go by the day of your troubles. She thinks it was green, but didn't pay it any mind.'

'Someone was poking around the cottage last night. Lost him in the fog.' Gray remembered in disgust. 'But he was close enough to leave a footprint in Brie's flower bed. Might have been kids.' Gray took a contemplative sip of beer. 'Has anyone been asking about me?'

'You're a daily topic of conversation,' Murphy said dryly.

'Ah, fame. No, I mean a stranger.'

'Not that I've heard. You'd better to ask over at the post office. Why?'

'I think it might be an overenthusiastic fan. I've run into it before. Then again . . .' He shrugged. 'It's the way my mind works, always making more out of what's there.'

'There's a dozen men or more a whistle away if anyone gives you or Brie any trouble.' Murphy glanced up as the door to the pub opened. Brianna came in, flanked by Rogan and Maggie. His brow lifted as he looked back at Gray. 'And a dozen men or more who'll haul you off to the altar if you don't mind that gleam in your eye.'

'What?' Gray picked up his beer again, and his lips curved. 'Just looking.'

'Aye. I'm a rover,' Murphy sang, 'and seldom sober, I'm a rover of high degree. For when I'm drinking, I'm always thinking, how to gain my love's company.'

'There's still half a pint in this glass,' Gray muttered, and rose to walk to Brianna. 'I thought you had mending.'

'I did.'

'We bullied her into coming out,' Maggie explained and gave a little sigh as she levered herself onto a stool.

'Persuaded,' Rogan corrected. 'A glass of Harp, Brie?'

'Thank you, I will.'

'Tea for Maggie, Tim,' Rogan began and grinned as his

wife muttered. 'A glass of Harp for Brie, a pint of Guinness for me. Another pint, Gray?'

'This'll do me.' Gray leaned against the bar. 'I remember the last time I went drinking with you.'

'Speaking of Uncle Niall,' Maggie put in. 'He and his bride are spending a few days on the island of Crete. Play something bright, will you, Murphy?'

Obligingly, he reeled into 'Whiskey in the Jar' and set her feet tapping.

After listening to the lyrics, Gray shook his head. 'Why is it you Irish always sing about war?'

'Do we?' Maggie smiled, sipping at her tea as she waited to join in the chorus.

'Sometimes it's betrayal or dying, but mostly it's war.'

'Is that a fact?' She smiled over the rim of her cup. 'I couldn't say. Then again, it might be that we've had to fight for every inch of our own ground for centuries. Or —'

'Don't get her started,' Rogan pleaded. 'There's a rebel's heart in there.'

'There's a rebel's heart inside every Irish man or woman. Murphy's a fine voice, he does. Why don't you sing with him, Brie?'

Enjoying the moment, she sipped her Harp. 'I'd rather listen.'

'I'd like to hear you,' Gray murmured and stroked a hand down her hair.

Maggie narrowed her eyes at the gesture. 'Brie has a voice like a bell,' she said. 'We always wondered where she got it, until we found out our mother had one as well.'

'How about "Danny Boy"?'

Maggie rolled her eyes. 'Count on a Yank to ask for it. A Brit wrote that tune, outlander. Do "James Connolly," Murphy. Brie'll sing with you.'

With a resigned shake of her head, Brianna went to sit with Murphy.

'They make lovely harmony,' Maggie murmured, watching Gray.

'Mmm. She sings around the house when she forgets someone's there.'

'And how long do you plan to be there?' Maggie asked, ignoring Rogan's warning scowl.

'Until I'm finished,' Gray said absently.

'Then onto the next?'

'That's right. Onto the next.'

Despite the fact that Rogan now had his hand clamped at the back of her neck, Maggie started to make some pithy comment. It was Gray's eyes rather than her husband's annoyance that stopped her. The desire in them had stirred her protective instincts. But there was something more now. She wondered if he was aware of it.

When a man looked at a woman that way, more than hormones were involved. She'd have to think it over, Maggie decided, and see how it set with her. In the meantime she picked up her tea again, still watching Gray.

'We'll see about that,' she murmured. 'We'll just see about it.'

One song became two, and two, three. The war songs, the love songs, the sly and the sad. In his mind Gray began to craft a scene.

The smoky pub was filled with noise and music – a sanctuary from the horrors outside. The woman's voice drawing the man who didn't want to be drawn. Here, he thought, just here was where his hero would lose the battle. She would be sitting in front of the turf fire, her hands neatly folded in her lap, her voice soaring, effortless and lovely, her eyes as haunted as the tune.

And he would love her then, to the point of giving his life if need be. Certainly of changing it. He could forget the past with her, and look toward the future.

'You look pale, Gray.' Maggie tugged on his arm until he backed onto a stool. 'How many pints have you had?'

'Just this.' He scrubbed a hand over his face to bring himself back. 'I was just . . . working,' he finished. That was it, of course. He'd only been thinking of characters, of crafting the lie. Nothing personal.

'Looked like a trance.'

'Same thing.' He let out a little breath, laughed at himself. 'I think I'll have another pint after all.'

Chapter Ten

With the pub scene he'd spun in his imagination replaying in his head, Gray did not spend a peaceful night. Though he couldn't erase it, neither could he seem to write it. At least not well.

The one thing he despised was even the idea of writer's block. Normally he could shrug it off, continue working until the nasty threat of it passed. Much, he sometimes thought, like a black-edged cloud that would then hover over some other unfortunate writer.

But this time he was stuck. He couldn't move into the scene, nor beyond it, and spent a great deal of the night scowling at the words he'd written.

Cold, he thought. He was just running cold. That's why the scene was cold.

Itchy was what he was, he admitted bitterly. Sexually frustrated by a woman who could hold him off with no more than one quiet look.

Served him right for obsessing over his landlady when he should be obsessing about murder.

Muttering to himself, he pushed away from his desk and stalked to the window. It was just his luck that Brianna should be the first thing he saw.

There she was below his window, neat as a nun in some prim pink dress, her hair all swept up and pinned into submission. Why was she wearing heels? he wondered and leaned closer to the glass. He supposed she'd call the unadorned pumps sensible shoes, but they did senselessly wonderful things to her legs.

As he watched, she climbed behind the wheel of her car, her movements both practical and graceful. She'd set her purse on the seat beside her first, he thought. And so she did. Then carefully buckle her seat belt, check her mirrors. No primping in the rearview for Brianna, he noted. Just a quick adjustment to be certain it was aligned properly. Now turn the key.

Even through the glass he could hear the coughing fatigue of the engine. She tried it again and a third time. By then Gray was shaking his head and heading downstairs.

'Why the hell don't you get that thing fixed?' he shouted at her as he strode out the front door.

'Oh.' She was out of the car by now and trying to lift the hood. 'It was working just fine a day or two ago.'

'This heap hasn't worked fine in a decade.' He elbowed her aside, annoyed that she should look and smell so fresh when he felt like old laundry. 'Look, if you need to go to the village for something, take my car. I'll see what I can do with this.'

In automatic defense against the terse words, she angled her chin. 'Thank you just the same, but I'm going to Ennistymon.'

'Ennistymon?' Even as he placed the village on his mental map, he lifted his head from under the hood long enough to glare at her. 'What for?'

'To look at the new gallery. They'll be opening it in a couple of weeks, and Maggie asked if I'd come see.' She stared at his back as he fiddled with wires and cursed. 'I left you a note and food you can heat since I'll be gone most of the day.'

'You're not going anywhere in this. Fan belt's busted, fuel line's leaking, and it's a pretty good bet your starter motor's had it.' He straightened, noted that she wore earrings today, thin gold hoops that just brushed the tips of her lobes. They added a celebrational air that irritated him unreasonably. 'You've got no business driving around in this junkyard.'

'Well, it's what I have to drive, isn't it? I'll thank you for your trouble, Grayson. I'll just see if Murphy can –'

'Don't pull that ice queen routine on me.' He slammed the hood hard enough to make her jolt. Good, he thought. It proved she had blood in her veins. 'And don't throw Murphy up in my face. He couldn't do any more with it than I can. Go get in my car, I'll be back in a minute.'

'And why would I be getting in your car?'

'So I can drive you to goddamn Ennistymon.'

Teeth set, she slapped her hands on her hips. 'It's so kind of you to offer, but –'

'Get in the car,' he snapped as he headed for the house. 'I need to soak my head.'

'I'd soak it for you,' she muttered. Yanking open her car door, she snatched out her purse. Who'd asked him to drive her, she'd like to know? Why she'd rather walk every step than sit in the same car with such a man. And if she wanted to call Murphy, well . . . she'd damn well call him.

But first she wanted to calm down.

She took a deep breath, then another, before walking slowly among her flowers. They soothed her, as always, the tender green just beginning to bud. They needed some work and care, she thought, bending down to tug out an invading weed. If tomorrow was fine, she'd begin. By Easter, her garden would be in its glory.

The scents, the colors. She smiled a little at a brave young daffodil.

Then the door slammed. Her smile gone, she rose, turned.

He hadn't bothered to shave, she noted. His hair was damp and pulled back by a thin leather thong, his clothes clean if a bit ragged.

She knew very well the man had decent clothes. Why, didn't she wash and iron them herself?

150

He flicked a glance at her, tugged the keys out of his jeans pocket. 'In the car.'

Oh, he needed a bit of a coming down, he did. She walked to him slowly, ice in her eyes and heat on her tongue. 'And what do you have to be so cheerful about this morning?'

Sometimes, even a writer understood that actions can speak louder than words. Without giving either of them time to think he hauled her against him, took one satisfied look at the shock that raced over her face, then crushed her mouth with his.

It was rough and hungry and full of frustration. Her heart leaped, seemed to burst in her head. She had an instant to fear, a moment to yearn, then he was yanking her away again.

His eyes, oh, his eyes were fierce. A wolf's eyes, she thought dully, full of violence and stunning strength.

'Got it?' he tossed out, furious with her, with himself when she only stared. Like a child, he thought, who'd just been slapped for no reason.

It was a feeling her remembered all too well.

'Christ, I'm going crazy.' He scrubbed his hands over his face and fought back the beast. 'I'm sorry. Get in the car, Brianna. I'm not going to jump you.'

His temper flashed again when she didn't move, didn't blink. 'I'm not going to fucking touch you.'

She found her voice then, though it wasn't as steady as she might have liked. 'Why are you angry with me?'

'I'm not.' He stepped back. Control, he reminded himself. He was usually pretty good at it. 'I'm sorry,' he repeated. 'Stop looking at me as if I'd just punched you.'

But he had. Didn't he know that anger, harsh words, hard feelings wounded her more than a violent hand? 'I'm going inside.' She found her defenses, the thin walls that blocked out temper. 'I need to call Maggie and tell her I can't be there.'

'Brianna.' He started to reach out, then lifted both hands in a gesture that was equal parts frustration and a plea for peace. 'How bad do you want me to feel?'

'I don't know, but I imagine you'll feel better after some food.'

'Now she's going to fix me breakfast.' He closed his eyes, took a steadying breath. 'Even tempered,' he muttered and looked at her again. 'Isn't that what you said I was, not too long ago? You were more than a little off the mark. Writers are miserable bastards, Brie. Moody, mean, selfish, self-absorbed.'

'You're none of those things.' She couldn't explain why she felt bound to come to his defense. 'Moody, perhaps, but none of the others.'

'I am. Depending on how the book's going. Right now it's going badly, so I behaved badly. I hit a snag, a wall. A goddamn fortress, and I took it out on you. Do you want me to apologize again?'

'No.' She softened, reached out and laid a hand on his stubbled cheek. 'You look tired, Gray.'

'I haven't slept.' He kept his hands in his pockets, his eyes on hers. 'Be careful how sympathetic you are, Brianna. The book's only part of the reason I'm feeling raw this morning. You're the rest of it.'

She dropped her hand as if she'd touched an open flame. Her quick withdrawal had his lips curling.

'I want you. It hurts wanting you this way.'

'It does?'

'That wasn't supposed to make you look pleased with yourself.'

Her color bloomed. 'I didn't mean to —'

'That's part of the problem. Come on, get in the car. Please,' he added. 'I'll drive myself insane trying to write today if I stay here.'

It was exactly the right button to push. She slipped into the car and waited for him to join her. 'Perhaps if you just murdered someone else.'

He found he could laugh after all. 'Oh, I'm thinking about it.'

Worldwide Gallery of Clare County was a gem. Newly constructed, it was designed like an elegant manor house, complete with formal gardens. It wasn't the lofty cathedral of the gallery in Dublin, nor the opulent palace of Rome, but a dignified building specifically conceived to house and showcase the work of Irish artists.

It had been Rogan's dream, and now his and Maggie's reality.

Brianna had designed the gardens. Though she hadn't been able to plant them herself, the landscapers had used her scheme so that brick walkways were flanked with roses, and wide, semi-circular beds were planted with lupins and poppies, dianthus and foxglove, columbine and dahlias, and all of her favorites.

The gallery itself was built of brick, soft rose in color, with tall, graceful windows trimmed in muted gray. Inside the grand foyer, the floor was tiled in deep blue and white, with a Waterford chandelier overhead and the sweep of mahogany stairs leading to the second floor.

' 'Tis Maggie's,' Brianna murmured, caught by the sculpture that dominated the entranceway.

Gray saw two figures intwined, the cool glass just hinting of heat, the form strikingly sexual, oddly romantic.

'It's her *Surrender*. Rogan bought it himself before they were married. He wouldn't sell it to anyone.'

'I can see why.' He had to swallow. The sinuous glass was an erotic slap to his already suffering system. 'It makes a stunning beginning to a tour.'

'She has a special gift, doesn't she?' Gently, with finger-tips only, Brianna stroked the cool glass that her sister had created from fire and dreams. 'Special gifts make a person moody, I suppose.' Smiling a little, she looked over her shoulder at Gray. He looked so restless, she thought. So impatient with everything, especially himself. 'And diffi-cult, because they'll always ask so much of themselves.'

'And make life hell for everyone around them when they don't get it.' He reached out, touched her instead of the glass. 'Don't hold grudges, do you?'

'What's the point in them?' With a shrug, she turned a circle, admiring the clean and simple lines of the foyer. 'Rogan wanted the gallery to be a home, you see, for art. So there's a parlor, a drawing room, even a dining room, and sitting rooms upstairs.' Brianna took his hand and drew him toward open double doors. 'All the paintings, the sculptures, even the furniture, are by Irish artists and crafts-men. And – oh.'

She stopped dead and stared. Cleverly arranged over the back and side of a low divan was a soft throw in bold teal that faded into cool green. She moved forward, ran her hand over it.

'I made this,' she murmured. 'For Maggie's birthday. They put it here. They put it here, in an art gallery.'

'Why shouldn't they? It's beautiful.' Curious, he took a closer look. 'Did you weave this?'

'Yes. I don't have much time for weaving, but . . .' She trailed off, afraid she might weep. 'Imagine it. In an art gallery, with all these wonderful paintings and things.'

'Brianna.'

'Joseph.'

Gray watched the man stride across the room and enve-lope Brianna in a hard and very warm embrace. Artistic type, Gray thought with a scowl. Turquoise stud in the ear, ponytail streaming down the back, Italian suit. The look clicked. He remembered seeing the man at the wedding in Dublin.

'You get lovelier every time I see you.'

'You get more full of nonsense.' But she laughed. 'I didn't know you were here.'

'I just came in for the day, to help Rogan with a few details.'

'And Patricia?'

'She's in Dublin still. Between the baby and the school, she couldn't get away.'

'Oh, the baby, and how is she?'

'Beautiful. Looks like her mother.' Joseph looked at Gray then, held out a hand. 'You'd be Grayson Thane? I'm Joseph Donahue.'

'Oh, I'm sorry. Gray, Joseph manages Rogan's gallery in Dublin. I thought you'd met at the wedding.'

'Not technically.' But Gray shook in a friendly manner. He remembered Joseph had a wife and daughter.

'I'll have to get it out of the way and tell you I'm a big fan.'

'It's never in the way.'

'It happens I brought a book along with me, thinking I could pass it along to Brie to pass it to you. I was hoping you wouldn't mind signing it for me.'

Gray decided he could probably learn to like Joseph Donahue after all. 'I'd be glad to.'

'It's kind of you. I should tell Maggie you're here. She wants to tour you about herself.'

'It's a lovely job you've done here, Joseph. All of you.'

'And worth every hour of insanity.' He gave the room a quick, satisfied glance. 'I'll fetch Maggie. Wander around if you like.' He stopped at the doorway, turned, and grinned. 'Oh, be sure to ask her about selling a piece to the president.'

'The president?' Brianna repeated.

'Of Ireland, darling. He offered for her *Unconquered* this morning.'

'Imagine it,' Brianna whispered as Joseph hurried off. 'Maggie being known to the president of Ireland.'

'I can tell you she's becoming known everywhere.'

'Yes, I knew it, but it seems . . .' She laughed, unable to describe it. 'How wonderful this is. Da would have been so proud. And Maggie, oh, she must be flying. You'd know how it feels, wouldn't you? The way it is when someone reads your books.'

'Yeah, I know.'

'It must be wonderful, to be talented, to have something to give that touches people.'

'Brie.' Gray lifted the end of the soft teal throw. 'What do you call this?'

'Oh, anyone can do that – just takes time. What I mean is art, something that lasts.' She crossed to a painting, a bold, colorful oil of busy Dublin. 'I've always wished . . . it's not that I'm envious of Maggie. Though I was, a little, when she went off to study in Venice and I stayed home. But we both did what we needed to do. And now, she's doing something so important.'

'So are you. Why do you do that?' he demanded, irritated with her. 'Why do you think of what you do and who you are as second place. You can do more than anyone I've ever known.'

She smiled, turning toward him again. 'You just like my cooking.'

'Yes, I like your cooking.' He didn't smile back. 'And your weaving, your knitting, your flowers. The way you make the air smell, the way you tuck the corners of the sheets in when you make the bed. How you hang the clothes on the line and iron my shirts. You do all of those things, more, and make it all seem effortless.'

'Well it doesn't take much to –'

'It does.' He cut her off, his temper rolling again for no reason he could name. 'Don't you know how many people can't make a home, or don't give a damn, who haven't a clue how to nurture. They'd rather toss away what they have instead of caring for it. Time, things, children.'

He stopped himself, stunned by what had come out of him, stunned it had been there to come out. How long had that been hiding? he wondered. And what would it take to bury it again?

'Gray.' Brianna lifted a hand to his cheek to soothe, but he stepped back. He'd never considered himself vulnerable, or not in too many years to count. But at the moment he felt too off balance to be touched.

'What I mean is what you do is important. You shouldn't forget that. I want to look around.' He turned abruptly to the side doorway of the parlor and hurried through.

'Well.' Maggie stepped in from the hallway. 'That was an interesting outburst.'

'He needs family,' Brianna murmured.

'Brie, he's a grown man, not a babe.'

'Age doesn't take away the need. He's too alone, Maggie, and doesn't even know it.'

'You can't take him in like a stray.' Tilting her head, Maggie stepped closer. 'Or can you?'

'I have feelings for him. I never thought I'd have these feelings for anyone again.' She looked down at her hands that she'd clutched together in front of her, deliberately loosened then. 'No, that's not true. It's not what I felt for Rory.'

'Rory be damned.'

'So you always say.' And because of it, Brianna smiled. 'That's family.' She kissed Maggie's cheek. 'Tell me, how does it feel having the president buy your work?'

'As long as his money's good.' Then Maggie threw back her head and laughed. 'It's like going to the moon and back. I can't help it. We Concannons just aren't sophisticated enough to take such things in stride. Oh, I wish Da . . .'

'I know.'

'Well.' Maggie took a deep breath. 'I should tell you that the detective Rogan hired hasn't found Amanda Dougherty as yet. He's following leads, whatever that may mean.'

'So many weeks, Maggie, the expense.'

'Don't start nagging me about taking your housekeeping money. I married a rich man.'

'And everyone knows you wanted only his wealth.'

'No, I wanted his body.' She winked and hooked her arm through Brianna's. 'And your friend Grayson Thane has one a woman wouldn't sneeze at, I've noticed.'

'I've noticed myself.'

'Good, shows you haven't forgotten how to look. I had a card from Lottie.'

'So did I. Do you mind if they stay the third week?'

'For myself Mother could stay in that villa for the rest of her natural life.' She sighed at Brianna's expression. 'All right, all right. It's happy I am that she's enjoying herself, though she won't admit to it.'

'She's grateful to you, Maggie. It's just not in her to say so.'

'I don't need her to say so anymore.' Maggie laid a hand on her belly. 'I have my own, and it makes all the difference. I never knew I could feel so strong about anyone. Then there was Rogan. After that, I thought I could never feel so strong about anything or anyone else. And now, I do. So maybe I understand a little how if you didn't love, and didn't want the child growing in you, it could blight your life as much as loving and wanting it can brighten it.'

'She didn't want me, either.'

'What makes you say such a thing?'

'She told me.' It was a load lifted, Brianna discovered, to say it aloud. 'Duty. 'Twas only duty, not even to Da, but to the Church. It's a cold way to be brought into the world.'

It wasn't anger Brianna needed now, Maggie knew, and bit back on it. Instead, she cupped Brianna's face. 'It's her loss, Brie. Not yours. Never yours. And for myself, if the duty hadn't been done, I'd have been lost.'

'He loved us. Da loved us.'

'Yes, he did. And that's been enough. Come, don't worry on it. I'll take you upstairs and show you what we've been up to.'

From the back of the hallway, Gray let out a long breath. The acoustics in the building were much too good for secrets to be told. He thought he understood now some of the sadness that haunted Brianna's eyes. Odd that they should have the lack of a mother's care in common.

Not that the lack haunted him, he assured himself. He'd gotten over that long ago. He'd left the scared, lonely child behind in the cheerless rooms of the Simon Brent Memorial Home for Children.

But who, he wondered, was Rory? And why had Rogan hired detectives to look for a woman named Amanda Dougherty?

Gray had always found the very best way to find the answers was to ask the questions.

'Who's Rory?'

The question snapped Brianna out from her quiet daydream as Gray drove easily down narrow winding roads away from Ennistymon. 'What?'

'Not what, who?' He nipped the car closer to the edge as a loaded VW rounded a curve on his side of the road.

Probably an inexperienced Yank, he thought with a superior degree of smugness. 'Who's Rory?' he repeated.

'You've been listening to pub gossip, have you?'

Rather than warn him off, the coolness in her voice merely egged him on. 'Sure, but that's not where I heard the name. You mentioned him to Maggie back at the gallery.'

'Then you were eavesdropping on a private conversation.'

'That's redundant. It's not eavesdropping unless it's a private conversation.'

She straightened in her seat. 'There's no need to correct my grammar, thank you.'

'That wasn't grammar, it was . . . never mind.' He let it, and her, stew a moment. 'So, who was he?'

'And why would it be your business?'

'You're only making me more curious.'

'He was a boy I knew. You're taking the wrong road.'

'There is no wrong road in Ireland. Read the guidebooks. Is he the one who hurt you?' He flicked a glance in her direction, nodded. 'Well, that answers that. What happened?'

'Are you after putting it in one of your books?'

'Maybe. But it's personal first. Did you love him?'

'I loved him. I was going to marry him.'

He caught himself scowling over that and tapping a finger against the steering wheel. 'Why didn't you?'

'Because he jilted me two paces from the altar. Does that satisfy your curiosity?'

'No. It only tells me that Rory was obviously an idiot.' He couldn't stop the next question, was surprised he wanted to. 'Do you still love him?'

'That would be remarkably idiotic of me as it was ten years ago.'

160

'But it still hurts.'

'Being tossed aside hurts,' she said tersely. 'Being the object of pity in the community hurts. Poor Brie, poor dear Brie, thrown over two weeks before her wedding day. Left with a wedding dress and her sad little trousseau while her lad runs off to America rather than make her a wife. Is that enough for you?' She shifted to stare at him. 'Do you want to know if I cried? I did. Did I wait for him to come back? I did that as well.'

'You can punch me if it makes you feel better.'

'I doubt it would.'

'Why did he leave?'

She made a sound that came as much from annoyance as memory. 'I don't know. I've never known. That was the worst of it. He came to me and said he didn't want me, wouldn't have me, would never forgive me for what I'd done. And when I tried to ask him what he meant, he pushed me away, knocked me down.'

Gray's hands tightened on the wheel. 'He what?'

'He knocked me down,' she said calmly. 'And my pride wouldn't let me go after him. So he left, went to America.'

'Bastard.'

'I've often thought so myself, but I don't know why he left me. So, after a time, I gave away my wedding dress. Murphy's sister Kate wore it the day she married her Patrick.'

'He isn't worth the sadness you carry around in your eyes.'

'Perhaps not. But the dream was. What are you doing?'

'Pulling over. Let's walk out to the cliffs.'

'I'm not dressed for walking over rough ground,' she protested, but he was already out of the car. 'I've the wrong shoes, Gray. I can wait here if you want a look.'

'I want to look with you.' He tugged her out of the car, then swung her up in his arms.

'What are you doing? Are you mad?'

'It's not far, and think of what nice pictures those nice tourists over there are going to take home of us. Can you speak French?'

'No?' Baffled, she angled back to look at his face. 'Why?'

'I was just thinking if we spoke French, they'd think we were – French, you know. Then they'd tell Cousin Fred back in Dallas the story about this romantic French couple they'd seen near the coast.' He kissed her lightly before setting her on her feet near the verge of a rocky slope.

The water was the color of her eyes today, he noted. That cool, misty green that spoke of dreaming. It was clear enough that he could see the sturdy humps of the Aran Islands, and a little ferryboat that sailed between Innismore and the mainland. The smell was fresh, the sky a moody blue that could, and would, change at any moment. The tourists a few yards away were speaking in a rich Texas twang that made him smile.

'It's beautiful here. Everything. You've only to turn your head in this part of the world to see something else breathtaking.' Deliberately, he turned to Brianna. 'Absolutely breathtaking.'

'Now you're trying to flatter me to make up for prying into my business.'

'No, I'm not. And I haven't finished prying, and I like to pry, so it'd be hypocritical to apologize. Who's Amanda Dougherty, and why is Rogan looking for her?'

Shock flashed over her face, had her mouth tremble open and closed. 'You're the most rude of men.'

'I know all that already. Tell me something I don't know.'

'I'm going back.' But as she turned, he simply took her arm.

'I'll carry you back in a minute. You'll break your ankle in those shoes. Especially if you're going to flounce.'

'I don't flounce as you so colorfully put it. And this is none of your . . .' She trailed off, blew out a huff of breath. 'Why would I waste my time telling you it's none of your business?'

'I haven't got a clue.'

Her gaze narrowed on his face. Bland was what it was, she noted. And stubborn as two mules. 'You'll just keep hammering at me until I tell you.'

'Now you're catching on.' But he didn't smile. Instead he tucked away a tendril of hair that fluttered into her face. His eyes were intense, unwavering. 'That's what's worrying you. She's what's worrying you.'

'It's nothing you'd understand.'

'You'd be surprised what I understand. Here, sit.' He guided her to a rock, urged her down, then sat beside her. 'Tell me a story. It comes easier that way.'

Perhaps it would. And perhaps it would help this heaviness in her heart to say it all. 'Years ago, there was a woman who had a voice like an angel – or so they say. And ambition to use it to make her mark. She was discontent with her life as an innkeeper's daughter and went roaming, paying her way with a song. One day she came back, for her mother was ailing and she was a dutiful daughter if not a loving one. She sang in the village pub for her pleasure, and the patron's pleasure, and a few pounds. It was there she met a man.'

Brianna looked out to sea as she imagined her father catching sight of her mother, hearing her voice.

'Something hot flashed between them. It might have been love, but not the lasting kind. Still, they didn't, or couldn't resist it. And so, before long, she found herself with child. The Church, her upbringing, and her own beliefs left her no choice but to marry, and give up the dream she'd had. She was never happy after that, and had

163

not enough compassion in her to make her husband happy. Soon after the first child was born, she conceived another. Not out of that flash of something hot this time, but out of a cold sense of duty. And that duty satisfied, she refused her husband her bed and her body.'

It was her sigh that had Gray reaching out, covering her hand with his. But he didn't speak. Not yet.

'One day, somewhere near the River Shannon, he met another. There was love there, a deep, abiding love. Whatever their sin, the love was greater. But he had a wife, you see, and two small daughters. And he, and the woman who loved him, knew there was no future for them. So she left him, went back to America. She wrote him three letters, lovely letters full of love and understanding. And in the third she told him that she was carrying his child. She was going away, she said, and he wasn't to worry, for she was happy to have a part of him inside her growing.'

A sea bird called, drew her gaze up. She watched it wing off toward the horizon before she continued her story.

'She never wrote to him again, and he never forgot her. Those memories may have comforted him through the chill of his dutiful marriage and all the years of emptiness. I think they did, for it was her name he said before he died. He said Amanda as he looked out to the sea. And a lifetime after the letters were written, one of his daughters found them, tucked in the attic where he'd kept them tied in a faded red ribbon.'

She shifted to Gray then. 'There's nothing she can do, you see, to turn back the clock, to make any of those lives better than they might have been. But doesn't a woman who was loved so deserve to know she was never forgotten? And hasn't the child of that woman, and that man, a right to know his own blood?'

'It may hurt you more to find them.' He looked down at

their joined hands. 'The past has a lot of nasty trapdoors. It's a tenuous tie, Brianna, between you and Amanda's child. Stronger ones are broken every day.'

'My father loved her,' she said simply. 'The child she bore is kin. There's nothing else to do but look.'

'Not for you,' he murmured as his eyes scanned her face. There was strength there mixed with the sadness. 'Let me help you.'

'How?'

'I know a lot of people. Finding someone's mostly research, phone tag, connections.'

'Rogan's hired a detective in New York.'

'That's a good start. If he doesn't turn up something soon, will you let me try?' He lifted a brow. 'Don't say it's kind of me.'

'All right I won't, though it is.' She brought their joined hands to her cheek. 'I was angry with you for pushing me to tell you. But it helped.' She tilted her face toward his. 'You knew it would.'

'I'm innately nosy.'

'You are, yes. But you knew it would help.'

'It usually does.' He stood, scooped her from the rock. 'It's time to go back. I'm ready to work.'

Chapter Eleven

The chain the story had around his throat kept Gray shackled to his desk for days. Curiosity turned the key in the lock now and again as guests came and went from the cottage.

He'd had it to himself, or nearly so for so many weeks, he thought he might find the noise and chatter annoying. Instead it was cozy, like the inn itself, colorful, like the flowers that were beginning to bloom in Brianna's garden, bright as those first precious days of spring.

When he didn't leave his room, he would always find a tray outside his door. And when he did, there was a meal and some new company in the parlor. Most stayed only a night, which suited him. Gray had always preferred quick, uncomplicated contacts.

But one afternoon he came down, stomach rumbling, and tracked Brianna to the front garden.

'Are we empty?'

She glanced up from under the brim of her garden hat. 'For a day or two, yes. Are you ready for a meal?'

'It can wait until you're finished. What are you doing there?'

'Planting. I want pansies here. Their faces always look so arrogant and smug.' She sat back on her heels. 'Have you heard the cuckoo calling, Grayson?'

'A clock?'

'No.' She laughed and patted earth tenderly around roots. 'I heard the cuckoo call when I walked with Con early this morning, so we're in for fine weather. And there were two magpies chattering, which means prosperity will follow.' She bent back to her work. 'So, perhaps another guest will find his way here.'

'Superstitious, Brianna. You surprise me.'

'I don't see why. Ah, there's the phone now. A reservation.'

'I'll get it.' As he was already on his feet, he beat her to the parlor phone. 'Blackthorn Cottage. Arlene? Yeah, it's me. How's it going, beautiful?'

With a faint frown around her mouth, Brianna stood in the doorway and wiped her hands on the rag she'd tucked in her waistband.

'Any place I hang my hat,' he said in response to her question of whether he was feeling at home in Ireland. When he saw Brianna start to step back and fade from the room, he held out a hand in invitation. 'What's it like in New York?' He watched Brianna hesitate, step forward. Gray linked his fingers with hers and began to nuzzle her knuckles. 'No, I haven't forgotten that was coming up. I haven't given it much thought. If the spirit moves me, sweetheart.'

Though Brianna tugged on her hand and frowned, he only grinned and kept his grip firm.

'I'm glad to hear that. What's the deal?' He paused, listening and smiling into Brianna's eyes. 'That's generous, Arlene, but you know how I feel about long-term commitments. I want it one at a time, just like always.'

As he listened, he made little sounds of agreement, hums of interest, and nipped his way down to Brianna's wrist. It didn't do his ego any harm to feel her pulse scrambling.

'It sounds more than fine to me. Sure, push the Brits a bit further if you think you can. No, I haven't seen the London *Times*. Really? Well, that's handy, isn't it? No, I'm not being a smartass. It's great. Thanks. I – what? A fax? Here?' He snickered, leaned forward, and gave Brianna a quick, friendly kiss on the mouth. 'Bless you, Arlene. No, just send

167

it through the mail, my ego can wait. Right back at you, beautiful. I'll be in touch.'

He said his goodbyes and hung up with Brianna's hand still clutched in his.

When she spoke, the chill in her voice lowered the temperature of the room by ten degrees. 'Don't you think it's rude to be flirting with one woman on the phone and kissing another?'

His already pleased expression brightened. 'Jealous, darling?'

'Certainly not.'

'Just a little.' He caught her other hand before she could evade and brought both to his lips. 'Now that's progress. I almost hate to tell you that was my agent. My very married agent, who though dear to my heart and my bank-book is twenty years older than I and the proud grandmother of three.'

'Oh.' She hated to feel foolish almost as much as she hated to feel jealous. 'I suppose you want that meal now.'

'For once, food's the last thing on my mind.' What was on it was very clear in his eyes as he tugged her closer. 'You look really cute in that hat.'

She turned her head just in time to avoid his mouth. His lips merely skimmed over her cheek. 'Was it good news then, her calling?'

'Very good. My publisher liked the sample chapters I sent them a couple weeks ago and made an offer.'

'That's nice.' He seemed hungry enough to her, the way he was nibbling at her ear. 'I suppose I thought you sold books before you wrote them, like a contract.'

'I don't do multiples. Makes me feel caged in.' So much so that he had just turned down a spectacular offer for three projected novels. 'We deal one at a time, and with Arlene in my corner, we deal nicely.'

A warmth was spreading in her stomach as he worked his leisurely way down her neck. 'Five million you told me. I can't imagine so much.'

'Not this time.' He cruised up her jaw. 'Arlene strong-armed them up to six point five.'

Stunned, she jerked back. 'Million? American dollars?'

'Sounds like Monopoly money, doesn't it?' He chuckled. 'She's not satisfied with the British offer – and since my current book is steady at number one on the London *Times*, she's squeezing them a bit.' Absently he nipped her by the waist, pressed his lips to her brow, her temple. '*Sticking Point* opens in New York next month.'

'Opens?'

'Mmm. The movie. Arlene thought I might like to go to the premiere.'

'Of your own movie. You must.'

'There's no musts. Seems like old news. *Flashback*'s now.'

His lips teased the corner of her mouth and her breath began to hitch. '*Flashback*?'

'The book I'm working on. It's the only one that matters.' His eyes narrowed, lost focus. 'He has to find the book. Shit, how could I have missed that? It's the whole thing.' He jerked back, dragged a hand through his hair. 'Once he finds it, he won't have any choice, will he? That's what makes it personal.'

Every nerve ending in her body was humming from the imprint of his lips. 'What are you talking about? What book?'

'Deliah's diary. That's what links past and present. There'll be no walking away after he reads it. He'll have to –' Gray shook his head, like a man coming out, or moving into a trance. 'I've got to get to work.'

He was halfway up the stairs, and Brianna's heart was still thudding dully. 'Grayson?'

'What?'

He was already steeped in his own world, she noted, torn between amusement and irritation. That impatient gleam was in his eyes, eyes she doubted were even seeing her. 'Don't you want some food?'

'Just leave a tray when you have a chance. Thanks.'

And he was gone.

Well. Brianna set her hands on her hips and managed to laugh at herself. The man had all but seduced her into a puddle, and didn't even know it. Off he went with Deliah and her diary, murder and mayhem, leaving her system ticking like an overwound watch.

For the best, she assured herself. All that hand kissing and nibbling had weakened her. And it was foolish, wasn't it, to go weak over a man who would be gone from her home and her country as carelessly as he'd gone from her parlor.

But oh, she thought as she walked to the kitchen, it made her wonder what it would be like. What it would be like to have all that energy, all that attention, all that skill focused only on her. Even for a short time. Even for only one night.

She would know then, wouldn't she, what it felt like to give pleasure to a man? And to take it. Loneliness might be bitter after, but the moment might be sweet.

Might. Too many mights, she warned herself and fixed Gray a generous plate of cold lamb and cheese croquettes. She carried it up, taking it into his room without speaking.

He didn't acknowledge her, nor did she expect it now. Not when he was hulked over his little machine, his eyes slitted, his fingers racing. He did grunt when she poured the tea and set a cup at his elbow.

When she caught herself smiling, checking an urge to run a hand down that lovely gold-tipped hair, she decided it was a very good time to walk over to Murphy's and ask him about fixing her car.

The exercise helped work out those last jittery frissons of need. It was her time of year, the spring, when the birds called, the flowers bloomed, and the hills glowed so green your throat ached to look at them.

The light was gilded, the air so clear that she could hear the *putt-putt* of Murphy's tractor two fields over. Charmed by the day, she swung the basket she carried and sang to herself. As she climbed over a low stone wall, she smiled at the spindly legged foal that nursed greedily while his mother cropped grass. She spent a moment in admiration, another few stroking both mother and baby before wandering on.

Perhaps she would walk to Maggie's after seeing Murphy, she thought. It was only a matter of weeks now before the baby was due. Someone needed to tend Maggie's garden, do a bit of wash.

Laughing, she stopped, crouching down when Con raced over the field toward her.

'Been farming, have you? Or just chasing rabbits. No, 'tisn't for you,' she said, hooking the basket higher as the dog sniffed around it. 'But I've a fine bone at home waiting.' Hearing Murphy's hail, she straightened, waved her arm in greeting.

He shut off his tractor and hopped down as she walked over the newly turned earth.

'A fine day for planting.'

'The finest,' he agreed and eyed the basket. 'What have you there, Brie?'

'A bribe.'

'Oh, I'm made of stronger stuff than that.'

'Sponge cake.'

He closed his eyes and gave an exaggerated sigh. 'I'm your man.'

'That you are.' But she held the basket tantalizingly out of reach. ''Tis my car again, Murphy.'

Now his look was pained. 'Brianna, darling, it's time for the wake there. Past time.'

'Couldn't you just take a peek?'

He looked at her, then at the basket. 'The whole of the sponge cake?'

'Every crumb.'

'Done.' He took the basket, set it up on the tractor seat. 'But I'm warning you, you'll need a new one before summer.'

'If I do, I do. But I've my heart set on the greenhouse, so the car has to last a wee bit longer. Did you have time to look at my drawings for the greenhouse, Murphy?'

'I did. Could be done.' Taking advantage of the break, he pulled out a cigarette, lighted it. 'I made a few adjustments.'

'You're a darling man, Murphy.' Grinning, she kissed his cheek.

'So all the ladies tell me.' He tugged on a loose curl of hair. 'And what would your Yank think if he came across you charming me in my own field?'

'He's not my Yank.' She shifted as Murphy only lifted one black brow. 'You like him, don't you?'

'Hard not to like him. Is he worrying you, Brianna?'

'Maybe a little.' She sighed, gave up. There was nothing in her heart and mind she couldn't tell Murphy. 'A lot. I care for him. I'm not sure what to do about it, but I care for him, so much. It's different than even it was with Rory.'

At the mention of the name, Murphy scowled and stared down at the tip of his cigarette. 'Rory's not worth a single thought in your head.'

'I don't spend time thinking of him. But now, with Gray, it brings it back, you see. Murphy . . . he'll leave, you know. As Rory left.' She looked away. She could say it, Brianna thought, but she couldn't deal with the sympathy in Murphy's eyes when she did. 'I try to understand that, to accept it. I tell myself it'll be easier for at least I'll know why. Not knowing, my whole life with Rory, what was lacking in me —'

'There's nothing lacking in you,' Murphy said shortly. 'Put it aside.'

'I have. I did — or nearly. But I . . .' Overwhelmed, she turned away to stare out over the hills. 'But what is it in me, or not in me, that sends a man away? Do I ask too much from him, or not enough? Is there a coldness in me that freezes them out?'

'There's nothing cold about you. Stop blaming yourself for someone else's cruelty.'

'But I've only myself to ask. Ten years, it's been. And this is the first time since I've felt any stirring. It frightens me because I don't know how I'll live through heartbreak again. He's not Rory, I know, and yet —'

'No, he's not Rory.' Furious at seeing her so lost, so unhappy, Murphy tossed his cigarette down and ground it out. 'Rory was a fool who couldn't see what he had, and wanted to believe whatever lies he heard. You should thank God he's gone.'

'What lies?'

The heat stirred in Murphy's eyes, then cooled. 'Whatever. The day's wasting, Brie. I'll come look at your car tomorrow.'

'What lies?' She put a hand on his arm. There was a faint ringing in her ears, a hard fist in her belly. 'What do you know about it, Murphy, that you haven't told me?'

'What would I know? Rory and I were never mates.'

'No, you weren't,' she said slowly. 'He never liked you. He was jealous, he was, because we were close. He couldn't see that it was like having a brother. He couldn't see that,' she continued, watching Murphy carefully. 'And once or twice we argued over it, and he said how I was too free with kisses when it came to you.'

Something flickered over Murphy's face before he checked it. 'Well, didn't I tell you he was a fool?'

'Did you say something to him about it? Did he say something to you?' She waited, then the chill that was growing in her heart spread and cloaked her. 'You'll tell me, by God you will. I've a right. I wept my heart out over him, I suffered from the pitying looks of everyone I knew. I watched your sister marry in the dress I'd made with my own hands to be a bride. For ten years there's been an emptiness in me.'

'Brianna.'

'You'll tell me.' Rigid, braced, she faced him. 'For I can see you have the answer. If you're my friend, you'll tell me.'

'That 'tisn't fair.'

'Is doubting myself all this time any fairer?'

'I don't want to hurt you, Brianna.' Gently he touched a hand to her cheek. 'I'd cut off my arm before.'

'I'll hurt less knowing.'

'Maybe. Maybe.' He couldn't know, had never known. 'Maggie and I both thought –'

'Maggie?' she broke in, stunned. 'Maggie knows as well?'

Oh, he was in it now, he realized. And there was no way out without sinking the lot of them. 'Her love for you is so fierce, Brianna. She'd do anything to protect you.'

'And I'll tell you what I've told her, time and again. I don't need protecting. Tell me what you know.'

Ten years, he thought, was a long time for an honest man to hold a secret. Ten years, he thought, was longer still for an innocent woman to hold blame.

'He came after me one day while I was out here, working the fields. He went for me, out of the blue, it seemed to me. And not being fond of him, I went for him as well. Can't say my heart was in it much until he said what he did. He said you'd been . . . with me.'

It embarrassed him still, and beneath the embarrassment, he discovered there remained that sharp-edged rage that had never dulled with time.

'He said that we'd made a fool of him behind his back and he'd not marry a whore. I bloodied his face for that,' Murphy said viciously, his fist curling hard in memory. 'I'm not sorry for it. I might have broken his bones as well, but he told me he'd heard it from your mother's own lips. That she'd told him you'd been sneaking off with me, and might even be carrying my child.'

She was dead pale now, her heart crackling with ice. 'My mother said this to him?'

'She said — she couldn't, in good conscience, let him marry you in church when you'd sinned with me.'

'She knew I hadn't,' Brie whispered. 'She knew we hadn't.'

'Her reasons for believing it, or saying it, are her own. Maggie came by when I was cleaning myself up, and I told her before I could think better of it. At first I thought she'd go deal with Maeve with her fists, and I had to hold her there until she'd calmed a bit. We talked, and it was Maggie's thinking that Maeve had done it to keep you at home.'

Oh, yes, Brianna thought. At home, that had never been a home. 'Where I'd tend her, and the house, and Da.'

'We didn't know what to do, Brianna. I swear to you I'd have dragged you away from the altar meself if you'd gone ahead and tried to marry that snake-bellied bastard. But he left the very next day, and you were hurting so. I didn't have the heart, nor did Maggie, to tell you what he'd said.'

'You didn't have the heart.' She pressed her lips together.

'What you didn't have, Murphy, you nor Maggie, was the right to keep it from me. You didn't have the right any more than my mother did to say such things.'

'Brianna.'

She jerked back before he could touch her. 'No, don't. I can't talk to you now. I can't talk to you.' She turned and raced away.

She didn't weep. The tears were frozen in her throat, and she refused to let them melt. She ran across the fields, seeing nothing now, nothing but the haze of what had been. Or what had nearly been. All innocence had been shattered now. All illusions crushed to dust. Her life was lies. Conceived on them, bred on them, nurtured with them.

By the time she reached the house, her breath was sobbing in her lungs. She stopped herself, fisting her hands hard until her nails dug into flesh.

The birds still sang, and the tender young flowers she'd planted herself continued to dance in the breeze. But they no longer touched her. She saw herself as she'd been, shocked and appalled as she'd felt Rory's hand strike her to the ground. All these years later she could visualize it perfectly, the bafflement she'd felt as she'd stared up at him, the rage and disgust in his face before he'd turned and left her there.

She'd been marked as a whore, had she? By her own mother. By the man she had loved. What a fine joke it was, when she had never felt the weight of a man.

Very quietly she opened the door, closed it behind her. So her fate had been decided for her on that long-ago morning. Well, now, this very day, she would take her fate into her own hands.

Deliberately she walked up the stairs, opened Gray's door. Closed it tight at her back. 'Grayson?'

'Huh?'

'Do you want me?'

'Sure. Later.' His head came up, his glazed eyes only half focused. 'What? What did you say?'

'Do you want me?' she repeated. Her spine was as stiff as the question. 'You've said you did, and acted as you did.'

'I . . .' He made a manful attempt to pull himself out of imagination into reality. She was pale as ice, he noted, and her eyes glittered with cold. And, he noted, hurt. 'Brianna, what's going on?'

'A simple question. I'd thank you for an answer to it.'

'Of course I want you. What's the − what in hell are you doing?' He was out of the chair like a shot, gaping as she began to briskly unbutton her blouse. 'Cut it out. Goddamn it, stop that now.'

'You said you want me. I'm obliging you.'

'I said stop.' In three strides he was to her, yanking her blouse together. 'What's gotten into you? What's happened?'

'That's neither here nor there.' She could feel herself beginning to shake and fought it back. 'You've been trying to persuade me into bed, now I'm ready to go. If you can't spare the time now, just say so.' Her eyes flared. 'I'm used to being put off.'

'It's not a matter of time −'

'Well, then.' She broke away to turn down the bed. 'Would you prefer the curtains open or closed? I've no preference.'

'Leave the stupid curtains.' The neat way she folded down the covers did what it always did. It made his stomach tighten into a slippery fist of lust. 'We're not going to do this.'

'You don't want me, then.' When she straightened her open blouse shifted, giving him a tantalizing peek of pale skin and tidy white cotton.

'You're killing me,' he murmured.

'Fine. I'll leave you to die in peace.' Head high, she marched for the door. He merely slammed a hand on it to keep it shut.

'You're not going anywhere until you tell me what's going on.'

'Nothing, it seems, at least with you.' She pressed herself back against the door, forgetting now to breathe slowly, evenly, to keep the wrenching pain out of her voice. 'Surely there's a man somewhere who might spare a moment or two to give me a tumble.'

He bared his teeth. 'You're pissing me off.'

'Oh, well, that's a pity. I do beg your pardon. It's sorry I am to have bothered you. It's only that I thought you'd meant what you'd said. That's my problem, you see,' she murmured as tears glistened in her eyes. 'Always believing.'

He would have to handle the tears, he realized, and whatever emotional tailspin she was caught in, without touching her. 'What happened?'

'I found out.' Her eyes weren't cold now, but devastated and desperate. 'I found out that there's never been a man who's loved me. Not really loved me ever. And that my own mother lied, lied hatefully, to take away even that small chance of happiness. She told him I'd slept with Murphy. She told him that, and that I might be carrying a child. How could he marry me believing that? How could he believe it loving me?'

'Hold on a minute.' He paused, waiting for her quick blur of words to register. 'You're saying that your mother told the guy you were going to marry, this Rory, that you'd been having sex with Murphy, might be pregnant?'

'She told him that so that I couldn't escape this house.' Leaning her head back she closed her eyes. 'This house as it was then. And he believed her. He believed I could have done that, believed it so that he never asked me if it was true. Only told me he wouldn't have me, and left. And all this time Maggie and Murphy have known it, and kept it from me.'

Tread carefully, Gray warned himself. Emotional quicksand. 'Look, I'm on the outside here, and I'd say, being a professional observer, that your sister and Murphy kept their mouths shut to keep you from hurting more than you already were.'

'It was my life, wasn't it? Do you know what it's like not to know why you're not wanted, to go through life only knowing you weren't, but never why?'

Yeah, he knew, exactly. But he didn't think it was the answer she wanted. 'He didn't deserve you. That should give you some satisfaction.'

'It doesn't. Not now. I thought you would show me.'

He stepped cautiously back as the breath clogged in his lungs. A beautiful woman, one who had, from the first instant, stirred his blood. Innocent. Offering. 'You're upset,' he managed in a tight voice. 'Not thinking clearly. And as much as it pains me, there are rules.'

'I don't want excuses.'

'You want a substitute.' The quick violence of the statement surprised both of them. He hadn't realized that little germ had been in his head. But he lashed out as it grew. 'I'm not a goddamn stand-in for some whiny, wimp-hearted jerk who tossed you over a decade ago. Yesterday sucks. Well, welcome to reality. When I take a woman to bed, she's going to be thinking about me. Just me.'

What little color that had seeped back into her cheeks drained. 'I'm sorry. I didn't mean it that way, didn't mean it to seem that way.'

'That's exactly how it seems, because that's exactly what it is. Pull yourself together,' he ordered, deadly afraid she would start to cry again. 'When you figure out what you want, let me know.'

'I only . . . I needed to feel as if something, you, wanted me. I thought – I hoped I'd have something to remember. Just once, to know what it was like to be touched by a man I cared for.' The color came back, humiliation riding her cheeks as Gray stared at her. 'Doesn't matter. I'm sorry. I'm very sorry.'

She yanked open the door and fled.

She was sorry, Gray thought, staring into the space where she'd been. He could all but see the air vibrate in her wake.

Good going, pal, he thought in disgust as he began to pace the room. Nice job. It always makes someone feel better when you kick them while they're down.

But damn it, damn it, she'd made him feel exactly as he'd told her. A convenient substitute for some lost love. He felt miserable for her, facing that kind of betrayal, that kind of rejection. There was nothing he understood better. But he'd patched himself up, hadn't he? So could she.

She'd wanted to be touched. She'd just needed to be soothed. Head pounding, he stalked to the window and back. She'd wanted him – a little sympathy, a little understanding. A little sex. And he'd brushed her off.

Just like the ever-popular Rory.

What was he supposed to do? How could he have taken her to bed when all that hurt and fear and confusion had been shimmering around her? He didn't need other people's complications.

He didn't want them.

He wanted her.

On an oath he rested his head against the window glass. He could walk away. He'd never had any trouble walking away. Just sit down again, pick up the threads of his story, and dive into it.

Or . . . or he could try something that might clear the frustration out of the air for both of them.

The second impulse was more appealing, a great deal more appealing, if a great deal more dangerous. The safe route was for cowards, he told himself. Snatching up his keys, he walked downstairs and out of the house.

Chapter Twelve

If there was one thing Gray knew how to do with style, it was set scenes. Two hours after he'd left Blackthorn Cottage, he was back in his room and putting the final touch on the details. He didn't think past the first step. Sometimes it was wiser – safer certainly – not to dwell on how the scene might unfold or the chapter close.

After a last glance around, he nodded to himself, then went downstairs to find her.

'Brianna.'

She didn't turn from the sink where she was meticulously frosting a chocolate cake. She was calmer now, but no less ashamed of her behavior. She had shuddered more than once over the past two hours over the way she'd thrown herself at him.

Thrown herself, she remembered again, and not been caught.

'Yes, dinner's ready,' she said calmly. 'Would you want it down here?'

'I need you to come upstairs.'

'All right, then.' Her relief that he didn't ask for a cozy meal in the kitchen was tremendous. 'I'll just fix a tray for you.'

'No.' He laid a hand on her shoulder, uneasy when he felt her muscles stiffen. 'I need you to come upstairs.'

Well, she would have to face him sooner or later. Carefully wiping her hands on her apron, she turned. She read nothing in his face of condemnation, or the anger he'd speared at her earlier. It didn't help. 'Is there a problem?'

'Come up, then you tell me.'

'All right.' She followed behind him. Should she apologize again? She wasn't sure. It might be best just to pretend nothing had been said. She gave a little sigh as they approached his room. Oh, she hoped it wasn't the plumbing. The expense just now would . . .

She forgot about plumbing as she stepped inside. She forgot about everything.

There were candles set everywhere, the soft light streaming like melted gold against the twilight gray of the room. Flowers spilled out of a half dozen vases, tulips and roses, freesia and lilacs. In a silver bucket rested an iced bottle of champagne, still corked. Music came from somewhere. Harp music. She stared, baffled, at the portable stereo on his desk.

'I like the curtains open,' he said.

She folded her hands under her apron where only she would know they trembled. 'Why?'

'Because you never know when you might catch a moonbeam.'

Her lips curved, ever so slightly at the thought. 'No, I mean why have you done all this?'

'To make you smile. To give you time to decide if it's what you really want. To help persuade you that it is.'

'You've gone to such trouble.' Her eyes skimmed toward the bed, then quickly, nervously onto the vase of roses. 'You didn't have to. I've made you feel obliged.'

'Please. Don't be an idiot. It's your choice.' But he moved to her, took the first pin from her hair, tossed it aside. 'Do you want me to show you how much I want you?'

'I –'

'I think I should show you, at least a little.' He took out another pin, a third, then simply combed his hands through her tumbling hair. 'Then you can decide how much you'll give.'

His mouth skimmed over hers, gentle as air, erotic as sin. When her lips trembled apart, he slipped his tongue between them, teasing hers.

'That should give you the idea.' He moved his lips along her jaw, up to her temple, then back to nip at the corner of her mouth. 'Tell me you want me, Brianna. I want to hear you say it.'

'I do.' She couldn't hear her own voice, only the hum of it in her throat where his mouth now nestled. 'I do want you. Gray, I can't think. I need —'

'Just me. You only need me tonight. I only need you.' Coaxing, he smoothed his hands down her back. 'Lie down with me, Brianna.' He lifted her, cradled her. 'There are so many places I want to take you.'

He laid her down on the bed where the sheets and quilt had been folded down in invitation. Her hair spilled like fired gold over the crisp linen, subtle waves of it catching glints from the candlelight. Her eyes were stormy with the war of doubts and needs.

And his stomach trembled, looking at her. From desire, yes, but also from fear.

He would be her first. No matter what happened after, through her life, she would remember tonight, and him.

'I don't know what to do.' She closed her eyes, excited, embarrassed, enchanted.

'I do.' He laid beside her, dipped his mouth to hers once more. She was trembling beneath him, a fact that had a hot ball of panic tightening in his gut. If he moved too fast. If he moved to slow. To soothe them both he pried her nervous fingers apart, kissed them one by one. 'Don't be afraid, Brianna. Don't be afraid of me. I won't hurt you.'

But she was afraid, and not only of the pain she knew went hand in hand with the loss of innocence. She was afraid of not being capable of giving pleasure, and of not being able to feel the full truth of it.

'Think of me,' he murmured, deepening the kiss degree by shuddering degree. If he did nothing else, he swore he would exorcise the last ghost of her heartache. 'Think of me.' And when he repeated it, he knew, from somewhere hidden inside that he needed this moment as much as she.

Sweet, she thought hazily. How odd that a man's mouth could taste so sweet, and could be firm and soft all at once. Fascinated by the taste and texture, she traced his lips with the tip of her tongue. And heard his quiet purr in answer.

One by one her muscles uncoiled as his flavor seeped into her. And how lovely it was to be kissed as if you would be kissed until time stopped. How solid and good his weight was, how strong his back when she dared let her hands roam.

He stiffened, bit back a moan as her hesitant fingers skimmed over his hips. He was already hard and shifted slightly, worried that he might frighten her.

Slowly, he ordered himself. Delicately.

He slipped the top strap of her apron over her head, untied the one around her waist and drew it off. Her eyes fluttered open, her lips curved.

'Will you kiss me again?' Her voice was honey thick now, and warm. 'It makes everything go gold behind my eyes when you do.'

He rested his brow on hers, waited a moment until he thought he could give her the gentleness she'd asked for. Then he took her mouth, swallowed her lovely, soft sigh. She seemed to melt beneath him, the tremblings giving way to pliancy.

She felt nothing but his mouth, that wonderful mouth that feasted so sumptuously on hers. Then his hand cupped her throat as if testing the speed of the pulse that fluttered there before he trailed down.

She hadn't been aware that he'd unfastened her blouse. As his fingers traced the soft swell of her breast above her bra, her eyes flew open. His were steady on hers, with a concentration so focused it brought the trembles back. She started to protest, to make some sound of denial. But his touch was so alluring, just a skim of fingertips against flesh.

It wasn't fearful, she realized. It was soothing, and just as sweet as the kiss. Even as she willed herself to relax again, those clever fingers slipped under the cotton and found the sensitive point.

Her first gasp ripped through him – the sound of it, the arousing sensation of her body arching in surprise and pleasure. He was barely touching her, he thought as his blood pounded. She had no idea how much more there was.

God, he was desperate to show her.

'Relax.' He kissed her, kissed her, as his fingers continued to arouse and his free hand circled back to unhook the barrier. 'Just feel it.'

She had no choice. Sensations were tearing through her, tiny arrows of pleasure and shock. His mouth swallowed her strangled breaths as he tugged away her clothes and left her bare to the waist.

'God, you're so beautiful.' His first look at that milk-pale skin, the small breasts that fit so perfectly into the cups of his palms nearly undid him. Unable to resist, he lowered his head and tasted.

She moaned, long, deep, throaty. The movements of her body under his were pure instinct, he knew, and not designed to deliberately claw at his control. So he pleased her, gently, and found his own pleasure growing from hers.

His mouth was so hot. The air was so thick. Each time he tugged, pulled, laved, there was an answering flutter in the pit of her stomach. A flutter that built and built into something too close to pain, too close to pleasure to separate them.

He was murmuring to her, lovely, soft words that circled

like rainbows in her head. It didn't matter what he said — she would have told him if she could. Nothing mattered as long as he never, never stopped touching her.

He tugged his own shirt over his head, craving the feel of flesh against flesh. When he lowered himself to her again, she made a small sound and wrapped her arms around him.

She only sighed again when his mouth roamed lower, over torso, over ribs. Her skin heated, muscles jerking, quivering under his lips and hands. And he knew she was lost in that dark tunnel of sensations.

Carefully he unhooked her slacks, baring new flesh slowly, exploring it gently. As her hips arched once in innocent agreement, he clamped his teeth and fought back the tearing need to take, just take and satisfy the grinding in his taut body.

Her nails dug into his back, drawing out a groan of dark delight from him as his hand skimmed down her bared hip. He knew she'd stiffened again and begged whatever god was listening for strength.

'Not until you're ready,' he murmured and brought his lips patiently back to hers again. 'I promise. But I want to see you. All of you.'

He shifted, knelt back. There was fear in her eyes again, though her body was quivering with suppressed needs. He couldn't steady his hands or his voice, but he kept them gentle.

'I want to touch all of you.' His eyes stayed on hers as he unsnapped his jeans. 'All of you.'

When he stripped, her gaze was drawn inexorably down. And her fear doubled. She knew what was to happen. She was, after all, a farmer's daughter, however poor a farmer he'd been. There would be pain, and blood, and . . .

'Gray —'

'Your skin's so soft.' Watching her, he skimmed a finger

up her thigh. 'I've wondered what you'd look like, but you're so much lovelier than I imagined.'

Unsettled, she'd crossed an arm over her breast. He left it there and went back to where he'd begun. With soft, slow, drugging kisses. And next caresses, patient, skilled hands that knew where a woman longed to be touched. Even when the woman didn't. Helplessly she yielded beneath him again, her breathing quickening into catchy pants as his hand roamed over the flat of her stomach toward the terrible, glorious heat.

Yes, he thought, fighting delirium. Open for me. Let me. Just let me.

She was damp and hot where he cupped her. The groan tore from his throat when she writhed and tried to resist.

'Let go, Brianna. Let me take you there. Just let go.'

She was clinging to the edge of some towering cliff by no more than her fingertips. Terror welled inside her. She was slipping. No control. There was too much happening inside her body all at once for her burning flesh to hold it all in. His hand was like a torch against her, firing her, searing her mercilessly until she would have no choice but to tumble free into the unknown.

'Please.' The word sobbed out. 'Oh, sweet God, please.'

Then the pleasure, the molten flood of it washed through her, over her, stealing her breath, her mind, her vision. For one glorious moment she was blind and deaf to everything but herself and the velvet shocks convulsing her.

She poured into his hand, making him moan like a dying man. He shuddered, even as she did, then with his face buried against her skin took her soaring again.

Straining against the chain of his own control, he waited until she was at peak. 'Hold me. Hold on to me,' he murmured, dizzy with his own needs as he struggled to ease gently into her.

She was so small, so tight, so deliciously hot. He used every ounce of willpower he had left not to thrust greedily inside as he felt her close around him.

'Only for a second,' he promised her. 'Only for a second, then it'll be good again.'

But he was wrong. It never stopped being good. She felt him break the barrier of her innocence, fill her with himself, and felt nothing but joy.

'I love you.' She arched up to meet him, to welcome him.

He heard the words dimly, shook his head to deny them. But she was wrapped around him, drawing him into a well of generosity. And he was helpless to do anything but drown.

Coming back to time and place was, for Brianna, like sliding weightlessly through a thin, white cloud. She sighed, let the gentle gravity take her until she was once more in the big old bed, candlelight flickering red and gold on her closed lids, and the truly incredible pleasure of Gray's weight pinning her to the mattress.

She thought hazily that no books she had read, no chatter she had heard from other women, no secret daydreaming could have taught her how simply good it was to have a man's naked body pressed onto hers.

The body itself was an amazing creation, more beautiful than she'd imagined. The long, muscled arms were strong enough to lift her, gentle enough to hold her as if she were a hollowed-out egg, easily broken.

The hands, wide of palm, long of finger, knew so cleverly just where to touch and stroke. Then there were the broad shoulders, the long, lovely, lean back, narrow hips leading down to hard thighs, firm calves.

Hard. She smiled to herself. Wasn't it a miracle that

something so hard, so tough and strong should be covered with smooth, soft skin?

Oh, indeed, she thought, a man's body was a glorious thing.

Gray knew if she kept touching him he'd go quietly mad. If she stopped, he was certain he'd whimper.

Those pretty tea-serving hands of hers were gliding over him, whispering touches, exploring, tracing, testing, as if she were memorizing each muscle and curve.

He was still inside her, couldn't bear to separate himself. He knew he should, should ease away and give her time to recover. However much he'd fought not to hurt her, there was bound to be some discomfort.

And yet, he was so content – she seemed so content. All those nerves that had sizzled through him at the thought of taking her the first time – her first time – had melted away into lazy bliss.

When those skimming caresses caused him to stir again, he forced himself to move, propping up on his elbows to look down at her.

She was smiling. He couldn't have said why he found that so endearing, so perfectly charming. Her lips curved, her eyes warmly green, her skin softly flushed. Now, with that first rush of needs and nerves calmed, he could enjoy the moment, the lights, the shadows, the rippling pleasure of fresh arousal.

He pressed his lips to her brow, her temples, her cheeks, her mouth.

'Beautiful Brianna.'

'It was beautiful for me.' Her voice was thick, still raspy with passion. 'You made it beautiful for me.'

'How do you feel now?'

He would ask, she thought, both in kindness and in curiosity. 'Weak,' she said. And with a quick laugh,

'Invincible. Why do you suppose such a natural thing as this should make such a difference in a life?'

His brows drew together, smoothed out again. Responsibility, he thought, it was his responsibility. He had to remind himself she was a grown woman, and the choice had been hers. 'Are you comfortable with that difference?'

She smiled up at him, beautifully, touched a hand to his cheek. 'I've waited so long for you, Gray.'

The quick inner defense signal flashed on. Even steeped in her, warm, damn, half aroused, it flashed. Step carefully, cautioned a cool, controlled part of his mind. *Warning: Intimacy Ahead*.

She saw the change in his eyes, a subtle but distinct distancing even as he took the hand against his cheek and shifted it so that his lips pressed to her palm.

'I'm crushing you.'

She wanted to say – no, stay – but he was already moving away.

'We haven't had any champagne.' Easy with his nakedness, he rolled out of bed. 'Why don't you go have a bath while I open the bottle?'

She felt odd suddenly, and awkward, where she'd felt nothing but natural with him atop and inside her. Now she fumbled with the sheets. 'The linen,' she began, and found herself flushing and tongue-tied. It would be soiled, she knew, with her innocence.

'I'll take care of it.' Seeing her color deepen and understanding, he moved to the bed again and cupped her chin in his hand. 'I can change sheets, Brie. And even if I didn't know how before, I'd have picked it up watching you.' His mouth brushed hers, his voice thickening. 'Do you know how often I've been driven insane watching you smooth and tuck my sheets?'

'No.' There was a quick lick of pleasure and desire. 'Really?'

He only laughed and laid his brow on hers. 'What wonderful good deed did I do to deserve this? To earn you?' He drew back, but his eyes had kindled again, making her heart drum slow and hard against her ribs. 'Go have your bath. I'm wanting to make love with you again,' he said, slipping into a brogue that made her lips quirk. 'If you'd like it.'

'I would, yes.' She drew a deep breath, bracing herself to climb naked from the bed. 'Very much I would. I won't be long.'

When she went into the bath, he took a deep breath himself. To steady his system, he told himself.

He'd never had anyone like her. It wasn't just that he'd never tasted innocence before – that would have been enormous enough. But she was unique to him. Her responses, that hesitation and eagerness playing at odds with each other. With her absolute trust shining over all.

'I love you,' she'd said.

It wouldn't do to dwell on that. Women tended to romanticize, emotionalize sex in most cases. Certainly a woman experiencing sex for the first time would be bound to mix lust with love. Women used words, and required them. He knew that. That was why he was very careful when choosing his.

But something had spurted through him when she'd whispered that overrated and overused phrase. Warmth and need and, for an instant, just a heartbeat, a desperate desire to believe it. And to echo her words.

He knew better, and though he would do anything and everything in his power to keep her from hurt, anything and everything to make her happy while they were together, there were limits to what he could and would give to her. To anyone.

Enjoy the moment, he reminded himself. That's all there was. He hoped he could teach her to enjoy it as well.

She felt odd as she wrapped the towel around her freshly scrubbed body. Different. It was something that could never be explained to a man, she supposed. They lost nothing when they gave themselves the first time. There was no sharp tearing of self to admit another. But it wasn't pain she remembered, even the soreness between her thighs didn't bring the violence of invasion to mind. It was the unity she thought of. The sweet and simple bond of mating.

She studied herself in the misty mirror. She looked warm, she decided. It was the same face, surely, that she'd glimpsed countless time in countless mirrors. Yet wasn't there a softness here she'd never noticed before? In the eyes, around the mouth? Love had done that. The love she held in her heart, the love she'd tasted for the first time with her body.

Perhaps it was only the first time that a woman felt so aware of herself, so stripped of everything but flesh and soul. And perhaps, she thought, because she was older than most, the moment was all the more overwhelming and precious.

He wanted her. Brianna closed her eyes, the better to feel those long, slow ripples of delight. A beautiful man with a beautiful mind and kind heart wanted her.

All of her life she'd dreamed of finding him. Now she had.

She stepped into the bedroom, and saw him. He'd put fresh linen on the bed and had laid one of her white flannel gowns at the foot of it. He stood now in jeans unsnapped and relaxed on his hips, with champagne bubbling in glasses and candlelight simmering in his eyes.

'I'm hoping you'll wear it,' he said when she saw her

gaze rest on the prim, old-fashioned nightgown. 'I've imagined getting you out of it since that first night. I watched you come down the stairs, a candle in one hand, a wolfhound in the other, and my head went spinning.'

She picked up a sleeve. How much she wished it was silk or lace or something that would make a man's blood heat. ' 'Tisn't very alluring, I think.'

'You think wrong.'

Because she had nothing else, and it seemed to please him, she slipped the gown over her head, letting the towel fall away as the flannel slid down. His muffled groan had her smiling over uncertainly.

'Brianna, what a picture you are. Leave the towel,' he murmured as she bent to retrieve it. 'Come here. Please.'

She stepped forward, that half smile on her face and nerves threatening to swallow her, to take the glass he held out. She sipped, discovered the frothy wine did nothing to ease her dry throat. He was looking at her, she thought, the way she imagined a tiger might look at a lamb just before he pounced.

'You haven't had dinner,' she said.

'No.' Don't frighten her, idiot, he warned himself and struggled back the urge to devour. He took a slow sample of champagne, watching her, wanting her. 'I was just thinking I wanted it. Thinking we could eat up here, together. But now . . .' He reached out to curl a damp tendril of her hair around his finger. 'Can you wait?'

So it was to be simple again, she thought. And again her choice. 'I can wait for dinner.' She could barely get the words passed the heat in her throat. 'But not for you.'

She stepped, quite naturally, into his arms.

Chapter Thirteen

An elbow in the ribs brought Brianna groggily out of sleep. Her first view of the morning after a night of love was floor. If Gray took up another inch of the bed, she'd be on it.

It took her only seconds, and a shiver in the chilly morning air, to realize she hadn't even the stingiest corner of sheet or blanket covering her.

Gray, on the other hand, was cozily wrapped beside her, like a contented moth in a cocoon.

Sprawled over the mattress, he slept like the dead. She wished she could have said his snuggled position, and the elbow lodged near her kidney, was loverlike, but it smacked plainly of greed. Her tentative pushes and tugs didn't budge him.

So that was the way of it, she thought. The man was obviously unaccustomed to sharing.

She might have stayed to tussle for her share — just on principle — but the sun was shining through the windows. And there were chores to do.

Her efforts to slip quietly from the bed so as not to disturb him proved unnecessary. The minute her feet were on the floor, he grunted, then shifted to lay claim to her small slice of mattress.

Still, the dregs of romance remained in the room. The candles had guttered out in their own wax sometime during the night. The champagne bottle was empty in its silver bucket, and flowers scented the air. The open curtain caught sunbeams, rather than moonbeams.

He'd made it perfect for her, she remembered. Had known how to make it perfect.

This morning business wasn't quite the way she'd

imagined it. In sleep, he didn't look like an innocent boy dreaming, but like a man well satisfied with himself. There hadn't been any gentle caresses or murmured good mornings to acknowledge their first day together as lovers. Just a grunt and a shove to send her on her way.

The many moods of Grayson Thane, she mused. Perhaps she could write a book on that subject herself.

Amused, she tugged her discarded nightgown over her head and headed downstairs.

She could do with some tea, she decided, to get the blood moving again. And since the sky looked promising, she'd do a bit of wash and hang it out to catch the morning air.

She thought the house could do with an airing as well and tossed open windows as she walked. Through the one in the parlor, she spotted Murphy bent under the hood of her car.

She watched him a moment, her emotions tangling. Her anger with him warred with loyalty and affection. Anger was already losing as she walked outside and moved along the garden path.

'I didn't expect to see you,' she began.

'I said I'd have a look.' He glanced back. She was standing in her nightgown, her hair tangled from the night, her feet bare. Unlike Gray, his blood didn't kindle. She was simply Brianna to him, and he took the moment to search out any sign of temper or forgiveness. He saw neither, so went back to his business.

'Your starter motor's in a bad way,' he muttered.

'So I've been told.'

'Your engine's sick as an old horse. I can get some parts, patch it back together. But it's good money after bad as I see it.'

'If it could last me through the summer, into the

autumn . . .' She trailed off as he cursed under his breath. She simply couldn't keep her heart cool from him. He'd been her friend as long as she remembered. And it was friendship, she knew, that had caused him to do what he'd done.

'Murphy, I'm sorry.'

He straightened then, and turned to her, with everything he felt naked in his eyes. 'So am I. I never meant to cause you hurt, Brie. God's witness.'

'I know that.' She took the step, crossing to him and slipping her arms around him. 'I shouldn't have been so hard, Murphy. Not on you. Never on you.'

'You scared me, I'll admit it.' His arms went tight around her. 'I spent the night worrying over it — afraid you wouldn't forgive me, and not bake me scones anymore.'

She laughed as he'd hoped. Shaking her head, she kissed him under the ear. 'I was so angry at the thought of it all more than at you. I know you acted out of caring. And Maggie, too.' Secure with her head on his shoulder, Brianna closed her eyes. 'But my mother, Murphy, what did she act out of?'

'I can't say, Brie.'

'You wouldn't say,' she murmured and eased back to study his face. Such a handsome one, she thought, with all that goodness inside. It wasn't right for her to ask him to condemn or defend her mother. And she wanted to see him smile again. 'Tell me, did Rory hurt you very much?'

Murphy made a sound of derision, purely male, Brianna thought. 'Soft hands is what he had, and not a bit of style. Wouldn't have laid the first one on me if I'd been expecting it.'

She tucked her tongue in her cheek. 'No, I'm sure of it. And did you bloody his nose for me, Murphy darling?'

'That and more. His nose was broke when I'd finished with him, and he'd lost a tooth or two.'

'That's a hero for you.' She kissed him lightly on both cheeks. 'I'm sorry she used you that way.'

He shrugged that off. 'I'm glad I was the one who plowed a fist in his face, and that's the truth. Never liked the bastard.'

'No,' Brianna said softly. 'You nor Maggie, either. It seems you both saw something I didn't, or I was seeing something that was never there.'

'Don't worry at it now, Brie. It was years ago.' He started to pat her and remembered the grease on his hands. 'Get back now, you'll make yourself filthy. What are you doing out here in your bare feet?'

'Making up with you.' She smiled, then looked toward the road at the sound of a car. When she spotted Maggie, Brianna folded her hands, lifted a brow. 'Warned her, did you?' she muttered to Murphy.

'Well, I thought it best.' And he thought it best now to step neatly back out of the line of fire.

'So.' Maggie walked around the nodding columbine, her eyes on Brianna's face. 'I thought you might want to talk to me.'

'I do, yes. Did you think I had no right to know, Maggie?'

'It wasn't rights I was worried about. 'Twas you.'

'I loved him.' The long breath she took was part relief that the emotion was fully past tense. 'I loved him longer than I would had I known the whole of it.'

'Maybe that's true, and I'm sorry for it. I couldn't bear to tell you.' To all three of their discomfort, Maggie's eyes filled. 'I just couldn't. You were so hurt already, so sad and lost.' Pressing her lips together, she struggled with the tears. 'I didn't know what was best.'

'It was both of our decision.' Murphy ranged himself with Maggie. 'There was no bringing him back for you, Brie.'

'Do you think I would have wanted him back?' A shimmer of heat, and more of pride seeped through as she tossed back her hair. 'Do you think so little of me? He believed what she told him. No, I'd not have had him back.' She let out a quick huff of breath, drew in another more slowly. 'And, I'm thinking, had it been me in your position, Margaret Mary, I might have done the same. I'd have loved you enough to have done the same.'

She rubbed her hands together, then held one out. 'Come inside, I'm going to make some tea. Have you had breakfast, Murphy?'

'Nothing to speak of.'

'I'll call you when it's ready then.' With Maggie's hand in hers, she turned and saw Gray standing in the doorway. There was no way to stop the color that flooded her cheeks, a combination of pleasure and embarrassment, that sent her pulse scrambling. But her voice was steady enough, her nod of greeting easy. 'Good morning to you, Grayson. I was about to start breakfast.'

So, she wanted to play it cool and casual, Gray noted, and returned the nod. 'Looks like I'll have company eating it. Morning, Maggie.'

Maggie sized him up as she walked with Brianna to the house. 'And to you, Gray. You look . . . rested.'

'The Irish air agrees with me.' He moved aside to let them through the door. 'I'll see what Murphy's up to.'

He strolled down the walk and stopped by the open hood of the car. 'So, what's the verdict?'

Murphy leaned on the car and watched him. 'You could say it's still out.'

Understanding that neither of them were discussing engines, Gray tucked his thumbs in his front pockets and rocked back on his heels. 'Still looking out for her? Can't blame you for that, but I'm not Rory.'

'Never thought you were.' Murphy scratched his chin, considered. 'She's a sturdy piece of work, our Brie, you know. But even sturdy women can be damaged if handled carelessly.'

'I don't intend to be careless.' He lifted a brow. 'Thinking of beating me up, Murphy?'

'Not yet.' And he smiled. 'I like you, Grayson. I hope I won't be called upon to break any of your bones.'

'That goes for both of us.' Satisfied, Gray glanced toward the engine. 'Are we going to give this thing a decent burial?'

Murphy's sigh was long and heartfelt. 'If only we could.'

In harmony they ducked under the hood together.

In the kitchen Maggie waited until coffee was scenting the air and Con was chomping happily at his breakfast. Brianna had dressed hastily and, with her apron in place, was busy slicing bacon.

'I've gotten a late start,' Brianna began, 'so there's no time for fresh muffins or buns. But I've plenty of bread.'

Maggie sat at the table, knowing her sister preferred that she stay out of the way. 'Are you all right, Brianna?'

'Why wouldn't I be? Will you be wanting sausage, too?'

'Doesn't matter. Brie . . .' Maggie dragged a hand through her hair. 'He was your first, wasn't he?' When Brianna set her slicing knife aside and said nothing, Maggie pushed away from the table. 'Did you think I wouldn't know, just seeing you together? The way he looks at you.' She rubbed her hands absently over her weighted belly as she paced. 'The way you look.'

'Have I a sign around my neck that says fallen woman?' Brianna said coolly.

'Damn it, you know that's not my meaning.' Exasperated, Maggie stopped to face her. 'Anyone with wit could see what was between you.' And their mother had wit, Maggie thought grimly. Maeve would be back in a matter of days. 'I'm not trying to interfere, or to give advice if advice isn't welcome. I just want to know . . . I need to know that you're all right.'

Brianna smiled then and let her stiff shoulders relax. 'I'm fine, Maggie. He was very good to me. Very kind and gentle. He's a kind and gentle man.'

Maggie touched a hand to Brianna's cheek, brushed at her hair. 'You're in love with him.'

'Yes.'

'And he?'

'He's used to being on his own, to coming and going as he pleases, without ties.'

Maggie tilted her head. 'And you're after changing that?'

With a little hum in her throat, Brianna turned back to her cooking. 'You don't think I can?'

'I think he's a fool if he doesn't love you. But changing a man's like walking through molasses. A lot of effort for little progress.'

'Well, it's not so much changing him as letting him see what choices there are. I can make a home for him, Maggie, if he'll let me.' Then she shook her head. 'Oh, it's too soon to be thinking so far. He's made me happy. That's enough for now.'

Maggie hoped that was true. 'What will you do about Mother?'

'As far as Gray's concerned, I won't let her spoil it.' Brianna's eyes frosted as she turned to add cubed potatoes to the pan. 'As to the other, I haven't decided. But I will handle it myself, Maggie. You understand me?'

'I do.' Giving in to eight months of pregnancy, she sat again. 'We heard from the New York detective yesterday.'

'You did? Did he find her?'

'It's a more complicated business than we might have thought. He found a brother — a retired policeman who still lives in New York.'

'Well, that's a start then, isn't it?' Eager for more, Brianna began to whip up batter for griddle cakes.

'More of a stop, I'm afraid. The man refused to admit he even had a sister at first. When the detective pressed — he had copies of Amanda's birth certificate and such — this Dennis Dougherty said he hadn't seen nor heard from Amanda in more than twenty-five years. That she was no sister to him and so forth as she'd gotten herself in trouble and run off. He didn't know where, or care to know.'

'That's sad for him, isn't it?' Brianna murmured. 'And her parents? Amanda's parents?'

'Dead, both of them. The mother only last year. There's a sister as well, married and living out in the West of the States. He's talked to her as well, Rogan's man, and though she seems softer of heart, she hasn't been any real help.'

'But she must know,' Brianna protested. 'Surely she'd know how to find her own sister.'

'That doesn't seem to be true. It appears there was a family ruckus when Amanda announced she was pregnant, and she wouldn't name the father.' Maggie paused, pressed her lips together. 'I don't know if she was protecting Da, or herself, or the child if it comes to it. But according to the sister, there were bitter words on all sides. They were lace-curtain Irish and saw a pregnant unwed daughter as a smear on the family name. They wanted her to go away, have the child, and give it up. It seems she refused and simply went away altogether. If she contacted her parents again, the brother isn't saying, and the sister isn't aware of it.'

'So we have nothing.'

'Next to it. He did find out — the detective — that she'd

visited Ireland all those years ago with a woman friend. He's working now on tracking her down.'

'Then we'll be patient.' She brought a pot of tea to the table and frowned at her sister. 'You look pale.'

'I'm just tired. Sleeping's not as easy as it once was.'

'When do you see the doctor again?'

'This very afternoon.' Maggie drummed up a smile as she poured herself a cup.

'Then I'll take you. You shouldn't be driving.'

Maggie sighed. 'You sound like Rogan. He's coming all the way back from the gallery to take me himself.'

'Good. And you're staying right here with me until he comes to get you.' More concerned than pleased when she got no argument, Brianna went to call the men to breakfast.

She spent the day happily enough, fussing over Maggie, welcoming an American couple who had stayed at her inn two years earlier. Gray had gone off with Murphy to look for car parts. The sky stayed clear, the air warm. Once she had seen Maggie safely off with Rogan, Brianna settled down for an hour of gardening in her herb bed.

Freshly washed linens were billowing on the line, music was trilling out through the open windows, her guests were enjoying tea cakes in her parlor, and her dog was snoozing in a patch of sunlight beside her.

She couldn't have been happier.

The dog's ears pricked, and her own head came up when she heard the sound of cars. 'That's Murphy's truck,' she said to Con, and indeed, the dog was already up, tail wagging. 'The other I don't recognize. Do you think we have another guest?'

Pleased with the prospect, Brianna rose, dusted the garden dirt from her apron and started around the house. Con raced ahead of her, already barking happily in greeting.

She spotted Gray and Murphy, both of them wearing silly grins as the dog welcomed them as if it had been days rather than hours since they'd parted. Her gaze skimmed over the neat, late-model blue sedan parked in front of Murphy's truck.

'I thought I heard two cars.' She looked around anxiously. 'Did they go inside already?'

'Who?' Gray wanted to know.

'The people who were driving this. Is there luggage? I should brew some tea fresh.'

'I was driving it,' Gray told her. 'And I wouldn't mind some tea.'

'You're a brave one, boy-o,' Murphy said under his breath. 'I don't have time for tea meself,' he went on, preparing to desert. 'My cows'll be looking for me by now.' He rolled his eyes at Gray, shook his head, and climbed back into his truck.'

'Now, what was that?' Brianna wondered as Murphy's truck backed into the road. 'What have the pair of you been up to, and why would you be driving this car when you've already got one?'

'Someone had to drive it, and Murphy doesn't like anyone else behind the wheel of his truck. What do you think of it?' In the way of men Gray ran a hand along the front fender of the car as lovingly as he would over a smooth, creamy shoulder.

'It's very nice, I'm sure.'

'Runs like a top. Want to see the engine?'

'I don't think so.' She frowned at him. 'Are you tired of your other one?'

'My other what?'

'Car.' She laughed and shook back her hair. 'What are you about, Grayson?'

'Why don't you sit in it? Get the feel of it?' Encouraged

by her laugh, he took her arm and tugged her toward the driver's side. 'It only has about twenty thousand miles on it.'

Murphy had warned him that bringing back a new car would be as foolish as spitting into the wind.

Willing to humor him, Brianna climbed in and set her hands on the wheel. 'Very nice. It feels just like a car.'

'But do you like it?' He propped his elbows on the base of the window and grinned at her.

'It's a fine car, Gray, and I'm sure you'll enjoy the driving of it.'

'It's yours.'

'Mine? What do you mean it's mine?'

'That old crate of yours is going to junkyard heaven. Murphy and I agreed it was hopeless, so I bought you this.'

He yelped when she jerked open the door and caught him smartly on the shin. 'Well, you can just take it back where it came from.' Her voice was ominously cool as he rubbed his throbbing shin. 'I'm not ready to buy a new car, and when I am I'll decide for myself.'

'You're not buying it. I'm buying it. I bought it.' He straightened and faced the ice with what he was certain was sheer reason. 'You needed reliable transportation, and I've provided it. Now stop being so stiff-necked.'

'Stiff-necked, is it? Well, 'tis you who's being arrogant, Grayson Thane. Going out and buying a car without a by-your-leave. I won't have such decisions taken out of my hands, and I don't need to be tended to like a child.'

She wanted to shout. He could see she was fighting the urge with every breath, covering raging temper with an icy dignity that made him want to smile. Being a wise man, he kept his expression sober.

'It's a gift, Brianna.'

'A box of chocolates is a gift.'

'A box of chocolates is a cliché,' he corrected, then

205

backtracked. 'Let's just say this is my version of a box of chocolates.' He shifted, cleverly trapping her between his body and the side of the car. 'Do you want me worried about you every time you drive off to the village?'

'There's no need for you to worry.'

'Of course there is.' Before she could evade, he slipped his arms around her. 'I visualize you tottering back up the road with nothing more than a steering wheel in your hand.'

'It's your imagination that's to blame for that.' She turned her head, but his lips managed to brush her neck. 'Stop it. You won't get around me that way.'

Oh, but he thought he would. 'Do you really have a hundred pounds to toss away on a lost cause, my practical Brianna? And do you really want to ask poor Murphy to tinker with that useless heap every other day just so you can keep your pride?'

She started to snarl, but he covered her lips firmly with his. 'You know you don't,' he murmured. 'It's just a car, Brianna. Just a thing.'

Her head was starting to spin. 'I can't accept such a thing from you. Will you stop nuzzling me! I've guests in the parlor.'

'I've been waiting all day to nuzzle you. Actually, I've been waiting all day to get you back in bed. You smell wonderful.'

'It's the rosemary from the herb bed. Stop this. I can't think.'

'Don't think. Just kiss me. Just once.'

If her head hadn't been reeling, she would have known better. But his lips were already on hers, and hers were softening, parting. Welcoming.

He took it slow, deepening the kiss degree by lazy degree, savoring her gradual warming, the delicate scent of the herbs that clung to the hands she lifted to his face, the gentle, almost reluctant yielding of her body to his.

For a moment he forgot the move had been one of persuasion, and simply enjoyed.

'You have such a wonderful mouth, Brianna.' He nibbled at it, pleasing himself. 'I wonder how I managed to stay away from it for so long.'

'You're trying to distract me.'

'I have distracted you. And myself.' He drew her back to arm's length, marveling that what he'd intended to be a playful kiss had set his heart thundering. 'Let's forget practicality, and all the other intellectual reasons I was going to use to convince you to take the damn car. I want to do this for you. It's important to me. It would make me happy if you'd accept it.'

She could have stood firm against the practical, ignored the reason of the intellect. But how could she refuse this quiet request, or hold back from the steady look in his eyes?

' 'Tisn't fair to use my heart,' she murmured.

'I know that.' He swore impatiently. 'I know it. I should walk away from you right now, Brianna. Pack up, move out and get gone.' He swore again as she kept her eyes level. 'There'll probably come a time you'll wish I had.'

'No, I won't.' She folded her hands together, afraid if she touched him she might cling. 'Why did you buy me this car, Grayson?'

'Because you needed it,' he tossed out, then steadied himself. 'Because I needed to do something for you. It's not that big a deal, Brie. The money's nothing to me.'

Her brow quirked. 'Oh, I know it. You're rolling in pound notes, aren't you? Do you think all your fine money matters to me, Grayson? That I care for you because you can buy me new cars?'

He opened his mouth, closed it again, oddly humbled. 'No, I don't. I don't think it matters to you in the least.'

'Well, then, we understand that.' He was so needy, she thought, and didn't even know. The gift had been as much for himself as it was for her. And that, she could accept. She turned around to take another look at the car. 'This was a kind thing you did, and I haven't been properly grateful – not for the thought or the deed.'

He felt oddly like a small boy about to be forgiven for some careless bit of mischief. 'So, you'll keep it.'

'Aye.' She turned back, kissed him. 'And thank you.'

His grin broke out. 'Murphy owes me five pounds.'

'Wagered on me, did you?' Amusement colored her voice. It was so typical.

'His idea.'

'Mmm. Well, why don't I go in and see if my guests are happy, then we can go for a little drive.'

He came to her that night, as she'd hoped he would, and again the night after, as guests slept peacefully upstairs. Her inn was full, as she liked it best. When she sat down with her accounts, it was with a light heart. She was nearly ready to buy her material for the greenhouse.

He found her at her little desk, bundled in her robe, tapping a pen against her lips, her eyes dreamy.

'Are you thinking of me?' he murmured, bending down to nuzzle her neck.

'Actually, I was thinking of southern exposure and treated glass.'

'Second place to a greenhouse.' He'd worked his way around to her jaw when his gaze skimmed over a letter she had spread open. 'What's this? An answer from that mining company.'

'Yes, at last. They've gotten their bookkeeping together. We'll get a thousand pounds when we turn in the stock.'

He drew back frowning. 'A thousand? For ten thousand shares? That doesn't seem right.'

She only smiled and rose to take down her hair. Normally it was a ritual he enjoyed, but this time he only continued to stare at the papers on her desk.

'You didn't know Da,' she told him. 'It's a great deal more than I expected. A fortune really, as his schemes usually cost much more than they ever gained.'

'A tenth of a pound per share.' He picked up the letter himself. 'What do they say he paid for it?'

'Half of that, as you can see. I can't remember anything he ever did that earned as well. I've only to tell Rogan to send them the certificate.'

'Don't.'

'Don't?' She paused, the brush in her hand. 'Why shouldn't we?'

'Has Rogan looked into the company?'

'No, he's enough on his mind with Maggie and the gallery opening next week. I only asked him to hold the certificate.'

'Let me call my broker. Look, it can't hurt to get a prospectus on the company, a little information. A few days won't matter to you, will they?'

'No. But it seems a lot of bother for you.'

'A phone call. My broker loves to bother.' Setting the letter down again, he crossed to her and took the brush. 'Let me do that.' He turned her to face the mirror and began to draw the brush through her hair. 'Just like a Titian painting,' he murmured. 'All these shades within shades.'

She stood very still, watching him in the glass. It shocked her to realize how intimate it was, how arousing, to have him tend to her hair. The way his fingers combed through after the brush. Much more than her scalp began to tingle.

Then his eyes lifted, met hers in the glass. Excitement arrowed into her when she saw the flare of need in his.

'No, not yet.' He held her as she was when she started to turn to him. He set the brush down, then drew her hair away from her face.

'Watch,' he murmured, then slid his fingers down her to the belt of her robe. 'Do you ever wonder how we look together?'

The idea was so shocking, so thrilling, she couldn't speak. His eyes stayed on hers as he unbelted the robe, drew it away. 'I can see it in my head. Sometimes it gets in the way of my work, but it's hard to mind.'

His hands trailed up lightly over her breasts, making her shiver before he began to unbutton the high-necked gown.

Speechless, helpless, she watched his hands move over her, felt the heat spread under her skin, over it. Her legs seemed to melt away so that she had no choice but to lean back against him. As if in a dream she saw him tug the gown from her shoulder, press his lips to the bared skin.

A jolt of pleasure, a flash of heat.

Her breath came out on a little purr of agreement as the tip of his tongue teased the curve of her neck.

It was so stunning to see as well as to feel. Though her eyes went wide when he slipped the gown up, over her head and away, she didn't protest. Couldn't.

She stared in amazement at the woman in the glass. At herself, she thought hazily. It was herself she watched, for she could feel that light, devastating touch as his hands curved up to take her breasts.

'So pale,' he said in a voice that had roughened. 'Like ivory, tipped with rose petals.' Eyes dark and intense, he rubbed his thumbs over her nipples, felt her tremble, heard her moan.

It was beautifully erotic to watch her body curve back,

to feel the soft, yielding weight of her sag against him as she went pliant with pleasure. Almost experimentally he took his hand down her torso, feeling each muscle quiver under his palm. The scent of her hair streamed through his senses, the silk of those long white limbs, and the sight of them trembling in the glass.

He wanted to give, to give to her as he'd never wanted to give to anyone before. To soothe and excite, to protect and inflame. And she, he thought, pressing his lips to her throat again, was so perfect, so outrageously generous.

A touch, he thought, at his touch all that cool dignity and calm manner melted away.

'Brianna.' His breath was backing up in his lungs, but he held on until her clouded eyes lifted once more to the reflection of his. 'Watch what happens to you when I take you up.'

She started to speak, but his hand glided smoothly down, cupping her, finding her already hot and wet. Even as she choked out his name, half in protest, half in disbelief, he stroked her, gently at first, persuasively. But his eyes were fierce with concentration.

It was staggering, shocking to see his hand possess her there, and to feel those long slow strokes that evoked an answering pull and tug in her center. Her own eyes showed her that she was moving against him now, willingly, eagerly, almost pleadingly. Any thought of modesty was forgotten, abandoned as she lifted her arms, hooking them back around his neck, her hips responding to his increasing rhythm.

And she was like a moth pinned by a sharp sweet spear of pleasure. Her body was still shuddering when he lifted her, carrying her to the bed to show her more.

Chapter Fourteen

'The opening's tomorrow, and he's barred me from the place.' With her chin on her fist, Maggie glared at Brianna's back. 'And he's plopped me down in your kitchen so you can be my keeper.'

Patiently Brianna finished icing the petit fours she'd baked for tea. She had eight guests, counting Gray, including three active children. 'Margaret Mary, didn't the doctor tell you to stay off your feet, and that since the baby's dropped, you could deliver earlier than you'd thought?'

'What does he know?' Cranky as a child herself, Maggie scowled. 'I'm going to be pregnant for the rest of my life. And if Sweeney thinks he's keeping me from the opening tomorrow, he'd best think again.'

'Rogan never said he intended to do that. He didn't want you . . .' She'd nearly said underfoot and took more care with her words. 'Overdoing today.'

'It's my gallery, too,' she muttered. Her back was paining her like a toothache, and she was having twinges. Just twinges, she assured herself. Probably the mutton she'd eaten that afternoon.

'Of course it is,' Brianna soothed. 'And we'll all be there tomorrow for the opening. The advertisements in the papers were lovely. It'll be a great success, I know.'

Maggie only grunted. 'Where's the Yank?'

'He's working. Locked himself in as defense against the little German girl who kept wandering into his room.' She smiled over it. 'He's a darling with children. He played Chutes and Ladders with her last night, so she's fallen in love with him and won't leave him in peace.'

'And you're thinking what a fine father he'll make.'

Brianna pokered up. 'I didn't say that. But he would. You

212

should see how he –' She broke off when she heard the front door open. 'If that's more guests, I'll have to give them my room and sleep in the parlor.'

'You can just stop playing musical beds and sleep in Gray's,' Maggie commented, then winced when she recognized the voices coming down the hall. 'Ah, perfect. I'd hoped she'd changed her mind and stayed in France.'

'Stop it,' Brianna warned and took out more cups for tea.

'The world travelers are back,' Lottie said cheerfully as she trailed Maeve into the kitchen. 'Oh, what a fine place you have there, Maggie. Like a palace it is. What a wonderful time we had.'

'Speak for yourself.' Maeve sniffed and set her purse on the counter. 'Bunch of foreign half-naked people running around on the beach.'

'Some of the men were built beautifully.' Lottie giggled. 'There was an American widower who flirted with Maeve.'

'Dallying.' Maeve waved a hand, but her cheeks had flushed. 'I paid no mind to his kind.' Sitting down, Maeve gave Maggie a hard stare. She covered the spurt of concern with a curl of the lip. 'Peaked you are. You'll soon appreciate what a mother suffers when you go into labor.'

'Thank you so much.'

'Ah, the girl's as strong as a horse.' Lottie's voice was bracing as she patted Maggie's hand. 'And young enough to have a half dozen children.'

Maggie rolled her eyes and managed a laugh. 'I don't know which of you depresses me more.'

'It's nice you're back in time for the gallery opening tomorrow.' Brianna tactfully changed subjects as she served the tea.

'Hah. What would I be doing wasting time at some art place?'

'We wouldn't miss it.' Lottie aimed a stern look in Maeve's direction. 'Maeve, you know very well you said you'd be pleased to see Maggie's work, and the rest.'

Maeve shifted uncomfortably. 'What I said was I was surprised there was so much fuss over bits of glass.' She frowned at Brianna before Lottie could embarrass her further. 'Your car wasn't out front. Has it fallen apart at last?'

'I'm told it was hopeless. I've a new one, the blue one out there.'

'A new one.' Maeve set her cup down with a clatter. 'Squandering your money on a new car?'

' 'Tis her money,' Maggie began heatedly, but Brianna cut her off with a look.

'It's not new, except to me. It's a used car, and I didn't buy it.' She braced herself. 'Grayson bought it for me.'

For a moment there was silence. Lottie stared down at her tea with her lips pursed. Maggie prepared to leap to her sister's defense and fought to ignore the twinges.

'Bought it for you?' Maeve's voice was hard as stone. 'You accepted such a thing from a man? Have you no care for what people will think, or say?'

'I imagine people will think it was a generous thing, and say the same.' She set aside her frosting knife and picked up her tea. Her hands would shake in a moment. She knew it, hated it.

'What they will think is that you sold yourself for it. And have you? Is that what you've done?'

'No.' The word was frigidly calm. 'The car was a gift, and accepted as such. It has nothing to do with our being lovers.'

There, she thought. She'd said it. Her stomach was clutched, her hands fit to tremble, but she'd said it.

White around the lips, her eyes burning blue, Maeve shoved away from the table. 'You've whored yourself.'

'I haven't. I've given myself to a man I care for and admire. Given myself for the first time,' she said and was surprised that her hands remained steady. 'Though you've told it differently.'

Maeve's gaze cut to Maggie, full of bitterness and temper.

'No, I didn't tell her,' Maggie said calmly enough. 'I should have, but I didn't.'

'It hardly matters how I found out.' Brianna folded her hands together. There was a coldness inside her, a horrible chill, but she would finish this. 'You saw that I lost whatever happiness I might have had with Rory.'

'He was nothing,' Maeve shot back. 'A farmer's son who never would have made a man. You'd have had nothing with him but a houseful of crying children.'

'I wanted children.' An ache shot through the ice. 'I wanted a family and a home, but we'll never know if I would have found that with him. You saw to that and dragged a good, fine man into your lies. To keep me safe, Mother? I don't think so. I wish I could think so. To keep me tied. Who would have tended to you and this house if I had married Rory? We'll never know that, either.'

'I did what was best for you.'

'What was best for you.'

Because her legs felt weak, Maeve sat again. 'So, this is the way you pay me back for it. By giving yourself in sin to the first man who strikes your fancy.'

'By giving myself in love to the first and only man who's touched me.'

'And what will you do when he plants a baby in your belly and goes off whistling?'

'That's my concern.'

'She's talking like you now.' Enraged, Maeve turned on Maggie. 'You've turned her against me.'

'You've done that yourself.'

'Don't bring Maggie into this.' In a protective move Brianna laid a hand on her sister's shoulder. 'This is you and me, Mother.'

'Any chance of getting a . . .' High on an afternoon of successful writing, Gray breezed into the kitchen and trailed off as he spotted the company. Though he felt the weight of tension in the room, he tried a friendly smile. 'Mrs. Concannon, Mrs. Sullivan, it's good to have you back.'

Maeve's hands curled into fists. 'Bloody bastard, you'll burn in hell with my daughter beside you.'

'Mind your tongue in my house.' Brianna's sharp order shocked them all more than Maeve's bitter prediction. 'I beg your pardon, Gray, for my mother's rudeness.'

'You'll beg no one's pardon on my account.'

'No,' Gray agreed, nodding at Maeve. 'There's no need. You can say what you like to me, Mrs. Concannon.'

'Did you promise her love and marriage, a lifetime of devotion to get her on her back? Do you think I don't know what men say to have their way?'

'He promised me nothing,' Brianna began, but Gray cut her off with one sharp look.

'No, I didn't make promises. Brianna's not someone I would lie to. And she's not someone I'd turn from if I was told something about her I didn't like.'

'You've shared family business with him, too?' Maeve whirled on Brianna. 'It's not enough for you to condemn your soul to hell?'

'Will you forever be damning your children to hell?' Maggie fired up before Brianna could speak. 'Because you couldn't find happiness, must you try to keep us both from finding it? She loves him. If you could see through your own bitterness, you'd know that, and that's what would matter to you. But she's been at your beck and call all her life and you can't stand the thought that she might find something, someone for herself.'

'Maggie, enough,' Brianna murmured.

' 'Tisn't enough. You won't say it, never would. But she'll hear it from me. She's hated me from the moment I was born, and she's used you. We're not daughters to her, but by turns a penance and a crutch. Has she once, even once wished me happy with Rogan, or with the baby?'

'And why should I?' Maeve shot back, lips trembling. 'And have my good wishes tossed back in my face. You've never given me the love that's a mother's right.'

'I would have.' Maggie's breath began to hitch as she shoved back from the table. 'God knows I've wanted to. And Brianna's tried. Have you ever been grateful for all she put aside for your comfort? Instead you ruined whatever chance she had for the home and family she wanted. Well, you'll not do it again, not this time. You won't come into her house and speak to her or the man she loves this way.'

'I'll speak as I choose to my own flesh and blood.'

'Stop it, the pair of you.' Brianna's voice was sharp as a whiplash. She was pale, icily so, and the trembling she'd managed to fight back had grown to shudders. 'Must you strike at each other this way, always? I won't be the club you use to hurt each other. I've guests in the parlor,' she said, drawing an unsteady breath. 'And I prefer they not be subjected to the misery of my family. Maggie, you sit down and calm yourself.'

'Fight your own battles, then,' Maggie said furiously. 'I'll leave.' Even as she said it, the pain struck and had her gripping the back of the chair.

'Maggie.' Panicked, Brianna grabbed her. 'What is it? Is it the baby?'

'Just a twinge.' But it built into a wave that stunned her.

'You've gone white. Sit down now. Sit, don't argue with me.'

Lottie, a retired nurse, rose briskly. 'How many twinges have you had, darling?'

'I don't know. On and off all afternoon.' She let out a relieved breath when the pain passed. 'It's nothing, really. I've two weeks yet, or nearly that.'

'The doctor said any time now,' Brianna reminded her.

'What does a doctor know?'

'True, true.' Smiling easily, Lottie skirted the table and began to massage Maggie's shoulders. 'Anything else paining you, love?'

'My back a bit,' Maggie admitted. 'It's been nagging me all day.'

'Mmmm. Well, you just breathe easy now and relax. No, no more tea for her just now, Brianna,' she said before Brianna could pour. 'We'll see by and by.'

'I'm not in labor.' Maggie's head went giddy at the idea. 'It's just the mutton.'

'Might be, yes. Brie, you haven't given your young man any tea.'

'I'm fine.' Gray looked from one woman to the other, wondering what move to make. Retreat, he decided, would probably be best for all of them. 'I think I'll go back to work.'

'Oh, I do enjoy your books,' Lottie said cheerfully. 'Two of them I read while we were on our holiday. I wonder how you can think up such tales and write them down in all those nice words.'

She chattered on, keeping him and everyone as they were until Maggie caught her breath. 'There you are, only about four minutes apart, I'd say. Breathe it out, love, that's a girl. Brie, I think you should call Rogan now. He'll want to meet us at the hospital.'

'Oh.' For an instant Brianna couldn't think, much less move. 'I should call the doctor.'

'That'll be fine.' Lottie took Maggie's hand, held it tight as Brianna dashed off. 'Now, don't you worry. I've helped bring many a baby into this world. Do you have a case packed, Maggie, at home?'

'In the bedroom, yes.' She shuddered out a breath as the contraction passed. Odd, she felt calmer now. 'In the closet.'

'The young man will go fetch it for you. Won't you, dear?'

'Sure.' He'd be glad to. It would get him out of the house, away from the terrifying prospect of childbirth. 'I'll go get it right now.'

'It's all right, Gray.' With the new calm cloaking her, Maggie managed a chuckle. 'I'm not going to deliver on the kitchen table.'

'Right.' He gave her an uncertain smile, and fled.

'I'm going to get your jacket now,' Lottie told Maggie, and sent Maeve a telling look. 'Don't forget your breathing.'

'I won't. Thank you, Lottie. I'll be fine.'

'You're scared.' Gently Lottie bent down to cup Maggie's cheek. ''Tis natural. But what's happening to you is just as natural. Something only a woman can do. Only a woman can understand. The good Lord knows if a man could do it, there'd be fewer people in the world.'

The thought made Maggie smile. 'I'm only a little scared. And not just of the pain. Of knowing what to do after.'

'You'll know. You'll be a mother soon, Margaret Mary. God bless you.'

Maggie closed her eyes when Lottie left the room. She could feel the changes inside her body, the magnitude of them. She imagined the changes in her life, the enormity of them. Yes, she would be a mother soon. The child she and Rogan had created would be in her arms instead of her womb.

I love you, she thought. I swear to you I'll only show you love.

The pain began to well again, drawing a low moan from her throat. She squeezed her eyes tighter, concentrated on breathing. Through the haze of pain she felt a hand cover hers. Opening her eyes she saw her mother's face, and tears, and perhaps for the first time in her life, a true understanding.

'I wish you happy, Maggie,' Maeve said slowly. 'With your child.'

For a moment at least, the gap was bridged. Maggie turned her hand over and gripped her mother's palm to palm.

When Gray hurried back, the overnight bag clutched in his hand, Lottie was helping Maggie toward Brianna's car. Every guest in the house was outside, waving them off.

'Oh, thank you for being quick.' Brianna snatched the case, then looked around distractedly. 'Rogan's on his way to the hospital. He hung up before I could even say goodbye. The doctor said to bring her right in. I have to go with her.'

'Of course you do. She'll be fine.'

'Yes, she'll be fine.' Brianna nibbled on her thumb nail. 'I have to leave — all the guests.'

'Don't worry about things here. I'll take care of it.'

'You can't cook.'

'I'll take the lot of them out to dinner. Don't worry, Brie.'

'No, it's silly of me. I'm so distracted. I'm so sorry, Gray.'

'Don't.' Steadier himself, he took her face in his hands.

'Don't even think about any of that now. Just go help your sister have a baby.'

'I will. Could you call Mrs. O'Malley, please? Her number's in my book. She'll come tend to things until I get home again. And if you'd call Murphy. He'd want to know. And –'

'Brie, go. I'll call the whole county.' Despite the audience, he gave her a quick, hard kiss. 'Have Rogan send me a cigar.'

'Yes. All right, yes, I'm going.' She hurried to the car.

Gray stood back and watched her drive away, with Lottie and Maeve following behind.

Families, he thought, with a shake of the head and a shudder. Thank Christ he didn't have to worry about one.

But he worried about her. As afternoon became evening and evening became night. Mrs. O'Malley had come, bustling into the kitchen barely half an hour after his SOS call. Rattling pans, she chattered cheerfully about the childbirth experience, until queasy, Gray had retreated to his room.

He fared better when Murphy came down and shared a glass of whiskey with him in toast to Maggie and the baby.

But as the inn grew quiet and the hour late, Gray wasn't able to work or sleep – two activities he'd always used for escape.

Being wakeful gave him too much time to think. However much he wanted to avoid it, the kitchen scene played over and over in his head. What kind of trouble had he caused Brianna simply by wanting her, then acting on the wanting? He hadn't considered her family, or her religion. Did she believe as her mother did?

It made him uneasy to think of souls and eternal

damnation. Anything eternal made him uneasy, and damnation certainly topped the list.

Or had Maggie spoken Brianna's mind? That was hardly less disturbing. All that talk of love. From his point of view love could be every bit as dangerous as damnation, and he preferred to dwell on neither on a personal level.

Why couldn't people keep things simple? he wondered as he wandered into Brianna's room. Complications were part and parcel of fiction, but in reality life was so much smoother one day at a time.

But it was stupid, he admitted, and incredibly naive to pretend that Brianna Concannon wasn't a complication. Hadn't he admitted already that she was unique? Restless, he lifted the top off a small bottle on her dresser. And smelled her.

He just wanted to be with her – for the time being, he told himself. They enjoyed each other, liked each other. At this particular time and this particular place, they suited each other well.

Of course, he could back off any time. Of course he could. With a little snarl he shot the top back in the bottle.

But her scent remained with him.

She wasn't in love with him. Maybe she thought she was, because he was her first. That was natural. And maybe, just maybe, he was a little more involved with her than he'd ever been with anyone else. Because she was unlike anyone else. So that was natural, too.

Still and all, when his book was finished, they would have to be finished as well. He'd be moving on. Lifting his head, he stared at himself in the mirror. No surprises there, he thought. It was same face. If there was a faint light of panic in the eyes, he chose to ignore it.

Grayson Thane looked back at him. The man he'd made from nothing. A man he was comfortable with. A man, he told himself now, who moved through life as he chose to move. Free, no baggage, no regrets.

There were memories. He could block the unpleasant ones. He'd been doing that for years. One day, he thought, he'd look back and remember Brianna, and that would be enough.

Why the hell hadn't she called?

He checked himself, turned away from the mirror before he could see something he preferred to avoid. No need for her to call, he told himself and poked through the books on her shelf. It was her business, family business, and he had no part in it. Wanted no part in it.

He was curious, that was all, about Maggie and the baby. If he was waiting up, it was only to satisfy that curiosity.

Feeling better, he chose a book, stretched out on her bed, and began to read.

Brianna found him there at three A.M. She staggered in on a wave of joy and fatigue to see him asleep on top of her blankets, an open book on his chest. She beamed at him, foolishly, she knew. But it was a night for foolishness.

Quietly she undressed, folded her clothes over a chair, slipped into a nightgown. In the adjoining bath she scrubbed the tiredness from her face. She caught her own grinning reflection in the mirror, and laughed.

Padding back into the bedroom, she bent down to pet Con, who was curled on the rug at the foot of the bed. With a sigh she turned off the light and laid down without bothering to turn down the covers.

He turned to her instantly, his arm draping over her, his face nuzzling her hair. 'Brie.' His voice was thick with sleep. 'Missed you.'

'I'm back now.' She shifted, curving to him. 'Just sleep.'

'Hard to sleep without you. Too many old dreams without you.'

'Ssh.' She stroked him, felt herself start to drift. 'I'm right here.'

He came fully awake with a snap, blinking, confused. 'Brie.' He cleared his throat and pushed himself up. 'You're back.'

'Yes. You fell asleep reading.'

'Oh. Yeah.' After scrubbing his hands over his face, he squinted to see her in the dim light. It came flooding back. 'Maggie?'

'She's fine, she's wonderful. Oh, it was beautiful to see, Gray.' Excited all over again, she sat up, wrapped her arms around her knees. 'She was cursing Rogan, vowing all sorts of hideous revenge on him. He just kept kissing her hands and telling her to breathe. Then she'd laugh, tell him she loved him, and curse him all over again. I've never seen a man so nervous and awed and loving all at once.'

She sighed again, not even aware her cheeks were wet. 'There was all this confusion and chattering, arguing, just as you'd expect. Whenever they tried to boot us out, Maggie would threaten to get up and leave herself. "My family stays," says she, "or I go with them." So we stayed. And it was so . . . marvelous.'

Gray wiped her tears himself. 'Are you going to tell me what she had?'

'A boy.' Brianna sniffled. 'The most beautiful boy. He has black hair, like Rogan's. It curls around his little head like a halo. And he has Maggie's eyes. They're blue now, of course, but the shape of them's Maggie's. And he wailed so, like he was cursing the lot of us for bringing him into this mess. His little fingers all clenched into fists. Liam, they named him. Liam Matthew Sweeney. They let me hold him.' She rested her head on Gray's shoulder. 'He looked at me.'

'Are you going to tell me he smiled at you?'

'No.' But she smiled. 'No, that he didn't. He looked at me, very serious like, as if he was after wondering what he was to make of all this business. I've never held a life so new before. It's like nothing else, nothing else in the world.' She turned her face into his throat. 'I wish you could have been there.'

To his amazement, he found he wished the same. 'Well, somebody had to mind the ranch. Your Mrs. O'Malley came on the fly.'

'Bless her. I'll call her up tomorrow to give her the news and thank her.'

'She doesn't cook as well as you.'

'You don't think so?' She grinned to herself, delighted. 'I hope you didn't say so.'

'I'm the soul of diplomacy. So.' He kissed Brianna's temple. 'She had a boy. What's the weight?'

'Seven pounds, one ounce.'

'And the time – you know, when she had it?'

'Oh, it was about half one.'

'Shit, looks like the German copped the pool.'

'Pardon?'

'The pool. We had a baby pool going. Sex, weight, time of birth. I'm pretty sure the German guy – Krause – hit the closest.'

'A betting pool, is it? And whose idea was that?'

Gray ran his tongue around his teeth. 'Murphy's,' he said. 'The man'll bet on anything.'

'And what was your guess?'

'Girl, seven and a half pounds, straight up midnight.' He kissed her again. 'Where's my cigar?'

'Rogan sent you along a fine one. It's in my purse.'

'I'll take it down to the pub tomorrow. Somebody's bound to be handing out free drinks.'

'Oh, you can bet on that as well.' She took a little breath, locked her fingers together. 'Grayson, about this afternoon. My mother.'

'You don't have to say anything about that. I walked in at a bad moment, that's all.'

'It's not all, and it's foolish to pretend it is.'

'All right.' He'd known she'd insist on hashing it out, but he couldn't bear to see her mood lowered. 'We won't pretend. Let's not think about it tonight, though. We'll talk about it later, as much as you need to. Tonight's for celebrating, don't you think?'

Relief warmed her. Her emotions had ridden on a roller coaster long enough that day. 'I do, yes.'

'I bet you haven't eaten.'

'I haven't.'

'Why don't I get us some of the cold chicken that's left over from dinner? We'll eat in bed.'

Chapter Fifteen

It was easy enough to avoid serious subjects over the next week. Gray buried himself in his work, and Brianna's time was stretched thin between her guests and her new nephew. Whenever she had a spare minute, she found some excuse to dart down to Maggie's cottage and fuss over the new mother and baby. Maggie was too enraptured with her son to do more than give a few token complaints about missing the opening of her new gallery.

Gray had to admit the kid was a winner. He'd wandered down to the cottage himself a time or two when he needed to stretch his legs and clear his mind.

Early evening was the best time, when the light took on that luminous glow so special to Ireland, and the air was so clear he could see for miles across the emerald hills with the sun striking down on the thin ribbon of river in the distance making it flash like a silver sword.

He found Rogan, dressed in a T-shirt and old jeans, in the front garden, plucking industriously at weeds. An interesting look, Gray mused, for a man who could likely afford a platoon of gardeners.

'Hiya, Pop.' Grinning, Gray leaned on the garden gate.

Rogan shifted back on the worn heels of his boots. 'Ah, a man. Come in and join me. I've been evicted. Women.' He jerked his head toward the cottage. 'Maggie and Brie and Murphy's sister Kate up for a visit, and some of the village ladies. Discussing breast feeding and delivery room war stories.'

'Yeah.' Gray gave the cottage a pained look as he swung through the gate. 'It sounds to me more like you escaped than got kicked out.'

'True enough. Being outnumbered I can't get near Liam.

And Brianna pointed out that Maggie shouldn't be doing the gardening yet, and it's getting overrun. Then she lifted her brow at me in that way of hers. So I took the hint.' He looked longingly back at the cottage. 'We could try sneaking into the kitchen for a beer.'

'It's safer out here.' Gray sat down, folded his legs. Companionably, he reached out and pulled a weed. At least it looked like a weed. 'I've been wanting to talk to you anyway. About that stock certificate.'

'Which stock certificate is that?'

'The Triquarter Mining thing.'

'Ah, yes. That business slipped my mind with all that's been going on. Brianna heard from them, didn't she?'

'She heard from someone.' Gray scratched his chin. 'I had my broker do a little digging. It's interesting.'

'Thinking of investing, are you?'

'No, and couldn't if I were. There is no Triquarter Mining – not in Wales or anywhere else he can locate.'

Rogan's brow creased. 'Folded, did they?'

'It doesn't appear there ever was a Triquarter Mining – which should mean the certificate you're holding is worthless.'

'Odd then, that someone would be willing to pay a thousand pounds for it. Your man might have missed something. The company might be quite small, not appear on any of the standard lists.'

'I thought of that. So did he. He was curious enough to dig a little deeper, even called the number that was printed on the letterhead.'

'And?'

'It isn't a working number. It occurs to me that anyone can have a sheet of letterhead printed up. Just as anyone can rent a post office box, like the one Brianna wrote to in Wales.'

'True enough. But it doesn't explain why someone would be willing to pay for something that doesn't exist.' Rogan frowned into middle distance. 'I've got some business in Dublin. Though I'm not sure Brie will forgive me for taking Maggie and Liam away, we need to leave at the end of the week. It should only take a few days, and I can look into this myself while I'm there.'

'I figure it's worth a trip to Wales.' Gray shrugged as Rogan looked at him. 'You're a little encumbered right now, but I'm not.'

'You're thinking of going to Wales yourself?'

'I've always wanted to play detective. It's kind of a coincidence, don't you think, that shortly after Brie found the certificate and sent off a letter, the cottage was broken into.' He moved his shoulders again. 'I make my living tying coincidences into plots.'

'And will you tell Brianna what you're up to?'

'Pieces of it anyway. I've been thinking about taking a quick trip to New York – Brianna might like a weekend in Manhattan.'

Now Rogan's brows lifted. 'I imagine she would – if you could convince her to leave the cottage during high season.'

'I think I've got that worked out.'

'And New York is a distance from Wales.'

'Wouldn't be hard to detour there on the way back to Clare, though. Add a couple days onto the trip. I thought about going on my own, but if I had to talk to anyone official, I think I'd need her – or Maggie or their mother.' He grinned again. 'I think Brie's the obvious choice.'

'When would you leave?'

'A couple of days.'

'You move fast,' Rogan commented. 'Do you think you can get Brianna to move as quickly?'

'It'll take a lot of charm. I've been saving up.'

'Well, if you manage it, keep in touch with me. I'll do what I can to look into the matter from my end. Oh, and if you need extra ammunition, you could mention we've several of Maggie's pieces displayed in Worldwide New York.'

The sound of women's laughter filled the air. They came outside, still circling Maggie, who had Liam in the crook of her arm. There were introductions, greetings, a lot of last-minute cooing over the baby before the visitors hopped on bicycles and pedaled off.

'Let's have him.' Gray reached out and took the baby from Maggie's arms. He always got a kick out of the way Liam stared up at him with solemn blue eyes. 'Hey, aren't you talking yet? Rogan, I think it's time we got this kid away from the women, took him down to the pub for a pint.'

'He's had his pint for the evening, thank you,' Maggie put in. 'Mother's milk.'

Gray tickled the baby's chin. 'How come he's wearing a dress? These women are making a sissy out of you, kid.'

' 'Tisn't a dress.' Brianna leaned forward to kiss the top of Liam's head. 'A saque is what it is. He'll be wearing trousers soon enough. Rogan, you've only to heat that dish I brought down when you're ready for dinner.' She scowled down at his gardening attempt. 'It's no good playing with the weeds. You have to get the roots.'

He grinned, kissed her. 'Yes, ma'am.'

Waving him away, she laughed. 'I'm going. Gray, give the baby back. The Sweeneys have had more than enough company for the day. You'll put your feet up?' she said to Maggie.

'I will. Make her do the same,' she ordered Gray. 'She's been running two households for days.'

Gray snatched Brianna's hand. 'I could carry you back.'

'Don't be foolish. You take care.' She let her hand stay in Gray's as they walked through the garden gate and onto the road. 'He's grown so much already,' she murmured. 'And he does smile now, right at you. Do you ever wonder what goes through a baby's mind when he's looking at you?'

'I figure he's wondering if this life is going to be much different from the last.'

Surprised, she turned her head. 'Do you believe in that sort of thing? Really?'

'Sure. One trip through never made sense to me. We'd never get it right with one try. And being in a place like this, you can feel the echo of old souls every time you take a breath.'

'Sometimes I feel I've walked along here before.' Idly she reached out, trailing her hand along the red blossoms of fuchsia that lined the road. 'Right here, but in a different time, in a different skin.'

'Tell me a story.'

'There's a stillness to the air, a peace. The road's only a path, very narrow but well trod. And I can smell turf fires burning. I'm tired, but it's good, because I'm going home to someone. Someone's waiting for me just up ahead. Sometimes I can almost see him standing there, lifting his hand to wave at me.'

She stopped, shook her head at her own nonsense. 'It's foolish. Just imagining.'

'Doesn't have to be.' He bent down, plucked a wild-flower from the side of the road, and handed it to her. 'The first day I walked here, I couldn't look at it all fast enough, long enough. It wasn't just because it was new. It was like remembering.' On impulse he turned, took her into his arms, and kissed her.

So was this, he realized. Now and then, when he held

her, when his mouth was on hers, there was a picture of it at the edge of his mind.

Like remembering.

He brushed off the feeling. It was time, he decided, to start charming her into doing what he wanted. 'Rogan told me he needs to go back to Dublin for a while. Maggie and Liam will go with him.'

'Oh.' There was a sharp, quick stab of regret before she found acceptance. 'Well, they have a life there as well. I tend to forget when they're here.'

'You'll miss them.'

'I will, yes.'

'I need to take a little trip myself.'

'A trip?' Now there was a jolt of panic she fought to control. 'Where are you going?'

'New York. The premiere, remember?'

'Your movie.' She managed a smile. 'It's exciting for you.'

'It could be. If you'd go with me.'

'Go with you?' Now she stopped dead in the road to gape at him. 'To New York City?'

'A couple of days. Three or four.' He scooped her into his arms again and led her into an impromtu waltz. 'We could stay at the Plaza like Eloise.'

'Eloise? Who –'

'Never mind. I'll explain later. We'll take the Concorde, be there before you know it. We could visit Worldwide there,' he added as extra incentive. 'Do all the tourist things, eat in ridiculously expensive restaurants. You might get some new menus out of it.'

'But I couldn't. Really.' Her head was spinning, and had nothing to do with the quick circles of the dance. 'The inn –'

'Mrs. O'Malley said she'd be glad to pinch hit.'

'To –'

'To help out,' he elaborated. 'I want you with me, Brianna. The movie's important, but it won't be any fun without you. It's a big moment for me. I don't want it to just be an obligation.'

'But, New York —'

'A wink away on the SST. Murphy's happy to look after Con, Mrs. O'Malley's bustling to take care of the inn.'

'You've talked to them already.' She tried to stop the whirling dance, but Gray kept spinning her.

'Sure. I knew you wouldn't go until everything was tidy.'

'I wouldn't. And I can't —'

'Do this for me, Brianna.' Ruthlessly he pulled out his best weapon. The trust. 'I need you there.'

Her breath came out on a long, slow sigh. 'Grayson.'

'Is that a yes?'

'I must be mad.' And she laughed. 'Yes.'

Two days later Brianna found herself on the Concorde, streaking across the Atlantic. Her heart was in her throat. Had been since she'd closed her suitcase. She was going to New York. Just like that. She'd left her business in the hands of another. Capable hands, to be sure, but not her hands.

She'd agreed to go to another country, to cross an entire ocean with a man who wasn't even kin, in a plane that was a great deal smaller than she'd imagined.

Surely she must have gone mad.

'Nervous?' He took her hand, brought it to his lips.

'Gray, I should never have done this. I don't know what got into me.' Of course, she knew. He had. He had gotten into her in every possible way.

'Are you worried about your mother's reaction?'

That had been hideous. The hard words, the accusations and predictions. But Brianna shook her head. She'd resigned herself to Maeve's feelings on Gray, and their relationship.

233

'I just packed and left,' she murmured.

'Hardly.' He laughed at her. 'You made at least a dozen lists, cooked enough meals for a month and stuck them in the freezer, cleaned the cottage from top to bottom –' He broke off because she didn't merely look nervous. She looked terrified. 'Honey, relax. There's nothing to be scared of. New York isn't nearly as bad as it's made out to be.'

It wasn't New York. Brianna turned her head, burying her face against his shoulder. It was Gray. She understood, if he didn't, that there was no one else in the world she would have done this for, but family. She understood, if he didn't, that he had become as intricate and vital a part of her life as her own flesh and blood.

'Tell me about Eloise again.'

He kept her hand in his, soothing. 'She's a little girl who lives at the Plaza with her Nanny, her dog Weenie, and her turtle Skipperdee.'

Brianna smiled, closed her eyes, and let him tell her the story.

There was a limo waiting for them at the airport. Thanks to Rogan and Maggie, Brianna had experienced a limo before and didn't feel a complete dolt. In the plush back-seat she found an elaborate bouquet of three dozen white roses and a chilled bottle of Dom Perignon.

'Grayson.' Overwhelmed, she buried her face in the blossoms.

'All you have to do is enjoy yourself.' He popped the cork on the champagne, let it fizz to the rim. 'And I, your genial host, will show you all there is to see in the Big Apple.'

'Why do they call it that?'

'I haven't got a clue.' He handed her a flute of wine,

tapped his against it. 'You are the most beautiful woman I've ever known.'

She flushed, fumbled, and pushed a hand through her travel-touseled hair. 'I'm sure I'm looking my best.'

'No, you look best in your apron.' When she laughed, he leaned closer, nibbled on her ear. 'In fact, I was wondering if you'd wear it for me sometime.'

'I wear it every day.'

'Uh-uh. I mean *just* the apron.'

Now color flooded her cheeks and she cast a distracted glance at the back of the driver's head through the security glass. 'Gray —'

'Okay, we'll deal with my prurient fantasies later. What do you want to do first?'

'I —' She was still stuttering over the idea of standing in her kitchen in nothing but her apron.

'Shopping,' he decided. 'After we check in, and I make a couple of calls, we'll hit the streets.'

'I should buy some souveniers. And there's that toy store, that important one.'

'F.A.O. Schwartz.'

'Aye. They'd have something wonderful for Liam, wouldn't they?'

'Absolutely. But I was thinking more about Fifth and Forty-Seventh.'

'What's that?'

'I'll take you.'

He barely gave her time to gawk, at the palacelike structure of the hotel itself, at the opulent lobby of the Plaza with its red carpeting and dazzling chandeliers, the spiffy uniforms of the staff, the magnificently ornate floral arrangements, and the glorious little display windows filled with stunning jewels.

They rode the elevator to the top, and she walked into

the sumptuous suite so high up that had a view of the lush green island of Central Park. He whirled her in, and by the time she'd freshened up from traveling, he was waiting impatiently to whirl her out again.

'Let's walk. It's the best way to see New York.' He took her purse, crossed the strap from her shoulder to her hip. 'Carry it like this, with your hand on it. Are those shoes comfortable?'

'Yes.'

'Then you're set.'

She was still trying to catch her breath when he pulled her out.

'It's a great town in the spring,' he told her as they began to walk down Fifth.

'So many people.' She watched a woman dash by, legs flashing under short, shimmering silk. And another in baggy red leather with a trio of earrings dangling from her left lobe.

'You like people.'

She stared at a man marching along, barking orders into a cellular phone. 'Yes.'

Gray shifted her out of the path of a zipping bike. 'Me, too. Now and then.'

He pointed out things to her, promised her as much time as she wanted in the grand toy store, enjoyed watching her gawk at store windows and the wonderfully varied people who hurried along the streets.

'I went to Paris once,' she told him, smiling at a sidewalk vender who hawked hot dogs. 'To see Maggie's show there. I thought then I'd never in my life see anything as grand as that.' Laughing, she squeezed his hand hard. 'But this is.'

She loved it. The constant and almost violent noise of traffic, the glittering offerings displayed in shop after shop, the people, self-absorbed and rushing away on their own business, and the towering buildings, spearing up everywhere and turning the streets into canyons.

'Here.'

Brianna stared at the building on the corner, each window dripping with jewels and gems. 'Oh, what is it?'

'It's a bazaar, darling.' Zooming on the excitement of just being there with her, he yanked open the door. 'A carnival.'

The air inside was alive with voices. Shoppers bumped along the aisles, peering into display cases. She saw diamonds, ring after ring flashing through glass. Colored stones like rainbows, the seductive gleam of gold.

'Oh, what a place.' She was pleased to wander along the aisle with him. It seemed otherworldly, all the sellers and buyers haggling over the price of ruby necklaces and sapphire rings. What a story she'd have to tell when she got back to Clare.

She stopped with Gray by a display case and chuckled. 'I doubt very much I'll find my souveniers in here.'

'I will. Pearls, I think.' He wagged a finger at the saleswoman to hold her off and studied the wares himself. 'Pearls would suit.'

'Are you buying a gift?'

'Exactly. This one.' He gestured to the clerk. He'd already had an image in his mind, and the three strands of milky pearls fit it perfectly.

He listened with half an ear as the clerk touted the beauty and worth of the necklace. Traditional, she said, simple and elegant. An heirloom. And, of course, a bargain.

Gray took the necklace himself, tested the weight, studied the glowing orbs. 'What do you think, Brianna?'

'It's stunning.'

'Of course it is,' the clerk said, sensing a sale rather than a browse. 'You won't find another to compare with it, certainly not at this price. A classic look like this, you can wear with anything, evening dress, day wear. A little cashmere sweater, silk blouse. Simple little black dress.'

'Black wouldn't suit her,' Gray said, looking at Brianna. 'Midnight blue, pastels, moss green maybe.'

Brianna's stomach began to jitter as the clerk picked up the theme. 'You know you're right. With her coloring, you want jewel tones or pastels. Not every woman can wear both. Try it on. You'll see for yourself how beautifully they drape.'

'Gray, no.' Brianna took a step back, bumped solidly into another shopper. 'You can't. It's ridiculous.'

'Dearie,' the clerk broke in. 'When a man wants to buy you a necklace like this, it's ridiculous to quibble. At forty percent off retail, too.'

'Oh, I think you can do better than that,' Gray said offhandedly. It wasn't the money, he'd hardly glanced at the tiny ticket tagged discreetly to the pave diamond clasp. It was the sport. 'Let's see how they look.'

Brianna stood, her eyes filled with distress, as Gray fastened the necklace around her. It lay like a miracle against her plain cotton blouse. 'You can't buy me something like this.' She refused, however much her fingers itched, to reach up and stroke the pearls.

'Sure I can.' He leaned over, gave her a casual kiss. 'Let me enjoy myself.' Straightening, he studied her through narrowed eyes. 'I think it's pretty much what I'm looking for.' He shot the clerk a look. 'Do better.'

'Dearie, I'm practically giving it away now. Those pearls are perfectly matched, you know.'

'Mmm-hmm.' He turned the little tabletop mirror toward Brianna. 'Take a look,' he suggested. 'Live with them for a minute. Let me see that pin there, the diamond heart.'

'Oh, that's a nice piece. You've got a good eye.' Revved,

the clerk reached for it, lay it on the counter on a black velvet pad. 'Twenty-four brilliant cut stones. Top quality.'

'Pretty. Brie, don't you think Maggie would like it? A new mom present.'

'Ah.' She was having a hard time keeping her mouth from hanging open. First the sight of herself in the mirror with pearls around her neck, then the idea that Gray would buy diamonds for her sister. 'She'd adore it, how couldn't she? But you can't —'

'What kind of deal are you going to make me for both?'

'Well . . .' the clerk drummed her fingers on her breast. As if pained, she picked up a calculator and started running figures. She wrote an amount on a pad that had Brianna's heart stopping.

'Gray, please.'

He just waved her to silence. 'I think you can do better than that.'

'You're killing me here,' the woman said.

'See if you can stand a little more pain.'

She grumbled, muttering about profit margins and the quality of her merchandise. But she juggled figures, sliced a bit, then patted a hand over her heart. 'I'm cutting my own throat.'

Gray winked at her, took out his wallet. 'Box them up. Send them to the Plaza.'

'Gray, no.'

'Sorry.' He unclasped the pearls, handed them negligently to the delighted clerk. 'You'll have them by tonight. It's not smart to walk around with them.'

'That's not what I mean, and you know it.'

'You have such a lovely voice,' the clerk said to distract her. 'Are you Irish?'

'I am, yes. You see —'

'It's her first trip to the States. I want her to have

something special to remember it by.' He took Brianna's hand, kissing her fingers in a way that made even the clerk's cynical heart sigh. 'I want that very much.'

'You don't have to buy me things.'

'That's part of the beauty of it. You never ask.'

'And what part of Ireland are you from, dearie?'

'County Clare,' Brianna murmured, knowing she'd lost again. 'It's in the west.'

'I'm sure it's lovely. And you're going to . . .' After taking Gray's credit card, the clerk read the name and yelped. 'Grayson Thane. God, I read all your books. I'm your biggest fan. Wait until I tell my husband. He's your biggest fan, too. We're going to see your movie next week. Can't wait. Can I have your autograph? Milt's just not going to believe it.'

'Sure.' He took the pad she shoved at him. 'This you, Marcia?' He tapped the business card displayed on the counter.

'That's me. Do you live in New York? It never says where on the back of your books.'

'No, I don't.' He smiled at her, handing her back the pad to distract her from asking more questions.

' "To Marcia," ' she read, ' "a gem among gems. Fondly, Grayson Thane." ' She beamed at him now, but not so brightly she forgot to have him sign the credit slip. 'You come back any time you're looking for something special. And don't you worry, Mr. Thane. I'll have these sent out to your hotel right away. You enjoy your necklace, dearie. And you enjoy New York.'

'Thanks, Marcia. Give my best to Milt.' Pleased with himself, he turned back to Brianna. 'Want to look around some more?'

Numb, she merely shook her head. 'Why do you do that?' she managed when they were on the street again.

'How do you make it impossible to say no when I mean no?'

'You're welcome,' he said lightly. 'Are you hungry? I'm hungry. Let's get a hot dog.'

'Gray.' She stopped him. 'It's the most beautiful thing I've ever had,' she said solemnly. 'And so are you.'

'Good.' He grabbed her hand and led her to the next corner, calculating that he'd softened her up enough so that she'd let him buy her the perfect dress for the premiere.

She argued. She lost. To balance things out Gray backed off when she insisted on paying for her trinkets for Ireland herself. He amused himself helping her figure her change with the unfamiliar American money she'd gotten at the airport bank. It fascinated him that she seemed more dazzled by the toy store than by the jewelry or dress shops they'd visited. And when inspiration hit, he discovered her even more enthralled with a kitchen specialty store.

Delighted with her, he carted her bags and boxes back to the hotel, then charmed her into bed, spinning out time with long, luxurious lovemaking.

He wined and dined her at Le Cirque, then in a rush of nostalgic romanticism, took her dancing at the Rainbow Room, enjoying as much as she the out-of-time decor and big band sound.

Then he loved her again, until she slept exhausted beside him, and he lay wakeful.

He lay wakeful a long time, smelling the roses he'd given her, stroking the silk of her hair, listening to her quiet, even breathing.

Somewhere during that twilight time of half sleep, he thought of how many hotels he'd slept in alone. How many mornings he'd awakened alone, with only the people he created inside his head for company.

He thought of how he preferred it that way. He always had. And how, with her curled beside him, he wasn't quite able to recapture that sensation of solitary contentment.

Surely he would again, when their time was up. Even half dreaming he warned himself not to dwell on tomorrow, and certainly not on yesterday.

Today was where he lived. And today was very nearly perfect.

Chapter Sixteen

By the following afternoon Brianna was still dazzled enough with New York to try to look everywhere at once. She didn't care if she appeared so obviously the tourist, snapping pictures with her camera, staring up, her neck craned back, to see the very top of the spearing buildings. If she gawked, what of it? New York was a noisy and elaborate sideshow designed to stun the senses.

She pored over the guidebook in their suite, making careful lists and dutifully crossing off each sight she'd seen.

Now she had to face the prospect of a business lunch with Gray's agent.

'Arlene's terrific,' Gray assured Brianna as he hustled her along the street. 'You'll like her.'

'But this lunch.' Though she slowed her pace, he didn't allow her to hang back as she would have preferred. 'It's like a business meeting. I should wait for you somewhere, or perhaps join you when you've finished. I could go to Saint Patrick's now, and —'

'I told you I'd take you to Saint Pat's after lunch.'

And he would, she knew. He was more than willing to take her anywhere. Everywhere. Already that morning she'd stood at the top of the Empire State Building, marvelling. She'd had a subway ride, eaten breakfast in a deli. Everything she'd done, everything she'd seen was whirling around in her head like a kaleidoscope of color and sound.

Still, he promised more.

But the prospect of having lunch with a New York agent, an obviously formidable woman, was daunting. She'd have found some firm way of excusing herself, perhaps even inventing a headache or fatigue, if Gray hadn't seemed so excited by the idea.

She watched as he casually stuffed a bill into a tin cup of a man dozing against the side of a building. He never missed one. Whatever the hand-printed sign might say – homeless, out of work, Vietnam vet – it got his attention. And his wallet.

Everything got his attention, she mused. He missed nothing and saw everything. And those small acts of kindness to strangers others seemed not even to admit existed were an innate part of him.

'Hey, bud, need a watch? Got some nice watches here. Only twenty bucks.' A slim black man opened a briefcase to display an array of Gucci and Cartier knockoffs. 'Got a real nice watch for the lady here.'

To Brianna's dismay, Gray stopped. 'Yeah? They got works?'

'Hey.' The man grinned. 'What do I look like? They keep the time, man. Look just like the ones you pay a thousand for down on Fifth.'

'Let's see.' Gray chose one while Brianna bit her lip. The man looked dangerous to her, the way his eyes were shifting right and left. 'Get hassled much on this corner?'

'Nah. I got a rep. Nice watch there, quality, look pretty on the lady. Twenty bucks.'

Gray gave the watch a shake, held it to his ear. 'Fine.' He passed the man a twenty. 'Couple of beat cops heading this way,' he said mildly and tucked Brianna's hand in his arm.

When she looked back, the man was gone.

'Were they stolen?' she asked, awed.

'Probably not. Here you go.' He fastened the watch on her wrist. 'It might run for a day – or a year. You can never tell.'

'Then why did you buy it?'

'Hey, the guy's got to make a living, doesn't he? The restaurant's up here.'

That distracted her enough to have her tug on the jacket of her suit. She felt drab and countrified, and foolish with her little I Love New York bag holding her Empire State souveniers.

Nonsense, she assured herself. She met new people all the time. She enjoyed new people. The problem was, she thought as Gray ushered her into the Four Seasons, this time it was Gray's people.

She tried not to stare as he led her up the steps.

'Ah, Mr. Thane.' The maître d' greeted him warmly. 'It's been too long. Ms. Winston is already here.'

They crossed the room with its long gleaming bar, the linen-decked tables already filled with the lunch crowd. A woman rose as she spotted Gray.

Brianna saw the gorgeous red suit first, the glint of gold at the lapel and at the ears. Then the short, sleek blond hair, the quick flashing smile before the woman was enveloped by Gray's enthusiastic embrace.

'Good to see you, beautiful.'

'My favorite globe trotter.' Her voice was husky, with a hint of gravel.

Arlene Winston was tiny, barely topping five feet, and athletically trim from her thrice weekly workouts. Gray had said she was a grandmother, but her face was almost unlined, the tawny eyes sharp in contrast to the soft complexion and pixie features. With her arm still around Gray's waist, she held out a hand to Brianna.

'And you're Brianna. Welcome to New York. Has our boy been showing you a good time?'

'He has, yes. It's a wonderful city. I'm pleased to meet you, Mrs. Winston.'

'Arlene.' She cupped Brianna's hand briefly between the two of hers, patted. However friendly the gesture, Brianna wasn't unaware of the quick and thorough measuring. Gray simply stood back beaming.

'Isn't she gorgeous?'

'She certainly is. Let's sit. I hope you don't mind, I've ordered champagne. A little celebration.'

'The Brits?' Gray asked, settling.

'There is that.' She smiled as their glasses were filled from the bottle of spring water already on the table. 'Do you want to get this business out of the way now, or wait until after lunch?'

'Let's get it out of the way.'

Obliging, Arlene dismissed the waiter, then reached into her briefcase and took out a file of faxes. 'Here's the British deal.'

'What a woman,' Gray said and winked at her.

'The other foreign offers are in there – and the audio. We've just started to pitch to the movie people. And I have your contract.' She shifted, letting Gray look over the papers while she smiled at Brianna. 'Gray tells me you're an incredible cook.'

'He likes to eat.'

'Doesn't he though? You run a B and B, delightfully from what I hear. Blackthorn, it's called.'

'Blackthorn Cottage, yes. It's not a large place.'

'Homey, I imagine.' Arlene studied Brianna over her water glass. 'And quiet.'

'Quiet, certainly. People come to the west for the scenery.'

'Which, I'm told, is quite spectacular. I've never been to Ireland, but Gray's certainly whetted my curiosity. How many people can you manage?'

'Oh, I've four guest rooms, so it varies depending on the size of families. Eight's comfortable, but I sometimes have twelve or more with children.'

'And you cook for them all, run the place by yourself?'

'It's a bit like running a family,' Brianna explained. 'Most people stay only a night or two, going on their way.'

Casually Arlene drew Brianna out, weighing each word, every inflection, judging. Gray was more than a client to her, much more. An interesting woman, she decided. Reserved, a bit nervous. Obviously capable, she mused, tapping a perfectly manicured nail against the cloth as she pumped Brianna for details of the countryside.

Neat as a pin, she observed, well mannered, and . . . ah . . . she watched Brianna's gaze wander — just for a fraction — and rest on Gray. And saw what she wanted to see.

Brianna looked back, saw Arlene's lifted brows, and struggled not to blush. 'Grayson said you have grandchildren.'

'I certainly do. And after a glass of champagne, I'm likely to drag out all their pictures.'

'I'd love to see them. Really. My sister just had a baby.' Everything about her warmed, her eyes, her voice. 'I've pictures of my own.'

'Arlene.' Gray looked up from the file, focused again. 'You're a queen among agents.'

'And don't you forget it.' She handed him a pen even as she signaled for the wine and the menus. 'Sign the contracts, Gray, and let's celebrate.'

Brianna calculated that she had sipped more champagne since meeting Grayson that she had in the whole of her life before him. While she toyed with a glass, she studied the menu and tried not to wince over the prices.

'We have drinks with Rosalie late this afternoon,' Gray was saying, referring to the meeting scheduled with his editor, 'then the premiere. You're going, aren't you?'

'Wouldn't miss it,' Arlene assured him. 'I'll have the chicken,' she added, passing her menu to the hovering waiter. 'Now,' she continued after their orders were placed. 'Tell me how the book's going.'

'It's going well. Incredibly well. I've never had anything fall into place like this. I've nearly got the first draft finished.'

'So quickly?'

'It's streaming out.' His gaze rested on Brianna. 'Almost like magic. Maybe it's the atmosphere. It's a magical place, Ireland.'

'He works hard,' Brianna put in. 'Sometimes he doesn't come out of his room for days at a time. And it doesn't do to disturb him. He'll snap at you like a terrier.'

'And do you snap back?' Arlene wanted to know.

'Not usually.' Brianna smiled as Gray covered her hand with his own. 'I'm used to that sort of behavior with my sister.'

'Oh, yes, the artist. You'd have experience with the artistic temperament.'

'I do, indeed,' Brianna said with a laugh. 'Creative people have a more difficult time than the rest of us, I think. Gray needs to keep the door of his world closed while he's in it.'

'Isn't she perfect?'

'I believe she is,' Arlene said complacently.

A patient woman, she waited until after the meal before making her next move. 'Will you have dessert, Brianna?'

'I couldn't, thank you.'

'Gray will. Never gains an ounce,' she said with a shake of her head. 'You order something sinful, Gray. Brianna and I will go into the ladies' room where we can talk about you in private.'

When Arlene rose, Brianna had little choice but to follow suit. She cast one confused glance at Gray over her shoulder as they walked away.

The ladies' lounge was as glamorous as the barroom. The counter was set with bottles of scent, lotions, even cosmetics. Arlene sat before the mirror, crossed her legs, and gestured for Brianna to join her.

'Are you excited about the premiere tonight?'

'Yes. It's a big moment for him, isn't it? I know they've made movies of his books before – I've seen one. The book was better.'

'Thatta girl.' Arlene laughed, tilted her head. 'Do you know Gray has never brought a woman with him to meet me before you?'

'I . . .' Brianna fumbled, wondered how best to respond.

'I find that a very telling thing. Our relationship goes beyond business, Brianna.'

'I know. He's so fond of you. He speaks of you like family.'

'I am family. Or as close as he'll let himself come to it. I love him dearly. When he told me he was bringing you to New York, I was more than surprised.' Casually Arlene opened her compact, dabbed powder under her eyes. 'I wondered just how some little Irish tart had gotten her hooks in my boy.'

When Brianna's mouth opened, her eyes iced, Arlene held up a hand.

'An overprotective mother's first reaction. And one that shifted as soon as I got a look at you. Forgive me.'

'Of course.' But Brianna's voice was stiff and formal.

'Now you're annoyed with me, and you should be. I've adored Gray for more than a decade, worried about him, harassed him, soothed him. I'd hoped he could find someone he could care for, someone who would make him happy. Because he's not.'

She snapped her compact closed and, out of habit, took out a tube of lipstick. 'Oh, he's probably the most well-adjusted person I know, but there's a lack of happiness in some corner of his heart.'

'I know,' Brianna murmured. 'He's too alone.'

'He was. Do you know the way he looks at you? He's almost giddy. That might have concerned me, if I hadn't seen the way you look at him.'

'I love him,' Brianna heard herself say.

'Oh, my dear, I can see that.' She reached out to clasp Brianna's hand. 'Has he told you about himself?'

'Very little. He holds that in, pretends it isn't there.'

Arlene's lips thinned as she nodded. 'He's not one to share. I've been as close to him as anyone can be for a long time, and I know next to nothing myself. Once, after his first million-dollar sale, he got a little drunk and told me more than he'd meant to.' She shook her head. 'I don't feel I can tell you. Something like a priest in confession – you'd understand that.'

'Yes.'

'I'll say this. He had a miserable childhood and a difficult life. Despite it, maybe because of it, he's a kind and generous man.'

'I know he is. Sometimes too generous. How do you make him stop buying you things?'

'You don't. Because he needs to do it. Money's not important to Gray. The symbol of it is vital, but the money itself is nothing more than a means to an end. And I'm about to give some unsolicited advice and tell you not to give up, to be patient. Gray's only home in his work. He sees to that. I wonder if he realizes yet you're making him a home in Ireland.'

'No.' Brianna relaxed enough to smile. 'He doesn't. Neither did I until a bit ago. Still, his book's almost finished.'

'But you're not. And you've got someone very much on your side now, if you feel the need for it.'

★

Hours later, as Gray tugged up the zipper of her dress, Brianna thought over Arlene's words. It was a lover's gesture, she thought as Gray planted a kiss on her shoulder. A husband's.

She smiled at him in the mirror. 'You look wonderful, Grayson.'

So he did in the black suit, tieless, with that casual sophistication she'd always associated with movie and music stars.

'Who's going to look at me when you're around?'

'All the women?'

'There's a thought.' He draped the pearls around her throat, grinning as he clasped them. 'Nearly perfect,' he judged, turning her to face him.

The tone of the midnight blue warmed against her creamy skin. The neckline was a low scoop that skimmed the soft curve of breasts and left her shoulders bare. She'd put her hair up so that he could play with the tendrils that escaped to tickle her ears and the nape of her neck.

She laughed as he turned her in a slow circle. 'Earlier you said I was perfect.'

'So I did.' He took a box out of his pocket, flipped open the top. There were more pearls inside, two luminous teardrops that dripped from single flashing diamonds.

'Gray –'

'Ssh.' He slipped the earrings over her lobes. A practiced move, she thought wryly, smoothly and casually done. '*Now*, you're perfect.'

'When did you get these?'

'I picked them out when we bought the necklace. Marcia was delighted when I called and had her send them over.'

'I bet she was.' Helpless to do otherwise, she lifted a hand and stroked an earring. It was real, she knew, yet she couldn't imagine it – Brianna Concannon standing in a luxurious New York hotel, wearing pearls and diamonds while the man she loved smiled at her.

'It's no use telling you that you shouldn't have done it?'

'No use at all. Say thank you.'

'Thank you.' Accepting, she pressed her cheek to his. 'This is your night, Grayson, and you've made me feel like a princess.'

'Just think how nifty we'll look if any of the press bothers to snap a picture.'

'Bothers to?' She grabbed her bag as he pulled her toward the door. 'It's your movie. You wrote it.'

'I wrote the book.'

'That's what I said.'

'No.' He slipped an arm around her shoulders as they walked to the elevator. She may have looked like a glamorous stranger, he noted, but she still smelled like Brianna. Soft, sweet, and subtle. 'You said it was my movie. It's not. It's the director's movie, the producer's movie, the actors' movie. And it's the screenwriter's movie.' As the doors opened he led her inside, pushed the button for lobby. 'The novelist is way down on the list, honey.'

'That's ridiculous. It's your story, your people.'

'Was.' He smiled at her. She was becoming indignant for him, and he found it charming. 'I sold it, so whatever they've done – for better or worse – you won't hear me complain. And the spotlight most certainly will not be on "based on the novel written by" tonight.'

'Well, it should be. They'd have nothing without you.'

'Damn right.'

She cut him a glance as they stepped into the lobby. 'You're making fun of me.'

'No, I'm not. I'm adoring you.' He kissed her to prove it, then led her outside where their limo was waiting. 'The trick to surviving a Hollywood sale is not to take it too personally.'

'You could have written the screenplay yourself.'

'Do I look like a masochist?' He almost shuddered at the thought. 'Thanks, but working with an editor is as close as I ever want to come to writing by committee.' He settled back as the car cruised through traffic. 'I get paid well, I get my name on the screen for a few seconds, and if the movie's a hit — and the early buzz seems to indicate this one will be — my sales soar.'

'Don't you have any temperament?'

'Plenty of it. Just not about this.'

Their picture was snapped the moment they alighted at the theater. Brianna blinked against the lights, surprised and more than a little disconcerted. He'd indicated that he'd be all but ignored, yet a microphone was thrust at him before they'd taken two steps. Gray answered questions easily, avoided them just as easily, all the while keeping a firm grip on Brianna as they made their way toward the theater.

Dazzled, she looked around. There were people here she'd only seen in glossy magazines, on movie and television screens. Some loitered in the lobby, as ordinary people might, catching a last smoke, chatting over drinks, gossiping or talking shop.

Here and there, Gray introduced her. She made whatever responses seemed right and filed away names and faces for the people back in Clare.

Some dressed up, some dressed down. She saw diamonds, and she saw denim. There were baseball caps and thousand-dollar suits. She smelled popcorn, as she might in any theater on any continent, and that bubble gum scent of candy along with subtle perfumes. And over it all was a thin, glossy coat of glamour.

When they took their seats in the theater, Gray draped his arm over the back of her chair, turned so that his mouth was at her ear. 'Impressed?'

'Desperately. I feel I've walked into a movie instead of coming to see one.'

'That's because events like this have nothing to do with reality. Wait until the party after.'

Brianna let out a careful breath. She'd come a long way from Clare, she thought. A long, long way.

She didn't have much time to chew over it. The lights dimmed, the screen lit. In only moments she felt the sharp, silvery thrill of seeing Gray's name flash, hold, then fade.

'That's wonderful,' she whispered. 'That's a wonderful thing.'

'Let's see if the rest is as good.'

She thought it was. The action swept by, that edge-of-the-seat pace that had her immersed. It didn't seem to matter that she'd read the book, already knew the twists of plot, recognized whole blocks of Gray's words in the dialogue. Her stomach still clenched, her lips still curved, her eyes still widened. Once Gray pressed a handkerchief into her hands so she could dry her cheeks.

'You're the perfect audience, Brie. I don't know how I've watched a movie without you.'

'Ssh.' She sighed, took his hand, and held it through the breathless climax and through the closing credits while applause echoed from the walls.

'I'd say we've got a hit.'

'They won't believe me,' Brianna said as they stepped out of the elevator in the Plaza hours later. '*I* wouldn't believe me. I danced with Tom Cruise.' Giggling, a little light-headed on wine and excitement, she turned a quick pirouette. 'Do you believe it?'

'I have to.' Gray unlocked the door. 'I saw it. He seemed very taken with you.'

'Oh, he just wanted to talk about Ireland. He has a fondness for it. He's charming, and madly in love with his wife. And to think they might actually come and stay at my house.'

'It wouldn't surprise me to find the place lousy with celebrities after tonight.' Yawning, Gray toed off his shoes. 'You enchanted everyone you spoke with.'

'You Yanks always fall for an Irish voice.' She unclasped her necklace, running the strands through her hands before she laid them in their box. 'I'm so proud of you, Gray. Everyone was saying how wonderful the movie was, and all that talk about Oscars.' She beamed at him as she slipped off her earrings. 'Imagine, you winning an Oscar.'

'I wouldn't.' He took off his jacket, tossed it carelessly aside. 'I didn't write the movie.'

'But . . .' She made a sound of disgust, stepping out of her shoes, lowering the zipper of her dress. 'That's just not right. You should have one.'

He grinned, and taking off his shirt glanced over his shoulder at her. But the quip dried like dust on the tip of his tongue.

She stepped out of her dress and was standing there in the little strapless fancy he'd bought to go under it. Midnight blue. Silk. Lace.

Unprepared, he was hard as iron as she bent to unsnap a smoky stocking from its garters. Pretty hands with their neat, unpainted nails skimmed down over one long smooth thigh, over the knee, the calf, tidily rolling the stocking.

She was saying something, but he couldn't hear it over the buzzing in his head. Part of his brain was warning him to get a choke hold on the violent flare of desire. Another part was urging him to take, as he'd wanted to take. Hard and fast and mindlessly.

Her stockings neatly folded, she reached up to unpin her hair. His hands fisted at his sides as those fired-gold tresses spilled down over bare shoulders. He could hear his own breathing, too quick, too harsh. And could almost, almost feel that silk rip in his hands, feel the flesh beneath go hot, taste that heat as his mouth closed greedily over her.

He forced himself to turn away. He needed only a moment, he assured himself, to reclaim control. It wouldn't be right to frighten her.

'And it'll be such fun to tell everyone.' Brianna set down her brush and giving into the new laugh, turned another pirouette. 'I can't believe it's the middle of the night and I'm so wide awake. Just like a little child who's had too many sweets. I don't feel as though I'll ever need to sleep again.' She spun toward him, wrapping her arms around his waist, pressing against his back. 'Oh, I've had such a wonderful time, Gray. I don't know how to thank you for it.'

'You don't have to.' His voice was rough, every cell in his body on full alert.

'Oh, but you're used to this sort of thing.' Innocently she planted a quick line of friendly kisses from shoulder to shoulder. He ground his teeth to hold back a moan. 'I don't suppose you can really imagine what a thrill all this has been for me. But you're all knotted up.' Instinctively she began to rub his back and shoulders. 'You must be tired, and here I am, chattering like a magpie. Lie down, won't you? And I'll work these kinks out for you.'

'Stop.' The order sliced out. He whirled quickly, gripping her wrists so that she could only stand and stare. He looked furious. No, she realized. He looked dangerous.

'Grayson, what is it?'

'Don't you know what you're doing to me?' When she shook her head, he jerked her against him, his fingers biting into flesh. He could see the puzzlement in her eyes

give way to dawning awareness, and to panic. And he
snapped.

'Goddamn it.' His mouth crushed down on hers, hungry,
desperate. If she'd pushed him away, he might have pulled
himself back. Instead she lifted a trembling hand to his
cheek, and he was lost.

'Just once,' he muttered, dragging her to the bed. 'Just
once.'

This wasn't the patient, tenderhearted lover she'd
known. He was wild, on the edge of violence with hands
that tugged and tore and possessed. Everything about him
was hard, his mouth, his hands, his body. For an instant, as
he used them all to batter her senses, she feared she might
simply break apart, like glass.

Then the dark tide of his need swept her along, shocked,
aroused, and terrified all at once.

She cried out, staggered, as those restless fingers shot her
mercilessly to peak and over. Her vision hazed, but she
could see him through it. In the lights they'd left blazing,
his eyes were fierce.

She said his name again, sobbed it out as he pulled her
up to her knees. They were torso to torso on the rumpled
bed, his hands molding her, pushing her ruthlessly toward
madness.

Helpless, she bowed back, shuddering when his teeth
scraped down her throat, over her breast. There he suckled
greedily, as if starved for her taste, while his impatient fingers drove her mercilessly higher.

He couldn't think. Each time he'd loved her he'd struggled to keep one corner of his mind cool enough to make
his hands gentle, his pace easy. This time there was only heat,
a kind of gleeful, glorious hell that seeped into mind as well
as body and burned away the civilized. Now bombarded by
his own lust, craving hers, control was beyond him.

257

He wanted her writhing, bucking, screaming.

And he had her.

Even the torn silk was too much of a barrier. Frantic now, he ripped it down the center, pushing her onto her back so that he could devour the newly exposed flesh. He could feel her hands drag through his hair, her nails score his shoulders as he worked his way down her, feasting.

Then her gasp, the jolt, the muffled scream when his tongue plunged into her.

She was dying. No one could live through this heat, through the pressure that kept building and exploding, building and exploding until her body was only a quivering mass of scored nerves and unspeakable needs.

The sensations pounded at her, massing too quickly to be separated. She only knew he was doing things to her, incredible, wicked, delicious things. The next climax slammed into her like a fist.

Rearing up, she grabbed at him, thrashing until they were rolling over the bed. Her mouth sprinted over him, just as greedy now, just as frenzied. Her questing hands found him, cupped him, so that her system shivered with fresh and furious pleasure when he groaned.

'Now. Now.' It had to be now. He couldn't stop himself. His hands slid off her damp skin, gripped hard at her hips to lift them. He drove himself inside her deep, panting as he positioned her to take even more of him.

He rode her hard, plunging further each time she rose to meet him. He watched her face as she plummeted over that final, vicious peak. The way her clouded eyes went dark as her muscles contracted around him.

With something perilously close to pain, he emptied himself into her.

Chapter Seventeen

He'd rolled off her and was staring at the ceiling. He could curse himself, he knew, but he couldn't take back what he'd done.

All of his care, all of his caution, and in an instant, he had snapped. And ruined it.

Now she was curled up beside him, quivering. And he was afraid to touch her.

'I'm sorry,' he finally said and tasted the uselessness of the apology. 'I never meant to treat you that way. I lost control.'

'Lost control,' she murmured and wondered how it could be a body should feel limp and energized all at once. 'Did you think you needed it?'

Her voice was shaky, he noted, and rough, he imagined, with shock. 'I know an apology's pretty lame. Can I get you something? Some water.' He squeezed his eyes shut and cursed himself again. 'Talk about lame. Let me get you a nightgown. You'll want a nightgown.'

'No, I don't.' She managed to shift enough to look up and study his face. He didn't look at her, she noted, but only stared at the ceiling. 'Grayson, you didn't hurt me.'

'Of course I did. You'll have bruises to prove it.'

'I'm not fragile,' she said with a hint of exasperation.

'I treated you like —' He couldn't say it, not to her. 'I should have been gentle.'

'You have been. I like knowing it took you some effort to be gentle. And I like knowing something I did made you forget to be.' Her lips curved as she brushed at the hair on his forehead. 'Did you think you frightened me?'

'I know I frightened you.' He shifted away, sat up. 'I didn't care.'

'You did frighten me.' She paused. 'I liked it. I love you.'

259

He winced, squeezed the hand she'd laid over his. 'Brianna,' he began without a clue how to continue.

'Don't worry. I don't need the words back.'

'Listen, a lot of times people get sex confused with love.'

'I imagine you're right. Grayson, do you think I would be here with you, that I would ever have been with you like this if I didn't love you.'

He was good with words. Dozens of reasonable excuses and ploys ran through his mind. 'No,' he said at length, settling on the truth. 'I don't. Which only makes it worse,' he muttered, and rose to tug on his trousers. 'I should never have let things go this far. I knew better. It's my fault.'

'There's no fault here.' She reached for his hand so that he would sit on the bed again rather than pace. 'It shouldn't make you sad to know you're loved, Grayson.'

But it did. It made him sad, and panicked, and for just a moment, wishful. 'Brie, I can't give you back what you want or should have. There's no future with me, no house in the country and kids in the yard. It's not in the cards.'

'It's a pity you think so. But I'm not asking you for that.'

'It's what you want.'

'It's what I want, but not what I expect.' She gave him a surprisingly cool smile. 'I've been rejected before. And I know very well what is it to love and not have the person love you back, at least not so much as you want, or need.' She shook her head before he could speak. 'As much as I might want to go on with you, Grayson, I'll survive without you.'

'I don't want to hurt you, Brianna. I care about you. I care for you.'

She lifted a brow. 'I know that. And I know you're worried because you care more for me than you've cared for anyone before.'

He opened his mouth, shut it, shook his head. 'Yes, that's

true. It's new ground for me. For both of us.' Still uncertain of his moves, he took her hand, kissed it. 'I'd give you more if I could. And I am sorry I at least didn't prepare you a little better for tonight. You're the first . . . inexperienced woman I've been with, so I've tried to take it slow.'

Intrigued, she cocked her head. 'You must have been as nervous as I was, the first time.'

'More.' He kissed her hand again. 'Much more, believe me. I'm used to women who know the ropes, and the rules. Experienced or pro, and you –'

'Pro? Professional?' Her eyes went huge. 'You've paid women to bed them?'

He stared back at her. He must have been even more befuddled than he'd realized to have come out with something like that. 'Not in recent memory. Anyway –'

'Why would you have to do that? A man who looks like you, who has your sensibility?'

'Look, it was a long time ago. Another life. Don't look at me like that,' he snapped. 'When you're sixteen and alone on the streets, nothing's free. Not even sex.'

'Why were you alone and on the street at sixteen?'

He stood, retreated, she thought. And there was shame in his eyes as much as anger.

'I'm not going to get into this.'

'Why?'

'Christ.' Shaken, he dragged both hands through his hair. 'It's late. We need to get some sleep.'

'Grayson, is it so hard to talk to me? There's hardly anything you don't know of me, the bad things and the good. Do you think I'd think less of you for knowing?'

He wasn't sure, and told himself he didn't care. 'It's not important, Brianna. It has nothing to do with me now, with us here.'

Her eyes cooled, and she rose to get the nightgown she'd

said she didn't want. 'It's your business, of course, if you choose to shut me out.'

'That's not what I'm doing.'

She tugged the cotton over her head, adjusted the sleeves. 'As you say.'

'Goddamn it, you're good, aren't you?' Furious with her, he jammed his hands into his pockets.

'I don't know your meaning.'

'You know my meaning exactly,' he tossed back. 'Lay on the guilt, spread on a little frost, and you get your way.'

'We've agreed it's none of my business.' Moving toward the bed, she began to tuck in the sheets they'd ripped out. 'If it's guilt you're feeling, it's not my doing.'

'You get to me,' he muttered. 'You know just how to get to me.' He hissed out a breath, defeated. 'You want it, fine. Sit down, I'll tell you a story.'

He turned his back on her, rummaging through the drawer for the pack of cigarettes he always carried and smoked only when working.

'The first thing I remember is the smell. Garbage just starting to rot, mold, stale cigarettes,' he added, looking wryly at the smoke that curled toward the ceiling. 'Grass. Not the kind you mow, the kind you inhale. You've probably never smelled pot in your life, have you?'

'I haven't, no.' She kept her hands in her lap, and her eyes on him.

'Well, that's my first real memory. The sense of smell's the strongest, stays with you − good or bad. I remember the sounds, too. Raised voices, loud music, someone having sex in the next room. I remember being hungry, and not being able to get out of my room because she'd locked me in again. She was stoned most of the time and didn't always remember she had a kid around who needed to eat.'

He looked around idly for an ashtray, then leaned back

against the dresser. It wasn't so hard to speak of it after all, he discovered. It was almost like making up a scene in his mind. Almost.

'She told me once she'd left home when she was sixteen. Wanted to get away from her parents, all the rules. They were square, she'd say. Went nuts when they found out she smoked dope and had boys up in her room. She was just living her own life, doing her own thing. So she just left one day, hitched a ride and ended up in San Francisco. She could play at being a hippie there, but she ended up on the hard edge of the drug culture, experimented with a lot of shit, paid for a lot of it by begging or selling herself.'

He'd just told her his mother was a prostitute, a junkie, and waited for some shocked exclamation. When she only continued to watch him with those cool, guarded eyes, he shrugged and went on.

'She was probably about eighteen when she got pregnant with me. According to her story, she'd already had two abortions and was scared of another. She could never be quite sure who the father was, but was pretty certain it was one of three guys. She moved in with one of them and decided to keep me. When I was about a year old, she got tired of him and moved in with somebody else. He pimped for her, supplied her with drugs, but he knocked her around a little too much, so she ditched him.'

Gray tapped his cigarette out, paused long enough for Brianna to comment. But she said nothing, only sat as she was on the bed, her hands folded.

'Anyway, we can fast forward through the next couple of years. As far as I can tell, things stayed pretty much as they were. She moved around from man to man, got hooked on the hard stuff. In enlightened times, I guess you could say she had an addictive personality. She knocked me around a little, but she never really beat me – that would have taken a little too much effort and interest. She locked me in to keep me from wandering when she was on the street or meeting her dealer. We lived in filth, and I remember the cold. It gets fucking cold in San Francisco. That's how the fire started. Somebody in the building knocked over a portable heater. I was five, and I was alone and locked in.'

'Oh, my God, Grayson.' She pressed her hands to her mouth. 'Oh, God.'

'I woke up choking,' he said in the same distant voice. 'The room was filled with smoke, and I could hear the sirens and the screaming. I was screaming, and beating at the door. I couldn't breathe, and I was scared. I remember just lying down on the floor and crying. Then a fireman crashed through the door, and he picked me up. I don't remember him carrying me out. I don't remember the fire itself, just the smoke in my room. I woke up in the hospital, and a social worker was there. A pretty young thing with big blue eyes and soft hands. And there was a cop. He made me nervous because I'd been taught to distrust anyone in authority. They asked me if I knew where my mother was. I didn't. By the time I was well enough to leave the hospital ward, I'd been scooped up in the system. They put me in a children's home while they looked for her. They never found her. I never saw her again.'

'She never came for you.'

'No, she never came. It wasn't such a bad deal. The home was clean, they fed you regular. The big problem for me was that it was structured, and I wasn't used to structure. There were foster homes, but I made sure that didn't work. I didn't want to be anyone's fake kid, no matter how good or how bad the people were. And some of them were really good people. I was what they call intractable. I liked it that way. Being a troublemaker gave me an identity, so I made plenty of trouble. I was a real tough guy with a smart mouth and a bad attitude. I liked to pick fights, because I was strong and fast and could usually win.

'I was predictable,' he said with a half laugh. 'That's the worst of it. I was a product of my early environment and damned proud of it. No fucking counselor or shrink or social worker was going to get through to me. I'd been taught to hate authority, and that was one thing she'd taught me well.'

'But the school, the home . . . they were good to you?'

A mocking light shimmered in his eyes. 'Oh, yeah, just peachy. Three squares and a bed.' He let out an impatient breath at her troubled expression. 'You're a statistic, Brianna, a number. A problem. And there are plenty of other statistics and numbers and problems to be shuffled around. Sure, in hindsight, I can tell you that some of them probably really gave a damn, really tried to make a difference. But they were the enemy, with their questions and tests, their rules and disciplines. So following my mother's example, I ran off at sixteen. Lived on the streets, by my wits. I never touched drugs, never sold myself, but there wasn't much else I didn't do.'

He pushed away from the dresser and began to prowl the room. 'I stole, I cheated, I ran scams. And one day I had an epiphany when a guy I was running a short con on got wise and beat the living shit out of me. It occurred to me, when I came to in an alley with blood in my mouth and several busted ribs, that I could probably find a better way to make a living. I headed to New York. I sold plenty of watches along Fifth Avenue,' he said with a hint of a smile. 'Ran a little three-card monte, and I started to write. I'd gotten a fairly decent education in the home. And I liked to write. I couldn't admit that at sixteen, being such a tough sonofabitch. But at eighteen, in New York, it didn't seem so bad. What seemed bad, what suddenly began to seem really bad, was that I was the same as she was. I decided to be somebody else.

'I changed my name. I changed myself. I got a legit job bussing tables at a little dive in the Village. I shed that little bastard layer by layer until I was Grayson Thane. And I don't look back, because it's pointless.'

'Because it hurts you,' Brianna said quietly. 'And makes you angry.'

'Maybe. But mostly because it has nothing to do with who I am now.'

She wanted to tell him it had everything to do with who he was, what he'd made himself. Instead she rose to face him. 'I love who you are now.' She felt a pang, knowing he was drawing back from what she wanted to give him. 'Is it so distressing to you to know that, and to know I can feel sorry for the child, for the young man, and admire what evolved from them?'

'Brianna, the past doesn't matter. Not to me,' he insisted. 'It's different for you. Your past goes back centuries. You're steeped in it, the history, the tradition. It's formed you, and because of it, the future's just as important. You're a planner, long term. I'm not. I can't be. Damn it, I don't want to be. There's just now. The way things are right now.'

Did he think she couldn't understand that, after all he'd told her? She could see him all too well, the battered little boy, terrified of the past, terrified there was no future, holding on desperately whatever he could grab in the present.

'Well, we're together right now, aren't we?' Gently she cupped his face. 'Grayson, I can't stop loving you to make you more comfortable. I can't do it to make myself more comfortable. It simply is. My heart's lost to you, and I can't take it back. I doubt I would if I could. It doesn't mean you have to take it, but you'd be foolish not to. It costs you nothing.'

'I don't want to hurt you, Brianna.' He linked his fingers around her wrists. 'I don't want to hurt you.'

'I know that.' He would, of course. She wondered that he couldn't see he would hurt himself as well. 'We'll take the now, and be grateful for it. But tell me one thing,' she said and kissed him lightly. 'What was your name?'

'Christ, you don't give up.'

'No.' Her smile was easy now, surprisingly confident. 'It's not something I consider a failing.'

'Logan,' he muttered. 'Michael Logan.'

And she laughed, making him feel like a fool. 'Irish. I should have known it. Such a gift of gab you've got, and all the charm in the world.'

'Michael Logan,' he said, firing up, 'was a small-minded, mean-spirited, penny-ante thief who wasn't worth spit.'

She sighed. 'Michael Logan was a neglected, troubled child who needed love and care. And you're wrong to hate him so. But we'll leave him in peace.'

Then she disarmed him by pressing against him, laying her head on his shoulder. Her hands moved up and down his back, soothing. She should have been disgusted by what he'd told her. She should have been appalled by the way he'd treated her in bed. Yet she was here, holding him and offering him a terrifying depth of love.

'I don't know what to do about you.'

'There's nothing you have to do.' She brushed her lips over his shoulder. 'You've given me the most wonderful months of my life. And you'll remember me, Grayson, as long as you live.'

He let out a long breath. He couldn't deny it. For the first time in his life, he'd be leaving a part of himself behind when he walked away.

It was he who felt awkward the next morning. They had breakfast in the parlor of the suite, with the view of the park out the window. And he waited for her to toss something he'd told her back in his face. He'd broken the law, he'd slept with prostitutes, he'd wallowed in the sewers of the streets.

Yet she sat there across from him, looking as fresh as a morning in Clare, talking happily about their upcoming trip to Worldwide before they went to the airport.

'You're not eating your breakfast, Grayson. Aren't you feeling well?'

'I'm fine.' He cut into the pancakes he'd thought he'd wanted. 'I guess I'm missing your cooking.'

It was exactly the right thing to say. Her concerned look transformed into a delighted smile. 'You'll be having it again tomorrow. I'll fix you something special.'

He gave a grunt in response. He'd put off telling her about the trip to Wales. He hadn't wanted to spoil her enjoyment of New York. Now he wondered why he'd thought he could. Nothing he'd dumped on her the night before had shaken that steady composure.

'Ah, Brie, we're actually going to take a little detour on the way back to Ireland.'

'Oh?' Frowning, she set her teacup down. 'Do you have business somewhere?'

'Not exactly. We're stopping off in Wales.'

'In Wales?'

'It's about your stock. Remember I told you I'd have my broker do some checking?'

'Yes. Did he find something unusual?'

'Brie, Triquarter Mining doesn't exist.'

'But of course it exists. I have the certificate. I've got the letter.'

'There is no Triquarter Mining on any stock exchange. No company by that name listed anywhere. The phone number on the letterhead is fake.'

'How can that be? They offered me a thousand pounds.'

'Which is why we're going to Wales. I think it would be worth the trip to do a little personal checking.'

Brianna shook her head. 'I'm sure your broker's very competent, Gray, but he must have overlooked something. If a company doesn't exist, they don't issue stock or offer to buy it back.'

'They issue stock if it's a front,' he said, stabbing at his meal as she stared at him. 'A scam, Brie. I have a little experience with stock cons. You get a post office box, a phone number, and you canvas for marks. For people who'll invest,' he explained. 'People looking to make a quick buck. You get a suit and a spiel, put some paperwork together, print up a prospectus and phony certificates. You take the money, and you disappear.'

She was quiet for a moment, digesting it. Indeed she could see her father falling for just such a trick. He'd always flung himself heedlessly into deals. In truth, she'd expected nothing when she'd first pursued the matter.

'I understand that part, I think. And it's in keeping with my father's luck in business. But how do you explain that they answered me, and offered me money?'

'I can't.' Though he had some ideas on it. 'That's why we're going to Wales. Rogan's arranged for his plane to meet us in London and take us. It'll bring us back to Shannon Airport when we're ready.'

'I see.' Carefully she set her knife and fork aside. 'You've discussed it with Rogan, him being a man, and planned it out between you.'

Gray cleared his throat, ran his tongue over his teeth. 'I wanted you to enjoy the trip here without worrying.' When she only pinned him with those cool green eyes, he shrugged. 'You're waiting for an apology, and you're not going to get one.' She folded her hands, rested them on the edge of the table, and said nothing. 'You're good at the big chill,' he commented, 'but it isn't going to wash. Fraud's out of your league. I'd have taken this trip by myself, but it's likely I'll need you since the stock's in your father's name.'

'And being in my father's name makes it my business. It's kind of you to want to help.'

'Fuck that.'

She jolted, felt her stomach shrivel at the inevitability of the argument. 'Don't use that tone on me, Grayson.'

'Then don't use that irritated schoolteacher's tone on me.' When she rose, his eyes flashed, narrowed. 'Don't you walk away, goddamn it.'

'I won't be sworn at or shouted at or made to feel inadequate because I'm only a farmer's daughter from the west counties.'

'What the hell does that have to do with anything?' When she continued to walk toward the bedroom, he shoved away from the table. He snatched her arm, whirled her back. A flicker of panic crossed her face before she closed up. 'I said don't walk away from me.'

'I come and go as I please, just as you do. And I'm going to dress now and get ready for the trip you've so thoughtfully arranged.'

'You want to take a bite out of me, go ahead. But we're going to settle this.'

'I was under the impression you already had. You're hurting my arm, Grayson.'

'I'm sorry.' He released her, jammed his hands in his pockets. 'Look, I figured you might be a little annoyed, but I didn't expect someone as reasonable as you to blow it all out of proportion.'

'You've arranged things behind my back, made decisions for me, decided I wouldn't be able to cope on my own, and

I'm blowing it all out of proportion? Well, that's fine, then. I'm sure I should be ashamed of myself.'

'I'm trying to help you.' His voice rose again, and he fought to bring it and his temper under control. 'It has nothing to do with your being inadequate; it has to do with you having no experience. Someone broke into your house. Can't you put it together?'

She stared, paled. 'No, why don't you put it together for me?'

'You wrote about the stock, then somebody searches your house. Fast, sloppy. Maybe desperate. Not long after that, there's somebody outside your window. How long have you lived in that house, Brianna?'

'All my life.'

'Has anything like that happened before?'

'No, but . . . No.'

'So it makes sense to connect the dots. I want to see what the whole picture looks like.'

'You should have told me all this before.' Shaken, she lowered to the arm of a chair. 'You shouldn't have kept it from me.'

'It's just a theory. Christ, Brie, you've had enough on your mind. Your mother, Maggie and the baby, me. The whole business about finding that woman your father was involved with. I didn't want to add to it.'

'You were trying to shield me. I'm trying to understand that.'

'Of course I was trying to shield you. I don't like seeing you worried. I —' He broke off, stunned. What had he almost said? He took a long step back, mentally from those tricky three words, physically from her. 'You matter to me,' he said carefully.

'All right.' Suddenly tired, she pushed at her hair. 'I'm sorry I made a scene about it. But don't keep things from me, Gray.'

271

'I won't.' He touched her cheek and his stomach trembled. 'Brianna.'

'Yes?'

'Nothing,' he said and dropped his hand again. 'Nothing. We'd better pull it together if we're going to get to Worldwide.'

It was raining in Wales and too late to do more than check into the drab little hotel where Gray had booked a room. Brianna had only a fleeting impression of the city of Rhondda, of the bleak row houses in the tight groups, the sorry skies that pelted the road with rain. They shared a meal she didn't taste, them tumbled exhausted into bed.

He expected her to complain. The accommodations weren't the best and the traveling had been brutal, even for him. But she said nothing the next morning, only dressed and asked him what they would do next.

'I figured we'd check the post office, see where that gets us.' He watched her pin up her hair, her movements neat, precise, though there were shadows under her eyes. 'You're tired.'

'A bit. All the time changing, I imagine.' She glanced out the window where watery sunlight struggled through the glass. 'I always thought of Wales as a wild and beautiful place.'

'A lot of it is. The mountains are spectacular, and the coast. The Lleyn Peninsula – it's a little touristy, full of Brits on holiday – but really gorgeous. Or the uplands, very pastoral and traditionally Welsh. If you saw the moorlands in the afternoon sun, you'd see just how wild and beautiful the country is.'

'You've been so many places. I'm surprised you can remember one from another.'

'There's always something that sticks in your mind.' He

looked around the gloomy hotel room. 'I'm sorry about this, Brie. It was the most convenient. If you want to take an extra day or two, I'll show you the scenery.'

She smiled over it, the thought of her tossing responsibility aside and traveling with Gray over foreign hills and shores. 'I need to get home, once we've finished what we've come for. I can't impose on Mrs. O'Malley much longer.' She turned from the mirror. 'And you're wanting to get back to work. It shows.'

'Got me.' He took her hands. 'When I finish the book, I'll have a little time before I tour for the one that's coming up. We could go somewhere. Anywhere you like. Greece, or the South Pacific. The West Indies. Would you like that? Some place with palm trees and a beach, blue water, white sun.'

'It sounds lovely.' He, she thought, he who never made plans was making them. She felt it wiser not to point it out. 'It might be difficult to get away again so soon.' She gave his hands a squeeze before releasing them to pick up her purse. 'I'm ready if you are.'

They found the post office easily enough, but the woman in charge of the counter appeared immune to Gray's charm. It wasn't her place to give out the names of people who rented post office boxes, she told them crisply. They could have one themselves if they wanted, and she wouldn't be discussing them with strangers, either.

When Gray asked about Triquarter, he received a shrug and a frown. The name meant nothing to her.

Gray considered a bribe, took another look at the prim set of the woman's mouth, and decided against it.

'Strike one,' he said as they stepped outside again.

'I don't believe you ever thought it would be so easy.'

'No, but sometimes you get a hit when you least expect it. We'll try some mining companies.'

'Shouldn't we just report everything we know to the local authorities?'

'We'll get to that.'

He checked tirelessly, office after office, asking the same questions, getting the same answers. No one in Rhondda had heard of Triquarter. Brianna let him take control, for the simple pleasure of watching him work. It seemed to her that he could adjust, chameleonlike, to whatever personality he chose.

He could be charming, abrupt, businesslike, sly. It was, she supposed, how he researched a subject he might write about. He asked endless questions, by turns cajoling and bullying people into answering.

After four hours she knew more about coal mining and the Welsh economy than she cared to remember. And nothing about Triquarter.

'You need a sandwich,' Gray decided.

'I wouldn't say no to one.'

'Okay, we refuel and rethink.'

'I don't want you to be disappointed we haven't learned anything.'

'But we have. We know without a shadow of doubt there is no Triquarter Mining, and never has been. The post office box is a sham and in all likelihood still being rented by whoever's fronting the deal.'

'Why would you think that?'

'They need it until they settle with you, and any other outstanding investors. I imagine they've cleaned most of that up. Let's try here.' He nudged her into a small pub.

The scents were familiar enough to make her homesick, the voices just foreign enough to be exotic. They settled at a table where Gray immediately commandeered the thin plastic menu. 'Mmm. Shepherd's Pie. It won't be as good as yours, but it'll do. Want to try it?'

'That'll be fine. And some tea.'

Gray gave their order, leaned forward. 'I'm thinking, Brie, that your father dying so soon after he bought the stock plays a part in it. You said you found the certificate in the attic.'

'I did, yes. We didn't go through all the boxes after he'd died. My mother – well, Maggie didn't have the heart to, and I let it go because –'

'Because Maggie was hurting and your mother would have hounded you.'

'I don't like scenes.' She pressed her lips together and stared at the tabletop. 'It's easier to step back from them, walk away from them.' She glanced up, then away again. 'Maggie was the light of my father's life. He loved me, I know he did, but what they had was very special. It was only between them. She was grieving so hard, and there was already a blowup about the house being left to me, instead of my mother. Mother was bitter and angry, and I let things go. I wanted to start my business, you see. So it was easy to avoid the boxes, dust around them from time to time, and tell myself I'd get to it by and by.'

'And then you did.'

'I don't know why I picked that day. I suppose because things were settled quite a bit. Mother in her own house, Maggie with Rogan. And I . . .'

'You weren't hurting so much over him. Enough time had passed for you to do the practical thing.'

'That's true enough. I thought I could go through the things up there that he'd saved without aching so much for him, or wishing so hard things had been different. And it was part ambition.' She sighed. 'I was thinking I could have the attic room converted for guests.'

'That's my Brie.' He took her hand. 'So he'd put the certificate up there for safekeeping, and years passed without anyone finding it, or acting on it. I imagine they wrote it off. Why should they take a chance of making contact? If they did any checking, they'd have learned that Tom Concannon had died, and his heirs hadn't dealt with the stock. It might have been lost, or destroyed, or tossed out my mistake. Then you wrote a letter.'

'And here we are. It still doesn't explain why they've offered me money.'

'Okay, we're going to suppose. It's one of my best things. Suppose when the deal was made, it was a fairly straight-forward scam, the way I explained in New York. Then suppose somebody got ambitious, or lucky. Expanded on it. Triquarter was out of the picture, but the resources, the profit, the organization was still there. Maybe you run another scam, maybe you even get into something legit. Maybe you're just playing with things on the right side of the law, using them as cover. Wouldn't it be a surprise if the legal stuff started to work? Maybe even made more of a profit than the cons. Now you've got to shed that shadowy stuff, or at least cover it up.'

Brianna rubbed her temple as their meal was served. 'It's too confusing for me.'

'Something about those loose stock certificates. Hard to say what.' He helped himself to a healthy bite. 'Nope, does-n't come close to yours.' And swallowed. 'But there's some-thing, and they want them back, even pay to get them back. Oh, not much, not enough to make you suspicious, or interested in further investing. Just enough to make it worth your while to cash in.'

'You do know how all this business works, don't you?'

'Too much. If it hadn't been for writing . . .' He trailed off, shrugged. It wasn't something to dwell on. 'Well, we can consider it luck that I happen to have some experience along these lines. We'll make a few stops after we eat, then run it by the cops.'

She nodded, relieved at the idea of turning the whole mess over to the authorities. The food helped pick up her spirits. By morning they'd be home. Over her tea she began to dream about her garden, greeting Con, working in her own kitchen.

'Finished?'

'Hmm?'

Gray smiled at her. 'Taking a trip?'

'I was thinking of home. My roses might be blooming.'

'You'll be in the garden by this time tomorrow,' he promised and, after counting out bills for the tab, rose.

Outside, he draped his arm over her shoulder. 'Want to try to local public transportation? If we catch a bus we'll get across town a lot quicker. I could rent a car if you'd rather.'

'Don't be silly. A bus is fine.'

'Then let's just . . . hold it.' He turned her around, nudging her back into the pub doorway. 'Isn't that interesting?' he murmured, staring down the street. 'Isn't that just fascinating?'

'What? You're crushing me.'

'Sorry. I want you to keep back as much as you can and take a look down there, just across the street.' His eyes began to gleam. 'Just on the way to the post office. The man carrying the black umbrella.'

She poked her head out, scanning. 'Yes,' she said after a moment. 'There's a man with a black umbrella.'

'Doesn't look familiar? Think back a couple of months. You served us salmon as I recall, and trifle.'

'I don't know how it is you can remember meals so.' She leaned out further, strained her eyes. 'He looks ordinary enough to me. Like a lawyer, or a banker.'

'Bingo. Or so he told us. Our retired banker from London.'

'Mr. Smythe-White.' It came to her in a flash, made her laugh. 'Well, that's odd, isn't it? Why are we hiding from him?'

'Because it's odd, Brie. Because it's very, very odd that your overnight guest, the one who happened to be out sightseeing when your house was searched, is strolling down the street in Wales, just about to go into the post office. What do you want to bet he rents a box there?'

'Oh.' She sagged back against the door. 'Sweet Jesus. What are we going to do?'

'Wait. Then follow him.'

Chapter Eighteen

They didn't have long to wait. Barely five minutes after Smythe-White walked into the post office, he walked out again. After taking one quick look right, then left, he hurried up the street, his umbrella swinging like a pendulum at his side.

'Damn it, she blew it.'

'What?'

'Come on, quick.' Gray grabbed Brianna's hand and darted after Smythe-White. 'The postmistress, or whatever she is. She told him we were asking questions.'

'How do you know?'

'Suddenly he's in a hurry.' Gray checked traffic, cursed, and pulled Brianna in a zigzagging pattern between a truck and a sedan. Her heart pounded in her throat as both drivers retaliated with rude blasts of their horns. Already primed, Smythe-White glanced back, spotted them, and began to run.

'Stay here,' Gray ordered.

'I'll not.' She sprinted after him, her long legs keeping her no more than three paces behind. Their quarry might have dodged and swerved, elbowing pedestrians aside, but it was hardly a contest with two younger, healthy pursuers on his heels.

As if he'd come to the same conclusion, he came to a stop just outside a chemist's, panting. He dragged out a snowy white handkerchief to wipe his brow, then turned, letting his eyes widen behind his sparkling lenses.

'Well, Miss Concannon, Mr. Thane, what an unexpected surprise.' He had the wit, and the wherewithal, to smile pleasantly even as he pressed a hand to his speeding heart. 'The world is indeed a small place. Are you in Wales on holiday?'

'No more than you,' Gray tossed back. 'We've got business to discuss, pal. You want to talk here, or should we hunt up the local constabulary?'

All innocence, Smythe-White blinked. In a familiar habit, he took off his glasses, polished the lenses. 'Business? I'm afraid I'm at a loss. This isn't about that unfortunate incident at your inn, Miss Concannon? As I told you, I lost nothing and have no complaint at all.'

'It's not surprising you'd have lost nothing, as you did the damage yourself. Did you have to dump all my dry goods on the floor?'

'Excuse me?'

'Looks like the cops, then,' Gray said and took Smythe-White by the arm.

'I'm afraid I don't have time to dally just now, though it is lovely to run into you this way.' He tried, and failed, to dislodge Gray's grip. 'As you could probably tell, I'm in a hurry. An appointment I'd completely forgotten. I'm dreadfully late.'

'Do you want the stock certificate back or not?' Gray had the pleasure of seeing the man pause, reconsider. Behind the lenses of the glasses he carefully readjusted, his eyes were suddenly sly.

'I'm afraid I don't understand.'

'You understand fine, and so do we. A scam's a scam in any country, any language. Now, I'm not sure what the penalty for fraud, confidence games, and counterfeiting stocks is in the United Kingdom, but they can be pretty rough on pros where I come from. And you used the mail, Smythe-White. Which was probably a mistake. Once you put a stamp on it and hand it over to the local post, fraud becomes mail fraud. A much nastier business.'

He let Smythe-White sweat that before he continued. 'And then there's the idea of basing yourself in Wales and doing scams across the Irish Sea. Makes it international. You could be looking at a very long stretch.'

'Now, now, I don't see any reason for threats.' Smythe-White smiled again, but sweat had begun to pearl on his brow. 'We're reasonable people. And it's a small matter, a very small matter we can resolve easily, and to everyone's satisfaction.'

'Why don't we talk about that?'

'Yes, yes, why don't we?' He brightened instantly. 'Over a drink. I'd be delighted to buy both of you a drink. There's a pub just around the corner here. A quiet one. Why don't we have a friendly pint or two while we hash all this business out?'

'Why don't we? Brie?'

'But I think we should –'

'Talk,' Gray said smoothly and, keeping one hand firm on Smythe-White's arm, took hers. 'How long have you been in the game?' Gray asked conversationally.

'Oh, dear, since before either of you were born, I imagine. I'm out of it now, truly, completely. Just two years ago, my wife and I bought a little antique shop in Surrey.'

'I thought your wife was dead,' Brianna put in as Smythe-White led the way to the pub.

'Oh, no, indeed. Iris is hale and hearty. Minding things for me while I put this little business to rest. We do quite well,' he added as they stepped into the pub. 'Quite well. In addition to the antique shop, we have interests in several other enterprises. All quite legal, I assure you.' Gentleman to the last, he held Brianna's chair out for her. 'A tour company, First Flight, you might have heard of it.'

Impressed, Gray lifted a brow. 'It's become one of the top concerns in Europe.'

Smythe-White preened. 'I like to think that my managerial skills had something to do with that. We started it as rather a clandestine smuggling operation initially.' He smiled apologetically at Brianna. 'My dear, I hope you're not too shocked.'

She simply shook her head. 'Nothing else could shock me at this point.'

'Shall we have a Harp?' he asked, playing the gracious host. 'It seems appropriate.' Taking their assent for granted, Smythe-White ordered for the table. 'Now then, as I said, we did do a bit of smuggling. Tobacco and liquor primarily. But we didn't have much of a taste for it, and the touring end actually made more of a profit with no risk, so to speak. And as Iris and I were getting on in years, we decided to retire. In a manner of speaking. Do you know the stock game was one of our last? She's always been keen on antiques, my Iris, so we used the profits from that to buy and stock our little shop.' He winced, smiled sheepishly. 'I suppose it's poor taste to mention that.'

'Don't let that stop you.' Gray kicked back in his chair as their beer was served.

'Well, imagine our surprise, our dismay, when we received your letter. I've kept that post office box open because we have interests in Wales, but the Triquarter thing was well in the past. All but forgotten really. I'm ashamed to say your father, rest him, slipped through the cracks in our reorganization efforts. I hope you'll take it as it's meant when I say I found him a thoroughly delightful man.'

Brianna merely sighed. 'Thank you.'

'I must say, Iris and I very near panicked when we heard from you. If we were connected with that old life, our reputation, the little businesses we've lovingly built in the past few years could be ruined. Not to mention then, ah . . .' He dabbed at his lip with a napkin. 'Legal ramifications.'

'You could have ignored the letter,' Gray said.

'And we considered it. Did ignore the first. But when

Brianna wrote again, we felt something had to be done. The certificate.' He had the grace to flush. 'It's lowering to admit it, but I actually signed my legal name to it. Arrogance, I suppose, and I wasn't using it at the time. Having it float to the surface now, come to the attention of the authorities could be rather awkward.'

'It's as you said,' Brianna murmured, staring at Gray. 'It's almost exactly as you said.'

'I'm good,' he murmured and patted her hand. 'So, you came to Blackthorn to check out the situation for yourself.'

'I did. Iris couldn't join me as we were expecting a rather lovely shipment of Chippendale. Admittedly, I got a charge out of going under again. A bit of nostalgia, a little adventure. I was absolutely charmed by your home, and more than a little concerned when I discovered that you were related by marriage to Rogan Sweeney. After all, he is an important man, a sharp one. It worried me that he would take charge. So . . . when the opportunity presented itself, I took a quick look around for the certificate.'

He put a hand over Brianna's, gave it an avuncular squeeze. 'I do apologize for the mess and inconvenience. I couldn't be sure how long I'd have alone, you see. I'd hoped if I could put my hands on it, we could put a period to the whole unhappy business. But —'

'I gave the certificate to Rogan for safekeeping,' Brianna told him.

'Ah. I was afraid of something like that. I find it odd he didn't follow up.'

'His wife was about to have a baby, and he had the opening of the new gallery.' Brianna stopped herself, realized she was very nearly apologizing for her brother-in-law. 'I could handle the matter myself.'

'I began to suspect that as well after only a few hours in your home. An organized soul is a dangerous one to someone in my former trade. I did come back once, think-ing I might have another go, but between your dog and your hero in residence, I had to take to my heels.'

Brianna's chin came up. 'You were looking in my win-dow.'

'With no disrespectful intent, I promise you. My dear, I'm old enough to be your father, and quite happily mar-ried.' He huffed a bit, as if insulted. 'Well, I offered to buy the stock back, and the offer holds.'

'A half pound a piece,' Gray reminded him dryly.

'Double what Tom Concannon paid. I have the paper-work if you need proof.'

'Oh, I'm sure someone with your talent could come up with any paper transaction he wanted.'

Smythe-White let out a long-suffering sigh. 'I'm sure you feel you have the right to accuse me of that sort of behavior.'

'I think the police would be fascinated by your behavior.'

Eyes on Gray, Smythe-White took a hasty sip of beer. 'What purpose would that serve, really now? Two people in their golden years, taxpayers, devoted spouses, ruined and sent to prison for past indiscretions.'

'You cheated people,' Brianna snapped back. 'You cheated my father.'

'I gave your father exactly what he paid for, Brianna. A dream. He walked off from our dealing a happy man, hop-ing, as too many hope, to make something out of next to nothing.' He smiled at her gently. 'He really only wanted the hope that he could.'

Because it was true, she could find nothing to say. 'It doesn't make it right,' she decided at length.

'But we've mended our ways. Changing a life is an effortful thing, my dear. It takes work and patience and determination.'

She lifted her gaze again as his words hit home. If what he said of himself was true, there were two people at that table who had made that effort. Would she condemn Gray for what he'd done in the past? Would she want to see some old mistake spring up and drag him back?

'I don't want you or your wife to go to prison, Mr. Smythe-White.'

'He knows the rules,' Gray interrupted, squeezing Brianna's hand hard. 'You play, you pay. Maybe we can bypass the authorities, but the courtesy is worth more than a thousand pounds.'

'As I explained –' Smythe-White began.

'The stock isn't worth dick,' Gray returned. 'But the certificate. I'd say that would come in at ten thousand.'

'Ten thousand *pounds*?' Smythe-White blustered while Brianna simply sat with her mouth hanging open. 'That's blackmail. It's robbery. It's –'

'A pound a unit,' Gray finished. 'More than reasonable with what you've got riding on it. And with the tidy profit you made from the investors, I think Tom Concannon's dream should come true. I don't think that's blackmail. I think it's justice. And justice isn't negotiable.'

Pale, Smythe-White sat back. Again, he took out his handkerchief and mopped his face. 'Young man, you're squeezing my heart.'

'Nope, just your bankbook. Which is fat enough to afford it. You caused Brie a lot of trouble, a lot of worry. You messed with her home. Now, while I might sympathize with your predicament, I don't think you realize just what that home means to her. You made her cry.'

'Oh, well, really.' Smythe-White waved the handkerchief, dabbed with it again. 'I do apologize, most sincerely. This is dreadful, really dreadful. I have no idea what Iris would say.'

'If she's smart,' Gray drawled, 'I think she'd say pay up and count your blessings.'

He sighed, stuffed the damp handkerchief into his pocket. 'Ten thousand pounds. You're a hard man, Mr. Thane.'

'Herb, I think I can call you Herb because, at this moment, we both know I'm your best friend.'

He nodded sadly. 'Unfortunately true.' Changing tactics, he looked hopefully at Brianna. 'I really have caused you distress, and I'm terribly sorry. We'll clear the whole matter up. I wonder, perhaps we could cancel the debt in trade? A nice trip for you? Or furnishings for your inn. We have some lovely pieces at the shop.'

'Money talks,' Gray said before Brianna could think of a response.

'A hard man,' Smythe-White repeated and let his shoulders sag. 'I suppose there's very little choice in the matter. I'll write you a check.'

'It's going to have to be cash.'

Another sigh. 'Yes, of course it is. All right then, we'll make arrangements. Naturally, I don't carry such amounts with me on business jaunts.'

'Naturally,' Gray agreed. 'But you can get it. By tomorrow.'

'Really, another day or two would be more reasonable,' Smythe-White began, then seeing the gleam in Gray's eyes, surrendered. 'But I can wire Iris for the money. It will be no trouble to have it here by tomorrow.'

'I didn't think it would.'

Smythe-White smiled wanly. 'If you'd excuse me. I need the loo.' Shaking his head, he rose and walked to the rear of the pub.

'I don't understand. I don't,' Brianna whispered when Smythe-White was out of earshot. 'I kept quiet because you kept kicking me under the table but –'

'Nudging you,' Gray corrected. 'I was only nudging you.'

'Aye, and I'll have a limp for a week. But my point is, you're letting him go, and you're making him pay such a huge amount. It doesn't seem right.'

'It's exactly right. Your father wanted his dream, and he's getting his dream. Good old Herb knows that sometimes a con goes sour and you count your loses. You don't want to send him to jail and neither do I.'

'No, I don't. But to take his money –'

'He took your father, and that five hundred pounds couldn't have been easy for your family to spare.'

'No, but –'

'Brianna. What would your father say?'

Beaten, she dropped her chin on her fist. 'He'd think it was a grand joke.'

'Exactly.' Gray cast his eyes toward the men's room, narrowed them. 'He's taking too long. Hang on a minute.'

Brianna frowned into her glass. Then her lips began to curve. It really was a grand joke. One her father would have greatly appreciated.

She didn't expect to see the money, not such a huge amount. Not really. It was enough to know they'd settled it all, with no real harm done.

Glancing up, she saw Gray, eyes hot, storm out of the men's room and head toward the bar. He had a quick conversation with the barman before coming back to the table.

His face had cleared again as he dropped into his chair and picked up his beer.

'Well,' Brianna said after the moment stretched out.

'Oh, he's gone. Right out the window. Canny old bastard.'

'Gone?' Staggered by the turn of events, she shut her eyes. 'Gone,' she repeated. 'And to think, he had me liking him, believing him.'

'That's exactly what a con artist's supposed to do. But in this case, I think we got more of the truth than not.'

'What do we do now? I just don't want to go to the police, Gray. I couldn't live with myself imagining that little man and his wife in jail.' A sudden thought stabbed through, making her eyes pop wide. 'Oh, bloody hell. Do you suppose he really has a wife at all?'

'Probably.' Gray took a sip of beer, considered. 'As to what we do now, now we go back to Clare, let him stew. Wait him out. It'll be easy enough to find him again if and when we want.'

'How?'

'Through First Flight Tours. Then there's this.' Before Brianna's astonished eyes, Gray drew out a wallet. 'I picked his pocket when we were out on the street. Insurance,' he explained when she continued to gape. 'After all these years, I'm not even rusty.' He shook his head at himself. 'I should be ashamed.' Then he grinned and tapped the billfold against his palm. 'Don't look so shocked, it's only a little cash and I.D.'

Calmly Gray took bills from the wallet and stuck them in his own pocket. 'He still owes me a hundred pounds, more or less. I'd say he keeps his real money in a clip. He's got a London address,' Gray went on, tucking the lifted wallet away. 'I glanced through it in the men's room. There's also a snapshot of a rather attractive, matronly looking woman. Iris, I'd think. Oh, and his name's Carstairs. John B., not Smythe-White.'

Brianna pressed her fingers between her eyes. 'My head's spinning.'

'Don't worry, Brie, I guarantee we'll be hearing from him again. Ready to go?'

'I suppose.' Still reeling from the events of the day, she rose. 'He's a nerve, that one. He clipped out, too, without buying us the drinks.'

'Oh, he bought them.' Gray hooked an arm through hers, sending a salute to the barman on the way out. 'He owns the damn pub.'

'He –' She stopped, stared, then began to laugh.

Chapter Nineteen

It was good to be home. Adventures and the glamour of traveling were all very fine, Brianna thought, but so were the simple pleasures of your own bed, your own roof, and the familiar view out your own window.

She would not mind winging off somewhere again, as long as there was home to come back to.

Content with routine, Brianna worked in her garden, staking her budding delphiniums and monkshood, while the scent of just blooming lavender honeyed the air. Bees hummed nearby busy flirting with her lupine.

From the rear of the house came the sound of children laughing, and Con's excited barks as he chased the ball her young American visitors tossed for him.

New York seemed very far away, as exotic as the pearls she'd tucked deep inside her dresser drawer. And the day she had spent in Wales was like some odd, colorful play.

She glanced up, adjusting the brim of her hat as she studied Gray's window. He was working, had been almost around the clock since they'd set down their bags. She wondered where he was now, what place, what time, what people surrounded him. And what mood would he be in when he came back to her?

Irritable if the writing went badly, she thought. Touchy as a stray dog. If it went well, he'd be hungry – for food, and for her. She smiled to herself and gently tied the fragile stems to the stakes.

How amazing it was to be wanted the way he wanted her. Amazing for both of them, she decided. He was no more used to it than she. And it worried him a bit. Idly she brushed her fingers over a clump of bellflowers.

He'd told her things about himself she knew he'd told

no one else. And that worried him as well. How foolish of him to have believed she would think less of him for what he'd been through, what he'd done to survive.

She could only imagine the fear and the pride of a young boy who had never known the love and demands, the sorrows and the comforts, of family. How alone he'd been, and how alone he'd made himself, out of that pride and fear. And somehow through it, he'd fashioned himself into a caring and admirable man.

No, she didn't think less of him. She only loved him more for the knowing.

His story had made her think of her own, and study on her life. Her parents hadn't loved each other, and that was hurtful. But Brianna knew she'd had her father's love. Had always known it and taken comfort from it. She'd had a home and roots that kept body and soul anchored.

And in her own way Maeve had loved her. At least her mother had felt the duty toward the children she'd borne enough to stay with them. She could have turned her back at any time, Brianna mused. That option had never occurred to Brianna before, and she mulled it over now as she enjoyed the gardening chores.

Her mother could have walked away from the family she'd created – and resented. Gone back to the career that had meant so much to her. Even if it was only duty that had kept her, it was more than Gray had had.

Maeve was hard, embittered; she too often twisted the heart of the scriptures she so religiously read to suit her own means and uses. She could use the canons of the Church like a hammer. But she had stayed.

With a little sigh Brianna shifted to stake the next plant. The time would come for forgiveness. She hoped she had forgiveness in her.

'You're supposed to look happy when you garden, not troubled.'

Putting a hand on top of her hat, Brianna lifted her head to look at Gray. A good day, she decided at once. When he'd had a good day, you could all but feel the pleasure of it vibrate from him.

'I was letting my mind wander.'

'So was I. I got up and looked out of the window and saw you. For the life of me I couldn't think of anything else.'

'It's a lovely day for being out-of-doors. And you started working at dawn.' With quick and oddly tender move-ments, she staked another stem. 'Is it going well for you, then?'

'It's going incredibly well.' He sat beside her, indulged himself with a gulp of the perfumed air. 'I can barely keep up with myself. I murdered a lovely young woman today.'

She snorted with laughter. 'And sound very pleased with yourself.'

'I was very fond of her, but she had to go. And her mur-der is going to spearhead the outrage that will lead to the killer's downfall.'

'Was it in the ruins we went to that she died?'

'No, that was someone else. This one met her fate in the Burren, near the Druid's Altar.'

'Oh.' Despite herself, Brianna shivered. 'I've always been fond of that spot.'

'Me, too. He left her stretched over the crown stone, like an offering to a bloodthirsty god. Naked, of course.'

'Of course. And I suppose some poor unfortunate tourist will find her.'

'He already has. An American student on a walking tour of Europe.' Gray clucked his tongue. 'I don't think he'll ever be the same.' Leaning over, he kissed her shoulder. 'So, how was your day?'

'Not as eventful. I saw off those lovely newlyweds from Limerick this morning, and I minded the American children while their parents had a lie-in.' Eagle-eyed, she spotted a tiny weed and mercilessly ripped it out of the bed. 'They helped me make hot cross buns. After, the family had a day at Bunratty, the folk park, you know. Only returned shortly ago. We're expecting another family this evening, from Edinburgh, who stayed here two years past. They've two teenagers, boys, who both fell a bit in love with me last time.'

'Really?' Idly he ran a fingertip down her shoulder. 'I'll have to intimidate them.'

'Oh, I imagine they're over it now.' She glanced up, smiled curiously at his snort of laughter. 'What?'

'I was just thinking you've probably ruined those boys for life. They'll never find anyone to compare with you.'

'What nonsense.' She reached for another stake. 'I talked to Maggie earlier this afternoon. They might be in Dublin another week or two. And we'll have the baptism when they get back. Murphy and I are to be godparents.'

He shifted, sat cross-legged now. 'What does that mean, exactly, in Catholic?'

'Oh, not much different, I'd imagine, than it means in any church. We'll speak for the baby during the service, like sponsors, you see. And we'll promise to look after his religious upbringing, if something should happen to Maggie and Rogan.'

'Kind of a heavy responsibility.'

'It's an honor,' she said with a smile. 'Were you not baptized ever, Grayson?'

'I have no idea. Probably not.' He moved his shoulders, then cocked a brow at her pensive frown. 'What now? Worried I'll burn in hell because nobody sprinkled water over my head?'

293

'No.' Uncomfortable, she looked away again. 'And the water's only a symbol, of cleansing away Original Sin.'

'How original is it?'

She looked back at him, shook her head. 'You don't want me explaining catechism and such, and I'm not trying to convert you. Still, I know Maggie and Rogan would like you at the service.'

'Sure, I'll go. Be interesting. How's the kid anyway?'

'She says Liam's growing like a weed.' Brianna concentrated on what her hands were doing and tried not to let her heart ache too much. 'I told her about Mr. Smythe-White – I mean Mr. Carstairs.'

'And?'

'She laughed till I thought she'd burst. She thought Rogan might take the matter a bit less lightly, but we both agreed it was so like Da to tumble into a mess like this. It's a bit like having him back for a time. "Brie," he might say, "if you don't risk something, you don't win something." And I'm to tell you she was impressed with your cleverness in tracking Mr. Carstairs down, and would you like the job we've hired that detective for.'

'No luck on that?'

'Actually, there was something.' She sat back again, laid her hands on her thighs. 'Someone, one of Amanda Dougherty's cousins, I think, thought she might have gone north in New York, into the mountains. It seems she'd been there before and was fond of the area. The detective, he's taking a trip there, to, oh, that place where Rip van Winkle fell asleep.'

'The Catskills?'

'Aye, that's it. So, with luck, he'll find something there.'

Gray picked up a garden stake himself, eyeing it down the length, wondering absently how successful a murder weapon it might be. 'What'll you do if you discover you've got a half brother or sister?'

'Well, I think I would write to Miss Dougherty first.' She'd already thought it through, carefully. 'I don't want to hurt anyone. But from the tone of her letters to Da, I think she'd be a woman who might be glad to know that she, and her child, are welcome.'

'And they would be,' he mused, setting the stake aside again. 'This, what – twenty-six-, twenty-seven-year-old stranger would be welcome.'

'Of course.' She tilted her head, surprised he would question it. 'He or she would have Da's blood, wouldn't they? As Maggie and I do. He wouldn't want us to turn our back on family.'

'But he –' Gray broke off, shrugged.

'You're thinking he did,' Brianna said mildly. 'I don't know if that's the way of it. We'll never know, I suppose, what he did when he learned of it. But turn his back, no, it wouldn't have been in him. He kept her letters, and knowing him, I think he would have grieved for the child he would never be able to see.'

Her gaze wandered, followed the flitting path of a speck-led butterfly. 'He was a dreamer. Grayson, but he was first and always a family man. He gave up a great deal to keep this family whole. More than I'd ever guessed until I read those letters.'

'I'm not criticizing him.' He thought of the grave, and the flowers Brianna had planted over it. 'I just hate to see you troubled.'

'I'll be less troubled when we find out what we can.'

'And your mother, Brianna? How do you think she's going to react if this all comes out?'

Her eyes cooled, and her chin took on a stubborn tilt. 'I'll deal with that when and if I have to. She'll have to accept what is. For once in her life, she'll have to accept it.'

'You're still angry with her,' he observed. 'About Rory.'

'Rory's over and done. And has been.'

He took her hands before she could reach for her stakes. And waited patiently.

'All right, I'm angry. For what she did then, for the way she spoke to you, and maybe most of all for the way she made what I feel for you seem wicked. I'm not good at being angry. It makes my stomach hurt.'

'Then I hope you're not going to be angry with me,' he said as he heard the sound of a car approaching.

'Why would I?'

Saying nothing, he rose, drawing her to her feet. Together they watched the car pull up, stop. Lottie leaned out with a hearty wave before she and Maeve alighted.

'I called Lottie,' Gray murmured, squeezing Brianna's hand when it tensed in his. 'Sort of invited them over for a visit.'

'I don't want another argument with guests in the house.' Brianna's voice had chilled. 'You shouldn't have done this, Grayson. I'd have gone to see her tomorrow and had words in her home instead of mine.'

'Brie, your garden's a picture,' Lottie called out as they approached. 'And what a lovely day you have for it.' In her motherly way she embraced Brianna and kissed her cheek. 'Did you have a fine time in New York City?'

'I did, yes.'

'Living the high life,' Maeve said with a snort. 'And leaving decency behind.'

'Oh, Maeve, leave be.' Lottie gave an impatient wave. 'I want to hear about New York City.'

'Come in and have some tea then,' Brianna invited. 'I've brought you back some souveniers.'

'Oh, what a sweetheart you are. Souveniers, Maeve, from America.' She beamed at Gray as they walked to the house. 'And your movie, Grayson? Was it grand?'

'It was.' He tucked her hand through his arm, gave it a pat. 'And after I had to compete with Tom Cruise for Brianna's attention.'

'No! You don't say?' Lottie's voice squeaked and her eyes all but fell out in astonishment. 'Did you hear that, Maeve? Brianna met Tom Cruise.'

'I don't pay mind to movie actors,' Maeve grumbled, desperately impressed. 'It's all wild living and divorces with them.'

'Hah! Never does she miss an Errol Flynn movie when it comes on the telly.' Point scored, Lottie waltzed into the kitchen and went directly to the stove. 'Now, I'll fix the tea, Brianna. That way you can go fetch our presents.'

'I've some berry tarts to go with it.' Brianna shot Gray a look as she headed for her bedroom. 'Baked fresh this morning.'

'Ah, that's lovely. Do you know, Grayson, my oldest son, that's Peter, he went to America. To Boston he went, to visit cousins we have there. He visited the harbor where you Yanks dumped the British tea off the boat. Gone back twice again, he has, and taken his children. His own son, Shawn, is going to move there and take a job.'

She chatted on about Boston and her family while Maeve sat in sullen silence. A few moments later Brianna came back in, carrying two small boxes.

'There's so many shops there,' she commented, determined to be cheerful. 'Everywhere you look something else is for sale. It was hard to decide what to bring you.'

'Whatever it is, it'll be lovely.' Eager to see, Lottie set down a plate of tarts and reached for her box. 'Oh, would you look at this?' She lifted the small, decorative bottle to the light where it gleamed rich blue.

''Tis for scent, if you like, or just for setting out.'

'It's lovely as it can be,' Lottie declared. 'Look how it's got flowers carved right into it. Lilies. How sweet of you, Brianna. Oh, and Maeve, yours is red as a ruby. With poppies. Won't these look fine, setting on the dresser?'

'They're pretty enough.' Maeve couldn't quite resist running her finger over the etching. If she had a weakness, it was for pretty things. She felt she'd never gotten her fair share of them. 'It was kind of you to give me a passing thought while you were off staying in a grand hotel and consorting with movie stars.'

'Tom Cruise,' Lottie said, easily ignoring the sarcasm. 'Is he as handsome a lad as he looks in the films?'

'Every bit, and charming as well. He and his wife may come here.'

'Here?' Amazed at the thought, Lottie pressed a hand to her breast. 'Right here to Blackthorn Cottage?'

Brianna smiled at Lottie. 'So he said.'

'That'll be the day,' Maeve muttered. 'What would so rich and high-flying a man want with staying at this place?'

'Peace,' Brianna said coolly. 'And a few good meals. What everyone else wants when they stay here.'

'And you get plenty of both in Blackthorn,' Gray put in. 'I've done a great deal of traveling, Mrs. Concannon, and I've never been to a place as lovely or as comfortable as this. You must be very proud of Brianna for her success.'

'Hmph. I imagine right enough you're comfortable here, in my daughter's bed.'

'It would be a foolish man who wasn't,' he said amiably before Brianna could comment. 'You're to be commended for raising such a warm-hearted, kind-natured woman who also has the brains and the dedication to run a successful business. She amazes me.'

Stumped, Maeve said nothing. The compliment was a curve she hadn't expected. She was still searching through it for the insult when Gray crossed to the counter.

'I picked up a little something for both of you myself.' He'd left the bag in the kitchen before he'd gone out to Brianna. Setting the scene, he thought now, as he wanted it to play.

'Why, isn't that kind.' Surprise and pleasure coursed through Lottie's voice as she accepted the box Gray offered.

'Just tokens,' Gray said, smiling as Brianna simply stared at him, baffled. Lottie's little gasp of delight pleased him enormously.

'It's a little bird. Look here, Maeve, a crystal bird. See how it catches the sunlight.'

'You can hang it by a wire in the window,' Gray explained. 'It'll make rainbows for you. You make me think of rainbows, Lottie.'

'Oh, go on with you. Rainbows.' She blinked back a film of moisture and rose to give Gray a hard hug. 'I'll be hanging it right in our front window. Thank you, Gray, you're a darling man. Isn't he a darling man, Maeve?'

Maeve grunted, hesitated over the lid of her gift box. By rights, she knew she should toss the thing into his face rather than take a gift from a man of his kind. But Lottie's crystal bird was such a pretty thing. And the combination of basic greed and curiosity had her flipping open the lid.

Speechless, she lifted out the gilt and glass shaped like a heart. It had a lid as well, and when she opened it, music played.

'Oh, a music box.' Lottie clapped her hands together. 'What a beautiful thing, and how clever. What's the tune it's playing?'

'*Stardust*,' Maeve murmured and caught herself just before she began to hum along with it. 'An old tune.'

'A classic,' Gray added. 'They didn't have anything Irish, but this seemed to suit you.'

The corners of Maeve's mouth turned up as the music charmed her. She cleared her throat, shot Gray a level look. 'Thank you, Mr. Thane.'

'Gray,' he said easily.

Thirty minutes later Brianna placed her hands on her hips. There was only she and Gray in the kitchen now, and the plate of tarts was empty. '"Twas like a bribe.'

'No, 'twasn't like a bribe,' he said, mimicking her. 'It *was* a bribe. Damn good one, too. She smiled at me before she left.'

Brianna huffed. 'I don't know who I should be more ashamed of, you or her.'

'Then just think of it as a peace offering. I don't want your mother giving you grief over me, Brianna.'

'Clever you were. A music box.'

'I thought so. Every time she listens to it, she'll think of me. Before too long, she'll convince herself I'm not such a bad sort after all.'

She didn't want to smile. It was outrageous. 'Figured her out, have you?'

'A good writer's a good observer. She's used to complaining.' He opened the refrigerator, helped himself to a beer. 'Trouble is, she doesn't have nearly enough to complain about these days. Must be frustrating.' He popped the top off the bottle, took a swig. 'And she's afraid you've closed yourself off to her. She doesn't know how to make the move that'll close the gap.'

'And I'm supposed to.'

'You will. It's the way you're made. She knows that, but she's worried this might be the exception.' He tipped up Brianna's chin with a fingertip. 'It won't. Family's too important to you, and you've already started to forgive her.'

Brianna turned away to tidy the kitchen. 'It's not always

comfortable, having someone see into you as though you were made of glass.' But she sighed, listened to her own heart. 'Perhaps I have started to forgive her. I don't know how long the process will take.' Meticulously she washed the teacups. 'Your ploy today has undoubtedly speeded that along.'

'That was the idea.' From behind her he slipped his arms around her waist. 'So, you're not mad.'

'No, I'm not mad.' Turning, she rested her head in the curve of his shoulder, where she liked it best. 'I love you, Grayson.'

He stroked her hair, looking out the window, saying nothing.

They had soft weather over the next few days, the kind that made working in his room like existing in endless twilight. It was easy to lose track of time, to let himself fall into the book with only the slightest awareness of the world around him.

He was closing in on the killer, on that final, violent meeting. He'd developed a respect for his villain's mind, mirroring perfectly the same emotions of his hero. The man was as clever as he was vicious. Not mad, Gray mused as another part of his mind visualized the scene he was creating.

Some would call the villain mad, unable to conceive that the cruelty, the ruthlessness of the murders could spring from a mind not twisted by insanity.

Gray knew better – and so did his hero. The killer wasn't mad, but was cold-bloodedly sane. He was simply, very simply, evil.

He already knew exactly how the final hunt would develop, almost every step and word was clear in his head. In the rain, in the dark, through the wind-swept ruins where blood had already been spilled. He knew his hero would see himself, just for one instant see the worst of himself reflected in the man he pursued.

And that final battle would be more than right against wrong, good against evil. It would be, on that rain-soaked, wind-howling precipice, a desperate fight for redemption.

But that wouldn't be the end. And it was in search of that unknown final scene that Gray raced. He'd imagined, almost from the beginning, his hero leaving the village, leaving the woman. Both of them would have been changed irrevocably by the violence that had shattered that quiet spot. And by what had happened between them.

Then each would go on with the rest of his life, or try. Separately, because he'd created them as two dynamically opposing forces, drawn together, certainly, but never for the long haul.

Now, it wasn't so clear. He wondered where the hero was going, and why. Why the woman turned slowly, as he'd planned, moving toward the door of her cottage without looking back.

It should have been simple, true to their characters, satisfying. Yet the closer he came to reaching that moment, the more uneasy he became.

Kicking back in his chair, he looked blankly around the room. He hadn't a clue what time of day it was, or how long he'd been chained to his work. But one thing was certain, he'd run dry.

He needed a walk, he decided, rain or no rain. And he needed to stop second-guessing himself and let that final scene unfold in its own way, and its own time.

He started downstairs, marveling at the quiet before he remembered the family from Scotland had gone. It had amused him, when he'd crawled out of his cave long enough to notice, how the two young men had sniffed around Brianna's heels, competing for her attention.

It was tough to blame them.

The sound of Brianna's voice had him turning toward the kitchen.

'Well, good day to you, Kenny Feeney. Are you visiting your grandmother?'

'I am, Miss Concannon. We'll be here for two weeks.'

'I'm happy to see you. You've grown so. Will you come in and have a cup of tea and some cake?'

'I wouldn't mind.'

Gray watched a boy of about twelve give a crooked-toothed grin as he stepped out of the rain. He carried something large and apparently heavy wrapped in newspaper. 'Gran sent you a leg of lamb, Miss Concannon. We slaughtered just this morning.'

'Oh, that's kind of her.' With apparent pleasure Brianna took the grisly package while Gray – writer of blood-thirsty thrillers – felt his stomach churn.

'I have a currant cake here. You'll have a piece, won't you, and take the rest back to her?'

'I will.' Dutifully stepping out of his wellies, the boy stripped off his raincoat and cap. Then he spotted Gray. 'Good day to you,' he said politely.

'Oh, Gray, I didn't hear you come down. This is young Kenny Feeney, grandson of Alice and Peter Feeney from the farm down the road a bit. Kenny, this is Grayson Thane, a guest of mine.'

'The Yank,' Kenny said as he solemnly shook Gray's hand. 'You write books with murders in them, my gran says.'

'That's right. Do you like to read?'

'I like books about cars or sports. Maybe you could write a book about football.'

'I'll keep it in mind.'

'Will you have some cake, Gray?' Brianna asked as she sliced. 'Or would you rather have a sandwich now?'

He cast a wary eye toward the lump under the newspaper. He imagined it baaing. 'No, nothing. Not now.'

'Do you live in Kansas City?' Kenny wanted to know. 'My brother does. He went to the States three years ago this winter. He plays in a band.'

'No, I don't live there, but I've been there. It's a nice town.'

'Pat, he says it's better than anywhere. I'm saving me money so I can go over when I'm old enough.'

'Will you be leaving us, then, Kenny?' Brianna ran a hand over the boy's carrotty mop.

'When I'm eighteen.' He took another happy bite of cake, washed it down with tea. 'You can get good work there, and good pay. Maybe I'll play for an American football team. They have one, right there in Kansas City, you know.'

'I've heard rumors,' Gray said and smiled.

'This is grand cake, Miss Concannon.' Kenny polished off his piece.

When he left a bit later, Brianna watched him dart over the fields, the cake bundled under his arm like one of his precious footballs.

'So many of them go,' she murmured. 'We lose them day after day, year after year. Shaking her head, she closed the kitchen door again. 'Well, I'll see to your room now that you're out of it.'

'I was going to take a walk. Why don't you come with me?'

'I could take a short one. Just let me –' She smiled apologetically as the phone rang. 'Good afternoon, Blackthorn Cottage. Oh, Arlene, how are you?' Brianna held out a hand for Gray's. 'That's good to hear. Yes, I'm fine and well. Gray's just here, I'll . . . oh?' Her brow cocked, then she smiled again. 'That would be grand. Of course, you and your husband are more than welcome. September's a lovely time of the year. I'm so pleased you're coming. Yes, I have it. September fifteenth, for five days. Indeed yes, you can make a number of day trips from right here. Shall I send you some information about it? No, it would be my pleasure. And I look forward to it as well. Yes, Gray's here as I said. Just a moment.'

He took the phone, but looked at Brianna. 'She's coming to Ireland in September?'

'On holiday, she and her husband. It seems I tickled her curiosity. She has news for you.'

'Mmm–hmmm. Hey, gorgeous,' he said into the receiver. 'Going to play tourist in the west counties?' He grinned, nodded when Brianna offered him tea. 'No, I think you'll love it. The weather?' He glanced out the window at the steadily falling rain. 'Magnificent.' He winked at Brianna, sipped his tea. 'No, I didn't get your package yet. What's in it?'

Nodding, he murmured to Brianna. 'Reviews. On the movie.' He paused, listening 'What's the hype? Mmm. Brilliant, I like brilliant. Wait, say that one again. "From the fertile mind of Grayson Thane," ' he repeated for Brianna's benefit. 'Oscar worthy. Two thumbs straight up.' He laughed at that. 'And the most powerful movie of the year. Not bad, even if it's only May. No, I don't have my tongue in my cheek. It's great. Even better. Early quotes on the new book,' he told Brianna.

'But you haven't finished the new book.'

'Not that new book. The one that's coming out in July. That's the new book, what I'm working on is the new manuscript. No, just explaining some basic publishing to the landlady.'

Pursing his lips, he listened. 'Really? I like it.'

With an eye on him Brianna went to the stove for her roaster. He was making noises, the occasional comment. Occasionally he'd grin or shake his head.

'It's a good thing I'm not wearing a hat. My head's getting big. Yeah, publicity sent me an endless letter about the plans for the tour. I've agreed to be at their mercy for three weeks. No, you make the decision on that sort of thing. It just takes too long for them to mail stuff. Yeah, you, too. I'll tell her. Talk to you later.'

'The movie's doing well,' Brianna said, trying to resist pumping him.

'Twelve million in its first week, which is nothing to sneeze at. And the critics are smiling on it. Apparently they like the upcoming book, too. I'm at the top of my form,' he said, reaching into a canister for a cookie. 'I've created a story dense in atmosphere with prose as sharp as a honed dagger. With, ah, gut-wrenching twists and dark, biting humor. Not too shabby.'

'You should be very proud.'

'I wrote it almost a year ago.' He shrugged, chewed. 'Yeah, it's nice. I have an affection for it that will dim considerably after thirty-one cities in three weeks.'

'The tour you were speaking of.'

'Right. Talk shows, bookstores, airports, and hotel rooms.' With a laugh he popped the rest of the cookie into his mouth. 'What a life.'

'It suits you well, I'd think.'

'Right down to the ground.'

She nodded, not wanting to be sad, and set the roaster on the counter. 'In July, you say.'

'Yeah. It's crept up on me. I've lost track. I've been here four months.'

'Sometimes it seems you've been here always.'

306

'Getting used to me.' He grazed an absent hand over his chin, and she could see his mind was elsewhere. 'How about that walk?'

'I really need to get dinner on.'

'I'll wait.' He leaned companionably against the counter. 'So, what's for dinner?'

'Leg of lamb.'

Gray gave a little sigh. 'I thought so.'

Chapter Twenty

On a clear day in the middle of May, Brianna watched the workmen dig the foundation for her greenhouse. A small dream, she thought, flipping the braid she wore from her shoulder to her back, come true.

She smiled down at the baby who gurgled in the portable swing beside her. She'd learned to be content with small dreams, she thought, bending to kiss her nephew on his curling black hair.

'He's grown so, Maggie, in just a matter of weeks.'

'I know. And I haven't.' She patted her belly, grimaced a little. 'I feel less of a sow every day, but I wonder if I'll ever lose all of it again.'

'You look wonderful.'

'That's what I tell her,' Rogan added, draping an arm around Maggie's shoulders.

'And what do you know? You're besotted with me.'

'True enough.'

Brianna looked away as they beamed at each other. How easy it was for them now, she mused. So comfortably in love with a beautiful baby cooing beside them. She didn't care for the pang of envy, or the tug of longing.

'So where's our Yank this morning?'

Brianna glanced back, wondering uneasily if Maggie was reading her mind. 'He was up and out at first light, without even his breakfast.'

'To?'

'I don't know. He grunted at me. At least I think it was at me. His moods are unpredictable these days. The book's troubling him, though he says he's cleaning it up. Which means, I'm told, tinkering with it, shining it up.'

'He'll be done before long, then?' Rogan asked.

'Before long.' And then . . . Brianna was taking a page out of Gray's book and not thinking of *and thens*. 'His publisher's on the phone quite a lot now, and sending packets by express all the time, about the book that's coming out this summer. It seems to irritate him to have to think of one when he's working on another.' She glanced back at the workmen. 'It's a good spot for the greenhouse, don't you think? I'll be pleased to be able to see it from my window.'

'It's the spot you've been talking of for months,' Maggie pointed out and refused to be turned from the topic. 'Are things well between you and Gray?'

'Yes, very well. He's a bit sulky right now as I said, but his moods never last very long. I told you how he engineered a truce with Mother.'

'Clever of him. A trinket from New York. She was pleasant to him at Liam's christening. I had to give birth before I could achieve close to the same.'

'She's mad for Liam,' Brianna said.

'He's a buffer between us. Ah, what's the trouble, darling,' she murmured as Liam began to fuss. 'His nappie's wet, that's all.' Lifting him, Maggie patted his back and soothed.

'I'll change it.'

'You're quicker to volunteer than his Da.' With a shake of her head, Maggie laughed. 'No, I'll do it. You watch your greenhouse. It'll only take a minute.'

'She knows I wanted to talk to you.' Rogan led Brianna toward the wooden chairs set near the blackthorns for which the cottage was named.

'Is something wrong?'

'No.' There was an edginess about her under a forced calm that was out of character. That, Rogan decided with a slight frown, would have to be Maggie's department. 'I wanted to talk with you about this Triquarter Mining business. Or the lack of it.' He sat, laid his hands on his knees. 'We haven't really had the chance to talk it through since I was in Dublin, then the baby's christening. Maggie's satisfied with the way things have shaken down. She's more interested in enjoying Liam and getting back to her glass than pursuing the matter.'

'That's how it should be.'

'For her, perhaps.' He didn't say what was obvious to both of them. Neither he nor Maggie required any of the monetary compensation that might result from a suit. 'I have to admit, Brianna, it doesn't sit well with me. The principle of it.'

'I can understand that, you being a businessman yourself.' She smiled a little. 'You never met Mr. Carstairs. It's difficult to hold a grudge once you have.'

'Let's separate emotion from legalities for a moment.'

Her smile widened. She imagined he used just that brisk tone with any inefficient underling. 'All right, Rogan.'

'Carstairs committed a crime. And while you might be reluctant to see him imprisoned, it's only logical to expect a penalty. Now I'm given to understand that he's become successful in the last few years. I took it on myself to make a few discreet inquiries, and it appears that his current businesses are aboveboard as well as lucrative. He's in the position to compensate you for the dishonesty in his dealings with your father. It would be a simple matter for me to go to London personally and settle it.'

'That's kind of you.' Brianna folded her hands, drew a deep breath. 'I'm going to disappoint you, Rogan, and I'm sorry for it. I can see your ethics have been insulted by this, and you want only to see justice served.'

'I do, yes.' Baffled, he shook his head. 'Brie, I can understand Maggie's attitude. She's focused on the baby and her work and has always been one to brush aside anything that interfered with her concentration. But you're a practical woman.'

'I am,' she agreed. 'I am, yes. But I'm afraid I have a bit of my father in me as well.' Reaching out, she laid a hand over Rogan's. 'You know, some people, for whatever reason, start out on unsteady ground. The choices they make aren't always admirable. A portion of them stay there because it's easier, or what they're used to, or even what they prefer. Another portion slide onto a stable footing, without much effort. A bit of luck, of timing. And another, a small, special portion,' she said, thinking of Gray, 'fight their way onto the solid. And they make something admirable of themselves.'

She fell into silence, staring out over the hills. Wishing.

'I've lost you, Brie.'

'Oh.' She waved a hand and brought herself back. 'What I mean to say is I don't know the circumstances that led Mr. Carstairs from one kind of life to another. But he's hurting no one now. Maggie has what she wants, and I what contents me. So why trouble ourselves?'

'That's what she told me you'd say.' He lifted his hands in defeat. 'I had to try.'

'Rogan.' Maggie called from the kitchen doorway, the baby bouncing against her shoulder. 'The phone. It's Dublin for you.'

'She won't answer the damn thing in our own house, but she answers it here.'

'I've threatened not to bake for her if she doesn't.'

'None of my threats work.' He rose. 'I've been expecting a call, so I gave the office your number if we didn't answer at home.'

'That's no problem. Take all the time you need.' She smiled as Maggie headed out with the baby. 'Well, Margaret Mary, are you going to share him now or keep him all to yourself?'

'He was just asking for you, Auntie Brie.' With a chuckle, Maggie passed Liam to her sister and settled in the chair Rogan had vacated. 'Oh, it's good to sit. Liam was fussy last night. I'd swear between us Rogan and I walked all the way to Galway and back.'

'Do you suppose he's teething already?' Cooing, Brianna rubbed a knuckle over Liam's gums, looking for swelling.

'It may be. He drools like a puppy.' She closed her eyes, let her body sag. 'Oh, Brie, who would have thought you could love so much? I spent most of my life not knowing Rogan Sweeney existed, and now I couldn't live without him.'

She opened one eye to be certain Rogan was still in the house and couldn't hear her wax so sentimental. 'And the baby, it's an enormous thing this grip on the heart. I thought when I was carrying him I understood what it was to love him. But holding him, from the very first time I held him, it was so much more.'

She shook herself, gave a shaky laugh. 'Oh, it's those hormones again. They're turning me to mush.'

''Tisn't the hormones, Maggie.' Brianna rubbed her cheek over Liam's head, caught the marvelous scent of him. 'It's being happy.'

'I want you to be happy, Brie. I can see you're not.'

'That isn't true. Of course I'm happy.'

'You're already seeing him walk away. And you're making yourself accept it before it even happens.'

'If he chooses to walk away, I can't stop him. I've known that all along.'

'Why can't you?' Maggie shot back. 'Why? Don't you love him enough to fight for him?'

'I love him too much to fight for him. And maybe I lack the courage. I'm not as brave as you, Maggie.'

'That's just as excuse. Too brave is what you've always been, Saint Brianna.'

'And if it is an excuse, it's mine.' She spoke mildly. She would not, she promised herself, be drawn into an argument. 'He has reasons why he'll go. I may not agree with them, but I understand them. Don't slap at me, Maggie,' she said quietly and averted the next explosion. 'Because it does hurt. And I could see this morning when he left the house that he was already walking away.'

'Then make him stop. He loves you, Brie. You can see it every time he looks at you.'

'I think he does.' And that only increased the pain. 'That's why he's in a hurry all at once to move on. And he's afraid, too. Afraid he'll come back.'

'Is that what you're counting on?'

'No.' But she wanted to count on it. She wanted that very much. 'Love isn't always enough, Maggie. We can see that from what happened with Da.'

'That was different.'

'It's all different. But he lived without his Amanda, and he made his life as best he could. I'm enough his daughter to do the same. Don't worry over me,' she murmured, stroking the baby. 'I know what Amanda was feeling when she wrote she was grateful for the time they had together. I wouldn't trade these past months for the world and more.'

She glanced over, then fell silent, studying the set look on Rogan's face as he came across the lawn.

'We may have found something,' he said, 'on Amanda Dougherty.'

Gray didn't come home for tea, and Brianna wondered but didn't worry as she saw that her guests had their fill of finger sandwiches and dundee cake. Rogan's report on Amanda Dougherty was always at the back of her mind as she moved through the rest of her day.

The detective had found nothing in his initial check of

the towns and villages in the Catskills. It was, to Brianna's thinking, hardly a surprise that no one remembered a pregnant Irishwoman from more than a quarter of a century in the past. But Rogan, being a thorough man, hired thorough people. Routinely, the detective made checks on vital statistics, reading through birth and death and marriage certificates for a five-year period following the date of Amanda's final letter to Tom Concannon.

And it was in a small village, deep in the mountains, where he had found her.

Amanda Dougherty, age thirty-two, had been married by a justice of the peace, to a thirty-eight-year-old man named Colin Bodine. An address was given simply as Rochester, New York. The detective was already on his way there to continue the search for Amanda Dougherty Bodine.

The date of the marriage had been five months after the final letter to her father, Brianna mused. Amanda would have been close to term, so it was most likely the man she had married had known she'd been pregnant by another.

Had he loved her? Brianna wondered. She hoped so. It seemed to her it took a strong, kind-hearted man to give another man's child his name.

She caught herself glancing at the clock again, wondering where Gray had gone off to. Annoyed with herself, she biked down to Murphy's to fill him in on the progress of the greenhouse construction.

It was time to finish dinner preparations when she returned. Murphy had promised to come by and check over the foundation himself the following day. But Brianna's underlying purpose, the hope that Gray had been visiting her neighbor as he often did, had been dashed.

And now, with more than twelve hours passed since he'd left that morning, she moved from wonder to worry.

She fretted, eating nothing herself as her guests feasted on mackerel with gooseberry sauce. She played her role as hostess, seeing there was brandy where brandy was wanted, an extra serving of steamed lemon pudding for the child who eyed it so hopefully.

She saw that the whiskey decanter in each guest room was filled, and towels were fresh for evening baths. She made parlor conversation with her guests, offered board games to the children.

By ten, when the light was gone and the house quiet, she'd moved beyond worry to resignation. He would come back when he would come, she thought, and settled down in her room, her knitting in her lap and her dog at her feet.

A full day of driving and walking and studying the countryside hadn't done a great deal to improve Gray's mood. He was irritated with himself, irritated by the fact that a light had been left burning for him in the window.

He switched it off the moment he came inside, as if to prove to himself he didn't need or want the homey signal. He started to go upstairs, a deliberate move, he knew, to prove he was his own man.

Con's soft woof stopped him. Turning on the stairs, Gray scowled at the dog. 'What do you want?'

Con merely sat, thumped his tail.

'I don't have a curfew, and I don't need a stupid dog waiting up for me.'

Con merely watched him, then lifted a paw as if anticipating Gray's usual greeting.

'Shit.' Gray went back down the stairs, took the paw to shake, and gave the dog's head a good scratch. 'There. Better now?'

Con rose and padded toward the kitchen. He stopped, looked back, then sat again, obviously waiting.

'I'm going to bed,' Gray told him.

As if in agreement, Con rose again as if waiting to lead the way to his mistress.

'Fine. We'll do it your way.' Gray stuffed his hands in his pockets and followed the dog down the hall, into the kitchen, and through to Brianna's room.

He knew his mood was foul, and couldn't seem to alter it. It was the book, of course, but there was more. He could admit, at least to himself, that he'd been restless since Liam's christening.

There'd been something about it, the ritual itself, that ancient, pompous, and oddly soothing rite full of words and color and movement. The costumes, the music, the lighting had all melded together, or so it had seemed to him, to tilt time.

But it had been the community of it, the belonging he'd sensed from every neighbor and friend who'd come to witness the child's baptism, that had struck him most deeply.

It had touched him, beyond the curiosity of it, the writer's interest in scene and event. It had moved him, the flow of words, the unshakable faith, and the river of continuity that ran from generation to generation in the small village church, accented by a baby's indignant wail, fractured light through stained glass, wood worn smooth by generations of bended knees.

It was family as much as shared belief, and community as much as dogma.

And his sudden, staggering wish to belong had left him restless and angry.

Irritated with himself, and her, he stopped in the doorway of Brianna's sitting room, watching her with her knitting needles clicking rhythmically. The dark green wool spilled over the lap of her white nightgown. The light beside her slanted down so that she could check her work, but she never looked at her own hands.

Across the room, the television murmured through an old black-and-white movie. Cary Grant and Ingrid Bergman in sleek evening dress embraced in a wine celler. *Notorious*, Gray thought. A tale of love, mistrust, and redemption.

For reasons he didn't choose to grasp, her choice of entertainment annoyed him all the more.

'You shouldn't have waited up.'

She glanced over at him, her needles never faltering. 'I didn't.' He looked tired, she thought, and moody. Whatever he'd searched for in his long day alone, he didn't appear to have found it. 'Have you eaten?'

'Some pub grub this afternoon.'

'You'll be hungry, then.' She started to set her knitting aside in its basket. 'I'll fix you a plate.'

'I can fix my own if I want one,' he snapped. 'I don't need you to mother me.'

Her body stiffened, but she only sat again and picked up her wool. 'As you please.'

He stepped into the room, challenging. 'Well?'

'Well what?'

'Where's the interrogation? Aren't you going to ask me where I was, what I was doing? Why I didn't call?'

'As you've just pointed out, I'm not your mother. Your business is your own.'

For a moment there was only the sound of her needles and the distressed commercial voice of a woman on television who'd discovered chip fat on her new blouse.

'Oh, you're a cool one,' Gray muttered and strode to the set to slam the picture off.

'Are you trying to be rude?' Brianna asked him. 'Or can't you help yourself?'

'I'm trying to get your attention.'

'Well, you have it.'

'Do you have to do that when I'm talking to you?'

Since there seemed no way to avoid the confrontation he so obviously wanted, Brianna let her knitting rest in her lap. 'Is that better?'

'I needed to be alone. I don't like being crowded.'

'I haven't asked for an explanation, Grayson.'

'Yes, you have. Just not out loud.'

Impatience began to simmer. 'So, now you're reading my mind, are you?'

'It's not that difficult. We're sleeping together, essentially living together, and you feel I'm obliged to let you know what I'm doing.'

'Is that what I feel?'

He began to pace. No, she thought, it was more of a prowl – as a big cat might prowl behind cage bars.

'Are you going to sit there and try to tell me you're not mad?'

'It hardly matters what I tell you when you read my unspoken thoughts.' She linked her hands together, rested them on the wool. She would not fight with him, she told herself. If their time together was nearing an end, she wouldn't let the last memories of it be of arguments and bad feelings. 'Grayson, I might point out to you that I have a life of my own. A business to run, personal enjoyments. I filled my day well enough.'

'So you don't give a damn whether I'm here or not?' It was his out, wasn't it? Why did the idea infuriate him?

She only sighed. 'You know it pleases me to have you here. What do you want me to say? That I worried? Perhaps I did, for a time, but you're a man grown and able to take care of yourself. Did I think it was unkind of you not to let me know you'd be gone so long when it's your habit to be here most evenings? You know it was, so it's hardly worth me pointing it out to you. Now, if that satisfies you, I'm going to bed. You're welcome to join me or go upstairs and sulk.'

Before she could rise, he slapped both hands on either arm of her chair, caging her in. Her eyes widened, but stayed level on his.

'Why don't you shout at me?' he demanded. 'Throw something? Boot me out on my ass?'

'Those things might make you feel better,' she said evenly. 'But it isn't my job to make you feel better.'

'So that's it? Just shrug the whole thing off and come to bed? For all you know I could have been with another woman.'

For one trembling moment the heat flashed into her eyes, matching the fury in his. Then she composed herself, taking the knitting from her lap and setting it in the basket. 'Are you trying to make me angry?'

'Yes. Damn it, yes.' He jerked back from her, spun away. 'At least it would be a fair fight then. There's no way to beat that iced serenity of yours.'

'Then I'd be foolish to set aside such a formidable weapon, wouldn't I?' She rose. 'Grayson, I'm in love with you, and when you think I'd use that love to trap you, to change you, then you insult me. It's for that you should apologize.'

Despising the creeping flow of guilt, he looked back at her. Never in the whole of his life had another woman made him feel guilt. He wondered if there was another person in existence who could, with such calm reason, cause him to feel so much the fool.

'I figured you'd find a way to get an I'm sorry out of me before it was over.'

She stared at him a moment, then saying nothing, turned and walked into the adjoining bedroom.

'Christ.' Gray scrubbed his hands over his face, pressed his fingers against his closed eyes, then dropped his hands. You could only wallow in your own idiocy so long, he decided.

'I'm crazy,' he said, stepping into the bedroom.

She said nothing, only adjusted one of her windows to let in more of the cool, fragrant night air.

'I am sorry, Brie, for all of it. I was in a pisser of a mood this morning, and just wanted to be alone.'

She gave him no answer, no encouragement, only turned down the bedspread.

'Don't freeze me out. That's the worst.' He stepped behind her, laid a tentative hand on her hair. 'I'm having trouble with the book. It was lousy of me to take it out on you.'

'I don't expect you to adjust your moods to suit me.'

'You just don't expect,' he murmured. 'It's not good for you.'

'I know what's good for me.' She started to move away, but he turned her around. Ignoring the rigid way she held herself, he wrapped his arms around her.

'You should have booted me out,' he murmured.

'You're paid up through the month.'

He pressed his face into her hair, chuckled. 'Now you're being mean.'

How was a woman supposed to keep up with his moods? When she tried to push away, he only cuddled her closer.

'I had to get away from you,' he told her, and his hand roamed up and down her back, urging her spine to relax. 'I had to prove I could get away from you.'

'Don't you think I know that?' Drawing back as far as he would permit, she framed his face in her hands. 'Grayson, I know you'll be leaving soon, and I won't pretend that doesn't leave a crack in my heart. But it'll hurt so much more, for both of us, if we spend these last days fighting over it. Or around it.'

'I figured it would be easier if you were mad. If you tossed me out of your life.'

'Easier for who?'

'For me.' He rested his brow on hers and said what he'd avoided saying for the last few days. 'I'll be leaving at the end of the month.'

She said nothing, found she could say nothing over the sudden ache in her chest.

'I want to take some time before the tour starts.'

She waited, but he didn't ask, as he once had, for her to come with him to some tropical beach. She nodded. 'Then let's enjoy the time we have before you go.'

She turned her face so that her mouth met his. Gray laid her slowly onto the bed. And when he loved her, loved her tenderly.

Chapter Twenty-One

For the first time since Brianna had opened her home to guests, she wished them all to the devil. She resented the intrusion on her privacy with Gray. Though it shamed her, she resented the time he spent closed in his room finishing the book that had brought him to her.

She fought the emotions, did everything she could to keep them from showing. As the days passed, she assured herself that the sense of panic and unhappiness would fade. Her life was so very nearly what she wanted it to be. So very nearly.

She might not have the husband and children she'd always longed for, but there was so much else to fullfill her. It helped, at least a little, to count those blessings as she went about her daily routine.

She carried linens, fresh off the line, up the stairs. Since Gray's door was open, she went inside. Here, she set the linens aside. It was hardly necessary to change his sheets since he hadn't slept in any bed but hers for days. But the room needed a good dusting, she decided, since he was out of it. His desk was an appalling mess, to be sure.

She started there, emptying his overflowing ashtray, tidying books and papers. Hoping, she knew, to find some little snatch of the story he was writing. What she found were torn envelopes, unanswered correspondence, and some scribbled notes on Irish superstitions. Amused, she read:

Beware of speaking ill of fairies on Friday, because they are present and will work some evil if offended.

For a magpie to come to the door and look at you is a sure death sign, and nothing can avert it.

A person who passes under a hempen rope will die
a violent death.

'Well, you surprise me, Brianna. Snooping.'

Blushing red, she dropped the notepad, stuck her hands behind her back. Oh, wasn't it just like Grayson Thane, she thought, to come creeping up on a person.

'I was not snooping. I was dusting.'

He sipped idly at the coffee he'd gone to the kitchen to brew. To his thinking, he'd never seen her quite so flummoxed. 'You don't have a dust rag,' he pointed out.

Feeling naked, Brianna wrapped dignity around her. 'I was about to get one. Your desk is a pitiful mess, and I was just straightening up.'

'You were reading my notes.'

'I was putting the notebook aside. Perhaps I glanced at the writing on it. Superstitions is all it is, of evil and death.'

'Evil and death's my living.' Grinning, he crossed to her, picked up the pad. 'I like this one. On Hallowtide – that's November first.'

'I'm aware of when Hallowtide falls.'

'Sure you are. Anyway, on Hallowtide, the air being filled with the presence of the dead, everything is a symbol of fate. If on that date, you call the name of a person from the outside, and repeat it three times, the result is fatal.' He grinned to himself. 'Wonder what the garda could charge you with.'

'It's nonsense.' And gave her the chills.

'It's great nonsense. I used that one.' He set the notebook down, studied her. Her high color hadn't quite faded. 'You know the trouble with technology?' He lifted one of his computer disks, tapping it on his palm as he studied her with laughing eyes. 'No balled up papers, discarded by the frustrated writer that the curious can smooth out and read.'

'As if I'd do such a thing.' She flounced away to pick up her linens. 'I've beds to make.'

'Want to read some of it?'

She paused halfway to the door, looking back over her shoulder suspiciously. 'Of your book?'

'No, of the local weather report. Of course of my book. Actually, there's a section I could use a local's spin on. To see if I got the rhythm of the dialogue down, the atmosphere, interactions.'

'Oh, well, if I could help you, I'd be glad.'

'Brie, you've been dying to get a look at the manuscript. You could have asked.'

'I know better than that, living with Maggie.' She set the linens down again. 'It's worth your life to go in her shop to see a piece she's working on.'

'I'm a more even-tempered sort.' With a few deft moves he booted his computer, slipped in the appropriate disk. 'It's a pub scene. Local color and some character intros. It's the first time McGee meets Tullia.'

'Tullia. It's Gaelic.'

'Right. Means peaceful. Let's see if I can find it.' He began flipping screens. 'You don't speak Gaelic, do you?'

'I do, yes. Both Maggie and I learned from our Gran.'

He looked up, stared at her. 'Son of a bitch. It never even occured to me. Do you know how much time I've spent looking up words? I just wanted a few tossed in, here and there.'

'You'd only to have asked.'

He grunted. 'Too late now. Yeah, here it is. McGee's a burned-out cop, with Irish roots. He's come to Ireland to look into some old family history, maybe find his balance, and some answers about himself. Mostly, he just wants to be left alone to regroup. He was involved in a bust that went bad and holds himself responsible for the bystander death of a six-year-old kid.'

'How sad for him.'

'Yeah, he's got his problems. Tullia has plenty of her own. She's a widow, lost her husband and child in an accident that only she survived. She's getting through it, but carrying around a lot of baggage. Her husband wasn't any prize, and there were times she wished him dead.'

'So she's guilty that he is, and scarred because her child was taken from her, like a punishment for her thoughts.'

'More or less. Anyway, this scene's in the local pub. Only runs a few pages. Sit down. Now pay attention.' He leaned over her shoulder, took her hand. 'See these two buttons?'

'Yes.'

'This one will page up, this one will page down. When you finished what's on the screen and want to move on, push this one. If you want to go back and look at something again, push that one. And Brianna?'

'Yes?'

'If you touch any of the other buttons, I'll have to cut all your fingers off.'

'Being an even-tempered sort.'

'That's right. The disks are backed up, but we wouldn't want to develop any bad habits.' He kissed the top of her head. 'I'm going to go back downstairs, check on the progress on your greenhouse. If you find something that jars, or just doesn't ring quite true, you can make a note on the pad there.'

'All right.' Already reading, she waved him off. 'Go away, then.'

Gray wandered downstairs, and outside. The six courses of local stone that would be the base for her greenhouse were nearly finished. It didn't surprise him to see Murphy setting stones in place himself.

'I didn't know you were a mason as well as a farmer,' Gray called out.

'Oh, I do a bit of this, a bit of that. Mind you don't make that mortar so loose this time,' he ordered the skinny teenager nearby. 'Here's my nephew, Tim MacBride, visiting from Cork. Tim can't get enough of your country music from the States.'

'Randy Travis, Wynonna, Garth Brooks?'

'All of them.' Tim flashed a smile much like his uncle's.

Gray bent down, lifted a new stone for Murphy, while he discussed the merits of country music with the boy. Before long he was helping to mix the mortar and making satisfying manly noises about the work with his companions.

'You've a good pair of hands for a writer,' Murphy observed.

'I worked on a construction crew one summer. Mixing mortar and hauling it in wheelbarrows while the heat fried my brain.'

'It's pleasant weather today.' Satisfied with the progress, Murphy paused for a cigarette. 'If it holds, we may have this up for Brie by another week.'

Another week, Gray mused, was almost all he had. 'It's nice of you to take time from your own work to help her with this.'

'That's *comhair*,' Murphy said easily. 'Community. That's how we live here. No one has to get by alone if there's family and neighbors. They'll be three men or more here when it's time to put up the frame and the glass. And others'll come along if help's needed to build her benches and such. By the end of it, everyone will feel they have a piece of the place. And Brianna will be giving out cuttings and plants for everyone's garden.' He blew out smoke. 'It comes round, you see. That's *comhair*.'

Gray understood the concept. It was very much what he had felt, and for a moment envied, in the village church during Liam's christening. 'Does it ever . . . cramp your style that by accepting a favor you're obliged to do one?'

'You Yanks.' Chuckling, Murphy took a last drag, then crushed the cigarette out on the stones. Knowing Brianna, he tucked the stub into his pocket rather than flicking it aside. 'You always reckon in payments. *Obliged* isn't the word. 'Tis a security, if you're needing a more solid term for it. A knowing that you've only to reach out a hand, and someone will help you along if you need it. A knowing that you'd do the same.'

He turned to his nephew. 'Well, Tim, let's clean up our tools. We need to be getting back. You'll tell Brie not to be after fiddling with these stones, will you, Grayson? They need to set.'

'Sure, I'll – Oh Christ, I forgot about her. See you later.' He hurried back into the house. A glance at the kitchen clock made him wince. He'd left her for more than an hour.

And she was, he discovered, exactly where he'd left her.

'Takes you a while to read half a chapter.'

However much his entrance surprised her, she didn't jolt this time. When she lifted her gaze from the screen to his face, her eyes were wet.

'That bad?' He smiled a little, surprised to find himself nervous.

'It's wonderful.' She reached into her apron pocket for a tissue. 'Truly. This part where Tullia's sitting alone in her garden, thinking of her child. It makes you feel her grief. It's not like she's a made-up person at all.'

His second surprise was that he should experience embarrassment. As far as praise went, hers had been perfect. 'Well, that's the idea.'

'You've a wonderful gift, Gray, for making words into emotions. I went a bit beyond the part you wanted me to read. I'm sorry. I got caught up in it.'

'I'm flattered.' He noted by the screen she'd read more than a hundred pages. 'You're enjoying it.'

'Oh, very much. It has a different . . . something,' she said, unable to pinpoint it, 'than your other books. Oh, it's moody, as they always are, and rich in detail. And frightening. The first murder, the one at the ruins. I thought my heart would stop when I was reading it. And gory it was, too. Gleefully so.'

'Don't stop now.' He ruffled her hair, dropped down on the bed.

'Well.' She linked her hands, laid them on the edge of the desk as she thought through her words. 'Your humor's there as well. And your eye, it misses nothing. The scene in the pub, I've walked into that countless times in my life. I could see Tim O'Malley behind the bar, and Murphy playing a tune. He'll like that you made him so handsome.'

'You think he'll recognize himself?'

'Oh, I do, yes. I don't know how he'll feel about being one of the suspects, or the murderer, if that's what you've done in the end.' She waited, hopeful, but he only shook his head.

'You don't really think I'm going to tell you who done it, do you?'

'Well, no.' She sighed and propped her chin on her fist. 'As to Murphy, probably he'll enjoy it. And your affection for the village, for the land here and the people shows. In the little things – the family hitching a ride home from church in their Sunday best, the old man walking with his dog along the roadside in the rain, the little girl dancing with her grandda in the pub.'

'It's easy to write things down when there's so much to see.'

'It's more than what you see, with your eyes, I mean.' She lifted her hands, let them fall again. She didn't have words, as he did, to juggle into the right meaning. 'It's the heart of it. There's a deepness to the heart of it that's different from what I've read of your writings before. The way McGee fights that tug of war within himself over what he should do. The way he wishes he could do nothing and knows he can't. And Tullia, the way she bears her grief when it's near to bending her in two, and works to make her life what it needs to be again. I can't explain it.'

'You're doing a pretty good job,' Gray murmured.

'It touches me. I can't believe it was written right here, in my home.'

'I don't think it could have been written anywhere else.' He rose then, disappointing her by hitting buttons that jangled the screen. She'd hoped he'd let her read more.

'Oh, you've changed the name of it,' she said when the title page came up. '*Final Redemption*. I like it. That's the theme of it, is it? The murders, what's happened to McGee and Tullia before, and what changes after they meet?'

'That's the way it worked out.' He hit another button, bringing up the dedication page. In all the books he'd written, it was only the second time he'd dedicated one. The first, and only, had been to Arlene.

To Brianna, for gifts beyond price.

'Oh, Grayson.' Her voice hitched over the tears rising in the back of her throat. 'I'm honored. I'll start crying again,' she murmured and turned her face into his arm. 'Thank you so much.'

'There's a lot of me in this book, Brie.' He lifted her face, hoping she'd understand. 'It's something I can give you.'

'I know. I'll treasure it.' Afraid she'd spoil the moment with tears, she ran her hands briskly over her hair. 'You'll want to get back to work, I'm sure. And I've whittled the day away.' She picked up her linens, knowing she'd weep the moment she was behind the first closed door. 'Shall I bring your tea up here when it's time?'

He tilted his head, narrowed his eyes as he studied her. He wondered if she'd recognized herself in Tullia. The composure, the quiet, almost unshakable grace. 'I'll come down. I'm nearly done all I need to do for today.'

'In an hour then.'

She went out, closing the door behind her. Alone, Gray sat, and stared, for a long time, at the brief dedication.

It was the laughter and the voices that drew Gray, when the hour was up, toward the parlor rather than the kitchen. Brianna's guests were gathered around the tea table, sampling or filling plates. Brianna herself stood, swaying gently from side to side to rock the baby sleeping on her shoulder.

'My nephew,' she was explaining. 'Liam. I'm minding him for an hour or two. Oh, Gray.' She beamed when she saw him. 'Look who I have here.'

'So I see.' Crossing over, Gray peeked at the baby's face. His eyes were open, and dreamy, until they latched onto Gray and stared owlishly. 'He always looks at me as if he knows every sin I commited. It's intimidating.'

Gray moved to the tea table and had nearly decided on his choices when he noted Brianna slipping from the room. He caught up with her near the kitchen door. 'Where are you going?'

'To put the baby down.'

'What for?'

'Maggie said he'd be wanting a nap.'

'Maggie's not here.' He took Liam himself. 'And we never get to play with him.' To amuse himself, he made faces at the baby. 'Where's Maggie?'

'She's fired up her furnace. Rogan had to run into the gallery to handle some problem, so she came dashing down here just a little bit ago.' With a laugh she bent her head close to Gray's. 'I thought it would never happen. Now I have you all to myself,' she murmured. She straightened at the knock on the door. 'Keep his head supported, mind,' she said as she went to answer.

'I know how to hold a baby. Women,' he said to Liam. 'They don't think we can do anything. They all think you're hot stuff right now, boy-o, but just wait. In a few years they'll figure your purpose in life is to fix small electrical appliances and kill bugs.'

Since no one was looking, he bent his head to press a light kiss on Liam's mouth. And watched it curve.

'That's the way. Why don't we go in the kitchen, and –'

He broke off at Brianna's startled exclamation. Shifting Liam more securely in the crook of his arm, he hurried back down the hallway.

Carstairs stood at the threshold, a tan bowler in his hands, a friendly smile on his face. 'Grayson, how nice to see you again. I wasn't certain you'd still be here. And what's this?'

'It's a baby,' Gray said shortly.

'Of course it is.' Carstairs tickled Liam's chin and made foolish noises. 'Handsome lad. I must say, he favors you a bit, Brianna. Around the mouth.'

'He's my sister's child. And what might you be doing here at Blackthorn, Mr. Carstairs?'

'Just passing through, as it were. I'd told Iris so much about the cottage, and the countryside, she wanted to see it for herself. She's in the car.' He gestured to the Bentley parked at the garden gate. 'Actually, we'd hoped you might have a room for us, for the night.'

She goggled at him. 'You want to stay here?'

'I've bragged, perhaps unwisely, about your cooking.' He leaned forward confidentially. 'I'm afraid Iris was a bit irked at first. She's quite a cook herself, you know. She wants to see if I was exaggerating.'

'Mr. Carstairs. You're a shameless man.'

'That may be, my dear,' he said, twinkling. 'That may be.'

She huffed, sighed. 'Well, don't leave the poor woman sitting in the car. Bring her in for tea.'

'Can't wait to meet her,' Gray said, jiggling the baby.

'She says the same of you. She's quite impressed that you could lift my wallet without me having a clue. I used to be much quicker.' He shook his head in regret. 'But then, I used to be much younger. Shall I bring in our luggage, Brianna?'

'I have a room. It's smaller than what you had last.'

'I'm sure it's charming. Absolutely charming.' He strolled off to fetch his wife.

'Can you beat it?' Brianna said under her breath. 'I don't know whether to laugh or hide the silver. If I had any silver.'

'He likes you too much to steal from you. So,' Gray mused, 'this is the famous Iris.'

The photograph from the pinched wallet had been a good likeness, Brianna discovered. Iris wore a flowered dress that ruffled in the breeze around excellent legs. To Brianna's eye, Iris had used the time in the car to freshen her hair and makeup and so looked fresh and remarkably pretty as she strolled up the walk beside her grinning husband.

'Oh, Miss Concannon. Brianna, I do hope I can call you Brianna. I think of you as Brianna, of course, after hearing so much about you and your charming inn.'

Her voice was smooth, cultured, despite the fact that her words all but tumbled over each other to get out. Before Brianna could respond, Irish flug out both hands, gripped hers, and barrelled on.

'You're very bit as lovely as Johnny told me. How kind of you, how sweet to find room for us when we've dropped so unexpectedly on your doorstep. And your garden, my dear, I must tell you I'm dizzy with admiration. Your dahlias! I never have a bit of luck with them myself. And your roses, magnificent. You really must tell me your secret. Do you talk to them? I chatter at mine day and night, but I never get blooms like that.'

'Well, I —'

'And you're Grayson.' Iris simply rolled over Brianna's response and turned to him. She freed one of Brianna's hands so that she could grip Gray's. 'What a clever, clever young man you are. And so handsome, too. Why, you look just like a film star. I've read all your books, every one. Frighten me to death, they do, but I can't put them down. Wherever do you come up with such thrilling ideas? I've been so anxious to meet both of you,' she continued, holding on to each of them. 'Badgering poor Johnny to death, you know. And now, here we are.'

There was a pause while Iris beamed at both of them. 'Yes.' Brianna discovered she could find little else to say. 'Here you are. Ah, please come in. I hope you had a pleasant trip.'

'Oh, I adore traveling, don't you? And to think with all the racketing around Johnny and I did in our misspent youth, we never came to this part of the world. It's pretty as a postcard, isn't it, Johnny?'

'It is, my sweet. It certainly is.'

'Oh, what a lovely home. Just charming.' Iris kept her hand firmly on Brianna's as she glanced around. 'I'm sure no one could be anything but comfortable here.'

Brianna gave Gray a helpless look, but he only shrugged. 'I hope you will be. There's tea in the parlor if you like, or I can show you your room first.'

'Would you do that? We'll put our bags away, shall we, Johnny? Then perhaps we can all have a nice chat.'

Irish exclaimed over the stairway as they climbed it, the upstairs hall, the room Brianna escorted them into. Wasn't the bedspread charming, the lace curtains lovely, the view from the window superb?

In short order Brianna found herself in the kitchen brewing another pot of tea while her new guests sat at the table making themselves at home. Iris happily bounced Liam on her lap.

'Hell of a team, aren't they?' Gray murmured, helping by getting out cups and plates.

'She makes me dizzy,' Brianna whispered. 'But it's impossible not to like her.'

'Exactly. You'd never believe there was an unscrupulous thought in her head. Everyone's favorite aunt or amusing neighbor. Maybe you should hide that silver after all.'

'Hush.' Brianna turned away to carry plates to the table. Carstairs immediately helped himself to the bread and jam.

'I do hope you'll join us,' Irish began, chosing a scone, dipping into the clotted cream. 'Johnny, dear, we do want to get business over with, don't we? So distressing to have business clouding the air.'

'Business?' Brianna took Liam again, settled him on her shoulder.

'Unfinished business.' Carstairs dabbed his mouth with a napkin. 'I say, Brianna, this bread is tasty. Have a bit, do, Iris.'

'Johnny rhapsodized over your cooking. I'm afraid I got a teeny bit jealous. I'm a fair cook myself, you know.'

'A brilliant cook,' a loyal Carstairs corrected, snatching his wife's hand and kissing it lavishly. 'A magnificent cook.'

'Oh, Johnny, you do go on.' She giggled girlishly before swatting him aside. Then she pursed her lips and blew him several quick kisses. The byplay had Gray wiggling his brows at Brianna. 'But I can see why he was so taken with the table you set, Brianna.' She nibbled delicately on her scone. 'We must find time to exchange some recipes while we're here. My speciality is a chicken and oyster dish. And if I do say so myself, it's rather tasty. The trick is to use a really good wine, a dry white, you see. And a hint of tarragon. But there I go, running on again, and we haven't dealt with our business.'

She reached for another scone, gesturing to the empty chairs. 'Do sit down, won't you? So much cozier to talk business over tea.'

Agreeably Gray sat and began to fill his plate. 'Want me to take the kid?' he asked Brianna.

'No, I've got him.' She sat with Liam resting comfortably in the curve of her arm.

'What an angel,' Iris cooed. 'And you've such an easy way with babies. Johnny and I always regretted not having any ourselves. But then, we were always off having an adventure, so our lives were full.'

'Adventures,' Brianna repeated. An interesting term, she thought, for bilking.

'We were a naughty pair.' Iris laughed, and the gleam in her eyes said she understood Brianna's sentiments exactly. 'But what fun we had. It wouldn't be quite right to say we were sorry for it, when we enjoyed it so much. But then, one does get older.'

'One does,' Carstairs agreed. 'And one sometimes loses the edge.' He sent Gray a mild look. 'Ten years ago, lad, you'd never have pinched my wallet.'

'Don't bet on it.' Gray sipped at his tea. 'I was even better ten years ago.'

Carstairs tossed back his head and laughed. 'Didn't I tell you he was a pistol, Iris? Oh, I wish you'd have seen him button me down in Wales, my heart. I was filled with admiration. I hope you'll consider returning the wallet to me, Grayson. At least the photographs. The identification is easily replaced, but I'm quite sentimental over the photos. And, of course, the cash.'

Gray's smile was quick and wolfish. 'You still owe me a hundred pounds. Johnny.'

Carstairs cleared his throat. 'Naturally. Unquestionably. I only took yours, you see, to make it seem like a burglary.'

'Naturally,' Gray agreed. 'Unquestionably. I believe we discussed compensation in Wales, before you had to leave so unexpectedly.'

'I do apologize. You'd pinned me down, you see, and I didn't feel comfortable coming to a firm agreement without consulting Iris first.'

'We're strong advocates of full partnership,' Iris put in.

'Indeed.' He gave his wife's hand an affectionate pat. 'I can truthfully say that all our decisions are a matter of teamwork. We feel that, combined with deep affection, is why we've had forty-three successful years together.'

'And, of course, a good sex life,' Iris said comfortably, smiling when Brianna choked over her tea. 'Marriage would be rather dull otherwise, don't you think?'

'Yes, I'm sure you're right.' This time Brianna cleared her throat. 'I think I understand why you've come, and I appreciate it. It's good to clear the air over it.'

'We did want to apologize in person for any distress we've caused you. And I wanted to add my sympathies over my Johnny's clumsy and completely ill-advised search of your lovely home.' She cut a stern look at her husband. 'It lacked all finesse, Johnny.'

'It did. Indeed it did.' He bowed his head. 'I'm thoroughly ashamed.'

Brianna wasn't entirely certain of that, but shook her head. 'Well, there was no real harm done, I suppose.'

'No harm!' Iris took up the gauntlet. 'Brianna, my dear girl, I'm sure you were furious, and rightly so. And distressed beyond belief.'

'It made her cry.'

'Grayson.' Embarrassed now, Brianna stared into her teacup. 'It's done.'

'I can only imagine how you must have felt.' Iris's voice had softened. 'Johnny knows how I feel about my things. Why, if I came home and found everything topsy–turvy, I'd be devastated. Simply devastated. I only hope you can forgive him for the regrettable impulse, and for thinking like a man.'

'I do. I have. I understand he was under a great deal of pressure, and –' Brianna broke off, lifting her head when she realized she was defending the man who had cheated her father and invaded her home.

'What a kind heart you have.' Iris streamed into the breech. 'Now if we could touch on this uncomfortable business of the stock certificate one last time. First, let me say it was very broad–minded, very patient of you not to contact the authorities after Wales.'

'Gray said you'd be back.'

'Clever boy,' Iris murmured.

'And I didn't see any point in it.' With a sigh Brianna picked up a finger of bread and nibbled. 'It was long ago, and the money my father lost was his to lose. Knowing the circumstances was enough to satisfy me.'

'You see, Iris, it's just as I told you.'

'Johnny.' Her voice was suddenly commanding. The look that passed between them held until Carstairs let out a long breath and dropped his gaze.

'Yes, Iris, of course. You're quite right. Quite right.' Rallying, he reached into the inside pocket of his jacket, drew out an envelope. 'Iris and I have discussed this at length, and we would very much like to settle the matter to everyone's satisfaction. With our apologies, dear,' he said, handing Brianna the envelope. 'And our best wishes.'

Uneasy, she lifted the flap. Her heart careened to her stomach and up to her throat. 'It's money. Cash money.'

'A check would make bookkeeping difficult,' Carstairs explained. 'And then there's the taxes that would be involved. A cash transaction saves us both from that inconvenience. It's ten thousand pounds. Irish pounds.'

'Oh, but I couldn't –'

'Yes, you can,' Gray interrupted.

'It isn't right.'

She started to hand the envelope back to Carstairs. His eyes lit up briefly, his fingers reached out. And his wife swatted them away.

'Your young man is correct in the matter, Brianna. This is quite right, for everyone involved. You needn't worry that the money will make an appreciable difference in our lives. We do quite well. It would ease my mind, and my heart, if you'd accept it. And,' she added, 'return the certificate to us.'

'Rogan has it,' Brianna said.

'No, I got it back from him.' Gray rose, slipped into Brianna's rooms.

'Take the money, Brianna,' Iris said gently. 'Put it away now, in your apron pocket. I'd consider it a great favor.'

'I don't understand you.'

'I don't suppose you do. Johnny and I don't regret the way we lived. We enjoyed every minute of it. But a little insurance toward redemption wouldn't hurt.' She smiled, reached over to squeeze Brianna's hand. 'I'd look on it as a kindness. Both of us would. Isn't that right, Johnny?'

He gave the envelope one last, longing look. 'Yes, dear.'

Gray walked back in, holding the certificate. 'Yours, I believe.'

'Yes. Yes, indeed.' Eager now, Carstairs took the paper. Adjusting his glasses, he peered at it. 'Iris,' he said with pride as he tilted the certificate for her to study as well. 'We did superior work, didn't we? Absolutely flawless.'

'We did, Johnny, dear. We certainly did.'

Chapter Twenty-Two

'I have never in the whole of my life had a finer moment of satisfaction.' All but purring, Maggie stretched out in the passenger seat of Brianna's car. She sent one last glance behind at their mother's house as her sister pulled into the street.

'Gloating isn't becoming, Margaret Mary.'

'Becoming or not, I'm enjoying it.' She shifted, reaching out to put a rattle in Liam's waving hand as he sat snug in his safety seat in the back. 'Did you see her face, Brie? Oh, did you see it?'

'I did.' Her dignity slipped just a moment, and a grin snuck through. 'At least you had the good sense not to rub her nose in it.'

'That was the bargain. We'd tell her only that the money came from an investment Da made before he died. One that recently paid off. And I would resist, no matter how it pained me, pointing out that she didn't deserve her third of it as she never believed in him.'

'The third of the money was rightfully hers, and that should be the end of it.'

'I'm not going to badger you about it. I'm much too busy gloating.' Savoring, Maggie hummed a little. 'Tell me what are your plans for yours?'

'I've some ideas for improvements on the cottage. The attic room for one, which started the whole business.'

As Liam cheerfully flung the first one aside, Maggie pulled out another rattle. 'I thought we were going to Galway to shop.'

'We are.' Grayson had badgered her into the idea and had all but booted her out of her own front door. She smiled now, thinking of it. 'I've a mind to buy me one of those professional food processors. The ones they use in restaurants and on the cookery shows.'

'That would have pleased Da very much.' Maggie's grin softened into a smile. 'It is like a gift from him, you know.'

'I'm thinking of it that way. It seems right if I do. What about you?'

'I'll shovel some into the glass house. The rest goes away for Liam. I think Da would have wanted it.' Idly she ran her fingers over the dashboard. 'It's a nice car you've got here, Brie.'

'It is.' She laughed and told herself she'd have to thank Gray for pushing her out of the house for the day. 'Imagine, me driving to Galway without worrying something's going to fall off. It's so like Gray to give outrageous gifts and make it seem natural.'

'That's the truth. The man hands me a diamond pin as cheerfully as if it's a clutch of posies. He has a lovely, generous heart.'

'He does.'

'Speaking of him, what's he up to?'

'Well, he's either working or being entertained by the Carstairs.'

'What characters. Do you know Rogan tells me when they went to the gallery, they tried to charm him into selling them the antique table in the upstairs sitting room?'

'Doesn't surprise me in the least. She's nearly talked me into buying, sight unseen, a lamp she says will be perfect for my parlor. A fine discount she'll give me, too.' Brianna chuckled. 'I'll miss them when they leave tomorrow.'

'I have a feeling they'll be back.' She paused. 'When does Gray go?'

'Probably next week.' Brianna kept her eyes on the road and her voice even. 'He's doing no more than tinkering on the book now, from what I can tell.'

'And do you think he'll be back?'

'I hope he will. But I won't count on it. I can't.'

'Have you asked him to stay?'

'I can't do that, either.'

'No,' Maggie murmured. 'You couldn't. Nor could I under the same circumstances.' Still, she thought, he's a bloody fool if he leaves. 'Would you like to close up the cottage for a few weeks, or have Mrs. O'Malley look after it? You could come to Dublin, or use the villa.'

'No, though it's sweet of you to think of it. I'll be happier at home.'

That was probably true, Maggie thought, and didn't argue. 'Well, if you change your mind, you've only to say.' Making a determined effort to lighten the mood, she turned toward her sister. 'What do you think, Brie? Let's buy something foolish when we get to Shop Street. The first thing that strikes our fancy. Something useless and expensive; one of those trinkets that we used to look at with our noses pressed up to a shop window when Da would bring us.'

'Like the little dolls with the pretty costumes or the jewelry cases with the ballerinas that spun around on top.'

'Oh, I think we can find something a little more suited to our ages, but yes, that's the idea.'

'All right, then. We'll do it.'

It was because they'd talked about their father that memories swarmed Brianna after they reached Galway. With the car parked, they joined the pedestrian traffic, the shoppers, the tourists, the children.

She saw a young girl laughing as she rode her father's shoulders.

He used to do that, she remembered. He'd give her and Maggie turns up, and sometimes he'd run so that they'd bounce, squealing with pleasure.

Or he'd keep their hands firmly tucked in his while they wandered, spinning them stories while they jostled along the crowded streets.

When our ship comes in, Brianna my love, I'll buy you pretty dresses like they have in that window there.

One day we'll travel up here to Galway City with coins leaking out of our pocket. Just you wait, darling.

And though she'd known even then they were stories, just dreaming, it hadn't diminished the pleasure of the seeing, the smelling, the listening.

Nor did the memories spoil it now. The color and movement of Shop Street made her smile as it always did. She enjoyed the voices that cut through the lilting Irish – the twangs and drawls of the Americans, the guttural German, the impatient French. She could smell a hint of Galway Bay that carried on the breeze and the sizzling grease from a nearby pub.

'There.' Maggie steered the stroller closer to a shop window. 'That's perfect.'

Brianna maneuvered through the crowd until she could look over Maggie's shoulder. 'What is?'

'That great fat cow there. Just what I want.'

'You want a cow?'

'Looks like porcelain,' Maggie mused, eyeing the glossy black-and-white body and foolishly grinning bovine face. 'I bet it's frightfully priced. Even better. I'm having it. Let's go in.'

'But what'll you do with it?'

'Give it to Rogan, of course, and see that he puts it in that stuffy Dublin office of his. Oh, I hope it weighs a ton.'

It did, so they arranged to leave it with the clerk while they completed the rest of their shopping. It wasn't until they'd eaten lunch and Brianna had studied the pros and cons of half a dozen food processors that she found her own bit of foolishness.

The fairies were made of painted bronze and danced on wires hung from a copper rod. At a flick of Brianna's fingers, they twirled, their wings beating together musically.

'I'll hang it outside my bedroom window. It'll make me think of all the fairy stories Da used to tell us.'

'It's perfect.' Maggie slipped an arm around Brianna's waist. 'No, don't look at the price,' she said when Brianna started to reach for the little tag. 'That's part of it all. Whatever it costs, it's the right choice. Go buy your trinket, then we'll figure out how to get mine to the car.'

In the end they decided that Maggie would wait at the shop with the cow, with Liam and the rest of their bags, while Brianna drove the car around.

In a breezy mood she strolled back to the car park. She would, she thought, hang her fairy dance as soon as she got home. And then she would play with her fine new kitchen toy. She was thinking how delightful it would be to create a salmon mousse or to finely dice mushrooms with such a precision instrument.

Humming, she slipped behind the wheel, turned the ignition. Perhaps there was a dish she could try to add to the grilled fish she intended to make for dinner. What would Gray enjoy especially? she wondered as she steered toward the exit to pay her fee. Colcannon, perhaps, and a gooseberry fool for dessert – if she could find enough ripe gooseberries.

She thought of the berries' season as those first days of June. But Gray would be gone then. She clamped down on the twinge around her heart. Well, it was nearly June in any case, she told herself and started to drive out of the lot. And she wanted Gray to have her special dessert before he went away.

Brianna heard the shout as she started into her turn. Startled, she jerked her head. She only had time to suck in a breath for the scream as a car, taking the turn too sharp and on the wrong side, crashed into hers.

She heard the screech of metal rending, of glass shattering. Then she heard nothing at all.

'So Brianna's gone shopping,' Iris commented as she joined Gray in the kitchen. 'That's lovely for her. Nothing puts a woman in a better frame of mind that a good shopping binge.'

He couldn't imagine practical Brianna binging on anything. 'She went off to Galway with her sister. I told her we could manage if she didn't make it home by tea.' Feeling a little proprietary about the kitchen, Gray heaped the food Brianna had prepared earlier onto platters. 'It's only the three of us tonight anyway.'

'We'll be cozy right here.' Iris set the teapot in its cozy on the table. 'You were right to convince her to take a day for herself with her sister.'

'I nearly had to drag her out to the car – she's so tied to this place.'

'Deep, fertile roots. It's why she blooms. Just like her flowers out there. Never in my life have I seen such gardens as hers. Why, just this morning, I was – Ah, there you are, Johnny. Just in time.'

'I had the most invigorating walk.' Carstairs hung his hat on a peg, then rubbed his hands together. 'Do you know, my dear, they still cut their own turf?'

'You don't say so.'

'I do indeed. I found the bog. And there were stacks of it, drying in the wind and sun. It was just like stepping back a century.' He gave his wife a peck on the cheek before turning his attention to the table. 'Ah, what have we here?'

'Wash your hands, Johnny, and we'll have a nice tea. I'll pour out, Grayson. You just sit.'

Enjoying them, and their way with each other, Gray obliged her. 'Iris, I hope you're not offended if I ask you something.'

'Dear boy, you can ask whatever you like.'

'Do you miss it?'

She didn't pretend to misunderstand as she passed him the sugar. 'I do. From time to time, I do. That life on the edge sort of feeling. So invigorating.' She poured her husband's cup, then her own. 'Do you?' When Gray only lifted a brow, she chuckled. 'One recognizes one.'

'No,' Gray said after a pause. 'I don't miss it.'

'Well, you'd have retired quite early, so you wouldn't have the same sort of emotional attachment. Or perhaps you do, and that's why you've never used any of your prior experience, so to speak, in your books.'

Shrugging, he lifted his cup. 'Maybe I just don't see the point in looking back.'

'I've always felt you never have a really clear view of what's coming up if you don't glance over your shoulder now and again.'

'I like surprises. If tomorrow's already figured out, why bother with it?'

'The surprise comes because tomorrow's never quite what you thought it would be. But you're young,' she said, giving him a motherly smile. 'You'll learn that for yourself. Do you use a map when you travel?'

'Sure.'

'Well, that's it, you see. Past, present, future. All mapped out.' With her bottom lip clamped between her teeth, she measured out a stingy quarter spoon of sugar for her own tea. 'You may plan a route. Now some people stick to it no matter what. No deviations to explore some little road, no unscheduled stops to enjoy a particularly nice sunset. A pity for them,' she mused. 'And oh, how they complain when they're forced to detour. But most of us like a little adventure along the way, that side road. Having a clear view of the ultimate destination doesn't have to keep one from enjoying the ride. Here you are, Johnny dear, your tea's just poured.'

'Bless you, Iris.'

'And with just a drop of cream, the way you like it.'

'I'd be lost without her,' Carstairs said to Gray. 'Oh, it appears we're having company.'

Gray looked toward the kitchen door as Murphy opened it. Con darted in ahead, sat at Gray's feet, laid his head in Gray's lap. Even as Gray lifted a hand to stroke the dog's ears, his smile of greeting faded.

'What is it?' He found himself springing to his feet, rattling the cups on the table. Murphy's face was too set, his eyes too dark. 'What's happened?'

'There's been an accident. Brianna's been hurt.'

'What do you mean she's hurt?' he demanded over Iris's murmur of distress.

'Maggie called me. There was an accident when Brie was driving from the car park to the shop where Maggie and the baby were waiting.' Murphy took off his cap, a matter of habit, then squeezed his fingers on the brim. 'I'll take you up to Galway. She's in hospital there.'

'Hospital.' Standing there Gray felt, physically felt, the blood draining out of him. 'How bad? How bad is it?'

'Maggie wasn't sure. She didn't think it was too bad, but she was waiting to hear. I'll take you to Galway, Grayson. I thought we'd use your car. It'd be faster.'

'I need the keys.' His brain felt dull, useless. 'I have to get the keys.'

'Don't let him drive,' Iris said when Gray streaked from the room.

'No, ma'am, I won't be letting him do that.'

Murphy didn't have to argue. He simply took the keys from Gray's hand and got behind the wheel. Since Gray said nothing, Murphy concentrated on finessing all the speed the Mercedes was built for. Another time, perhaps, he would have appreciated the response the sleek car offered. For now he simply used it.

For Gray the trip was endless. The glorious scenery of the west rushed by, but they seemed to make no progress. It was like animation, he thought dimly, run over and over again, cel by cel, while he could do nothing but sit.

And wait.

She wouldn't have gone if he hadn't bullied her into it. But he'd pressured her to go out, to take a day. So she'd gone to Galway, and now she was . . . Christ, he didn't know what she was, how she was, and couldn't bear to imagine it.

'I should have gone with her.'

With the car cruising near ninety, Murphy didn't bother to glance over. 'You'll make yourself sick thinking that way. We're nearly there now, then we'll see.'

'I bought her the fucking car.'

'True enough.' The man didn't need sympathy, Murphy thought, but practicality. 'And you weren't driving the one who hit it. To my way of thinking, if she'd been in that rusted bucket she had before, things would be worse.'

'We don't know how bad they are.'

'We soon will. So hang on to yourself until we do.' He slipped off an exit, slowed, and began to maneuver through denser traffic. 'It's likely she's fine and will give us grief for driving all this way.'

He turned into the hospital car park. They'd no more climbed out and started for the doors when they spotted Rogan walking the baby.

'Brianna.' It was all Gray could say.

'She's all right. They want to keep her through the night at least, but she's all right.'

The feeling went out of Gray's legs so that he took Rogan's arm as much for balance as for emphasis. 'Where? Where is she?'

'They've just put her in a room on the sixth floor. Maggie's with her yet. I brought her mother and Lottie along with me. They're up there as well. She's –' He broke off, shifting to block Gray from rushing the entrance. 'She's banged up, and I think she's hurting more than she's letting on. But the doctor told us she's very lucky. Some bruises from the seat belt, which kept it from being worse. Her shoulder's wrenched, and that's causing the most pain. She's a knot on her head, and some cuts. They want her kept quiet for twenty-four hours.'

'I need to see her.'

'I know that.' Rogan stood his ground. 'But she doesn't need to see how upset you are. She's one who'll take that to heart and worry over it.'

'Okay.' Fighting for balance, Gray pressed his fingers to his eyes. 'All right. We'll keep it calm, but I have to see her for myself.'

'I'll go up with you,' Murphy said and led the way in. Keeping his own counsel, he said nothing as they waited for the elevator.

'Why are they all here?' Gray demanded when the elevator opened. 'Why are they here, Maggie, her mother. Rogan, Lottie, if she's all right?'

'They're family.' Murphy pushed the button for six. 'Where else would they be? Now, about three years past I broke an arm and cracked my head playing football. I couldn't get rid of one sister, but another would be at the door. My mother stayed for two weeks, no matter what I did to boost her on her way. And to tell the truth, I was glad to have them fussing around me. Don't go off in a mad rush,' Murphy warned as the elevator stopped. 'Irish nurses run a tight ship. And here's Lottie.'

'Gracious, you must have flown all the way.' She came forward, her smile all reassurance. 'She's doing fine, they're taking grand care of her. Rogan arranged for her to have a private room so she'd have quiet and privacy. She's already fretting about going home, but with the concussion, they'll want to keep an eye on her.'

'Concussion?'

'A mild one, really,' she soothed, leading them down the hallway. 'It doesn't seem she was unconscious for more than a few moments. And she was lucid enough to tell the man at the car park where Maggie was waiting. Look here, Brianna, you've more visitors already.'

All Gray could see was Brianna, white against white sheets.

'Oh, Gray, Murphy, you shouldn't have come all this way. I'll be going home shortly.'

'You'll not.' Maggie's voice was firm. 'You're staying the night.'

Brianna started to turn her head, but the throbbing made her think better of it. 'I don't want to stay the night. Bumps and bruises is all it is. Oh, Gray, the car. I'm so sorry about the car. The side of it's all bent in, and the headlamp's smashed, and —'

'Shut up, will you, and let me look at you?' He took her hand, held on.

She was pale, and a bruise had bloomed along her cheekbone. Above it, on the brow side of the temple was a neat white bandage. Beneath the shapeless hospital gown he could see more bandages at her shoulder.

Because his hand began to tremble, he drew it away,

jammed it in his pocket. 'You're hurting. I can see it in your eyes.'

'My head aches.' She smiled weakly, lifting a finger to the bandage. 'I feel a bit like I've been run over by an entire rugby team.'

'They should give you something.'

'They will, if I need it.'

'She's skittish of needles,' Murphy said and leaned over to kiss her lightly. His own relief at seeing her whole showed itself in a wide, cheeky grin. 'I remember hearing you howl, Brianna Concannon, when I was in Dr. Hogan's waiting room and you were getting a shot.'

'And I'm not ashamed of it. Horrible things, needles. I don't want them poking me more than they already have. I want to go home.'

'You'll stay just where you are.' Maeve spoke from a chair beneath the window. 'It's little enough to have a needle or two after the fright you've given us.'

'Mother, it's hardly Brianna's fault that some idiot Yank couldn't remember which side of the road to drive on.' Maggie's teeth clenched at the thought of it. 'And they, with barely a scratch between them.'

'You mustn't be so hard on them. It was a mistake, and all but frightened them to death.' The drumming in Brianna's head increased at the idea of an argument. 'I'll stay if I must, but if I could just ask the doctor again.'

'You'll leave the doctor be and rest as he told you.' Maeve pushed herself to her feet. 'And there's no rest with all these people fussing around. Margaret Mary, it's time you took your baby home.'

'I don't want Brie to be alone here,' Maggie began.

'I'm staying.' Gray turned, met Maeve's gaze steadily. 'I'm staying with her.'

She jerked a shoulder. 'Sure it's no business of mine what

you do. We missed our tea,' she said. 'Lottie and I will have something downstairs while Rogan arranges to have us taken home. Do as you're told here, Brianna, and don't make a fuss.'

She leaned over, a bit stiffly, and kissed Brianna's uninjured cheek. 'You were ever a fast healer, so I don't expect this time to be any different.' Her fingers rested, for just an instant where her lips had, then she turned and hurried out, calling Lottie to follow.

'She said two rosaries on the drive here,' Lottie murmured. 'Rest yourself.' After a parting kiss, she trailed after Maeve.

'Well.' Maggie let out a long breath. 'I think I can trust Grayson to see that you behave yourself. I'll find Rogan and see how we'll deal with getting them both home again. I'll come back before we go, in case Grayson needs help.'

'I'll go with you, Maggie.' Murphy patted Brianna's sheet-draped knee. 'If they come to poke you, just turn your head away and close your eyes. That's what I do.'

She chuckled and, when the room emptied, looked up at Gray. 'I wish you'd sit down. I know you're upset.'

'I'm fine.' He was afraid if he sat, he'd go one better and just slide bonelessly to the floor. 'I'd like to know what happened if you're up to telling me.'

'It was all so fast.' Indulging the discomfort and fatigue, she closed her eyes a moment. 'We'd bought too much to carry, and I was going to fetch the car and drive it around to the shop where Maggie was waiting. Just as I pulled out of the car park, I heard someone shout. It was the attendant. He'd seen the other car coming for mine. There was nothing anyone could do then. There wasn't time. It hit on the side.'

She started to shift and her shoulder twanged in protest. 'They were going to tow the car away. I can't remember where.'

'It doesn't matter. We'll take care of it later. You hit your head.' Gently he reached down but kept his fingertips a breath away from the bandage.

'I must have, for the next thing I remember, there was a crowd around, and the American woman was crying and asking me if I was all right. Her husband had already gone to call an ambulance. I was fuddled. I think I asked that somebody get my sister, and then the three of us – Maggie, the baby and me – were riding off in an ambulance.'

She didn't add that there been a great deal of blood. Enough to terrify her until the medical attendant had staunched the flow.

'I'm sorry Maggie wasn't able to tell you more when she called. If she'd waited until the doctor had finished looking me over, she'd have saved you a lot of worry.'

'I'd have worried anyway. I don't – I can't –' He shut his eyes and struggled to find the words. 'It's hard for me to handle the idea of you being hurt. The reality of it is even tougher.'

'It's just bruises and bumps.'

'And a concussion, a pulled shoulder.' For both of their sakes, he yanked himself back. 'Tell me, is it truth or myth about not falling asleep with a concussion because you might not wake up?'

'It's a myth.' She smiled again. 'But I'm thinking seriously of staying awake for a day or two, just in case.'

'Then you'll want company.'

'I'll love company. I think I'd go mad lying in this bed alone, with nothing to do and no one to see.'

'How's this?' Careful not to jar her, he sat on the side of the bed. 'The food probably sucks here. It's hospital law in every developed country. I'll go out, hunt us up some burgers and chips. We'll have dinner together.'

'I'd like that.'

'And if they come in and try to give you a shot, I'll beat them up.'

'I wouldn't mind if you did. Would you do something else for me?'

'Name it.'

'Would you call Mrs. O'Malley? I've haddock waiting to be grilled for dinner. I know Murphy will see to Con, but the Carstairs need to be served, and there's more guests coming tomorrow.'

Gray lifted her hand to his lips, then rested his brow on it. 'Don't worry about it. Let me take care of you.'

It was the first time in his life he'd ever made the request.

Chapter Twenty-Three

By the time Gray got back with dinner, Brianna's hospital room resembled her garden. Sprays of roses and freesia, spears of lupine and lilies, blooms of cheerful daisies and carnations banked her window, filled the table beside the bed.

Gray shifted the enormous bouquet he held so that he could see over it and shook his head. 'Looks like these are superfluous.'

'Oh, no, they aren't. They're lovely. Such a fuss really for a bump on the head.' She held the bouquet in her unin-jured arm, much like she held a child, then buried her face in it. 'I'm enjoying it. Maggie and Rogan brought those, and Murphy those. And the last ones there were sent up from the Carstairs. Wasn't that sweet of them?'

'They were really worried.' He set down the large paper bag he held. 'I'm to tell you they're going to stay over another night, maybe two, depending on when you get out of here.'

'That's fine, of course. And I'll be out tomorrow, if I have to climb through the window.' She shot a wistful look at the bag. 'Did you really bring dinner?'

'I did. Managed to sneak it past the big, eagle-eyed nurse out there.'

'Ah, Mrs. Mannion. Terrifying, isn't she?'

'Scares me.' He pulled a chair close to the bed, then sat to dig into the bag. 'Bon appetite,' he said, handing her a burger. 'Oh, here, let me take those.' He rose again to lift the bouquet from her arm. 'I guess they need water, huh? Here, you eat.' He pulled out a bag of chips for her. 'I'll go find a vase.'

When he left again, she tried to shift to see what else was

355

in the bag he'd set on the floor. But the shoulder made movement awkward. Settling back again, she nibbled on the burger and tried not to pout. The sound of footsteps returning had her pasting a smile on her face.

'Where do you want them?' Gray asked.

'Oh, on that little table on there. Yes, that's lovely. Your dinner'll be cold, Gray.'

He only grunted, then sitting again took his own share of the meal from the bag. 'Feeling any better?'

'I don't feel nearly bad enough to be pampered this way, but I'm glad you stayed to have dinner with me.'

'Only the beginning, honey.' He winked and with the half-eaten burger in one hand, reached into the bag.

'Oh, Gray – a nightgown. A real nightgown.' It was plain, white, and cotton and all but brought tears of gratitude to her eyes. 'I can't tell you how much I appreciate that. This awful thing they put on you.'

'I'll help you change after dinner. There's more.'

'Slippers, too. Oh, a hairbrush. Thank God.'

'Actually, I can't take credit for all this. It was Maggie's idea.'

'Bless her. And you.'

'She said your blouse was ruined.' Bloody, he remembered she'd told him and took a moment to steady himself. 'We'll take care of that tomorrow, if they spring you. Now what else do we have here? Toothbrush, a little bottle of that cream you use all the time. Almost forgot the drinks.' He handed her a paper cup, topped with plastic with a hole for the straw. 'An excellent vintage, I'm told.'

'You thought of everything.'

'Absolutely. Even the entertainment.'

'Oh, a book.'

'A romance novel. You have several on your shelf at the cottage.'

'I like them.' She didn't have the heart to tell him the headache would make reading impossible. 'You went to a lot of trouble.'

'Just a quick shopping spree. Try to eat a little more.'

Dutifully she bit into a chip. 'When you get home will you thank Mrs. O'Malley for me, and tell her please, not to bother with the wash.'

'I'm not going back until you go.'

'But you can't stay here all night.'

'Sure I can.' Gray polished off the burger, balled the wrapper, and tossed it into the waste can. 'I've got a plan.'

'Grayson, you need to go home. Get some rest.'

'Here's the plan,' he said, ignoring her. 'After visiting hours, I'll hide out in the bathroom until things settle down. They probably make a sweep, so I'll wait until they come in and check on you.'

'That's absurd.'

'No, it'll work. Then the lights go off, and you're all tucked in. That's when I come out.'

'And sit in the dark for the rest of the night? Grayson, I'm not on my deathbed. I want you to go home.'

'Can't do it. And we won't sit in the dark.' With a smug grin, he pulled his last purchase from the bag. 'See this? It's a book light, the kind you clip on so you don't disturb your bed partner if you want to read late.'

Amazed, she shook her head. 'You've lost your mind.'

'On the contrary, I'm extremely clever. This way I won't be at the cottage worrying, you won't be here, alone and miserable. I'll read to you until you're tired.'

'Read to me?' she repeated in a murmur. 'You're going to read to me?'

'Sure. Can't have you trying to focus on this little print with a concussion, can we?'

'No.' She knew nothing, absolutely nothing in her life

had ever touched her more. 'I should make you go, but I so very much want you to stay.'

'That makes two of us. You know, this sounded pretty good from the back cover copy. "A deadly alliance," ' he read. ' "Katrina – she would never be tamed. The fiery-haired beauty with the face of a goddess and the soul of a warrior would risk everything to avenge the murder of her father. Even wed and bed her fiercest enemy." ' He lifted a brow. 'Hell of a gal, that Katrina. And the hero's no slouch, either. "Ian – he would never surrender. The bold and battle-scarred highland chief known as the Dark Lord would fight friend and foe to protect his land, and his woman. Sworn enemies, sworn lovers, they form an alliance that sweeps them toward destiny and into passion." '

He flipped the book over to the front cover, reaching idly for a chip. 'Pretty good, huh? And a fine-looking couple they are, too. See, it takes place in Scotland, twelfth century. Katrina's the only child of this widowed laird. He's let her run pretty wild, so she does a lot of guy stuff. Sword-play and archery, hunting. Then there's this evil plot and he's murdered, which makes her the laird and prey for the vicious and slightly insane villain. But our Katrina's no doormat.'

Brianna smiled, reached for Gray's hand. 'You've read it?'

'I paged through it when I was waiting to pay for it. There's this incredibly erotic scene on page two fifty-one. Well, we'll work our way up to that. They're probably going to come in and check your blood pressure, and we don't want it elevated. Better get rid of the evidence here, too.' He gathered up the wrappings from the smuggled dinner.

He'd barely hidden them in the bag when the door opened. Nurse Mannion, big as a halfback, bustled in. 'Visiting hours are nearly over, Mr. Thane.'

'Yes, ma'am.'

'Now, Miss Concannon, how are we doing? Any dizziness, nausea, blurred vision?'

'No, not at all. I'm feeling fine, really. In fact, I was wondering if –'

'That's good, that's good.' Nurse Mannion easily overroad the expected request to leave as she made notes on the chart at the foot of the bed. 'You should try to sleep. We'll be checking on you through the night, every three hours.' Still moving briskly, she set a tray on the table beside the bed.

Brianna only had to take one look to go pale. 'What's that? I told you I feel fine. I don't need a shot. I don't want one. Grayson.'

'I, ah –' One steely glance from Nurse Mannion had him fumbling in the role of hero.

'It's not a shot. We just need to draw a little blood.'

'What for?' Abandoning any pretense of dignity, Brianna cringed back. 'I lost plenty. Take some of that.'

'No nonsense now. Give me your arm.'

'Brie. Look here.' Gray linked his fingers with hers. 'Look at me. Did I ever tell you about the first time I went to Mexico? I hooked up with some people and went out on their boat. This was in the Gulf. It was really beautiful. Balmy air, crystal blue seas. We saw this little barricuda swimming along the port side.'

Out of the corner of his eye he saw Nurse Mannion slide the needle under Brianna's skin. And his stomach turned.

'Anyway, anyway,' he said, speaking quickly. 'One of the guys went to get his camera. He comes back, leans over the rail, and the mama barricuda jumps right up out of the water. It was like freeze frame. She looked right at the lens of the camera and smiled with all those teeth. Like a pose.

Then she plopped back into the water, got her baby, and they swam away.'

'You're making it up.'

'God's truth,' he said, lying desperately. 'He got the picture, too. I think he sold it to *National Geographic*, or maybe it was the *Enquirer*. Last I heard he was still out in the Gulf of Mexico, hoping to repeat the experience.'

'That's done.' The nurse patted a bandage in the crook of Brianna's elbow. 'Your dinner's on its way, miss, if you have room for it after your hamburger.'

'Ah, no, thank you just the same. I think I'll just rest now.'

'Five minutes, Mr. Thane.'

Grayson scratched his chin when the door swung shut behind her. 'Guess we didn't quite pull that off.'

Now Brianna did pout. 'You said you'd beat them up if they came in with needles.'

'She's a lot bigger than me.' He leaned over, kissed her lightly. 'Poor Brie.'

She tapped a finger on the book that lay on the bed beside her. 'Ian would never have backed down.'

'Well, hell, look how he's built. He could wrestle a horse. I'll never qualify for Dark Lord.'

'I'll take you just the same. Grinning barricudas,' she said and laughed. 'How do you think of such things?'

'Talent, sheer talent.' He went to the door, peeked out. 'Don't see her. I'm going to turn off the light, duck into the bathroom. We'll give it ten minutes.'

He read to her for two hours, taking her through Katrina's and Ian's perilous and romantic adventures by the tiny light of the book lamp. Now and again his hand would reach out and brush over hers, lingering over the moment of contact.

She knew she would always remember the sound of his voice, the way he slipped into a Scottish burr for the dialogue to amuse her. And the way he looked, she thought, the way his face was lit by the small bulb so that his eyes were dark, his cheekbones shadowed.

Her hero, she thought. Now and always. Closing her eyes, Brianna let the words he read drift over her.

'You're mine.' Ian swept her into his arms, strong arms that trembled from the need that gripped him. 'By law and by right, you're mine. And I am pledged to you, Katrina, from this day, from this hour.'

'And are you mine, Ian?' Fearlessly she speared her fingers into his hair, drew him closer. 'Are you mine, Dark Lord?'

'No one has ever loved you more than I.' He swore it. No one ever will.

Brianna fell asleep wishing the words Gray read could be his own.

Gray watched her, knowing from the slow, steady sound of her breathing that she'd drifted off. He indulged himself then and buried his face in his hands. Keep it light. He'd promised himself he'd keep it light, and the strain was catching up with him.

She wasn't badly hurt. But no matter how often he reminded himself of that, he couldn't shake the bone-deep terror that had gripped him from the moment Murphy had stepped into the kitchen.

He didn't want her in a hospital, bruised and bandaged. He never wanted to think of her hurt in any way. And now he would always remember it, he would always know that something could happen to her. That she might not be, as he wanted her always to be, humming in her kitchen or babying her flowers.

It infuriated him that he would have this picture of her to carry with all the others. And it infuriated all the more that he'd come to care so much he knew those pictures wouldn't fade as hundreds of other memories had.

He'd remember Brianna, and that tie would make it difficult to leave. And necessary to do so quickly.

He brooded over it as he waited for the night to pass. Each time a nurse would come to check Brianna, he listened to their murmured questions, her sleepy responses. Once, when he came back out, she called for him softly.

'Go back to sleep.' He brushed the hair away from her brow. 'It's not morning yet.'

'Grayson.' Drifting again, she reached for his hand. 'You're still here.'

'Yeah.' He looked down at her, frowned. 'I'm still here.'

When she awoke again, it was light. Forgetting, she started to sit up, and the dull ache in her shoulder jarred her memory. More annoyed now than distressed, she touched her fingertips to the bandage on her head and looked around for Gray.

She hoped he'd found some empty bed or waiting room couch to sleep on. She smiled at his flowers and wished she'd asked him to put them closer so that she could touch them as well.

Warily she tugged out the bodice of her nightgown, bit her lip. There was a rainbow of bruises down her breastbone and torso where the seat belt had secured her. Seeing them, she was grateful Gray had helped her change into the nightgown in the dark.

It wasn't fair, she thought. It wasn't right that she should look so battered for the last few days they had together. She wanted to be beautiful for him.

'Good morning, Miss Concannon, so you're awake.' A nurse breezed in, all smiles and youth and blooming health. Brianna wanted to hate her.

'I am, yes. When will the doctor come to release me?'

'Oh, he'll be making his rounds soon, don't worry. Nurse Mannion said you passed a peaceful night.' As she spoke, she strapped a blood pressure cuff on Brianna's arm, stuck a thermometer under her tongue. 'No dizziness then? Good, good,' she said when Brianna shook her head. She checked the blood pressure gauge, nodded, slipped the thermometer back out and nodded again at the results. 'Well, you're doing fine, then, aren't you?'

'I'm ready to go home.'

'I'm sure you're anxious.' The nurse made notes on the chart. 'Your sister's called already this morning, and a Mr. Biggs. An American. He said he was the one who hit your car.'

'Yes.'

'We reassured them both that you're resting comfortably. The shoulder paining you?'

'A bit.'

'You can have something for that now,' she said, reading the chart.

'I don't want a shot.'

'Oral.' She smiled. 'And your breakfast is coming. Oh, Nurse Mannion said you'd need two trays. One for Mr. Thane?' Obviously enjoying the joke, she glanced toward the bathroom. 'I'll be leaving in just a moment, Mr. Thane, and you can come out. She says he's a most handsome man,' the nurse murmured to Brianna. 'With the devil's own smile.'

'He is.'

'Lucky you. I'll get you something for the pain.'

When the door closed again, Gray stepped out of the bathroom, scowled. 'What, does that woman have radar?'

'Were you really in there? Oh, Gray, I thought you'd found a place to sleep. Have you been up all night?'

'I'm used to being up all night. Hey, you look better.' He came closer, his scowl fading into a look of sheer relief. 'You really look better.'

'I don't want to think of how I look. And you look tired.'

'I don't feel tired now. Starving,' he said, pressing a hand to his stomach. 'But not tired. What do you think they'll feed us?'

'You are not going to carry me into the house.'

'Yes, I am.' Gray skirted the hood of his car and opened the passenger door. 'The doctor said you could come home, *if* you took it easy, rested every afternoon, and avoided any heavy lifting.'

'Well, I'm not lifting anything, am I?'

'Nope. I am.' Careful of her shoulder, he slipped an arm behind her back, another behind her knees. 'Women are supposed to think this kind of stuff's romantic.'

'Under different circumstances. I can walk, Grayson. There's nothing wrong with my legs.'

'Not a thing. They're great.' He kissed her nose. 'Haven't I mentioned that before?'

'I don't believe you have.' She smiled, despite the fact that he'd bumped her shoulder and the bruises on her chest were aching. It was the thought, after all, that counted. 'Well, since you're playing at being Dark Lord, sweep me inside, then. And I expect to be kissed. Well kissed.'

'You've gotten awfully demanding since you got hit on the head.' He carried her up the walk. 'But I guess I have to indulge you.'

Before he could reach for the door, it swung open and Maggie rushed out. 'There you are. It seems we've been waiting forever. How are you?'

'I'm being pampered. And if all of you don't watch out, I'll get used to it.'

'Bring her inside, Gray. Is there anything in the car she needs?'

'About an acre of flowers.'

'I'll fetch them.' She dashed off as the Carstairs hurried into the hall from the parlor.

'Oh, Brianna, you poor, dear thing. We've been so worried. Johnny and I barely slept a wink thinking of you lying in hospital that way. Such depressing places, hospitals. I can't think why anyone would choose to work in one, can you? Do you want some tea, a nice cool cloth? Anything at all?'

'No, thank you, Iris,' Brianna managed when she could get a word in. 'I'm sorry you were worried. It was only a little thing, really.'

'Nonsense. A car accident, a night in the hospital. A concussion. Oh, does your poor head ache?'

It was beginning to.

'We're glad you're home again,' Carstairs put in, and patted his wife's hand to calm her.

'I hope Mrs. O'Malley made you comfortable.'

'She's a treasure, I assure you.'

'Where do you want these flowers, Brie?' Maggie asked from behind a forest of posies.

'Oh, well –'

'I'll put them in your room,' she decided for herself. 'Rogan'll be up to see you as soon as Liam wakes from his nap. Oh, and you've had calls from the whole village, and enough baked goods sent over to feed an army for a week.'

'There's our girl.' Drying her hands on a towel, Lottie bustled out from the kitchen.

'Lottie. I didn't realize you were here.'

'Of course I am. I'm going to see your settled and cared for. Grayson, take her right on into her room. She needs rest.'

365

'Oh, but no. Grayson, put me down.'

Gray only shifted his grip. 'You're outnumbered. And if you don't behave, I won't read you the rest of the book.'

'This is nonsense.' Over her protests Brianna found herself in her room being laid on the bed. 'I might as well be back in the hospital.'

'Now, don't make a fuss. I'm going to make you a nice cup of tea.' Lottie began arranging pillows, smoothing sheets. 'Then you'll nap. You're going to be flooded with visitors before long and you need your rest.'

'At least let me have my knitting.'

'We'll see about that later. Gray, you can keep her company. See that she stays put.'

Brianna poked out a lip, folded her arms. 'Go away,' she told him. 'I don't need you about if you won't stand up for me.'

'Well, well, the truth comes out.' Eyeing her, he leaned comfortably on the doorjamb. 'You're quite a shrew, aren't you?'

'A shrew, is it? I complain at being bullied and ordered about and that makes me a shrew?'

'You're pouting and complaining about being cared for and looked after. That makes you a shrew.'

She opened her mouth closed it again. 'Well, then, I am.'

'You need your pills.' He took the prescription bottle out of his pocket, then walked into the bathroom to fill a glass with water.

'They make me groggy,' she muttered when he came back, holding out the capsule.

'Do you want me to have to pinch your nose to get you to open up and swallow.'

The notion of that humiliation had her snatching the pill, then the glass. 'There. Happy?'

'I'll be happy when you stop hurting.'

The fight went out of her. 'I'm sorry, Gray. I'm behaving so badly.'

'You're in pain.' He sat on the side of the bed, took her hand. 'I've been battered a couple of times myself. The first day's a misery. The second's hell.'

She sighed. 'I thought it would be better, and I'm angry it's not. I don't mean to snap at you.'

'Here's your tea now, lamb.' Lottie came in and balanced the saucer in Brianna's hands. 'And let's get these shoes off so you'll be comfortable.'

'Lottie. Thank you for being here.'

'Oh, you don't have to thank me for that. Mrs. O'Malley and I'll keep things running around here till you're feeling yourself again. Don't you fret over a thing.' She spread a light blanket over Brianna's legs. 'Grayson, you see that she rests now, won't you?'

'You can count on it.' On impulse he rose to kiss Lottie's cheek. 'You're a sweetheart, Lottie Sullivan.'

'Oh, go on.' Flushing with pleasure, she bustled back into the kitchen.

'So are you, Grayson Thane,' Brianna murmured. 'A sweetheart.'

'Oh, go on,' he said. He tilted his head. 'Can she cook?'

She laughed as he'd hoped she would. 'A fine cook is our Lottie, and it wouldn't take much to charm a cobbler from her. If you've a taste for one.'

'I'll keep that in mind. Maggie brought in the book.' He picked it up from where Maggie had set it on Brianna's night table. 'Are you up for another chapter of blistering medieval romance?'

'I am.'

'You fell asleep while I was reading last night,' he said as he paged through the book. 'What's the last thing you remember?'

'When he told her he loved her.'

'Well, that certainly narrows it down.'

'The first time.' She patted the bed, wanting him to sit beside her again. 'No one forgets the first time they hear it.' His fingers fumbled on the pages, stilled, and he said nothing. Understanding, Brianna touched his arm. 'You mustn't let it worry you, Grayson. What I feel for you isn't meant to worry you.'

It did. Of course it did. But there was something else, and he thought he could give her that, at least. 'It humbles me, Brianna.' He lifted his gaze, those golden-brown eyes uncertain. 'And it staggers me.'

'One day, when you remember the first time you heard it, I hope it pleasures you.' Content for now, she sipped her tea, smiled. 'Tell me a story, Grayson.'

Chapter Twenty-Four

He didn't leave on the first of June as he'd planned. He could have. Knew he should have. But it seemed wrong, certainly cowardly, to go before he was positive Brianna was well on the mend.

The bandages came off. He'd seen for himself the bruises and had iced down the swelling of her shoulder. He'd suffered when she turned in her sleep and caused herself discomfort. He scolded when she overdid.

He didn't make love with her.

He wanted her, hourly. At first he'd been afraid even the most gentle of touches would hurt her. Then he decided it was best as it was. A kind of segue, he thought, from lover, to friend, to memory. Surely it would be easier for them both if his remaining days with her were spent in friendship and not in passion.

His book was finished, but he didn't mail it. Gray convinced himself he should take a quick detour to New York before his tour and hand it over to Arlene personally. If he thought, from time to time, how he had asked Brianna to go off with him for a little while, he told himself it was best forgotten.

For her sake, of course. He was only thinking of her.

He saw, through the window, that she was taking down the wash. Her hair was loose, blowing back from her face in the stiff western breeze. Behind her, the finished greenhouse glistened in the sunlight. Beside her, flowers she'd planted swayed and danced. He watched as she unhooked a clothespin, popped it back on the line, moved onto the next, gathering billowing sheets as she went.

She was, he thought, a postcard. Something that personified a place, a time, a way of life. Day after day, he thought, year after year, she would hang her clothes and linens to dry in the wind and the sun. And gather them up again. And with her, and those like her, the repetition wouldn't be monotony. It would be tradition – one that made her strong and self-reliant.

Oddly disturbed, he walked outside. 'You're using that arm too much.'

'The doctor said exercise was good for it.' She glanced over her shoulder. The smile that curved her lips didn't reach her eyes, and hadn't for days. He was moving away from her so quickly, she couldn't keep up. 'I barely have a twinge now. It's a glorious day, isn't it? The family staying with us drove to Ballybunion to the beach. Da used to take Maggie and me there sometimes, to swim and eat ice-cream cones.'

'If you'd wanted to go to the beach, you'd only had to ask. I'd have taken you.'

The tone of his voice had her spine stiffening. Her movements became more deliberate as she unpinned a pillow-slip. 'That's kind of you, I'm sure, Grayson. But I don't have time for a trip to the sea. I've work to do.'

'All you do is work,' he exploded. 'You break your back over this place. If you're not cooking, you're scrubbing, if you're not scrubbing, you're washing. For Christ's sake, Brianna, it's just a house.'

'No.' She folded the pillowslip in half, then half again before laying it in her wicker basket. ''Tis my home, and it pleases me to cook in it, and scrub in it, and wash in it.'

'And never look past it.'

'And where are you looking, Grayson Thane, that's so damned important?' She choked off the bubbling temper, reverted to ice. 'And who are you to criticize me for making a home for myself.'

'Is it a home – or a trap?'

She turned then, and her eyes were neither hot nor cold, but full of grief. 'Is that how you think, really, in your heart? That one is the same as the other, and must be? If it is, truly, I'm sorry for you.'

'I don't want sympathy,' he shot back. 'All I'm saying is that you work too hard, for too little.'

'I don't agree, nor is that all you said. Perhaps it was all you meant to say.' She bent down and picked up her basket. 'And it's more than you've said to me for these past five days.'

'Don't be ridiculous.' He reached out to take the basket from her, but she jerked it away. 'I talk to you all the time. Let me take that.'

'I'll take it myself. I'm not a bloody invalid.' Impatiently she set the basket at her hip. 'You've talked at me and around me, Grayson, these last days. But to me, and of anything you were really thinking or feeling, no. You haven't talked to me, and you haven't touched me. Wouldn't it be more honest to just tell me you don't want me anymore?'

'Don't –' She was already stalking past him toward the house. He'd nearly grabbed at her before he stopped himself. 'Where did you get an idea that like?'

'Every night.' She let the door swing back and nearly caught him in the face with it. 'You sleep with me, but you don't touch me. And if I turn to you, you turn away.'

'You're just out of the fucking hospital.'

'I've been out of the hospital for nearly two weeks. And don't swear at me. Or if you must swear, don't lie.' She slapped the basket onto the kitchen table. 'Anxious to be gone is what you are, and not sure how to be gracious about it. And you're tired of me.' She snapped a sheet out of the basket and folded it neatly, corner to corner. 'And haven't figured out how to say so.'

'That's bullshit. That's just bullshit.'

'It's funny how your way with words suffers when you're angry.' She flipped the sheet over her arm in a practiced move, mating bottom to top. 'And you're thinking, poor

Brie, she'll be breaking her heart over me. Well, I won't.' Another fold, and the sheet was a neat square to be laid on the scrubbed kitchen table. 'I did well enough before you came along, and I'll do well enough after.'

'Very cool words from someone who claims to be in love.'

'I am in love with you.' She took out another sheet, calmy began the same routine. 'Which makes me a fool to be sure for loving a man so cowardly he's afraid of his own feelings. Afraid of love because he didn't have it as a boy. Afraid to make a home because he never knew one.'

'We're not talking about what I was,' Gray said evenly.

'No, you think you can run away from that, and do every time you pack your bag and hop on the next plane or train. Well, you can't. Any more than I can stay in one place and pretend I grew up happy in it. I missed my share of love, too, but I'm not afraid of it.'

Calmer now, she laid the second sheet down. 'I'm not afraid to love you, Grayson. I'm not afraid to let you go. But I'm afraid we'll both be sorry if we don't part honestly.'

He couldn't escape that calm understanding in her eyes. 'I don't know what you want, Brianna.' And he was afraid, for the first time in his adult memory, that he didn't know what he wanted himself. For himself.

It was hard for her to say it, but she thought it would be harder not to. 'I want you to touch me, to lie with me. And if you've no desire for me anymore, it would hurt much less if you'd tell me so.'

He stared at her. He couldn't see what it was costing her. She wouldn't let him see, only stood, her back straight, her eyes level, waiting.

'Brianna, I can't breathe without wanting you.'

'Then have me now, in the daylight.'

Defeated, he stepped forward, cupped her face in his hands. 'I wanted to make it easier for you.'

'Don't. Just be with me now. For now.'

He picked her up, made her smile as she pressed her lips to his throat. 'Just like in the book.'

'Better,' he promised as he carried her into the bedroom. 'This will be better than any book.' He set her on her feet, combing her wind-tossed hair back from her face before reaching for the buttons of her blouse. 'I've suffered lying beside you at night and not touching you.'

'There was no need.'

'I thought there was.' Very gently he traced a fingertip over the yellowing marks on her skin. 'You're still bruised.'

'They're fading.'

'I'll remember how they looked. And how my stomach clenched when I saw them. How I'd tighten up inside when you'd moan in your sleep.' A little desperate, he lifted his gaze to hers. 'I don't want to care this much about anyone, Brianna.'

'I know.' She leaned forward, pressed her cheek to his. 'Don't worry on it now. There's only us two, and I've been missing you so.' With her eyes half closed, she ran a line of kisses up his jaw while her fingers worked on the buttons of his shirt. 'Come to bed, Grayson,' she murmured, sliding the shirt from his shoulders. 'Come with me.'

A sigh of the mattress, a rustle of sheets, and they were in each other's arms. She lifted her face, and her mouth sought his. The first frisson of pleasure shuddered through her, then the next as the kiss went deep.

His fingertips were cool against her flesh, soft strokes as he stripped her. And his lips were light over the fading bruises, as if by wish alone he could vanish them.

A bird sang in the little pear tree outside, and the breeze sent the fairy dance she'd hung singing, billowed the delicate lace of her curtains. It fluttered over his bare back as he shifted over her, as he laid his cheek under her heart. The gesture made her smile, cradle his head in her hands.

It was all so simple. A moment of gold she would treasure. And when he lifted his head, and his lips sought hers again, he smiled into her eyes.

There was need, but no hurry, and longing without desperation. If either of them thought this might be their last time together, they looked for savoring rather than urgency.

She sighed out his name, breath hitching. He trembled.

Then he was inside her, the pace achingly slow. Their eyes remained open. And their hands, palm to palm, completed the link with interlacing fingers.

A shaft of light through the window, and dust motes dancing in the beam. The call of a bird, the distant bark of a dog. The smell of roses, lemon wax, honeysuckle. And the feel of her, the warm, wet feel of her yielding beneath him, rising to meet him. His senses sharpened on it all, like a microscope just focused.

Then there was only pleasure, the pure and simple joy of losing everything he was, in her.

She knew by dinnertime that he was leaving. In her heart she had known when they had lain quiet together after loving, watching the sunlight shift through her window.

She served her guests, listened to their bright talk of their day at the seaside. As always, she tidied her kitchen, washing her dishes, putting them away again in the cupboards. She scrubbed off her stove, thinking again that she should replace it soon. Perhaps over the winter. She would have to start pricing them.

Con was sniffing around the door, so she let him out for his evening run. For a time she just stood there, watching him race over the hills in the glowing sunlight of the long summer evening.

She wondered what it would be like to run with him. To just race as he was racing, forgetting all the little details of settling the house for the night. Forgetting most of all what she had to face.

But, of course, she would come back. This was where she would always come back.

She turned, closing the door behind her. She went into her room briefly before going up to Gray.

He was at his window, looking out at her front garden. The light that hung yet in the western sky gilded him and made her think, as she had so many months before, of pirates and poets.

'I was afraid you'd have finished packing.' She saw his suitcase open on the bed, nearly full, and her fingers tightened on the sweater she carried.

'I was going to come down and talk to you.' Braced for it, he turned to her, wishing he could read her face. But she'd found a way to close it off from him. 'I thought I could make Dublin tonight.'

'It's a long drive, but you'll have light for a while yet.'

'Brianna —'

'I wanted to give you this,' she said quickly. Please, she wanted to beg, no excuses, no apologies. 'I made it for you.'

He looked down at her hands. He remembered the dark green wool, how she'd been knitting with it the night he'd come into her room late and picked a fight with her. The way it had spilled over the white of her nightgown.

'You made it for me?'

'Yes. A sweater. You might find use for it in the fall and winter.' She moved toward him, holding it up to measure. 'I added to the length of the sleeves. You're long in the arm.'

His already unsteady heart shifted as he touched it. In the whole of his life, no one had ever made him anything. 'I don't know what to say.'

'Whenever you gave me a gift, you'd always tell me to say thank you.'

'So I did.' He took it, felt the softness and warmth on the palms of his hands. 'Thank you.'

'You're welcome. Do you need some help with your packing?' Without waiting for an answer, she took the sweater back and folded it neatly into his suitcase. 'You've more experience with it, I know, but you must find it tedious.'

'Please don't.' He laid a hand on her shoulder, but when she didn't look up, dropped it again. 'You've every right to be upset.'

'No, I don't. And I'm not. You made no promises, Grayson, so you've broken none. That's important to you, I know. Have you checked the drawers? You'd be amazed at what people forget.'

'I have to go, Brianna.'

'I know.' To keep her hands busy, she opened the dresser drawers herself, painfully distressed to find them indeed empty.

'I can't stay here. The longer I do now, the harder it is. And I can't give you what you need. Or think you need.'

'Next you'll be telling me you've the soul of a gypsy, and there's no need for that. I know it.' She closed the last drawer and turned around again. 'I'm sorry for saying what I did earlier. I don't want you to go remembering hard words between us, when there was so much more.'

Her hands were folded again, her badge of control. 'Would you like me to pack you some food for the trip, or a thermos of tea perhaps?'

'Stop being the gracious hostess. For Christ's sake, I'm leaving you. I'm walking out.'

'You're going,' she returned in a cool and steady voice, 'as you always said you would. It might be easier on your conscience if I wept and wailed and made a scene, but it doesn't suit me.'

'So that's that.' He tossed some socks into the case.

'You've made your choice, and I wish you nothing but

happiness. You're welcome back, of course, if you travel this way again.'

His gaze cut to hers as he snapped the case closed. 'I'll let you know.'

'I'll help you down with your things.'

She reached for his duffel, but he grabbed it first. 'I carried them in. I'll carry them out.'

'As you please.' Then she cut out his heart by coming to him and kissing him lightly on the cheek. 'Keep well, Grayson.'

'Goodbye, Brie.' They went down the steps together. He said nothing more until they'd reached the front door. 'I won't forget you.'

'I hope not.'

She walked part way with him to the car, then stopped on the garden path, waiting while he loaded his bag, climbed behind the wheel. She smiled, lifted her hand in a wave, then walked back into the cottage without looking back.

An hour later she was alone in the parlor with her mending basket. She heard the laughter through the windows and closed her eyes briefly. When Maggie came in with Rogan and the baby, she was nipping a thread and smiling.

'Well, now, you're out late tonight.'

'Liam was restless.' Maggie sat, lifting her arms so Rogan could pass the baby to her. 'We thought he'd like some company. And here's a picture, the mistress of the house in the parlor mending.'

'I'm behind in it. Would you like a drink? Rogan?'

'I wouldn't turn one down.' He moved toward the decanter. 'Maggie?'

'Aye, a little whiskey would go down well.'

'And Brie?'

'Thank you. I think I will.' She threaded a needle, knotted the end. 'Is your work going well, Maggie?'

'It's wonderful to be back at it. Yes, it is.' She planted a noisy kiss on Liam's mouth. 'I finished a piece today. It was Gray talking about those ruins he's so fond of that gave me the notion for it. Turned out well I think.'

She took the glass Rogan handed her, lifted hers. 'Well, here's to a restful night.'

'I'll give you no argument there,' her husband said with fervor and drank.

'Liam doesn't think the hours between two and five A.M. should be for sleeping.' With a laugh Maggie shifted the baby onto her shoulder. 'We wanted to tell you, Brie, the detective's tracking Amanda Dougherty to – where is that place, Rogan?'

'Michigan. He has a lead on her, and the man she married.' He glanced at his wife. 'And the child.'

'She had a daughter, Brie,' Maggie murmured, cuddling her own baby. 'He located the birth cirtificate. Amanda named her Shannon.'

'For the river,' Brianna whispered and felt tears rise up in her throat. 'We have a sister, Maggie.'

'We have. We may find her soon, for better or worse.'

'I hope so. Oh, I'm glad you came to tell me.' It helped a little, took some of the sting out of her heart. 'It'll be good to think of it.'

'It may just be thinking for a while,' Rogan warned. 'The lead he's following is twenty-five years old.'

'Then we'll be patient,' Brianna said simply.

Far from certain of her own feelings, Maggie shifted the baby, and the topic. 'I'd like to show the piece I've finished to Gray, see if he recognizes the inspiration. Where is he? Working?'

'He's gone.' Brianna sent the needle neatly through a buttonhole.

'Gone where? To the pub?'

'No, to Dublin, I think, or wherever the road takes him.'

'You mean he's gone? Left?' She rose then, making the baby chortle with glee at the sudden movement.

'Yes, just an hour ago.'

'And you sit here sewing?'

'What should I be doing? Flogging myself?'

'Flogging him's more like. Why, that Yank bastard. To think I'd grown fond of him.'

'Maggie.' Rogan laid a warning hand on her arm. 'Are you all right, Brianna?'

'I'm fine, thank you, Rogan. Don't take on so, Maggie. He's doing what's right for him.'

'To hell with what's right for him. What about you? Take the baby, will you?' she said impatiently to Rogan, then, arms free, went to kneel in front of her sister. 'I know how you feel about him, Brie, and I can't understand how he could leave this way. What did he say when you asked him to stay?'

'I didn't ask him to stay.'

'You didn't – Why the devil not?'

'Because it would have made us both unhappy.' She jabbed the needle, swore lightly at the prick on her thumb. 'And I have my pride.'

'A fat lot of good that does you. You probably offered to fix him sandwiches for the trip.'

'I did.'

'Oh.' Disgusted, Maggie rose, turned around the room. 'There's no reasoning with you. Never has been.'

'I'm sure you're making Brianna feel much better by having a tantrum,' Rogan said dryly.

'I was just –' But catching his eye, Maggie bit her tongue. 'You're right, of course. I'm sorry, Brie. If you like I can stay awhile, keep you company. Or I'll pack up some things for the baby, and we'll both stay the night.'

'You both belong at home. I'll be fine, Maggie, on my own. I always am.'

Gray was nearly to Dublin and the scene kept working on his mind. The ending of the book, the damn ending just wouldn't settle. That's why he was so edgy.

He should have mailed the manuscript off to Arlene and forgotten it. That last scene wouldn't be digging at him now if he had. He could already be toying with the next story.

But he couldn't think of another when he wasn't able to let go of the last.

McGee had driven away because he'd finished what he'd come to Ireland to do. He was going to pick up his life again, his work. He had to move on because . . . because he had to, Gray thought irritably.

And Tullia had stayed because her life was in the cottage, in the land around it, the people. She was happy there the way she never would be anywhere else. Brianna – Tullia, he corrected, would wither without her roots.

The ending made sense. It was perfectly plausible, fit both character and mood.

So why was it nagging at him like a bad tooth?

She hadn't asked him to stay, he thought. Hadn't shed a tear. When he realized his mind had once again shifted from Tullia to Brianna, he swore and pressed harder on the accelerator.

That's the way it was supposed to be, he reminded himself. Brianna was a sensible, levelheaded woman. It was one of the things he admired about her.

If she'd loved him so damn much, the least she could have done was said she'd miss him.

He didn't want her to miss him. He didn't want a light burning in the window, or her darning his socks or ironing his shirts. And most of all, he didn't want her preying on his mind.

He was footloose and free, as he'd always been. As he needed to be. He had places to go, a pin to stick in a map. A little vacation somewhere before the tour, and then new horizons to explore.

That was his life. He tapped his fingers impatiently on the steering wheel. He liked his life. And he was picking it up again, just like McGee.

Just like McGee, he thought with a scowl.

The lights of Dublin glowed in welcome. It relaxed him to see them, to know he'd come where he'd intended to go. He didn't mind the traffic. Of course he didn't. Or the noise. He'd just spent too long away from cities.

What he needed was to find a hotel, check in. All he wanted was a chance to stretch his legs after the long drive, to buy himself a drink or two.

Gray pulled over to a curb, let his head fall back against the seat. All he wanted was a bed, a drink, and quiet room.

The hell it was.

Brianna was up at dawn. It was foolish to lie in bed and pretend you could sleep when you couldn't. She started her bread and set it aside to rise before brewing the first pot of tea.

She took a cup for herself into the back garden, but couldn't settle. Even a tour of the greenhouse didn't please her, so she went inside again and set the table for breakfast.

It helped that her guests were leaving early. By eight, she'd fixed them a hot meal and bid them on their way.

But now she was alone. Certain she would find contentment in routine, she set the kitchen to rights. Upstairs, she stripped the unmade beds, smoothed on the sheets she'd taken fresh from the line the day before. She gathered the damp towels, replaced them.

And it couldn't be put off any longer, she told herself. Shouldn't be. She moved briskly into the room where Grayson had worked. It needed a good dusting, she thought and ran a finger gently over the edge of the desk.

Pressing her lips together, she straightened the chair.

How could she have known it would feel so empty?

She shook herself. It was only a room, after all. Waiting now for the next guest to come. And she would put the very next one into it, she promised. It would be wise to do that. It would help.

She moved into the bath, taking the towels he'd used from the bar where they'd dried.

And she could smell him.

The pain came so quickly, so fiercely, she nearly staggered under it. Blindly she stumbled back into the bedroom, sat on the bed, and burying her face in the towels, wept.

Gray could hear her crying as he came up the stairs. It was a wild sound of grieving that stunned him, made him slow his pace before he faced it.

From the doorway he saw her, rocking herself for comfort, with her face pressed into towels.

Not cool, he thought, or controlled. Not levelheaded.

He rubbed his hands over his own face, scraping away some of the travel fatigue and the guilt.

'Well,' he said in an easy voice, 'you sure as hell had me fooled.'

Her head shot up, and he could see now the heartbreak in her eyes, the shadows under them. She started to rise, but he waved a hand.

'No, don't stop crying, keep right on. It does me good to know what a fake you are. "Let me help you pack, Gray. Why don't I fix you some food for your trip? I'll get along just dandy without you." '

She struggled against the tears, but couldn't win. As they poured out, she buried her face again.

'You had me going, really had me. You never even looked back. That's what was wrong with the scene. It didn't play. It never did.' He crossed to her, pulled the towels away. 'You're helplessly in love with me, aren't you, Brianna? All the way in love, no tricks, no traps, no trite phrases.'

'Oh, go away. Why did you come back here?'

'I forgot a few things.'

'There's nothing here.'

'You're here.' He knelt down, taking her hands to keep her from covering the tears. 'Let me tell you a story. No, go on crying if you want,' he said when she tried to pull away. 'But listen. I thought he had to leave. McGee.'

'You've come back to talk to me about your book?'

'Let me tell you a story. I figured he had to leave. So what if he'd never cared for anyone the way he cared for Tullia. So what if she loved him, had changed him, changed his whole life. Completed it. They were miles apart in every other way, weren't they?'

Patiently he watched another tear run down her cheek. She was struggling against them, he knew. And she was losing.

'He was a loner,' Gray continued. 'Always had been. What the hell would he be doing, planting himself in some little cottage in the west of Ireland? And she let him go, because she was too damn stubborn, too proud, and too much in love to ask him to stay.

'I worried over that,' he continued. 'For weeks. It drove me crazy. And all the way to Dublin I chewed on it – figured I wouldn't think of you if I was thinking of that. And I suddenly realized that he wouldn't go, and she wouldn't let him. Oh, they'd survive without each other, because they're born survivors. But they'd never be whole. Not the way they were together. So I did a rewrite, right there in the lobby of the hotel in Dublin.'

She swallowed hard against tears and humiliation. 'So you've solved your problem. Good for you.'

'One of them. You're not going anywhere, Brianna.' He tightened his grip until she stopped dragging at her hands. 'When I finished the rewrite, I thought, I'll get a drink somewhere, and go to bed. Instead, I got in the car, turned around, and came back here. Because I forgot that I spent the happiest six months of my life here. I forgot that I wanted to hear you singing in the kitchen in the morning or see you out of the bedroom window. I forgot that surviving isn't always enough. Look at me. Please.'

When she did, he rubbed one of her tears away with his thumb, then linked his hands with hers again. 'And most of all, Brianna, I forgot to let myself tell you that I love you.'

She said nothing, couldn't as her breath continued to hitch. But her eyes widened and two new tears plopped onto their joined hands.

'It was news to me, too,' he murmured. 'More of a shock. I'm still not sure how to deal with it. I never wanted to feel this way about anyone, and it's been easy to avoid it until you. It means strings, and responsibilities, and it means maybe I can live without you, but I'd never be whole without you.'

Gently he lifted their joined hands to his lips and tasted her tears. 'I figured you'd gotten over me pretty quick with that send-off last night. That started me panicking. I was all set to beg when I came in and heard you crying. I have to say, it was music to my ears.'

'You wanted me to cry.'

'Maybe. Yeah.' He rose then, releasing her hands. 'I figured if you'd done some sobbing on my shoulder last night, if you'd asked me not to leave you, I'd have stayed. Then I could have blamed you if I screwed things up.'

After a short laugh she wiped at her cheeks. 'I've accommodated you, haven't I?'

'Not really.' He turned back to look at her. She was so perfect, he realized, with her tidy apron, her hair slipping from its pins, and tears drying on her cheeks. 'I had to come around to this on my own, so I've got no one else to blame if I mess it up. I want you to know I'm going to try hard not to mess it up.'

'You want to come back.' She gripped her hands tight together. It was so hard to hope.

'More or less. More, actually.' The panic was still there, brewing inside him. He only hoped it didn't show. 'I said I love you, Brianna.'

'I know. I remember.' She managed a smile as she rose. 'You don't forget the first time you hear it.'

'The first time I heard it was the first time I made love to you. I was hoping I'd hear it again.'

'I love you, Grayson. You know I do.'

'We're going to see about that.' He reached into his pocket and took out a small box.

'You didn't have to buy me a gift. You only had to come home.'

'I thought about that a lot, driving back from Dublin. Coming home. It's the first time I have.' He handed her the box. 'I'd like to make it a habit.'

She opened the box and, bracing a hand on the bed behind her, sat again.

'I harassed the manager of the hotel in Dublin until he had the gift shop opened. You Irish are so sentimental, I didn't even have to bribe him.' He swallowed. 'I thought I'd have better luck with a traditional ring. I want you to marry me, Brianna. I want us to make a home together.'

'Grayson –'

'I know I'm a bad bet,' he hurried on. 'I don't deserve

you. But you love me anyway. I can work anywhere, and I can help you here, with the inn.'

As she looked at him, her heart simply overflowed. He loved her, wanted her, and would stay. 'Grayson —'

'I'll still have to travel some.' He plowed over her, terrified she'd refuse him. 'But it wouldn't be like before. And sometimes you could come with me. We'd always come back here, Brie. Always. This place, it means almost as much to me as it does to you.'

'I know. I —'

'You can't know,' he interrupted. 'I didn't know myself until I'd left. It's home. You're home. Not a trap,' he murmured. 'A sanctuary. A chance. I want to make a family here.' He dragged a hand through his hair as she stared at him. 'Jesus, I want that. Children, long-term plans. A future. And knowing you're right there, every night, every morning. No one could ever love you the way I do, Brianna. I want to pledge to you.' He drew an unsteady breath. 'From this day, from this hour.'

'Oh, Grayson.' She choked out his name. Dreams, it seemed, could come true. 'I've wanted —'

'I've never loved anyone before, Brianna. In my whole life there's been no one but you. So I'll treasure you. I swear it. And if you'd just —'

'Oh, be quiet, will you,' she said between laughter and tears, 'so I can say yes.'

'Yes?' He plucked her off the bed again, stared into her eyes. 'No making me suffer first?'

'The answer's yes. Just yes.' She put her arms around him, laid her head on his shoulder. And smiled. 'Welcome home, Grayson.'

Turn the page for an extract from
Born in Shame
Nora Roberts' romantic conclusion
to the Born In trilogy

Prologue

Amanda dreamed dreadful dreams. Colin was there, his sweet, well loved face crushed with sorrow. *Mandy,* he said. He never called her anything but Mandy. His Mandy, my Mandy, darling Mandy. But there'd been no smile in his voice, no laugh in his eyes.

Mandy, we can't stop it. I wish we could. Mandy, my Mandy, I miss you so. But I never thought you'd have to come so soon after me. Our little girl, it's so hard for her. And it'll get harder. You have to tell her, you know.

He smiled then, but it was sad, so sad, and his body, his face, that had seemed so solid, so close that she'd reached out in sleep to touch him, began to fade and shimmer away.

You have to tell her, he repeated. *We always knew you would. She needs to know where she comes from. Who she is. But tell her, Mandy, tell her never to forget that I loved her. I loved my little girl.*

Oh, don't go, Colin. She moaned in her sleep, pining for him. Stay with me. I love you, Colin. My sweet Colin. I love you for all you are.

But she couldn't bring him back. And couldn't stop the dream.

Oh, how lovely to see Ireland again, she thought, drifting like mist over the green hills she remembered from so long ago. See the river gleam, like a ribbon all silver and bright around a gift without price.

And there was Tommy, darling Tommy, waiting for her. Turning to smile at her, to welcome her.

Why was there such grief here, when she was back and felt so young, so vibrant, so in love?

I thought I'd never see you again. Her voice was breathless, with a laugh on the edges of it. *Tommy, I've come back to you.*

He seemed to stare at her. No matter how she tried she

could get no closer than an arm span away from him. But she could hear his voice, as clear and sweet as ever.

I love you, Amanda. Always. Never has a day passed that I haven't thought of you, and remembered what we found here.

He turned in her dream to look out over the river where the banks were green and soft and the water quiet.

You named her for the river, for the memory of the days we had.

She's so beautiful, Tommy. So bright, so strong. You'd be proud.

I am proud. And how I wish . . . But it couldn't be. We knew it. You knew it. He sighed, turned back. *You did well for her, Amanda. Never forget that. But you're leaving her now. The pain of that, and what you've held inside all these years, makes it so hard. You have to tell her, give her her birthright. And let her know, somehow let her know that I loved her. And would have shown her if I could.*

I can't do it alone, she thought, struggling out of sleep as his image faded away. Oh, dear God, don't make me do it alone.

'Mom.' Gently, though her hands shook, Shannon stroked her mother's sweaty face. 'Mom, wake up. It's a dream. A bad dream.' She understood what it was to be tortured by dreams, and knew how to fear waking – as she woke every morning now afraid her mother would be gone. There was desperation in her voice. Not now, she prayed. Not yet. 'You need to wake up.'

'Shannon. They're gone. They're both of them gone. Taken from me.'

'Ssh. Don't cry. Please, don't cry. Open your eyes now, and look at me.'

Amanda's lids fluttered open. Her eyes swam with grief. 'I'm sorry. So sorry. I did only what I thought right for you.'

'I know. Of course you did.' She wondered frantically if the delirium meant the cancer was spreading to the brain. Wasn't it enough that it had her mother's bones? She cursed the greedy disease, and cursed God, but her voice was soothing when she spoke. 'It's all right now. I'm here. I'm with you.'

With an effort, Amanda drew a long, steadying breath. Visions swam in her head – Colin, Tommy, her darling girl. How anguished Shannon's eyes were – how shattered they had been when she'd first come back to Columbus.

'It's all right now.' Amanda would have done anything to erase that dread in her daughter's eyes. 'Of course, you're here. I'm so glad you're here.' And so sorry, darling, so sorry I have to leave you. 'I've frightened you. I'm sorry I frightened you.'

It was true – the fear was a metallic taste in the back of Shannon's throat, but she shook her head to deny it. She was almost used to fear now, it had ridden on her back since she'd picked up the phone in her office in New York and been told her mother was dying. 'Are you in pain?'

'No, no, don't worry.' Amanda sighed again. Though there was pain, hideous pain, she felt stronger. Needed to, with what she was about to face. In the few short weeks Shannon had been back with her, she'd kept the secret buried, as she had all of her daughter's life. But she would have to open it now. There wasn't much time. 'Could I have some water, darling?'

'Of course.' Shannon picked up the insulated pitcher near the bed, filled a plastic glass, then offered the straw to her mother.

Carefully, she adjusted the back of the hospital style bed to make Amanda more comfortable. The living room in the lovely house in Columbus had been modified for hospice care. It had been Amanda's wish, and Shannon's, that she come home for the end.

There was music playing on the stereo, softly. The book Shannon had brought into the room with her to read aloud had fallen where she'd dropped it in panic. She bent to retrieve it, fighting to hold on.

When she was alone, she told herself there was improvement, that she could see it every day. But she had only to look at her mother, see the graying skin, the lines of pain, the gradual wasting, to know better.

There was nothing to do now but make her mother comfortable, to depend, bitterly, on the morphine to dull the pain that was never completely vanquished.

She needed a minute, Shannon realized as panic began to bubble in her throat. Just a minute alone to pull her weary courage together. 'I'm going to get a nice cool cloth for your face.'

'Thank you.' And that, Amanda thought as Shannon hurried away, would give her enough time, please God, to choose the right words.

Amanda had been preparing for this moment for years, knowing it would come, wishing it wouldn't. What was fair and right to one of the men she loved was an injustice to the other, whichever way she chose.

But it was neither of them she could concern herself with now. Nor could she brood over her own shame.

There was only Shannon to think of. Shannon to hurt for.

Her beautiful, brilliant daughter who had never been anything but a joy to her. A pride to her. The pain rippled through her like a poisoned stream, but she gritted her teeth. There would be hurt now, for what would happen soon, from what had happened all those years ago in Ireland. With all her heart she wished she could find some way to dull it.

She watched her daughter come back in, the quick, graceful movements, the nervous energy beneath. Moves

like her father, Amanda thought. Not Colin. Dear, sweet
Colin had lumbered, clumsy as an overgrown pup.

But Tommy had been light on his feet.

Shannon had Tommy's eyes, too. The vivid moss green,
clear as a lake in the sun. The rich chestnut hair that swung
silkily to her chin was another legacy from Ireland. Still,
Amanda liked to think that the shape of her daughter's face,
the creamy skin and soft full mouth had been her own
gifts.

But it was Colin, bless him, that had given her determination, ambition and a steady sense of self.

She smiled as Shannon bathed her clammy face. 'I haven't
told you enough how proud you make me, Shannon.'

'Of course you have.'

'No, I let you see I was disappointed you didn't choose
to paint. That was selfish of me. I know better than most
that a woman's path must be her own.'

'You never tried to talk me out of going to New York, or
moving into commercial art. And I do paint still,' she added
with a bolstering smile. 'I've nearly finished a still life I
think you'll like.'

Why hadn't she brought the canvas with her? Damn it,
why hadn't she thought to pack up some paints, even a
sketch book so that she could have sat with her mother and
given her the pleasure of watching?

'That's one of my favorites there.' Amanda gestured to
the portrait on the parlor wall. 'The one of your father,
sleeping in the chaise in the garden.'

'Gearing himself up to mow the lawn,' Shannon said
with a chuckle. Setting the cloth aside, she took the seat
beside the bed. 'And every time we said why didn't he hire
a lawn boy, he'd claim that he enjoyed the exercise, and go
out and fall asleep.'

'He never failed to make me laugh. I miss that.' She

brushed a hand over Shannon's wrist. 'I know you miss him, too.'

'I still think he's going to come busting in the front door. "Mandy, Shannon," he'd say, "get on your best dresses, I've just made my client ten thousand on the market, and we're going out to dinner." '

'He did love to make money,' Amanda mused. 'It was such a game to him. Never dollars and cents, never greed or selfishness there. Just the fun of it. Like the fun he had moving from place to place every couple of years. "Let's shake this town, Mandy. What do you say we try Colorado? Or Memphis?" '

She shook her head on a laugh. Oh, it was good to laugh, to pretend for just a little while they were only talking as they always had. 'Finally when we moved here, I told him I'd played gypsy long enough. This was home. He settled down as if he'd only been waiting for the right time and place.'

'He loved this house,' Shannon murmured. 'So did I. I never minded the moving around. He always made it an adventure. But I remember, about a week after we'd settled in, sitting up in my room and thinking that I wanted to stay this time.' She smiled over at her mother. 'I guess we all felt the same way.'

'He'd have moved mountains for you, fought tigers.' Amanda's voice trembled before she steadied it. 'Do you know, Shannon, really know how much he loved you?'

'Yes.' She lifted her mother's hand, pressed it to her cheek. 'I do know.'

'Remember it. Always remember it. I've things to tell you, Shannon, that may hurt you, make you angry and confused. I'm sorry for it.' She drew a breath.

There'd been more in the dream than the love and the grief. There had been urgency. Amanda knew she wouldn't have even the stingy three weeks the doctor had promised her.

'Mom, I understand. But there's still hope. There's always hope.'

'It's nothing to do with this,' she said, lifted a hand to encompass the temporary sick room. 'It's from before, darling, long before. When I went with a friend to visit Ireland and stayed in County Clare.'

'I never knew you'd been to Ireland.' It struck Shannon as odd to think of it. 'All the traveling we did, I always wondered why we never went there, with you and Dad both having Irish roots. And I've always felt this – connection, this odd sort of pull.'

'Have you?' Amanda said softly.

'It's hard to explain,' Shannon murmured. Feeling foolish, for she wasn't a woman to speak of dreams, she smiled. 'I've always told myself, if I ever take time for a long vacation, that's where I'd go. But with the promotion and the new account –' She shrugged off the idea of an indulgence. 'Anyway, I remember, whenever I brought up going to Ireland, you'd shake your head and say there were so many other places to see.'

'I couldn't bear to go back, and your father understood.' Amanda pressed her lips together, studying her daughter's face. 'Will you stay here beside me and listen? And oh, please, please, try to understand?'

There was a new and fresh frisson of fear creeping up her spine. What could be worse than death? she wondered. And why was she so afraid to hear it?

But she sat, keeping her mother's hand in hers. 'You're upset,' she began. 'You know how important it is for you to keep calm.'

'And use productive imagery,' Amanda said with a hint of smile.

'It can work. Mind over matter. So much of what I've been reading —'

'I know.' Even the wisp of a smile was gone now. 'And right way. When I was a few years older than you, I traveled with a good friend — her name was Kathleen Reilly — to Ireland. It was a grand adventure for us. We were grown women, but we had both come from strict families. So strict, so sure that I was more than thirty before I had the gumption to make such a move.'

She turned her head so that she could watch Shannon's face as she spoke. 'You wouldn't understand that. You've always been sure of yourself, and brave. But when I was your age, I hadn't even begun to struggle my way out of cowardice.'

'You've never been a coward.'

'Oh, but I was,' Amanda said softly. 'I was. My parents were lace curtain Irish, righteous as three popes. Their biggest disappointment — more for reasons of prestige than religion — was that none of their children had the calling.'

'But you were an only child,' Shannon interrupted.

'One of the truths I broke. I told you I had no family, let you believe there was no one. But I had two brothers and a sister, and not a word has there been between us since before you were born.'

'But why —' Shannon caught herself. 'I'm sorry. Go on.'

'You were always a good listener. Your father taught you that.' She paused a moment, thinking of Colin, praying that what she was about to do was right for all of them. 'We weren't a close family, Shannon. There was a . . . a stiffness in our house, a rigidity of rules and manners. It was over fierce objections that I left home to travel to Ireland with Kate. But we went, as excited as schoolgirls on a picnic. To Dublin first. Then on, following our maps and our noses. I felt free for the first time in my life.'

It was so easy to bring it all back, Amanda realized. Even

after all these years that she'd suppressed those memories they could swim back now, clear and pure as water. Kate's giggling laugh, the cough of the tiny car they'd rented, the wrong turns and the right ones they'd made.

And her first awed look of the sweep of hills, the spear of cliffs of the west. The sense of coming home she'd never expected, and had never felt again.

'We wanted to see all we could see, and when we'd reached the west, we found a charming inn that overlooked the River Shannon. We settled there, decided we could make it a sort of base while we drove here and there on day trips. The Cliffs of Mohr, Galway, the beach at Ballybunion, and all the little fascinating places you find off the roads where you least expect them.'

She looked at her daughter then, and her eyes were sharp and bright. 'Oh, I wish you would go there, see, feel for yourself the magic of the place, the sea spewing like thunder up on the cliffs, the green of the fields, the way the air feels when it's raining so soft and gentle – or when the wind blows hard from the Atlantic. And the light, it's like a pearl, just brushed with gold.'

Here was love, Shannon thought, puzzled, and a longing she'd never suspected. 'But you never went back.'

'No.' Amanda sighed. 'I never went back. Do you ever wonder, darling, how it is that a person can plan things so carefully, all but see how things will be the next day, and the next, then some small something happens, some seemingly insignificant something, and the pattern shifts. It's never quite the same again.'

It wasn't a question so much as a statement. So Shannon simply waited, wondering what small something had changed her mother's pattern.

The pain was trying to creep back, cunningly. Amanda closed her eyes a moment, concentrating on beating it. She would hold it off, she promised herself, until she had finished what she'd begun.

'One morning – it was late summer now and the rain came and went, fitful – Kate was feeling poorly. She decided to stay in, rest in bed for the day, read a bit and pamper herself. I was restless, a feeling in me that there were places I had to go. So I took the car, and I drove. Without planning it, I took myself to Loop Head. I could hear the waves crashing as I got out of the car and walked toward the cliffs. The wind was blowing, humming through the grass. I could smell the ocean, and the rain. There was a power there, drumming in the air even as the surf drummed on the rocks.

'I saw a man,' she continued, slowly now, 'standing where the land fell away to the sea. He was looking out over the water, into the rain – west toward America. There was no one else but him, hunched in his wet jacket, a dripping cap low over his eyes. He turned, as if he'd only been waiting for me, and he smiled.'

Suddenly Shannon wanted to stand, to tell her mother it was time to stop, to rest, to do anything but continue. Her hands had curled themselves into fists without her being aware. There was a larger, tighter one lodged in her stomach.

'He wasn't young,' Amanda said softly. 'But he was handsome. There was something so sad, so lost in his eyes. He smiled and said good morning, and what a fine day it was as the rain beat on our head and the wind slapped our faces. I laughed, for somehow it was a fine day. And though I'd grown used to the music of the brogue of western Ireland, his voice was so charming, I knew I could go on listening to it for hours. So we stood there and talked, about my travels, about America. He was a farmer, he said. A bad one, and he was sorry for that as he had two baby daughters to provide for. But there was no sadness in his face when he spoke of them. It lit. His Maggie Mae and Brie, he called them. And about his wife, he said little.

'The sun came out,' Amanda said with a sigh. 'It came out slow and lovely as we stood there, sort of slipping through the clouds in little streams of gold. We walked along the narrow paths, talking, as if we'd known each other all our lives. And I fell in love with him on the high, thundering cliffs. It should have frightened me.' She glanced at Shannon, tentatively reached out a hand. 'It did shame me, for he was a married man with children. But I thought it was only me who felt it, and how much sin can there be in the soul of an old maid dazzled by a handsome man in one morning?'

It was with relief she felt her daughter's fingers twine with hers. 'But it wasn't only me who'd felt it. We saw each other again, oh, innocently enough. At a pub, back on the cliffs, and once he took both me and Kate to a little fair outside of Ennis. It couldn't stay innocent. We weren't children, either of us, and what we felt for each other was so huge, so important, and you must believe me, so right. Kate knew – anyone who looked at us could have seen it – and she talked to me as a friend would. But I loved him, and I'd never been so happy as when he was with me. Never once did he make promises. Dreams we had, but there were no promises between us. He was bound to his wife who had no love for him, and to the children he adored.'

She moistened her dry lips, took another sip from the straw when Shannon wordlessly offered the glass. Amanda paused again, for it would be harder now.

'I knew what I was doing, Shannon, indeed it was more my doing than his when we became lovers. He was the first man to touch me, and when he did, at last, it was with such gentleness, such care, such love, that we wept together afterwards. For we knew we'd found each other too late, and it was hopeless.

399

'Still we made foolish plans. He would find a way to leave his wife provided for and bring his daughters to me in America where we'd be a family. The man desperately wanted family, as I did. We'd talk together in that room overlooking the river and pretend that it was forever. We had three weeks, and every day was more wonderful than the last, and more wrenching. I had to leave him, and Ireland. He told me he would stand at Loop Head, where we'd met, and look out over the sea to New York, to me.

'His name was Thomas Concannon, a farmer who wanted to be a poet.'

'Did you . . .' Shannon's voice was rusty and unsteady. 'Did you ever see him again?'

'No. I wrote him for a time, and he answered.' Pressing her lips together, Amanda stared into her daughter's eyes. 'Soon after I returned to New York, I learned I was carrying his child.'

Shannon shook her head quickly, the denial instinctive, the fear huge. 'Pregnant?' Her heart began to beat thick and fast. She shook her head again and tried to draw her hand away. For she knew, without another word being said, she knew. And refused to know. 'No.'

'I was thrilled.' Amanda's grip tightened, though it cost her. 'From the first moment I was sure, I was thrilled. I never thought I would have a child, that I would find someone who loved me enough to give me that gift. Oh, I wanted that child, loved it, thanked God for it. What sadness and grief I had came from knowing I would never be able to share with Tommy the beauty that had come from our loving each other. His letter to me after I'd written him of it was frantic. He would have left his home and come to me. He was afraid for me, and what I was facing alone. I knew he would have come, and it tempted me. But it was wrong, Shannon, as loving him was never wrong. So I wrote him a last time, lied to him for the first time, and told him I wasn't afraid, nor alone, and that I was going away.'

'You're tired.' Shannon was desperate to stop the words. Her world was tilting, and she had to fight to right it again. 'You've talked too long. It's time for your medicine.'

'He would have loved you,' Amanda said fiercely. 'If he'd had the chance. In my heart I know he loved you without ever laying eyes on you.'

'Stop.' She did rise then, pulling away, pushing back. There was a sickness rising inside her, and her skin felt so cold and thin. 'I don't want to hear this. I don't need to hear this.'

'You do. I'm sorry for the pain it causes you, but you need to know it all. I did leave,' she went on quickly. 'My family was shocked, furious when I told them I was pregnant. They wanted me to go away, give you up, quietly, discreetly, so that there would be no scandal and shame. I would have died before giving you up. You were mine, and you were Tommy's. There were horrible words in that house, threats, ultimatums. They disowned me, and my father, being a clever man of business, blocked my bank account so that I had no claim on the money that had been left to me by my grandmother. Money was never a game to him, you see. It was power.

'I left that house with never a regret, with the money I had in my wallet, and a single suitcase.'

Shannon felt as though she were underwater, struggling for air. But the image came clearly through it, of her mother, young, pregnant, nearly penniless, carrying a single suitcase. 'There was no one to help you?'

'Kate would have, and I knew she'd suffer for it. This had been my doing. What shame there was, was mine. What joy there was, was mine. I took a train north, and I got a job waiting tables at a resort in the Catskills. And there I met Colin Bodine.'

Amanda waited while Shannon turned away and walked to the dying fire. The room was quiet, with only the hiss of embers and the brisk wind at the windows to stir it. But beneath the quiet, she could feel the storm, the one swirling inside the child she loved more than her own life. Already she suffered, knowing that storm was likely to crash over both of them.

'He was vacationing with his parents. I paid him little mind. He was just one more of the rich and privileged I was serving. He had a joke for me now and again, and I smiled as was expected. My mind was on my work and my pay, and on the child growing inside me. Then one afternoon there was a thunderstorm, a brute of one. A good many of the guests chose to stay indoors, in their rooms and have their lunch brought to them. I was carrying a tray, hurrying to one of the cabins, for there would be trouble if the food got cold and the guest complained of it. And Colin comes barreling around a corner, wet as a dog, and flattens me. How clumsy he was, bless him.'

Tears burned behind Shannon's eyes as she stared down into the glowing embers. 'He said that was how he met you, by knocking you down.'

'So he did. And we always told you what truths we felt we could. He sent me sprawling in the mud, with the tray of food scattering and ruined. He started apologizing, trying to help me up. All I could see was that food, spoiled. And my back aching from carrying those heavy trays, and my legs so tired of holding the rest of me up. I started to cry. Just sat there in the mud and cried and cried and cried. I couldn't stop. Even when he lifted me up and carried me to his room, I couldn't stop.

'He was so sweet, sat me down on a chair despite the mud, covered me with a blanket and sat there, patting my hand till the tears ran out. I was so ashamed of myself, and he was so kind. He wouldn't let me leave until I'd promised to have dinner with him.'

It should have been romantic and sweet, Shannon thought while her breath began to hitch. But it wasn't. It was hideous. 'He didn't know you were pregnant.'

Amanda winced as much from the accusation in the words as she did from a fresh stab of pain. 'No, not then. I was barely showing and careful to hide it or I would have lost my job. Times were different then, and an unmarried pregnant waitress wouldn't have lasted in a rich man's playground.'

'You let him fall in love with you.' Shannon's voice was cold, cold as the ice that seemed slicked over her skin. 'When you were carrying another man's child.'

And the child was me, she thought, wretched.

'I'd grown to a woman,' Amanda said carefully, searching her daughter's face and weeping inside at what she read there. 'And no one had really loved me. With Tommy it was quick, as stunning as a lightning bolt. I was still blinded by it when I met Colin. Still grieving over it, still wrapped in it. Everything I felt for Tommy was turned toward the child we'd made together. I could tell you I thought Colin was only being kind. And in truth, at first I did. But I saw, soon enough that there was more.'

'And you let him.'

'Maybe I could have stopped him,' Amanda said with a long, long sigh. 'I don't know. Every day for the next week there were flowers in my room, and the pretty, useless things he loved to give. He found ways to be with me. If I had a ten minute break, there he would be. Still it took me days before I understood I was being courted. I was terrified. Here was this lovely man who was being nothing but kind, and he didn't know I had another man's child in me. I told him, all of it, certain it would end there, and sorry for that because he was the first friend I'd had since I'd left Kate in New York. He listened, in that way he had, without interruption, without questions, without condemnations. When I was finished, and weeping again, he took my hand "You'd better marry me, Mandy," he said. "I'll take care of you and the baby." '

The tears had escaped, ran down Shannon's cheeks as she turned back. They were running down her mother's cheeks as well, but she wouldn't allow herself to be swayed by them. Her world was no longer tilted; it had crashed.

'As simple as that? How could it have been so simple?'

'He loved me. It was humbling when I realized he truly loved me. I refused him, of course. What else could I do? I thought he was being foolishly gallant, or just foolish altogether. But he persisted. Even when I got angry and told him to leave me alone, he persisted.' A smile began to curve her lips as she remembered it. 'It was as if I were the rock and he the wave that patiently, endlessly sweeps over it until all resistance is worn away. He brought me baby things. Can you imagine a man courting a woman by bringing her gifts for her unborn child? One day he came to my room, told me we were going to get the license now and to get my purse. I did it. I just did it. And found myself married two days later.'

She looked over sharply, anticipating the question before it was asked. 'I won't lie to you and tell you I loved him then. I did care. It was impossible not to care for a man like that. And I was grateful. His parents were upset, naturally enough, but he claimed he would bring them around. Being Colin, I think he would have, but they were killed on their drive home. So it was just the two of us, and you. I promised myself I would be a good wife to him, make him a home, accept him in bed. I vowed not to think of Tommy again, but that was impossible. It took me years to understand there was no sin, no shame in remembering the first man I'd loved, no disloyalty to my husband.'

'Not my father,' Shannon said through lips of ice. 'He was your husband, but he wasn't my father.'

'Oh, but he was.' For the first time there was a hint of temper in Amanda's voice. 'Don't ever say different.'

Bitterness edged her voice. 'You've just told me different, haven't you?'

'He loved you while you were still in my womb, took both of us as his without hesitation or false pride.' Amanda spoke as quickly as her pain would allow. 'I tell you it shamed me, pining for a man I could never have, while one as fine as was ever made was beside me. The day you were born, and I saw him holding you in those big clumsy hands, that look of wonder and pride on his face, the love in his eyes as he cradled you against him as gently as if you were made of glass, I fell in love with him. I loved him as much as any woman ever loved any man from that day till this. And he was your father, as Tommy wanted to be and couldn't. If either of us had a regret, it was that we couldn't have more children to spread the happiness we shared in you.'

'You just want me to accept this?' Clinging to anger was less agonizing than clinging to grief. Shannon stared. The woman in bed was a stranger now, just as she was a stranger to herself. 'To go on as if it changes nothing.'

'I want you to give yourself time to accept, and understand. And I want you to believe that we loved you, all of us.'

Her world was shattered at her feet, every memory she had, every belief she'd fostered in jagged shards. 'Accept? That you slept with a married man and got pregnant, then married the first man who asked you to save yourself. To accept the lies you told me all my life, the deceit.'

'You've a right to your anger.' Amanda bit back the pain, physical, emotional.

'Anger? Do you think what I'm feeling is as pale as anger? God, how could you do this?' She whirled away, horror and bitterness biting at her heels. 'How could you have kept this from me all these years, let me believe I was someone I wasn't?'

'Who you are hasn't changed,' Amanda said desperately. 'Colin and I did what we thought was right for you. We were never sure how or when to tell you. We –'

'You discussed it?' Swamped by her own churning emotions, Shannon spun back to the frail woman on the bed. There was a horrible, shocking urge in her to snatch that shrunken body up, shake it. 'Is today the day we tell Shannon she was a little mistake made on the west coast of Ireland. Or should it be tomorrow?'

'Not a mistake, never a mistake. A miracle. Damn it, Shannon –' She broke off, gasping as the pain lanced through her, stealing her breath, tearing like claws. Her vision grayed. She felt a hand lift her head, a pill being slipped between her lips, and heard the voice of her daughter, soothing now.

'Sip some water. A little more. That's it. Now lie back, close your eyes.'

'Shannon.' The hand was there to take hers when she reached out.

'I'm here, right here. The pain'll be gone in a minute. It'll be gone, and you'll sleep.'

It was already ebbing, and the fatigue was rolling in like fog. Not enough time, was all Amanda could think. Why is there never enough time?

'Don't hate me,' she murmured as she slipped under the fog. 'Please, don't hate me.'

Shannon sat, weighed down by her own grief long after her mother slept.

She didn't wake again.